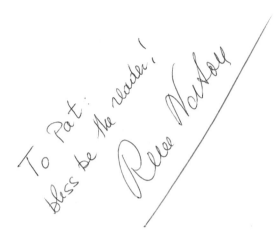

To Pat:
bless be the reader!
Rene Natan

The Bricklayer

RENE NATAN

ISBN: 1466404019
ISBN 13: 9781466404014

To the memory of Martin Gerardus Strybosch,
the bricklayer of my heart

The author gratefully acknowledges the contribution of the former Strybosch Construction Company, the late John E. Bennett, Dennis Rivest of the London Police Service (Media Relations) and Giovanni Rodriguez of Simar Developments.

Special thanks to Sharon Crawford and Harvey Stanbrough for the editing.

List of Characters

Alstein, Alain	Employee of The Werkstein Company
Alstein, Jeanette	Alain's wife
Bompiani, Alicia	Nurse
Bristol, Verge	Employee of The Werkstein Company
Clark, Oscar	Boat's owner
Dalton, Frederick (Fred)	Protagonist
Dalton, Deborah	Fred's wife
Fairweather, Lucy	Charlotte's maid
Falcone, Nicholas	Fred's friend
Father Thomas	Priest
The Gardeners	Young couple
Gassman, Charlotte	Fred's sister
Gassman, Werner	Charlotte's defunct husband
Gervasio, Mary	Fred's secretary
Hamilton, Ross	Employee of the funeral home
Heisman, Bruno	Criminal lawyer
Holton, Rose	Secretary of a school in Barrie
Johnson, Charles	Moira's brother
Johnson, Moira	Employee of The Werkstein Company
Lopes, Santos	Constable
Maclaren, Victor	Fred's lawyer
Manson, Beatrice	Caregiver
Morteson, Bernard	Bill Morteson's father
Morteson, Bill	Charlotte's doctor
Norton, Donald	Lawyer
O'Brian, Peggy	Policewoman
Orlandi, Harvey	OPP officer
Parker, Amanda	Crown prosecutor
Ross, Elisabeth	Charlotte's friend
Rowe, Brad	Charlotte's neighbor
Saldini, Arthur	Owner of the hangar
Smith, Louis	OPP officer
Stevenson, Gordon	Detective with the London Police Service
Tremonti, Sandra	Director of The Safe Harbor
Wilson, Walter	Tessa's ex-husband
Wilson, Theresa (Tessa)	Deborah's closest friend

One

Near Midland, Ontario, beginning of July, 2009

"Dust to dust, ashes to ashes," Father Thomas repeated for the third time, and swung the church bell up and down.

The priest, a small man with tortoise-shell-rimmed glasses that covered half of his face, tiredly shuffled one foot after the other as he led the mourning crowd up the hill. He wore an ivory cope festooned with gold trim, and the traditional black biretta. From time to time he turned around to make sure the congregation was following him.

Frederick Elliot Dalton, walking with his arm linked with his sister Charlotte's, was right behind him. He was in silent anguish. Deborah, his late wife, had arranged for her own funeral to be held on top of the cemetery hill that overlooked the village where she had been born and raised.

The priest slipped on a clump of grass and the bell fell to the ground. Fred freed his arm from Charlotte's, and stretched to catch him, but there was no need; the priest straightened himself up and retrieved the bell. Father Thomas resumed his walk and swung the bell one more time.

On top of the incline stood an improvised altar and, in front of it, the coffin of Deborah Dalton. Two altar boys, dressed in the customary surplices struggled to light the big candles lying on top of the altar—a losing fight against the prevailing wind. Stepping on high grass, Father Thomas took his place behind the altar. There were no chairs, no pews, not even stumps of old trees to sit on.

"Did you know of this arrangement?" Charlotte whispered in Fred's ear.

She had walked up the hill sustained on the left by Fred and on the right by Theresa "Tessa" Wilson, Deborah's closest friend. Charlotte, fifty-six years old, suffered with osteoporosis, which often sent blades of pain into every joint of her body.

"Not a single clue. I didn't even know she was in contact with her hometown's parish. It must have been one of her latest fancies." He looked at his sister, concerned. "Is this too much for you?"

"Oh no, but I'll hang onto both your arms, if you don't mind." She gave Fred and Tessa a grateful smile.

Fred extended his free arm and squeezed her hand. "Thank you, big sister."

Finally the entire crowd reached the top of the hill and slowly formed a circle around the altar; most people stood, but a few sat on the ground.

Father Thomas's voice was remarkably loud. "By the expressed desire of the deceased, the Requiem Mass will be held in Latin."

Charlotte gave Fred a quizzical look. "What's this all about?"

Fred shrugged.

As the Tridentine Mass unfolded—not a word of it understandable to him—Fred's mind again wandered. How could he reconcile this display of attachment to religious beliefs and tradition with Deborah's suicide? She had mentioned she would rather be dead than confined in a wheelchair, but that was right after the accident.

A small choir which seemed to come from nowhere formed a semicircle right behind the priest, and they accompanied the memorial service with litanies and religious songs.

Then the words of the *Pater Noster* resounded in the air, echoed by some voices from the church's oldest members. Fred looked around and then behind him. How could anybody think of holding a ceremony on top of a hill with no place to sit? He had assessed the number of people walking up the hill to be a couple of hundred, but the lack of seating accommodations coupled with a religious ceremony nobody could understand had reduced that number by half; those who remained had closed up around the altar, from time to time shifting their weight from one foot to the other.

The noise of vanes droning in the nearby village became more intense as a helicopter hovered above the hill. It drowned out the priest's words, but by that time, nobody in the crowd appeared to care. The chopper moved away, continuing its journey along the valley.

Finally the priest pronounced the last amen of the day, and six pallbearers approached the coffin. Fred let go of Charlotte's arm and neared Father Thomas.

"Thank you for the service, Father," he said. "Is there anything I can do? Any money to be paid?"

The priest gave him a severe look, and shook his head. "Your wife took care of everything. You don't owe me a penny."

"I see."

"You didn't know her well, did you?"

"I thought I did. I thought she'd come to terms with—I mean, I didn't think she would—"

"Commit suicide?"

Fred nodded, embarrassed.

"Maybe she didn't," the priest said, and moved away from him.

Fred froze. What was the priest implying? Did anybody doubt his wife's cause of death? He looked around just as Charlotte collapsed at Tessa's feet, exhausted. A man pushed a wheelchair up the hill. He placed it close to Charlotte and helped her into it.

"Thanks," Fred said. "I should have thought of it, but neither Charlotte nor I had any idea what was going to happen. And your name is...?"

"Donald Hamilton. I'm the funeral director's assistant. When I saw the lady coming up, heavily weighing on your arm, I should have thought of a wheelchair right away. Occasionally religious services are held on this ground, but we've never had a funeral. I guess Father Thomas forgot to order the chairs." He gestured toward the sudden clouds that amassed on top of the hill. "It is already drizzling; I'd better hurry before the grass gets slippery." He unfolded an umbrella to protect Charlotte.

"Certainly, and thanks again, Mr. Hamilton." Fred turned to Charlotte. "I'd like to be present at the internment. Father Thomas is going down fast, probably because of the weather. See you later, Charlotte."

The altar was being dismantled, and the six pallbearers were taking hold of the coffin, ready to carry it down the hill and to the burial ground.

He quickened his steps down the steep path, which abruptly twisted to the left to end up at the graveyard. Copious sheets of rain started to fall, swirling in the gusty wind. When he joined the funeral procession he was

soaked to the bones. The pallbearers hastily deposited the coffin on the provided harness and worked the lever that lowered Deborah's mortal remains
into the ground. Protected by a huge umbrella held by an altar boy, Father
Thomas swiftly pronounced a last blessing and left.

Low clouds, the color of lead, grazed the tall pine trees that marked the
cemetery's entrance; lighting bolts punctuated the dark sky and thunder
resounded in the nearby valley of Midland.

Fred took the flowers that had fallen off the coffin and lowered them
into Deborah's grave. Heedless of the raging storm, he genuflected in
prayer.

Moments later a thunderbolt resounded behind him, shaking the
ground underneath his body. Fred rose, murmured goodbye to Deborah,
and walked away from the grave and to the parking lot. Strangely, joyful
memories flashed before his mind's eye: Deborah playing volleyball on the
beach, her body stretched up in the air to score the winning goal; Deborah
giving him a kiss after their first dance together; Deborah clutching her
wedding bouquet and smiling at him...

A car horn called him back to reality and made him quicken his steps
back to the car. Charlotte sat on the passenger side and leaned over toward
the steering wheel.

"Sorry about making you wait," Fred said, opening the car door.
Charlotte straightened as Fred slid into the driver's seat.

"You are soaked to the bones!" Charlotte said. "You're going to catch
pneumonia!"

Fred took off his coat, tossed it onto the backseat, and turned on the
heat.

"I had to stay a few moments close to the tomb," he said. "After that
strange ceremony I wanted to give Deborah my personal farewell."

"Strange is not the right word," whispered Charlotte, and sighed.
"Didn't you check with the funeral home?"

"I did, but they told me Deborah had arranged everything and asked
them to follow her will to the letter." Fred sighed. "So they did."

"You didn't know of her arrangements?" Charlotte asked, sounding
flabbergasted.

"Heck, no! I know she went back to her village a few times. She didn't
want me to go with her and asked me to provide her with transportation—

that is, a van with a wheelchair lift—so I did. I was happy she wanted to get out of the house for a change."

"Of course, you've always given in to her desires, no matter how strange they were. She should have been grateful to you, instead of—" She paused. "Instead of doing what she did." She sighed again. "Well her funeral is something I'll never forget. Let's go to the reception hall. They're waiting for us."

Two

A five-foot cedar fence surrounded the Dalton property, interrupted only by the wrought-iron, spear-tipped gate that marked the entrance to the premises. The driveway wound left and then right, to end in a paved area where the garage door opened. A sidewalk stemmed off of the driveway, led to a side door near the garage, and continued toward a fenced patio. On the western wall of the house a large sliding glass door, flanked by two windows on each side, opened onto the fenced area, giving direct access to a whirlpool. The house was one-story, and sported a roof of black shingles and walls made of natural beige, purple, and pink stones. On the northwest side, several larch trees brushed against the wall, creating a big splash of soft green.

Fred had built the house to suit his wife's needs, and he had chosen a location that was only a ten-minute drive from where he worked. At one time he had thought of moving away from the commotion of a densely populated urban centre, but London, Ontario offered too many advantages. It was a vibrant city that fostered a variety of cultural and sports activities, and encouraged the establishment of new business. Fred had never regretted his decision.

The day after Deborah's funeral he drove to his house from Charlotte's, where he had spent the night. He had just set foot inside, when a strange feeling pervaded him.

This wasn't his place anymore. Actually, it had been nobody but Deborah's place, and now Deborah was no more. He threw his coat on the coat rack and walked into the large room where she had spent most of her days.

For a while after the accident, they had lived in the house they had built together. Deborah's condition, unfortunately, had inexorably deteriorated, both physically and mentally. A paraplegic, she would never again do any of the things she had previously enjoyed. Organizing and attending parties had been her main pleasure. They called her Party Girl Deborah, always out for a good time. At first, friends had come to visit her, but she would hardly say a word or, even worse, replied rudely when people asked her how she was doing. Her childhood friend Tessa was one of the few people who managed to cope with her outbursts of anger.

Fred pushed open the sliding door that opened onto the patio. In the whirlpool, now empty, the little, silvery blue ceramic tiles shone in the afternoon sun; the clear plastic dome was folded unevenly at the far end.

He had built the house to suit Deborah's needs after her accident. Plunging into the whirlpool with the help of a therapist was a daily ritual that appeased her anxiety for a couple of hours. Her living quarters and the adjacent large room took up the western side of the house; on the eastern side were the kitchen and the dining area that she had insisted on, even if they scarcely used it. Of late, very few friends came to the house. Fred had built a den for himself on the northern side, with a double bed in one corner. He spent most of his solitary evenings there, working on a project or watching a sporting event on television.

He looked a second time at the whirlpool, the place where Deborah had found death. He sighed deeply. *This house has to go.* He retreated inside and went directly to his den.

On one wall hung his civil engineering degree from the University of Western Ontario, and the multiple awards he had received for trap shooting. On the opposite wall were pictures of his father and mother, now deceased, and a family picture portraying his parents with their two kids, Fred and Charlotte, at Christmas. On his oak desk stood two pictures: a radiant Deborah and a serious Fred on the day of their wedding, and the two of them again in Aspen, wrapped in a single furry coat, smiling at the world.

All this is history, Fred thought. He had tried to take care of Deborah, but recently she had started to resent him, as if he sinned in his good health and mobility. He had coped with all the shortcomings that had come with Deborah's condition: the lack of a social life, the lack of any vacation and her angry scenes when he went out in the evening—something that seldom happened. He had buried himself in his work, and carried his cross with composure.

He exited the den and locked up the house. As he drove to his car, his mind wandered back to Deborah's funeral and the humiliation he had suffered because of the way it had been orchestrated. He shouldn't wait any longer. Although an important tender would close in a week, and an internal investigation required his attention, Fred had to know why Deborah had arranged for such a strange farewell. Feeling an irrepressible urgency, he called Father Thomas and asked him for an appointment; at the same time he let him know that he was pressed for time.

When he arrived at St. Mary of the Hurons, the priest's assistant ushered him into the sacristy.

"Father Thomas will see you soon," the assistant said.

But Fred was left waiting for an hour, seated on a hardwood chair. The place smelled of incense, and the lit candles beside the altar were clearly visible from where he sat. The scanty furnishings puzzled him. On a table set flush against one of the walls lay religious items, from pictures of popes to statuettes of saints. On a bench opposite the table, vestments lay stacked one on top of the other. He saw not a single magazine or a book he could use to entertain himself. He was at the end of his patience and about to leave, when Father Thomas entered the sacristy and sat on a chair opposite him.

"So, you came here to talk about your wife?" the priest asked. He removed his heavy eyeglasses and rubbed his eyes.

"I just wanted to know a bit more about what she said when she came to see you, and how she came to the decision of holding the ceremony on top of the cemetery hill." As the priest didn't utter a sound, Fred continued. "We have always been active members of our parish, so I was surprised that the service wasn't held there."

"I know. Your pastor called me the day Mrs. Dalton died. I had a long conversation with him." Father Thomas put his glasses back on and gave Fred a severe look. "Your wife was suffering; had you ever noticed?"

"Yes, she was, and of course I noticed. I felt sorry for her." Fred paused. "But that isn't the reason I came here. I wanted to know if you could tell me how many times she came, and how she came to choose those peculiar funeral arrangements."

"Not interested in her feelings?"

"Yes, I am, if you want to elaborate on that. But let me tell you, I couldn't do anything to repair the physical damage that the accident inflicted upon her. Deborah couldn't accept her...her condition...her fate. She got counseling, and I tried to provide for her needs." Fred avoided Father Thomas' eyes. "So how many times did she come here?"

"Four."

"Four?"

"Yes."

"Did you provide her with the name of the funeral home?"

"No, she had it written on a piece of paper."

Written? By whom? Deborah couldn't write! Somebody must have given her that information and written it down for her. "Do you have that paper, by any chance?"

"No. Why are you so interested in this issue?"

"Because I think somebody influenced her, actually took advantage of her frail state of mind."

"Maybe it was the woman who came with her."

"A woman? What woman? The driver of the van for the handicapped was a man."

Once again Father Thomas removed his heavy eyeglasses and rubbed his eyes. "Ah, yes, she always came in a special van and the driver waited in the vehicle. The woman I mentioned before drove here by herself, but they came to see me together. Not the first time, just the last three times." He closed his eyes. "Theresa...Tessa was her name. They grew up together. They went to school here."

"Tessa? I see," Fred said, more surprised than ever. "Did Tessa or Deborah give you any reason for the choice?"

"No. Your wife did most of the talking; Tessa kept quiet." Father Thomas reopened his eyes and resumed his belligerent attitude. "Of course,

I asked why her husband hadn't come with her. She said you were too busy to take care of family affairs."

At this point Fred had enough of Father Thomas's accusatory attitude.

"Thank you, Father." He rose.

"Don't you want to confess?"

Fred gave him a dirty look.

"The rite of reconciliation, you know, relieves people's souls of their worst burdens. And you, my son, have a big sin weighing on your soul."

Fred summoned all the charity he had in his heart. "Thanks for the offer. As I said, I already belong to a parish." He strode out of the sacristy.

Three

Fred hadn't slept much for the last few days; visions of Deborah in distress had taken over his heart and mind. Last night had been no exception. Although not rested, he kicked the sheets to the side and climbed out of bed. *Better go to the office and get things moving*, he thought. His construction company, The Werkstein Company Ltd., was in the process of bidding for two housing developments; there was frantic work at the office, but only moderate action in the field. Most of the equipment and construction workers were underutilized, a phenomen4on that occurred whenever some projects were at the point of completion, and new ones had not started yet.

Many called Fred *The Bricklayer*, even though he was an engineer and a general contractor. He had worked in the construction industry for eight years while going to school, and he had learned to lay bricks quickly and with expertise. The work had made him a lot of money, and had earned him his nickname. His specialty, however, was working with natural stone, a rare expertise that required a particular talent. The stones had to be lined up properly so that the walls stood up straight; on the other hand, to take advantage of the stones' natural look, size, shape, and color, their position had to alternate constantly. It was an art more than a craft, and it had earned Fred praise and extra money.

As soon as he entered his office, he called in Verge Bristol, his second in command. An engineer from the University of Saskatchewan, Verge was in his mid-fifties, almost completely bald, of medium height, with a weight problem. He usually tightened his belt as much as he could, giving more evidence of his growing stomach. He had been with the company since the beginning, eighteen years ago, and together with Alain Alstein he was in charge of pricing new projects and supervising the job sites.

Verge came in. "I didn't expect you in today." He sat in front of Fred's desk.

"Well, at the moment I can hardly eat or sleep, so I thought at least I could try to work." He shuffled a couple of pages inside a folder. "These two jobs are almost completed, so some men and equipment are probably going to be free for a while. Correct?"

"Yes. I checked with the two foremen. A couple days' work at full speed, and then the subs will come in to do the painting. We'll be out by then."

"Great. I'd like you to put a crew to work on my house. I want the whirlpool ripped out. I'd like to replace it with a nice garden. Get one of our usual landscapers to submit a couple of designs. Then ready a sketch for the inside of the house. I want to change the layout—carve a couple of bedrooms, one big and one small, out of the large recreational room Deborah used to spend her days in." Fred tossed a piece of paper to Verge. "Something along these lines."

"But...but we're busy pricing two new projects. We're speaking of multimillion-dollar projects. We can't do anything for a couple of weeks, until we close."

"I thought Moira did most of the pricing."

Verge swayed his head left and right. "Ms. Johnson makes herself out to be a pro, but she just joined the company; she needs a lot of advice and help...a *lot* of help." Verge stirred, making his chair screech.

"I see," Fred said coolly. He arched his eyebrows. He wanted to make sure Verge understood that he wasn't convinced of his reasoning. "Then I'll do the drawing. Just send a crew to dismantle the whirlpool as soon as a backhoe is available. I want that thing out of the way as soon as possible."

Verge didn't move.

"That's all for the moment."

After Verge left, Fred paced back and forth. The room was a working area more than an office, containing a drawing desk with an attached lamp, a counter with computer equipment and boxes of CDs and DVDs, and a sitting area with a low table and four chairs. Not far from the entrance stood his desk, with an off-white plastic top that was washable—an important quality, because he carelessly used markers of different colors to underline important features on drawings or documents. In front of the desk were two upholstered chairs, seldom used, as most employees who came to his office looked at blueprints and, therefore, stood and leaned over the desk or the drawing table. The two metal cabinets lined up along one wall contained mainly legal documents. In one corner, a large box overflowed with rolled-up blueprints of different sizes and thicknesses.

Two flat-screen monitors tilted down from the ceiling in front of his desk; one tuned to the job site with the most action, the other to his house to monitor the large room where Deborah used to spend most of her time. *No need for that anymore*, he realized with a pang. He switched it off.

Deborah's death, or rather the way it had happened, had hit him hard. The police had taken plenty of pictures of the accident and shown them to him. He could still see her emaciated body floating in the pool; her long, dark hair spread over the water; her legs—those legs that had once wanted to dance without stopping—reduced to bones covered by skin; the wheel-chair at the bottom of the pool.

Fred swept his forehead as if to brush away those images. *Could I have done anything to prevent her death? Was I responsible for what happened?* He had no answers to these questions.

He should focus on his work, especially on the problem he had with his two key people. He needed to examine the facts with a clear mind, and evaluate the consequences of his actions. He wanted to avoid bad publicity or, even worse, litigation.

A knock at the door brought him back to reality. It was Mary Gervasio, his secretary.

"The grand opening of the new long-term care facility is scheduled at 10:30 a.m.," she said.

"Long-term care facility" was the fancy name the government had decided to call the nursing home. The Werkstein had completed that building a month ago.

For a few seconds Fred looked at her blankly, then scouted the wall where the calendar hung.

"Oh, right…today is the day," he said. "I get it."

Mary gave him a look of concern. "Would you prefer to be represented by Verge or Alain?"

"No. The mayor and a provincial representative will be present, so I should go." He looked at his wristwatch. "Get the car ready at the front door, please. I'll put on a tie and clean up a bit. I'll be down in a few minutes."

The inauguration of any sizable government facility was always a big event, and an occasion for politicians to promote themselves and their party. The celebrations followed a traditional procedure: the committee in charge of the project's realization introduced the elected officials in ascending order of importance and invited them to speak in the reverse order. So the federal representative opened the ceremony, taking credit for providing part of the funding; the minister of Health and Long-Term Care spelled out that the majority of the capital came from the province through his office; the mayor praised her own office for initiating the project of the much-needed long-term health resource, and thanked the architect's office and the construction company for the design and its realization.

Fred barely followed each of the speeches, refraining from yawning. As he had experienced in the past, they were all much the same. When his name was called, he rose and approached the podium to receive a certificate with an attached blue ribbon. His public speech contained only a few words of thanks.

After the ceremony, the crowd spread out and hastened to the refreshment table. Fred took the occasion to leave, almost unnoticed.

It was late afternoon when he returned to the office. He tiptoed along the corridor and stopped to look into the room that Verge Bristol, Alain Alstein, and Moira Johnson shared. Moira, her back to the door, hunched over a desk computer and alternated between clicking and typing. The two men weren't present; they had probably taken off already, thinking he would not return for the day. Fortunately, he could count on Ms. Johnson, the junior member of the company.

Alain Alstein and Verge Bristol sipped on beers, waiting for their chicken wraps to come. They had taken a late lunch break; the Blackfriars Bistro was almost deserted at that time—an ideal situation for talking freely.

"I need that twenty thousand," Alain Alstein said. "I need it by the end of the month."

"I know, I know, to pay for the cruise and your mortgage," Verge Bristol replied. "You told me. I need money too, but we have to be careful; two police officers were around asking questions."

"But that was about Fred and his wife."

"About Fred, his married life and *his work*, Alain. They interviewed everybody. I gathered that they wanted to know whether Fred was in need of money. He's his wife's beneficiary. She was a well-to-do woman." He picked up a napkin and began folding it in different ways.

"Yes, but that was before the accident," Alain said. "I heard that between the therapist for the daily whirlpool treatment and the twenty-four hour surveillance, the cost was over a hundred and fifty thousand dollars a year. Deborah had a bit of money, but I heard it was all gone by the end of last year."

Their lunch arrived, and for a while the two friends savored their meals in silence. Soon afterward the waiter approached their table and asked them if they cared for dessert. They both declined, and he quietly retrieved their plates.

"Let's go back to our problem," said Verge Bristol. "Due to the situation, the best thing would be to do nothing and wait for the next tender." Bristol almost seemed to talk to himself.

"No! We can't do that. We never know whether the company will get the next job. A bid is a bid. If somebody comes in with a lower price, we're done—a full month of work down the drain!"

"That's true, unfortunately." Verge spent a moment in silence, absorbed in thought. "If we decide to go for it, we can choose between changing the subs before the contract is signed and altering the quality of the material."

"Both!" Alain spelled out clearly, but kept the tone of his voice down. "The one due soon isn't a very big job; we can't skim much off of it."

"No, but we can still go to jail for it," Verge said, once again pensive.

"We've been doing it for four years and nobody's caught us."

"True, but we didn't do it in grand style until Moira came. It was her work that inspired us." Verge grinned. "If she knew, she'd report us for sure."

"She doesn't know," Alain said.

"I really like the way she prices: using the material specified by the architect, using material of better quality of the same cost, and using material of same quality, but available through a different vendor, at a lower price. Neat."

"Don't think she's a genius. The computer does it all. She went to school for that, and she worked on the same kind of job for two years before coming here. She just knows the trade."

"But we don't. If Fred knew the truth, he'd fire us."

"But he doesn't. Let's not be distracted from the real issue. We have to make a decision."

Verge Bristol sighed. "Okay. Let's go full steam ahead. We can change the prices for both the electrical and the plumbing. I know of two that are reasonable. We'll use them instead of the higher subs, and pocket the difference. Our old accountant is very accommodating."

"Since he's getting a piece of the action, he'd better be." Alain scowled, and tossed his crimpled napkin on the table.

"Leave everything up to me," Verge said.

"Fine, but remember that the tender closes the day after tomorrow."

They both left the bistro and returned to their office.

Alain had just settled at his desk when Verge called him on his personal cell. "I need to see you. Go to the Men's."

Alain didn't want to move. He had a long lunch break, and it would soon be closing time. What would Moira think of all this time away, when they were supposed to be busy pricing? He rose from his chair, opened a file cabinet, extracted a folder, and looked at it for a few minutes. He glanced at Moira, but she was busy entering data in the company server and had her back to him. He deposited the folder on his desk and strode off as inconspicuously as he could.

"What now?" he asked Verge, as he entered the Men's room. "We just had a talk!"

"That was then. Fred called me. He went through the details of the bid; he asked how reliable the companies we chose were, and whether we'd used them in the past."

"Oh...well, he won't remember them once everything is finalized."

"That's the problem. He wrote them down on a separate sheet of paper and asked me to notify him if there were any last-minute changes."

"Shit! He's never done that. What do you think triggered his new attitude?"

"Actually, he used to check every detail, before his wife's accident. It's only in the last four years that he slacked off."

"That's a big problem." Alain sighed. "We could avoid notifying him of the changes; if he gets wind of them, we could always claim we forgot."

"That's a possibility, but we need to keep him busy so he doesn't have time to poke into our little side business."

Steps resounded outside and both men rushed to rinse their hands. The janitor came in pushing a cart full of disinfectants, mops, and tools needed to perform a thorough cleaning.

"I can come back later," he said when he saw Verge and Alain.

"No need. We're done." On the way out he whispered to Verge, "I have a good idea how to keep Fred on his toes so that he won't have time to do much checking."

Four

The Latin adage *Facta non verba credo* had trickled through the centuries to become the London Police Service's motto, translated as *Deeds not Words* on all cruisers. With six hundred and sixty officers and about two hundred civilians, Headquarters—as the Police Service was referred to—extended their invisible shield over almost half a million square kilometers and three hundred fifty-five thousand inhabitants. Headquarters, housed in a two-story, red-brick building on Dundas Street, was currently undergoing a major expansion and renovation, due for completion by the middle of 2011.

Inside his office, Detective Gordon Stevenson, a member of the Investigation Response Unit, had turned his chair around to look at Constable Santos Lopes.

"What?" Stevenson cried so loud that the two officers seated at the desks adjoining his jerked their heads.

Constable Santos Lopes had just joined the force. Thin, with a baby face, Santos had been the target of one joke after the other because of his shyness. His Adam's apple bounced up and down as he uttered an incomprehensible answer.

"What did you say happened?" Stevenson asked, in a milder tone.

Santos visibly swallowed. "Mr. Dalton's entire backyard has been dug out. There's no more whirlpool, and even the stones used for the path that led to the pool have been loaded and trucked away." He swallowed again, and his eyes shifted away from his boss.

"Not your fault," Stevenson said. "The man is a fast operator."

"We should have kept an eye on him," said Peggy O'Brian, another officer.

Peggy was tall, with curly blond hair that framed an oval face. The standard dark blue uniform, that hid a bullet-proof vest underneath the shirt, didn't hide her feminine figure.

"Yeah. Easy talking. If it wasn't for the two anonymous calls we received yesterday, we wouldn't have even thought of looking into this case again." He drummed his fingers on the desk. "Mr. Dalton had an airtight alibi; he was in a meeting with a bunch of people." Stevenson paused. "His wife talked about committing suicide with the caregivers; the video, which is still in our possession, didn't show anything suspicious; her diary, which is also in our possession, revealed a mind on the brink of madness; the laptop in her name was used only by her caregivers. We had no reason to suspect anything other than suicide."

"Should we try to get at the material Mr. Dalton trucked away?" Peggy O'Brian asked.

Detective Stevenson shrugged. "No. We examined that area carefully after the death, and we didn't notice anything suspicious." He sighed. "The speed with which the man cleaned up the place where his wife died isn't a good sign, but it doesn't make him guilty—insensitive, maybe, or maybe oversensitive. Maybe he didn't want to look at it every day. And the material of the old pool and backyard can't convey much more information than what we got at the inquest, which was zilch." Stevenson twisted his dark moustaches with both hands. "No. Somebody seems to know something we don't. We should find out who these people are. Let's start with the caregivers—there were two main ones—and then let's go and have another chat with the people working at his company, The Werkstein. Maybe he had a girlfriend that they knew of." He looked at Peggy. "Let's put a tail on our Mr. Dalton and find out how he spends his time now that he's free as a bird." He twisted around to look at Santos again. "Go, Santos. Go back to work."

Santos left the room.

Stevenson rose, his massive frame imposing. He had joined the force ten years ago, and had proceeded through the ranks in record time. He was well known for his dedication and keen perception, and also for considering crimes against people who couldn't defend themselves as the most heinous of all.

Santos was back, breathing heavily. "Detective?" he asked in a soft voice.

"Yes?"

"Mr. Dalton is in the waiting room. He asked if he could have his wife's diary."

Detective Stevenson slumped back into his chair. "Ask him in." Santos had already turned his back when Stevenson called out, "No. wait; wait a minute. Go downstairs and photocopy the diary. Bring it back as soon as you're done. On the double!"

Santos almost tripped as he disappeared from sight. Detective Stevenson turned to Peggy O'Brian. "Usher Mr. Dalton into the conference room, and get us two coffees."

A few minutes later he joined Fred Dalton.

"Mr. Dalton," Detective Stevenson said in an amiable tone. "Let me offer my condolences one more time." He stretched out his hand, and Fred gave it a firm shake.

"Thank you."

In denim jeans and a leather coat, Dalton looked ready to go to work in the field, and the tan that stopped just above his eyes, gave him away as a man accustomed to wearing a hat or a helmet. There was an air of urgency in the way he stood.

"Please, sit down," Stevenson said, then sat.

"Actually, I just came for my wife's diary." Fred sighed, hesitated, but finally sat. "I didn't even know she kept one until recently. After the accident you asked me for a few things that were in her room, and you took it along with the rest."

"Yes, I remember. When did you find out about its existence?"

"When I talked with Bea...Beatrice Manson, one of the caregivers. She was the one who transcribed what Deborah...well, what Deborah dictated to her, I guess. My wife couldn't write. The use of her right hand was compromised."

"I see."

Peggy came in and deposited the coffees in front of the two men.

Fred glanced at the female officer and gave her a tiny smile. "Thanks, but at the moment I've banned coffee from my diet. I can't sleep much, you see."

Peggy shot him a sympathetic look and retreated quietly.

For a brief moment Fred followed her silhouette, then turned to look at Stevenson.

"Deborah talked of suicide immediately after the accident, four years ago, but—"

"Excuse me, but what kind of accident did she have?"

"She was pushed off the road at night...she hit a tree. They found her only in the morning and took her to the hospital. By then she had lost a lot of blood." Fred sighed. "They saved her life, but the doctors couldn't do anything about a spine lesion. She lost the use of both legs and her left arm, and almost all use of her right arm." Fred's shoulders heaved, as if to relieve them of a load.

"And where were you when this happened?"

"On a trip. I was attending a workshop on new heating systems in Detroit. Anyway, Deborah went through a period when she wouldn't talk at all. When her condition began to sink in, she became very agitated, angry at the world. The doctor put her on medication and that seemed to calm her a bit...she slept a lot." Fred looked at Stevenson. "Physically, there was nothing the doctors could do to help her, and I couldn't reason with her." He paused. "There was nothing I could do to ease her anxiety or anger."

"It must have been hard for you."

Fred nodded. "The diary?"

"Oh, how forgetful of me. Let me go and get it."

Detective Stevenson descended the stairs that led to the basement, where printers and other computer equipment were kept.

"Santos?"

"Finished, sir. I had a hard time copying two pages onto one...to save paper," he said with a satisfied tone. "I checked page by page. They're all in."

"Thank you, son. Put the photocopy on my desk."

He doubled back and handed the pink book to Fred.

"Here it is," he said, and looked at Fred to capture any reaction. There wasn't any.

"Thanks," Fred said, and turned toward the exit.

When Stevenson returned to his office, many eyes were riveted on him. "Impression?" Peggy asked.

"Cool. He seemed genuinely interested in his wife's diary. The wife dictated her thoughts to one of the nurses, one Beatrice Manson. We interviewed her, and she didn't mention anything different from what appeared to have happened. Mrs. Dalton wanted to die." He paused, and twisted his long moustache. "Peggy, ask Ms. Manson if she can come in again. And here…" He tossed her the photocopy Santos had just made. Peggy grabbed it in mid-air. "Read the diary and tell me what you think. I went through it already, and I got a good idea of its content and who wrote it. However, you may see something that I missed."

"Consider it done. One more thing: should we interview Alicia Bompiani, again? She's the nurse who was on watch when the accident occurred."

Detective Stevenson hesitated, drumming his fingers on the desk. "She was a nervous wreck when I talked to her last time. But, yes, since new factors have emerged. Peggy, you do it this time."

"Fine. Could I hear the two anonymous calls again?"

Stevenson took a digital recorder out of his main drawer and pushed the *Play* button. "Here's the first."

A disembodied voice crackled, "Why were the police so hasty to conclude that the death of Deborah Dalton was suicide? If they had looked more closely around the pool, they'd have discovered something interesting."

Stevenson cut it off. "I sent Santos to take another look at the whirlpool area our man was so eager to clear out. Nothing. We watched the video in triplicate. The camera was set up at a fixed angle to allow Fred's wife to communicate directly with him from inside the large room where she spent most of her time, and the camera's range covered the patio door going onto the pool area. The last few frames showed Deborah opening the door and going through the threshold. Nothing else. There was nobody else around either."

"And the second call?" Peggy asked.

Again, Stevenson clicked *Play*.

A different disembodied voice, more terse, said, "Mr. Fred Dalton killed his wife. He plays the pious husband, but he's known to pick up girls at the Red Baron downtown."

Peggy frowned, staring at the recorder. "And they were sent from where?"

"The first one from a booth at the bus station on Talbot; the second from a restaurant downtown." Stevenson opened the folder that lay on his desk. "The Elephant, that's the name of the restaurant."

"Both men's voices?"

"I'd say so."

"Not much to go on," Peggy said, lost in thought. "The nurses, the caregivers...I mean, they seem to be the only reliable sources. I'll see if I can talk to them tomorrow. I'll go see Alicia; she might be more relaxed being interviewed at home than when you talked to her at Dalton's house or at the station."

Five

.

Peggy entered her Ford pickup, whistling the famous march from Verdi's
Aida. When she arrived at her destination, she parked on the roadside.
Alicia Bompiani lived in a semi-detached house, one of the many lined up
on Gainsborough Road in the northwestern part of London.

She picked up the folder she had previously deposited on the passenger
seat. It contained a report about Alicia Bompiani, and the transcripts of the
two interviews Detective Stevenson had conducted.

A single mother, Alicia had raised two children on the salary she earned
working as a nurse at the London Health Centre. When she reached sixty
and the children were on their own, she had retired and looked for a less-
stressful job. Two years ago she had come across a job assisting a paraplegic
woman. She had contacted Fred Dalton and joined the group of caregivers who orbited around Deborah Dalton. The group was coordinated by
Beatrice Manson, a former caregiver from the Victorian Order of Nurses.
Alicia bathed and dressed Deborah each morning, serving her breakfast and
later, lunch. The eight hours she spent at the house cleared her a hundred
and sixty dollars whether Deborah slept, screamed, or wheeled like mad in
circles in her big room. Alicia had concluded that the woman was totally
nuts and, after the first few days, had managed to do her job without getting upset.

Peggy closed the folder. Today she would gather her own impression of the nurse, and of her charge. From her cell she called Alicia.

"Ms. Bompiani, it's Constable Peggy O'Brian from the London Police Service. Might I have a word with you? It's about our recent investigation into the suicide of Deborah Dalton."

Alicia seemed to hesitate. Was Alicia stalling until she thought of an excuse to avoid seeing another police officer?

"Ms. Bompiani," Peggy rushed to say, "It's really important."

Peggy heard her sighing. "Fine...come over."

"Actually I'm just out front."

Peggy stepped out of her pickup, walked to the ranch-style house, and ascended the few steps in front of the recessed entrance. When the door opened she moved into a large living room. The thick drapes were closed, and a floor lamp bathed a low table and a rumpled sofa in light. A smell of fried onions and meat fanned out from the kitchen.

"Good afternoon, Ms. Bompiani," Peggy said cordially.

"Take a seat," Alicia said, gesturing toward the only straight-back chair available. "Coffee? It's ready. I have a pot on."

"It'd be wonderful. Thank you."

Alicia returned with two mugs and placed them on the coffee table; with a second trip she provided creamer, sugar, and two spoons. She dropped two full spoons of sugar into her coffee, stirred it, and then sat in the rocking chair close to Peggy.

"I told everything I knew to the other officer...your boss?"

"Yes. It was my boss who interviewed you."

Peggy sipped her coffee to have time to observe the woman. Heavy around the hips, with curved shoulders, she looked older than sixty-three. Her short grey hair was thin, and receded at the front hairline; her chin sagged.

"Can you tell me in your own words what happened that day? The day Mrs. Dalton died?"

Alicia waited for a long moment, and then said, "It was the worst day of my life. Everything that could go wrong did."

"Such as?"

"My car didn't start, so I called Jennifer—the girl on duty before me—and asked her if she could stay until I found a ride. She couldn't; she had to take her child to the doctor. I begged her, but she wouldn't budge."

"My understanding is that you're supposed to call Ms. Manson; she was in charge of coordinating the shifts."

After some hesitation Alicia said, "Yes...I should have called her."

"So why didn't you?"

Alicia sighed. "Bea had already told me I had to get another car. There were other times when I couldn't—" She stopped and finished her coffee. "I didn't want to invest money in a new car."

"I see. Continue, please."

"I called Mr. Dalton's office. He's a really nice man. I wanted to speak to him directly, but he was out of town so I left a message with the man who picked up the phone. He told me not to worry, that he'd send somebody over."

"Do you remember the name of the person you spoke to?"

"No."

"Nobody remembered your call."

"Too bad, because I did call The Werkstein." She paused for a moment.

"What can you tell me about Mrs. Dalton?"

"Crazy. That's the only word I can think of. She couldn't move her body, but her tongue! Profanities! She didn't seem to know any other words."

"Do you think she wanted to die?"

"Who knows? Sometimes she wanted to kill everybody around her, and other times she said she wanted to kill herself so Fred would feel guilty about it. She resented people who could walk...so pretty much everybody." She stopped. "That day marked me; I won't be able to find work now. But for poor Mr. Dalton...I'm happy for him."

Peggy hesitated, but her job was to find out the truth. "Do you think Mr. Dalton had a friend...a girlfriend?"

Alicia shrugged. "I don't know anything about that, but I wouldn't blame him if he had."

Peggy rose. "Thank you, Alicia, for your time and the coffee."

When she returned to Headquarters, she found Beatrice Manson waiting for her. Peggy invited her into the conference room and went to the vending machine to get two cans of tea. Beatrice had been trained in England and presented herself in a very professional way. Her navy blue suit was impeccably tailored, and the white top peeping through the front was perfectly ironed. Peggy grabbed a cup for her, certain she wouldn't drink out of a can. For a moment she was tempted to get a recording machine, but Stevenson had advised her to keep this second round of interviews as informal as possible. She should make an effort to ask clear questions that would elicit straight answers.

"Thank you for coming on such short notice," Peggy said as she opened the can for her and poured its content into a paper cup. "We'd like to tie up some loose ends about the death of Mrs. Deborah Dalton."

"I already told the police everything I know. I wasn't there that day."

"We know that. We're just curious about the arrangement Mr. Dalton made with you. You were in charge of providing continuous care through a number of people, mostly nurse-aides or retired nurses, is that right?"

"Right. That was what Mr. Dalton wanted."

Peggy paused, detecting some veiled antagonism. There was an edge she could exploit.

"In your professional opinion, was this kind of arrangement adequate for Mrs. Dalton's needs?"

"No. Mrs. Dalton should have been institutionalized. She should have been in a place where she couldn't hurt herself."

Oh-oh, Peggy thought. *No need to be careful here. She's ready to talk…more than that, she's eager to let it all out.*

"Can you elaborate?"

Beatrice leaned toward Peggy. "Deborah was left to do whatever she liked: screaming, if that pleased her; running around in circles in that big room of hers—have you seen the hardwood floor of that room? Trampled into traffic patterns she made with her wheelchair. I tell you, she was allowed everything, even throwing food at the help if she felt like it. Anything to keep her satisfied."

"Did you talk to Mr. Dalton about it?"

"Yes."

"And…?"

"He replaced the flooring twice. That was his way of handling the situation!" She paused, ready to get more steam out. "The problem was, Deborah didn't want to hear about being locked up, so Mr. Dalton accommodated her."

"What difference would it have made had she been in, let's say, a proper facility?"

"They'd have given her strong meds, the ones that can be administrated only under medical supervision," Bea said in a low voice.

"Did you explain that to the husband?"

"Yes. More than once."

"And his reaction?'

"He said that Deborah would become a zombie, and he didn't want that for his wife."

Peggy looked at Bea for a moment.

"How much did he pay you for assisting Deborah four times a week for eight hours and coordinating the shifts of the other nurses?"

"Four thousand, four hundred and eighty dollars a month."

For a moment Peggy didn't talk. "He was quite generous."

"I was worth every penny of it."

"Did you write in Deborah's diary under her dictation?"

Bea nodded.

"Did Deborah check?"

"Of course she did. Every single time."

"So what's in the diary is what she wanted to be recorded; correct?"

"Yes. Every word."

"Do you think Mrs. Dalton loved her husband?"

"She didn't love anybody; her husband wasn't singled out. She hated most of the help."

"But not the husband?"

"No. She had a great time with him when they were first married. It's in the diary."

"Were there any other incidents in which Deborah got hurt?"

"No. None that I know of."

Peggy thought it was time to explore her relationship with Alicia Bompiani.

"You hired Alicia. Did she miss a shift any other times? What I mean is, did she have problems with not showing up or showing up late?"

"Yes. Nine times. Each time her car wouldn't start. She'd call me and I'd cover up for her until she showed up."

"Didn't you make clear to her that Mrs. Dalton couldn't be left alone?"

"Yes. I told her to get a new car."

Peggy was thoughtful for a moment. Then she asked, "Why didn't you fire her?"

Bea gave her an icy look and stood up, tipping over her drink in the process. "I didn't come here to be professionally insulted! The responsibility of not showing up lies with Ms. Alicia Bompiani!" Without another word she stomped out of the conference room.

Peggy was so surprised that she almost didn't notice that the liquid was trickling near the edge of the table. She quickly rose and got a roll of paper towels. *Deborah Dalton wasn't the only person with a bad temper*, she thought as she cleaned up the spill. *At least Deborah had a reason to resent the world.* She had been pushed off the road and the vehicle that did it had never been identified.

She began to consider Mr. Dalton a victim of circumstances. She would take a second look at the diary's contents and then report her findings to Detective Stevenson.

Six

When Fred left Headquarters, he held tight onto his late wife's diary. He was eager to see whether Deborah had left any record of the visits to her hometown, her renewed friendship with Tessa Wilson, her contacts with Father Thomas and the strange funeral arrangement. Unfortunately, an accident had occurred on one of the job sites, and he had to rush there to see what had happened. Nobody was hurt, but the collapse of the formwork had required the temporary suspension of the construction. He had spent a full day analyzing the problem, until he discovered that unfit material had been used. New material had to be ordered, so it was only two days later that he had time to think about Deborah's diary, which he had left in his car.

He eased into his white Lexus and began reading. There were brief remarks about her unfortunate condition and the inability of people around her to remedy it. *Over and over again…* He shook his head. He was very familiar with Deborah's feelings; they were no different from those she broadcast aloud, at times for half a day. Four years had passed since the accident; those four years had reduced her to a shadow of herself. He could hardly associate the image that emerged from the diary with the woman he had married, who had been so full of *joie de vivre*. Destiny had been cruel to her, and he hadn't been able to bring her comfort. He still felt a pang when he thought of her condition. He kept reading until the end. With disappointment he realized there was nothing about her visit to her home-town or the funeral arrangements.

He closed the diary and drove to his office.

On his desk rested two copies of the bid for a housing compound of twenty units. On top of one copy was a yellow Post-it: *Your copy. I high-lighted the items more likely to be altered. M.*

Fred sat in his swivel chair and went through his copy, page by page. He took a pocket calculator from the main drawer and added the amounts corre-sponding to the highlighted items. They totaled one hundred fifty thousand dollars, and the proposed cost of the project was just over five million. He'd realized some time back that crooks had been operating with impunity inside his company, probably for years. This project might help him to catch them.

Now it was time to talk to Moira, the junior engineer who had discov-ered the doctored amounts in previous projects, and, at his request, had conducted a discreet, unofficial investigation. He clicked on her stored phone number and asked her to come to his office.

Moira Johnson was barely over five feet tall, thin, with an unruly mass of red curls that added an inch to her height. Freckles covered her face, with particular intensity on the nose. Her light gray eyes were magnified by the lenses of her eyeglasses, which often slid to the tip of her petite nose. Usually she dressed casually in jeans and a bright top underneath a white coat she left open at the front. She had joined The Werkstein Company a year ago, and the other employees, all male except the secre-tary, had not welcomed her. She came with unusual expertise: as well as holding a university degree, she had worked in a small company until the owner had died and his company consequently disbanded. She was famil-iar with the software used to price a project, from the different materials used to the estimation of the labor hours. She prepared her reports using the materials listed in the specifications, but she also suggested alternate choices which, if approved by the architect or the owner, would bring the cost down. In the short time she had been with The Werkstein, she had made the two people previously in charge of pricing obsolete.

"Come in," Fred called, responding to a soft knock. He stood.

Moira entered and stretched her hand to Fred. "Once again, condo-lences. How have you been?"

"Destroyed. Can't sleep; have a hard time concentrating. I can't believe I let it happen, with all the help I hired and the precautions I took."

"It was a fatality. Stop blaming yourself."

"There's something I've been meaning to ask you, Moira. Do you know whether Verge got a call from Alicia Bompiani that morning?"

"I wouldn't know. I called in sick that morning. I had to make a few calls that could have raised suspicion. You know what I mean."

"Yes, yes, I know." He looked at the papers on his desk. "Let's get to work. When do you think our men will go into action? Swapping subs isn't easy after the contract is signed."

"In the past job, two subs were substituted after the bidding but before the contract was signed—the contract you signed. Then material of inferior quality was ordered. I caught that one and played it as if an error had occurred. I didn't say anything to Verge or Alain; I sent back the material and ordered the material specified by the architect." Moira sighed. "I overheard them calling me names, but they couldn't do anything about it."

"Good girl."

"My feeling is that this time they're going for the kill. I know they're in contact with five companies The Werkstein normally doesn't use because they're not bonded. You should be able to nail them."

"I know Alain had problems with his previous employer—I checked with them after you pointed out the scam—but are you sure about Verge?"

"Unfortunately, yes. He supervises what happens in the field. He knows who's supposed to supply the construction materials, and he's often present when it's delivered. He's in it, too."

Fred raked his graying hair. "I have to clean up this mess, and all I feel like doing is leaving everything and going up north to live with the Inuit."

Moira was motionless for a moment.

"Well...you *are* finally free, Fred." She looked at him from above her glasses.

"Yes, but the way it happened left me with a bitter taste." He slumped in his swivel chair. "Let's make a list of the companies that might be involved in this scam. We should also try to find out whether the company as a whole is involved or whether it's the isolated work of one person."

Moira's cell rang and she opened it. "Yes, I know we have a meeting. I'll be there right away," she said into the speaker. She looked at Fred. "It was Alain. I'd better go. Let me know if there's anything else I can do."

✳ ✳ ✳

Seven

The storm had finally subsided and most of the officers on duty at Headquarters had returned to the station. Heavy wind and rain had caused branches to fall and a series of thunderbolts had severed entire trees, causing several accidents and blocking traffic in vital points of the city. There were reports to be filed, and for hours everybody was busy on one computer or another. It was only the day after that Detective Stevenson had time to talk to Constable O'Brian.

"Peggy," Stevenson called out. "You interviewed the two nurses involved in Mrs. Dalton's case. What's your conclusion?"

"Nothing substantial. The professionalism of the person in charge of the assistance, Beatrice Manson, is questionable, but two facts emerged: one, there hadn't been one single accident in which Deborah was involved before the one that caused her death; two, the husband refused to lock up his wife in a mental institution. He realized, I believe, that his wife was wild and difficult to manage, but that she was not crazy. Apparently he coped, for four years, with a very difficult situation."

"And the diary? What do you think of it?"

"Several notes on the inefficiency of the authorities in finding the vehicle that caused her invalidism. Remarks against friends who were unkind to her, complaints about some of the nurses. I couldn't find a thing that can enlighten us." She looked at her boss. "Did you discover anything interesting?"

"Nothing at the night club. Nobody remembers having seen him. I did hear one minor fact that might turn out to be interesting. At the moment our man has set up living quarters in his sister's apartment, located in a very exclusive building off Wonderland Road. Fred's sister, Charlotte Gassman, owns it, but doesn't live there. Her usual residence is in Port Franks."

"So?"

"I talked with the superintendent. Fred Dalton went there almost regularly, say once a week, even when the sister wasn't there."

"Alone?"

"We don't know for sure. The building had two entrances: one at the front and one at the back. The one at the back opens only with a digital card, which provides access to a private elevator. Mr. Dalton always used the front one, but the superintendent suspects somebody came to visit him the nights he was there, sneaking in through the back door."

"Interesting," Peggy said.

"It surely is. The sister was down for the funeral and stayed in London for a few days. She's gone now. Fred seems to have set up camp there alone."

"He may be cautious; he might suspect that we're keeping an eye on him."

"It could be," Stevenson said. "We'll have to wait and see."

"Any other phone calls hinting on Dalton's guilt?"

"No. I had a friendly chat with some of The Werkstein employees in the eatery across the road where some of them have lunch. Dalton's secretary, Mary Gervasio, considers him a saint. She said the wife would often call him even in the middle of a business meeting and he always tried to listen to her and soothe her. He needed to work, he would tell her, to provide her with the assistance she got, which was very expensive. I approached the two top employees, but they claimed they were too busy at the moment: two big jobs closing within days. I'll go see them when the rush is over." He paused and twisted his long moustache. "Tomorrow I'll go to the company's job sites and talk to the foremen. Mr. Dalton worked in the field as a bricklayer when he was young. I might get a feeling for the man."

Constable Lopes quietly entered and sat at his desk.

"Hello Santos. You were gone all day yesterday following Dalton. Where did he take you?"

"To a small village past Midland and then to the cemetery. He said a prayer over on his wife's, I mean his late wife's tomb."

Both Detective Stevenson and Peggy O'Brian laughed.

"If he knew he was being shadowed, that was a nice way to pull our leg," Stevenson said.

Carrying a bottle of Gray Goose Vodka, Fred entered his sister's apartment. It was totally dark at that time of night. He moved to one side and turned on the floor lamp. It arched over half the room; its shade, a huge daisy, sheltered a halogen bulb that spread bright light over a love seat, two upholstered chairs and a side table.

Fred deposited the bottle on the floor, sat in one of the chairs and stretched his legs over the table. He looked for the remote and turned on the television, not bothering to select a channel. He just wanted some background noise to keep him company. For two weeks he had dug into Deborah's last days, still puzzled by her suicide. The caregivers had said she had talked about it more than once; however, she hadn't mentioned it to him. Her talk of suicide dated back four years, to the time when she realized that she would never be mobile again.

Then there was Father Thomas, whose attitude toward him was only an inch away from being insulting. Fred sighed, and rose to get a glass from the lacquered bar situated in a corner. He poured himself a generous portion of vodka and sipped from it. He couldn't help feeling guilty; he wondered whether that feeling would ever leave him. He remembered Deborah attracting attention in the circle of their friends, ready to spring up to go places or play a game of tennis. He remembered the time when, after their honeymoon, she had come to a construction site for the first time. The sound of nailing shingles on the roof had stopped instantly as the workers gazed in awe at the tall, slender woman getting out of the car, her dark hair in a ponytail, her shapely legs stretching down from a white miniskirt that adhered perfectly to her little rump. The car accident had occurred six years later, and it had shattered not only her life but also his, albeit it in a different way. He wondered whether he would ever recover from those four long years of watching her suffer.

A soft knock on the door dispelled his memories.

He rose and opened the door. "Moira?"

"Hi, Fred." Moira waved a bag from KFC with one hand and a manila envelope with the other. "I got chicken nuggets with three sauces. Mary fell sick, so I offered to come over since I thought you might want to look at the document I have with me."

"Thank you," Fred said, and closed the door.

Moira deposited both the box with the food and the envelope on the table. "They told me you wouldn't be going to the party."

"Right."

"We'll miss you." Moira stood in front of him. Her pleated skirt and ruffled blouse made her look younger than her twenty-eight years.

"Believe me, I'd drag everybody down if they glimpsed my face."

"But the awarding of the two new contracts—totaling over ten million—is something worth celebrating!" She cocked her head and smiled. "You always did, before." As Fred shook his head vigorously she said, "Well, I should be going." She pointed at the envelope. "All you need to know about the illegal changes the two men plan to introduce is in there." At the door, she turned back. "Don't forget to eat."

And she was gone.

Detective Stevenson rolled back the latest film that had been taken near the rear entrance of Charlotte Gassman's apartment.

"Nothing," he said, discouraged. "Nothing of substance."

The film taken at the front entrance hadn't revealed any strange visitors either—just family, long-term friends of the Dalton's family or employees. Stevenson wiggled in his chair and watched the last two films once again.

"Two weeks of surveillance and absolutely zilch," he said.

Constable Santos was waiting for his boss to dictate the last words to include in the report.

"Did you record the time and place and everything I dictated to you?" Stevenson asked.

"Yes, sir."

"Write down the name and action of the last visitor: Ms. Moira Johnson visited the suspect, carrying a box from KFC and a manila envelope. She stayed in the apartment for about ten minutes and returned without the box and the envelope. She then drove away, probably to join the party held to celebrate the two new jobs The Werkstein Company managed to land, beating out stiff competition."

What a waste of city resources to put a tail on The Bricklayer. The man was leading the life of a recluse. Either he was very cunning or he was innocent, but it was impossible to determine which. Stevenson thought maybe he should let go of the issue, considering that there had not been any other calls insinuating his involvement in Deborah Dalton's death. He drummed his fingers on the desk, pondering the case.

Suppose Mr. Dalton was guilty and there was a third party involved—he would be careful at the beginning, but not forever. *Maybe I should extend the surveillance a little longer.* He looked at the timetable with the scheduled assignments for his unit. With no pressing matters coming up, he could spare a bit more spying.

"Anything else?" Santos asked.

"No. You can file the update on the case. You and Peggy will keep alternating the surveillance in the evening." As Santos looked at him questionably, he added, "One more week…less if something urgent comes up."

Eight

Tessa Wilson headed for Port Franks with the roof of her red Corvette convertible completely retracted. She enjoyed the rough caress of the wind. She had spent wonderful vacations on the stunning beach that ran along Lake Huron, practicing boogie boarding and body surfing. At night she and her friends used to gather on Charlotte Gassman's vast property to play music, make a bonfire and, often, smoke weed. Even if Fred joined them only rarely, his friends had permission to enjoy his sister's hospitality.

Fun memories of those times accompanied Tessa until she arrived at her destination. She parked her car near the entrance to the Gassman estate and tugged at the door. As she expected, it was open; she entered the house without hesitation. Her heels resounded crisply off the marble floor as she crossed a parlor and a long corridor to reach the patio of Charlotte's house. Charlotte Gassman called it a cottage, but in both architecture and furnishing the dwelling was luxurious. It was one-story, with a master bedroom, two guest bedrooms, a den, and a kitchen-dining room that shared a fireplace with a family room, and a solarium. The patio graded smoothly into the sandy beach that recent erosion had reduced to a depth of only fifty feet. Half a dozen fuchsia plants suspended from the overhead girders; their buds and flowers varied from bright red to soft pink.

Charlotte turned her head as Tessa approached the lounge chair where she leisurely stretched out. A huge black cat rested on her lap.

"Nice of you to come," Charlotte said in response to Tessa's hello, and tossed the *Vogue* magazine she was reading onto the nearby table. As Tessa came near her, Charlotte straightened up in her chair and deposited the cat on the ground opposite Tessa. The cat mewed a nasty complaint and arched her back. "Sultana is getting old and mean. Lately, she seems to hate visitors." Charlotte rose, picked up the cat and took it inside. She returned soon afterward. "Now we can visit in peace," she said, and sat again in the lounge chair. "What's new?"

"I went to Fred's house to help out." Tessa sighed. "A full day—I tell you, it took me a full day to go through the last part of Deborah's stuff. Sometimes Fred came in to help, but most of the time I had to do it by myself." She sat in a chair close to Charlotte, took off her high-heel shoes, and threw her straw hat onto the table. "It's so peaceful here. You live in a beautiful place."

"Beautiful, but isolated," Charlotte said. "But you didn't come here to hear me complaining about the location of my house, I guess."

"No. I wanted to spend some time with you." She poured herself a glass of water from the pitcher that was on the table. "To be honest, I'm worried about Fred. He seems moody. I think he's lost twenty pounds since the accident. He eats little and talks even less…monosyllables, most of the time."

Charlotte adjusted the straps of her bathing suit, which had slipped down her forearms. "Not much we can do, Tessa. He needs time to reconcile with himself, time to convince himself that he's not responsible for what happened to Deborah."

"You may be right. But…I thought there was something else bugging him…perhaps something about the present, not the past." She paused and moved her chair out from under the awning so she would be exposed to the morning sun, then slipped off her dress, underneath which she wore a black bikini. "He's living in your apartment now, right?"

"Yes. His most recent house was never a home to him. He's going to renovate it and sell it as fast as he can."

"I understand." Tessa sipped the water slowly, staring at the boats leaving the harbor, navigating slowly through the channel marked by the red and green buoys.

Charlotte adjusted the pillow behind her back.

"Tell me something, Tessa. I know your divorce became final a year ago." She gave Tessa a penetrating look. "You're only forty-four. You don't intend to stay single for long, I hope." Tessa didn't reply and Charlotte continued. "Don't do what I did. I lost my husband eight years ago. Not only did I bury him, but I also buried myself in total solitude. It was a mistake."

"Well, I wouldn't mind dating. You remember Nick Falcone? He was Fred's buddy in high school and beyond; they chummed around all the time."

"Do I remember! They almost drowned in this bay, going out wind-surfing in bad weather! First Nick's board broke to pieces. Then, when Fred took him aboard, *his* cracked in the middle. They made it ashore up to their knees in water with a sail that had been reduced to a quarter its size."

Tessa laughed. "Don't forget the adventure with the sand buggy they made themselves. Remember? They chose to test it on the highest sand dune they could find, and it capsized on the first run."

"Fred was on it. He had sand all over: in his clothes and shoes, even in his ears, he told me." Charlotte paused, immersed in her remembrance. "They stayed friends for some time, I believe."

"Oh, yes. Nick was still around when Deborah got engaged to Fred," Tessa said. "Then Nick moved out west."

"He wasn't a bad character, just a bit rough," Charlotte said.

"Well...he liked Deborah and he wasn't too happy when she started going steady with Fred." She paused. "He came back last month. He intends to stay around."

"Oh..."

"His parents died and left him the family house off Highway 21, not far from the lake."

Charlotte gave her a scrutinizing look. "Interested in him?"

"Oh, no. As you said before, he was a bit rough, and he still is. Maybe for going out and listening to music—we both love dancing." She paused again. "Do you think Fred would ever marry again?"

Charlotte rose, gathered their glasses and the carafe, and set them on a tray. "I wouldn't know." She strode inside. Over her shoulder, she hollered, "If you'd like to have a nice swim, this is the best time. Go ahead while I fix lunch."

"I'll swim later," Tessa said and followed Charlotte inside. "I'd like to ask you a favor."

"Yes?"

"Invite me one evening when Fred is here. I'd really like that."

Charlotte hesitated. "Well, he comes over often now that the weather is nice, but I don't know that he's ready for company. Mostly he just sits in a chair and stares at the lake."

"Please, Charlotte. It means a lot to me."

"Okay, then. I'll call you one of these days."

The dining area was a natural extension of the kitchen, the two partially separated by a counter with a white-and-green granite top. A bay window offered a skewed view of the lake and a snapshot of the garden overwhelmed with flowerbeds and colorful bushes. Along one wall a china cabinet paraded Delft blue dishes on the bottom shelves and Royal Doulton figurines on the top one. A big oval table and a three-level chandelier dominated the central space. The carpet was vivid green, and the crown moldings at the ceiling corners were gold on an ivory backdrop.

Charlotte had served supper on the table, where three blue place mats coordinated well with the china dishes. Dinner had been a luxurious rarity for Fred: pheasant, asparagus, and fried portabella mushrooms. A Black Forest cake stood in the middle of the table, almost untouched.

Fred filled the flutes with champagne for Charlotte and himself.

"What was the idea of inviting Tessa?" Fred asked, his tone between curt and bitter.

Charlotte didn't answer.

"Since she came back to live in town she's been around a lot. First, with the excuse of keeping Deborah company, and then with helping me move out."

"She begged me," Charlotte replied sheepishly. "She insisted and insisted, and I finally caved in. I didn't know it'd upset you."

"I can't explain, but her presence irritates me. Do you know what she did?"

Charlotte shook her head.

"She was with Deborah when Deborah went to her old hometown and arranged that farce of a funeral with Father Thomas!" Fred threw the blue paper napkin that was beside him to the far side of the table.

"I didn't know."

"I thought you didn't."

"But how do *you* know?"

"I went to see Father Thomas. Deborah went there four times, but on three occasions Tessa was with her; she followed Deborah in her car at Deborah's request."

"She should have told you of Deborah's intentions." Charlotte remained pensive for a minute. "Probably she didn't take Deborah's idea seriously. I know I wouldn't have."

"You may be right. I also got annoyed with her when one day she showed up at the house. I was busy with the foreman in charge of restructuring the old place and she went through Deborah's belongings without my permission, packing stuff in boxes. Then she got upset when I told her I had to close up and go back to my office. She didn't want to leave!" Fred sipped his wine. "Did she come to visit you often?"

"Yes, and I didn't know what to make of it. She talked a lot about the times you two were in high school, and then the summers she spent here at the lake. She remembered the Saturday nights when you, Deborah, Nick, and she partied on the beach until late at night. You dated her, right?"

"Yes. We went out a couple of times. She talked incessantly about money—she didn't need to work, she would say. She'd marry somebody who'd strike it rich."

"She married Walter Wilson. He *was* rich."

"Well, his parents were, but I heard he went through the family fortune at record speed." Fred laughed. "She had to divorce him quickly or she wouldn't have gotten a cent."

"Right," Charlotte said, and paused. "By the way, she told me Nick is back in town."

"Nick Falcone? I thought he was out west."

"His parents died two months ago. He lives on the family farm."

"Does he plan to farm?"

"I wouldn't know."

"I don't see Nick settling down. And farming? He isn't the type; he likes to be free. He was a lot of fun to be with. A bit risky at times, especially when he was at the wheel. He loved to speed." Fred rose and cut a piece of the chocolate cake. "Want some?" he asked Charlotte.

"Not at the moment. Maybe later." She sipped from her flute. "I gather you aren't interested in seeing any of the old gang. Tessa was thinking of throwing a party, a kind of reunion with all the people you used to chum around with."

"Not right now. I'm still in mourning."

"Right. By the way, did you ask her what she knew about the arrangement of Deborah's funeral?"

"No. What I learned is based on Father Thomas' recollection. The fellow seems to have a grudge against me. I don't want to stir up something that won't go anywhere. What's done is done."

"True." For a while nobody spoke, then Charlotte asked, "How Deborah paid for the funeral?"

"With her credit card. I never cancelled it; once in a blue moon she went out to do a bit of shopping. A nurse would be with her, and the stores gladly accepted her scribbling."

Charlotte rose and covered the cake with the plastic top on the table.

"Let me help you," Fred said.

"No need. I'll just put the cake away. Lucy comes in every night to check up on me. She'll clear the table."

Fred left Charlotte's house and drove home, or at least to his temporary home. Tessa's insistence on hanging around Charlotte and trying to extend that to him was puzzling. Tessa would flirt with any man within a radius of a few feet, but as a young girl she was never seriously interested in him. He'd had to support himself while going to the university, and Tessa liked money.

Is she interested in me now?

Charlotte had married a businessman who had made profitable investments and founded a construction company, The Werkstein. He had hired Fred and, a few years later, Fred had become the general manager of the company. When Werner Gassman, Charlotte's husband, had died, Charlotte had inherited everything—a fortune in the millions—and there were no children.

Fred tried to make some sense of Tessa's sudden interest in him. For the last decade business had been booming, allowing him to earn a good million every year; he had also invested most of his earnings in the company's shares and was now the major stockholder. But he didn't own the company; forty percent of the shares were still in Charlotte's name. *She probably consider me a good catch,* Fred thought. For the moment he would count on his sister to keep Tessa at bay.

✵ ✵ ✵

Nine

The Werkstein Company Ltd. had offices on the third floor of a high-rise on Trafalgar Street in London East and a building yard only fifteen kilometers out of town. With twenty full-time employees and an annual gross income averaging twenty million, the company was ranked mid-size by the Ontario Association of General Contractors and fell in that particular statistical bracket where the profit-investment ratio was high while the danger of going broke was low. When he took over the company, Fred had made two minor changes: he had requested major subcontractors be bonded, thus protecting the company against the risk that some would go broke, and he had improved the company's efficiency by inspecting each job site often and in person. These, of course, had been the dynamics until the accident that left Deborah paralyzed.

For the last four years he had relied heavily on Verge Bristol and Alain Alstein, and last year he had agreed to hire another engineer, Moira Johnson. He had done so with reluctance, but the need to get new blood into the company had been real. Competitors used advanced software to estimate the cost of each component, thus making the entire process of pricing faster and more accurate. For a while Fred had thought of acquiring the new skill himself, but hours outside of work were spent taking care of Deborah's problems.

He also knew that his two key men had passed the age in which learning came easy and appealing. Both Bristol and Alstein were marking time,
and didn't hide their desire to retire as soon as a good occasion presented
itself. Fred had, therefore, agreed to hire a person familiar with Autodesk,
Pro/ENGINEER and other computer-assisted-design software. He hadn't
been ready, however, to get a female engineer. Except for his secretary, Mary
Gervasio, his employees were all men.

He didn't think of himself as a sexist; he was more concerned about
whether a woman would feel out of place, rather than about the way the
men would treat her. After he had interviewed several candidates, though,
Moira Johnson had emerged as the best person available on the market
for the fifty-thousand dollar salary The Werkstein was prepared to pay. A
graduate from the University of Windsor, Moira had spent two years in a
small company where she had consolidated the trade learned in school.

And so a year ago little redhead Moira had joined the company; her
duties dealt, almost exclusively, with pricing and visualizing the projects
the company bid for.

"This had better be important," Alain Alstein said, as he slumped in
his chair. "My wife and I are ready to take off for Vegas."

Verge's eyes grew wide. "But it's only Friday!"

"There's nothing to do at the office; if they ask for me, tell them I'm
on job site number five." He wiggled in his chair. "There was a sensational
promotion for the weekend: two hundred dollars each, flight and accommodations included. We couldn't pass it up." He glimpsed at his wristwatch and sighed.

"Sure, and they're going to get your money when you gamble! Well, I'll
make it brief. Fred's checking the contract related to the first job."

"What do you mean?"

"He went through it with a marker and highlighted all the subs we'd
listed."

"Oh, he wants to check, eh? But he's never done that!"

"Yes, he has, before Deborah had the accident." Verge sat behind his
desk. "Now that she's gone he has time to do it again."

"What do you propose?"

"Two options—either we tell our friends we can't do it this time and
give them back the money or..."

Alain's face flushed red with anger. "I can't afford that! I already spent that money!"

"You didn't let me finish. The other possibility is to falsify the document; that is, we can replace the listed subs with the ones we want to use and exchange his copy with a new one."

"But there're seals!"

"Of course there're seals. That's why falsifying it can get us in deep trouble."

"Where does he keep the contract?"

"Main drawer of his desk; he locks it, but I know where he keeps the key, so there would be no problem in getting the one out and replacing it with the other. The seal is also there."

Alain glimpsed again at his watch. "What about the contract for the second job? Did he check that one too?"

"I don't know."

Alain shook his head. "He has too much time on his hands now that his wife is gone."

"Agreed, but what can we do? Find him a girlfriend?"

Alain's cell rang. He only listened and rose.

"It was my wife," he said. "She's downstairs, ready to go to the airport." He thought for a moment. "Falsify. That's the only choice we have at the moment. I'll think of something else for the second job."

"Fine," Verge said.

Alain was already out of the office.

A two-by-three foot *For Sale* sign hung on the wrought-iron gate of the Dalton's property. Fred checked its position and made sure it was well visible from the road, then left for the office, satisfied that the work on the house was proceeding as planned. There were two crews at work: one laying fresh sod where the whirlpool had once been; the other just starting to restructure the interior. It had taken three weeks to get the building permit.

This was his chance for a new life, and for the first time since Deborah's death, he felt energized. As he entered his office Fred looked at his planner and the incoming tray. *Not much in it*, he realized with satisfaction. Finally he felt he was on top of things, instead of running after them.

He neared the large window and looked outside. It was a beautiful sunny day and one of the warmest. A breeze bowed the young trees on the front lawn of the building; they had been planted only last spring. Summer was at its peak, and he looked forward to spending some time on the lake, swimming or body surfing again.

It felt good to be alive.

Ten

Bertoldi's, the Italian Trattoria on Richmond Street, was getting more full by the minute. In a corner, Tessa Wilson and Nick Falcone took turns dipping a slice of bread into the aromatic oil the house offered to customers who waited to order.

"You look fantastic," Nick said. "Aging seems to agree with you. You were such a skinny girl when you were young." He winked. "You've filled out nicely in all the right spots. And that miniskirt suits you perfectly."

"Thanks. I've been divorced for more than a year," she said, and smiled at him. "I haven't heard such a nice compliment for a long time."

"You know, I'm a specialist in consoling widows and divorcees." He took her hand and kissed it. "Tell me what's on your mind."

"I'm upset," Tessa said. "Apparently Fred doesn't want to have a reunion with his old friends."

"We can do it without him," Nick said. With his rugged face, drooping eyes and thin hair Nick looked older than his forty-four years.

"It'd be difficult. I was counting on his sister's house for the party. It's on the lake, and the beach is private. There's even an outdoor fireplace and two grills for barbecuing. It'd be fabulous, like old times."

"Why don't you ask her directly?"

"I did. I thought the two of us were close friends, but she gave me a flat-out no. She claimed that she's too old to throw a big party."

A waiter came to the table and took their orders, ricotta gnocchi for Tessa and Margherita pizza for Nick. They both chose a glass of the house white wine.

"How much is Charlotte worth?" Nick asked.

"In the two-digit millions...I don't know how much precisely. She inherited everything from her husband, industrialist Werner Gassman. He had investments all over."

"I see. And who is her heir?"

"Fred. When I saw her last time we chatted a lot. She talked about how much she and Werner regretted not having children. She said her brother Fred would inherit everything." Tessa paused and sipped her wine. "Fred was the poorest of our gang. He went to work while we partied, but he might end up being the richest of us all, and not too late either. Charlotte is only in her fifties, but she isn't in good health and he isn't even forty."

"It'll be a big coup when the old lady croaks."

"It surely will be," Tessa said. "Anyway, we have to find another place for our reunion. Maybe the Pinery. There're strict rules about drinking, though."

"We could do it at my place. It isn't fancy, but we can have a bonfire. We'd need only a couple of extra picnic tables. The house is away from the road, so we can have loud music."

"Is that your late parents' farm?"

"Yes. I got the house and a tiny parcel of land around it."

The waiter came and set a big plate in front of each. "Enjoy your meal," he said, and disappeared.

"I never thought they'd do that to me," Nick said. "My fucking parents! They sold their six hundred acres of farming land and used the money to travel around the world, and left me with a dilapidated house."

"That was terrible; I agree."

They savored their food in silence for a while.

"But it'd be nice to hold the party on the lake," Tessa said. "We could go windsurfing like old times."

"You're right," Nick said. "I may go see Charlotte myself. She was always nice to us and never made a fuss if we messed up her lawn or got a few beers out of her fridge. Besides, I have a way with old ladies." He winked.

Tessa pushed her plate, still half-full, to the middle of the table. "Good idea. Maybe you can get her to change her mind about the party."

A waiter deposited the bill on the table and walked away to take the order from the next customer. Tessa looked at it.

"Who pays the bill?" she asked.

"You do, of course."

Tessa threw two twenties and a ten on the table.

"See you Saturday," she said, and left.

A week later Tessa and Nick sat on a bench in the shady area surrounding the marina in Port Franks, their legs stretched out on top of the big blue cooler they had brought with them. Tessa wore white slacks and a vivid yellow tank top, Nick just a pair of shorts. It was mid-afternoon and the place was quiet. Most boats were still on the lake.

"So you'd like to get close to Fred...How close?" Nick asked.

"Well, I'd like to marry him, of course. He has status and money. And he'll be loaded when dear Charlotte departs."

Nick laughed. "You always looked at the almighty dollar. Didn't you take your ex for a couple million?"

"Don't mention that fucking cheat. Fancy cars and a yacht in the family...they talked a good show, but they didn't have damn-all. I didn't get any alimony, just a lump sum: four-hundred thousand, not enough to live on."

"But you have the house in London. That's around another eight hundred thousand, isn't it?"

She shrugged. "Something like that."

Nick looked at a boat coming in and waved at the skipper. "That's an old friend of mine." He stood up. "Be right back."

Tessa waited a while; then walked to the ramp. Nick was helping to pull his friend's boat ashore. When he had finished he exchanged a last greeting with the skipper and rejoined Tessa. Together they strolled back to the bench.

"He gave me a joint," he said. "Wanna drag?"

"No. I don't do it anymore."

"Oh, I didn't know." He lit it. "So let's get back to your problem. You want to get close to Fred, and you found out that Charlotte doesn't want to collaborate. Is that about right?"

"Yes."

Nick pondered the problem for a moment.

"You know how much I'd like to get even with Fred—after all, he literally stole Deborah from me—but our world is far away from his. It'd be difficult to create occasions where the two of you meet. His sister isn't willing to host even an innocent barbecue dinner, and I don't know anybody in the construction business." He looked at Tessa for a long time. "You told me you kept Deborah company in the last few months on and off. Isn't he grateful to you for that?"

"I suspect he found out I knew about the funeral arrangements and resents the fact that I didn't say anything. Of course I thought Deborah was joking. She'd become particularly wild in those days at the end." Tessa sighed. "Everybody I talked to at the reception following the ceremony said both Fred and Charlotte were appalled at the arrangements."

"I don't blame them. Why didn't you talk to Fred about it in advance?"

Tessa shrugged. "I thought it was one of her crazy ideas, and it'd end there, all talk, no action."

He shook his head. "I don't know how to help you out; the entire situation seems out of reach."

Tessa posed a hand on his bare arm. "There is one thing you can do for me: find out whether he's seeing another woman."

Nick laughed. "You were in and out of his house quite often and couldn't find out?"

"Fred made a point of having supper with Deborah and one of the nurses. He kept it intimate, if you can call that intimate."

"I see; the super-dedicated husband. I don't buy it."

"I don't either, but I couldn't very well check up on his activities day and night."

"And you want me to?"

"Yes." She caressed his arm once more. "I can be very, *very* nice, if you know what I mean."

Nick roared with laughter. "I know that very well. But if you marry Fred, I want a piece of the action: money, to be precise."

The sun was close to setting and swimmers and boaters alike started to pack their belongings and leave the marina. A yacht approached the oldest ramp where Port Franks' icon, an imposing big anchor, stood. Two men jumped ashore and waved at Nick.

"Ah, a couple more old friends of mine," said Nick. "Come, Tessa, let's join them. I'd like to know what they've been doing while I was out west."

✳ ✳ ✳

Eleven

When the red Corvette stopped near the entrance of Charlotte Gassman's house the sun had just set, leaving a deep rose glow on the sandy dunes. Tessa looked at Nick.

"Do you think it's a good idea to drop in without calling first?" she asked.

Nick emitted a sharp, raspy laugh. "That's the only way to prevent her saying she doesn't want to see me." He got out of the car. "Stay here. I work better alone in a case like this." He winked at her. "Trust me."

"If you insist."

Nick took a small comb out of his jeans pocket and ran it through his thin hair. He bent to use the car's side mirror to check on his image.

"Good enough for any woman on the planet, and surely extra good for a fifty-six-year-old wreck." With one easy hop over the white picket fence he entered Charlotte's premises.

Tessa followed Nick's masculine figure as he approached the patio at the back of the house. When he wasn't stoned out of his mind from booze or drugs, he was a lot of fun. He was also a good fuck. She was using him to get close to Fred, but there might be problems down the road. They had struck a deal: if she reached her goal of marrying Fred, she would give him half a million dollars. He hadn't promised, however, that he would stay out of sight. Tessa sighed. She would have preferred not to involve Nick in her scheme, but she had no other way to get close to Fred.

Yesterday, they had decided they would convince Charlotte to give a big surprise party for Fred's upcoming fortieth birthday. That would provide a good opportunity for Tessa to exercise her charms. After all, she was better looking than Deborah had ever been.

Tessa glanced toward the house. Somebody had turned on a light, probably the big chandelier in the dining area. She sighed, a bit worried about what Nick had in mind to convince dear Charlotte to host the party. She would have liked to spend more time with Nick and discuss the matter in greater detail, but Fred's birthday was less than three weeks away. Time was running short and Nick's idea to go see Charlotte and convince her to host the surprise party seemed a viable solution.

Tessa stepped out of the car, stretched her limbs, and took a short stroll down the road. It was getting dark and she wasn't pleased at being by herself. Half an hour later, as she walked back, Nick quickly vaulted over the fence. He opened the passenger door of the Corvette and jumped inside.

Tessa hurried back to the car. "What's going on?"

"Drive! Let's get out of here!"

Tessa turned the car around and took the road for London.

"I want to know what happened," Tessa asked with a tone that demanded an answer.

"Nothing of importance…a little accident, that's all."

"I want to know!" Tessa shouted.

Nick glared at her. "Shut up and drive!"

It was wise to avoid fighting with Nick. When he was in a foul mood he was capable of violent acts, as she had experienced more than once. She kept quiet. A few moments later Nick lowered his seat and stretched out. She breathed a sigh of relief when she heard a light snore.

She turned smoothly onto Highway 81 and drove without uttering a sound. In Mt. Bridges she turned on County Road 14 and headed to the west side of London, where her house was located. She parked her car parallel to Nick's pickup, turned off the engine and glanced at her passenger. Nick's head lay sideways on the headrest, his left arm hanging relaxed on the side. There were two long scratches on it; wide around his elbow, they thinned down toward his wrist. Probably Charlotte's old cat had left its imprint. No need to wake Nick up.

Once inside the house, Tessa locked her door and got a glass of warm milk. For the time being she wouldn't bother to ask Nick about the result of his encounter with dear Charlotte. Clearly he had failed. *No surprise*, Tessa thought as she headed for her bedroom. *After all, he's a born loser.*

Fred unfolded the last roll of blueprints and laid them on the floor. Two other sets were spread on the sofa and the kitchen table. Crouched on his knees, he used a pencil to make a modification to the floor plan. This was a project of the design-and-build type, the kind that raked in a lot of money even if the job itself wasn't very big; the one at hand consisted of a 12,000 square-foot hangar commissioned by Mr. Saldini. The Werkstein was responsible for all the work, from inception to realization; it required only the building owner's approval. Fred had hired an architect for the design; the blueprints he looked at were the first phase of the project. He had been working on it for two hours straight, from time to time sipping on a cup of coffee.

He needed a break and a snack. As he walked toward the fridge, his phone rang. At first he couldn't understand a word of what was said on the other end of the line, then he recognized the voice of Lucy Fairweather, Charlotte's part-time maid.

"Calm down, calm down, Lucy," he said. "Is it about Charlotte?"

"Yes, yes. She can't breathe, Mr. Dalton. And there's blood—"

"You called 911?"

"Yes...she looks bad, Mr. Dalton."

"Did they say when the ambulance would come?"

"No, I don't think so. They said they were coming. That's all."

"I'm on my way, Lucy. You just stay there until I arrive."

Fred grabbed his coat and descended to the underground garage. In no time he was on the road to Port Franks.

The traffic of vacationers coming from the lake was heavy, but only a few vehicles were on the road in his direction. He made sure to avoid speeding. In summer the police came out in force and he didn't want to be delayed. Charlotte was very dear to him; she had encouraged him in his undertakings after their father had died at the age of forty-five and she had taken care of their sick mother almost single-handed.

At the entrance of Charlotte's house the ambulance was flashing its lights, the rear door wide open. Fred parked his Lexus and rushed into the house.

Charlotte lay on a stretcher, an oxygen mask on her mouth.

"Is she alive?" Fred asked the paramedics.

"She's breathing," one of the paramedics said. "She has arrhythmia, and on top of that she's lost plenty of blood."

"Where will you take her?" Fred asked.

"Sarnia General Hospital."

The paramedics exited the house and loaded the stretcher into the ambulance. Their siren on, they disappeared into the night.

Fred turned to Lucy, who had retreated into a corner of the dining area, her eyes and nose red, a frightened look on her face.

"Do you have any idea what happened?" he asked.

She shook her head. "I came in to check up on her, as usual. I was a bit late, a quarter past nine, maybe. She was half on the floor, her head on that little table." She pointed at the green marble table, which was low to the ground. "I checked her pulse, and when I touched her, she opened her eyes." Lucy sobbed and snorted. "She tried to talk, but she couldn't."

"That's okay, Lucy. Go home. I'll go to the hospital." He hugged her. "Thank you for looking after her."

"Mr. Dalton?"

"Yes?"

"I'd better take Sultana with me. She was curled at Mrs. Gassman's feet when I came in."

"Great," Fred said. "See you tomorrow."

When Fred arrived at the hospital Charlotte was in surgery and nobody could tell him anything about her condition. He sat in the waiting room and wondered what might have happened. Charlotte suffered from osteoporosis and took medications for both the illness and the pain. *Did she faint and hit the edge of that marble table? But why would she be in that area with the big chandelier all lit up if she didn't have guests? Or did she have a guest and he or she had been the cause of the injury?* The appearance of two men in uniform stopped his musings.

"Harvey Orlandi, OPP officer. And this is Louis Smith."

"Fred Dalton."

"Sorry for the delay," Orlandi said. "There was a big accident on the 402. Some of our people are still there. So it's your sister who was injured?"

"Yes, but why are you here?"

"Routine. We come to check on all the accidents reported through 911." He paused and seemed to scrutinize Fred. "Were you with your sister when it happened?"

"No. She lived alone."

"Who reported the accident?" Orlandi opened a notebook and got out a pen.

"Lucy Fairweather, my sister's help."

"Where is she now?"

"At home."

"Address and phone number, please."

Fred opened his cell phone and looked up Lucy's phone number. He gave it to the officer.

"I don't know her address off hand," he said. "She lives a five-minute walk from my sister's place." He gave the officer Charlotte Gassman's address. He opened his arms in dismay. "That's all I know."

Orlandi turned to face his colleague. "Let's go talk to her."

"At this time?" Fred asked. "It's two o'clock in the morning! She was distressed, and she may have gone to bed. I think your inquiry can easily wait a few more hours, until later in the morning, I mean."

There was silence for a moment

"You have a point," Orlandi said. "Tomorrow morning will be early enough."

They saluted Fred and strode off.

✳ ✳ ✳

Twelve

At Tim Hortons', Verge Bristol and Alain Alstein were having the special of the day, the hot chili bowl with a bun. They decided to take their lunch early, when the place wouldn't be too busy and they could sit in a corner and talk freely.

"So, if the sister is out of the way, our beloved boss gets rich," Alain said.

"He isn't poor now," Verge replied.

"No, by no means, and with that new job, the design-and-build, he'll cash in two hundred thousand."

"More, if it's like all the previous ones. First, the architect is a friend of his; second, he can choose the subs he wants who, in return, will give him an excellent price. I bet he'll clear a quarter-million," Verge said.

"And we'll only get our salary," Alain said.

"Yeah. And pray that Moira comes back to work soon. She's been sick for three days. Otherwise we'll have to do the work."

There was silence for a while as the two friends ate their chili, one scoop after the other.

"Do you think Fred will find out that we changed some pages of the contract?" Alain asked.

"Not now. He's too busy going back and forth to the hospital. His sister can't be moved and Sarnia's over an hour away. Then he's following that project for the hangar in person." He paused. "Not a chance he has the time to do any checking. We'll get away with this job, I'm sure of it."

"And the next one? We should go ahead with the second one while he's still busy."

"No rush. Let's see how things work out. We still have a week to manipulate subs and prices." Verge looked at his wristwatch. "Time to go back. I'm going to call Moira at home. Yesterday she said she'd be in today."

"Let's check with Mary first, maybe she knows something we don't."

They walked back to The Werkstein and stopped at the secretary's desk.

Mary Gervasio was on the phone, but she gestured them to come close. She finished dictating a phone number, said goodbye and closed the communication.

"Moira called," she said. "She'll be in later today. She'd learned of Mrs. Gassman's accident only today and she wanted to go to the hospital to see her. She'll work late, she said. Just leave all the papers on her desk."

"Thanks, Mary," Verge said, and together with Alain he walked to their office. "The super-dedicated, efficient employee. She also goes to see the boss' sick sister. Do you buy that?"

"Yes, I do," Alain said. "She's still paid half of what we are. She has to play politics if she wants a raise."

At Sarnia General Hospital, Moira couldn't find out much about the condition of Fred's sister except that Charlotte was in intensive care and her vital signs were constantly monitored. She had seen Fred only briefly. He was in the company of an older man he had introduced as Bill Morteson, Charlotte's doctor. He had asked her to wait for him and said he would return within minutes.

That had been three-quarters of an hour ago. Finally the elevator door opened and Fred appeared. He stretched his hand toward Moira.

"Nice to see you, Moira," he said. "Let me just have a word with the nurse on the new shift, and then I'll be right with you." He walked toward the nurse's station, Moira in tow. "Please call if there's any change," he said to the nurse on duty. "I'll be at the Holiday Inn for the night." He pulled out the hotel card. "Here's my cell number," he said, and scribbled it on the card.

"Will do, Mr. Dalton. Have some rest. You look very tired."

"I am. Thanks."

Fred took Moira by the arm and they walked out of the hospital without talking.

Once outside, Fred said, "My car is just over there. Let's go have something to eat. I don't remember the last time I had a full meal."

"I can't." Moira stopped. "I told at the office I'd be back late, and it's already four o'clock."

"Work can wait another couple of hours. I talked with Mr. Saldini. He's the man I'm building the hangar for. I got a couple days' extension. He's in a hurry, but he understands the predicament I'm in, especially so soon after my wife's death." As Moira hadn't moved, he let go of her arm. "Something's wrong?"

Moira looked at him, her gray eyes intense. "I have problems..."

"Well, this is a good time to talk about them. Let's go."

Together they walked to his Lexus.

The lounge of the On the Front Restaurant offered a magnificent view of Sarnia's waterfront, and the furniture and decor made the area cozy yet elegant. Fred and Moira sat facing each other at a table near one of the big windows. A waiter immediately glided to the table, offering a variety of cocktails.

"No cocktail, thanks," they both said.

"Wine?"

Moira declined, "Oh no. I'm driving."

"Nothing for me either," Fred said.

The waiter nodded and picked up the lists of cocktails and wines. He deposited a menu in front of each of them.

"I'll give you a few minutes to decide." He retreated toward the bar.

It took only a glance for Fred to choose his entree. "I go for pasta; fettuccine Alfredo will do. What about you?"

"The halibut filet with rice and vegetables looks interesting."

They closed their menus and the waiter promptly reappeared at their table. They placed their orders, together with an herbal tea each.

"So what was troubling you, Moira?"

"I felt down...maybe I was a little sick...then my brother called me and said he'd like to come live in London. Right now he lives in a community home in Barrie. He's free to come and go, but they keep an eye on him. I wouldn't be able to take care of him...not properly, I mean."

"I understand. No other relatives?"

"None."

"I can see you're worried."

"But let's forget about my problems. How is your sister?"

"Not good. The brain damage was severe. She's comatose."

"And how are you holding up?" Moira asked.

He shook his head. "Just trying to keep my sanity. It's bad enough having to travel that far every day, but I can't even count on my two oldest collaborators. And the police are giving my sister's maid all kinds of trouble. She found her lying on the marble table, almost totally unconscious. She asked me to be with her when they questioned her. The first time they almost accused her of negligence."

"I'm sorry to hear that."

"First, they didn't come right away and then they wanted to speak with her in the middle of the night; well, I managed to dissuade them from doing that. The following morning, when they went to see her they accused Lucy—that's her name—of having moved some furniture around. All the poor girl did was lift Charlotte's head from the table and slip a couple of pillows underneath."

"They gave her trouble because of that?"

"Oh, yes, and the second time, when I was with her, they scolded her because she took the cat with her."

The entrees came. They tasted their food and waited to resume their conversation until the waiter was out of earshot.

"What did the cat have to do with Charlotte's fall?" Moira asked.

"That's what I asked too. No answer; and different policemen each time. I called my lawyer this morning and he's going to be with Lucy the next time they give her the third degree."

"No wonder you look tired."

"I'll stay at the hotel tonight and come to the office tomorrow morning if Charlotte's condition is stable. There're a few papers I have to sign."

Moira glanced at her watch. "I'll finish my meal and then I'll hightail it to London." She looked at Fred and laughed a little. "Your employee is very serious about her job."

"Fortunately so. At the moment you're the only person I can count on."

Moira ate the last bit of her fish, then dubbed her lips with the colorful napkin and grabbed her purse. She rose and waved Fred goodbye.

"See you tomorrow, boss."

Fred slowly finished his tea, his gaze following Moira as she walked out of the restaurant.

His cell rang. It was the hospital.

✳ ✳ ✳

Thirteen

"*Finally home!*" Moira cried as she entered her apartment on King Street.

She dropped her bag on the console table, tired but satisfied with what she had accomplished. She had stayed at the office until the pricing for the hangar, Fred's design-and-build project, was completed. Fred had given her a list of the most competitive subcontractors, and that had made her work easier. Tomorrow she would check all the figures once more and then the bid would be ready for Fred to sign.

She kicked off her shoes and walked into the small kitchen, which had a distinctive décor: white countertops and cupboards, and black metal appliances. She opened the fridge, realizing the sparseness of her food supply; she had been very busy with little time to shop. The carton with yesterday's pizza took a prominent space on the middle shelf; she lifted off the carton top and set the two leftover slices on a dish; a warm up in the oven would make them more palatable.

Moira disposed of the carton, took a beer out of the fridge, and sat at the round table just outside the kitchen area, waiting for the oven alarm to announce the end of its job. When it was ready, she placed her improvised meal in front of her. *Finally a moment of relaxation*, she thought.

She wolfed the first slice and was ready to tackle the second one when the intercom rang. Without a second thought she rose and clicked the *Listen* button.

It was her brother, Charlie.

"I need to see you." His voice betrayed distress. "It's urgent."

Oh my God, he's here!

"Charlie, do you realize it's one o'clock in the morning and I've worked until midnight?"

"I guessed you had. You weren't home when I came by earlier."

Moira hesitated. She loved Charlie, but she had come to the conclusion that she couldn't have a peaceful life with her brother around. She had lived with him for a while, but when she met his friends, she had gathered that he was involved in shadowy business. Then Charlie started bumming around and she had tried to distance herself from him.

"Are you going to open the damned door or not?"

Moira sighed and pressed the button that unlocked the main entrance.

"Make it fast," she shouted.

As she lived on the first floor, she went to open her door.

Charlie was five foot eight, with a broad chest and narrow hips. In spite of the warm season, he wore a coat. His baseball cap was plunked on his head with the rim low over his eyes and his blond-reddish, untidy beard covered most of his face. He entered the apartment, kicked off his dirty boots and slumped on one of the upholstered chairs.

Moira stood in front of him, her arms crossed over her chest.

"You smell terrible!" she said. "Where have you been?"

Charlie waved off the question. "I need money. One thousand by tomorrow."

"A thousand? I gave you a thousand four months ago. Do you think I print them out at night?"

"You have a good job. You can ask for a loan. I don't work anymore."

"What? Let me get this straight. You said you were coming down for a couple of weeks on vacation, and now you tell me that you aren't working anymore?"

Charlie took off his cap and threw it across the room.

"Right, and my unemployment benefits have expired."

"You lost your job? Again?"

He'd been delivering mail on one of those routes that the post office contracted out.

"You liked walking and you knew all the roads well. What happened?"

He shrugged. "I didn't feel well for a few days, so I didn't show up."

"Without calling in?"

"I forgot. I was sick."

It could be true, Moira thought. Since childhood Charlie suffered with seizures and ADHD—attention-deficit hyperactivity disorder. At times his mind wandered and his memory failed him.

"Could I come to live with you? When we stayed at the house together, you woke me up, filled my lunch box and sent me off." He smiled, showing yellow teeth. "It worked pretty well."

Moira closed her eyes, thinking of the countless times she'd had to rescue Charlie, lost on the other side of town, or worse, in the woods.

Charlie raised his voice. "I *have* to have that money or he'll kill me."

"Who is he?" She shot him an inquisitive look.

"You don't need to know."

"Good."

Moira strode off and sat at the table. Her brother was a helpless case, deteriorating with the advance of years.

Charlie neared her from behind and shook her shoulders.

"Did you hear what I said?"

"Stop hurting me! It won't do you any good." Moira took a morsel of her now-cold pizza and drank half of her beer. "If somebody's blackmailing you, you should go to the police. Now sit down and tell me who wants the thousand, and why. And what you've done to be in such deep trouble."

Charlie didn't utter a sound. As he sat opposite her, Moira finished her skimpy meal, rose, and cleaned up the table.

"You have five minutes to start talking. Then you either leave or I'll call the police."

"Bring me a beer, and I'll tell you."

Moira weighed the situation; finally she slid a bottle of Bud Light across the round table and stood in front of him, looking down on him, her back rod straight.

Unhurried, Charlie took off his coat and uncapped the beer.

"It seemed such a good idea," he said. "I met this guy at the bowling alley on Oxford West. There were a bunch of guys and we made two teams and played against each other. It was fun and we played for only a dollar a game. At closing time, this guy asked me if I wanted to make a fast buck. I didn't ever reply. I just walked outside, thinking about going home." Charlie paused and downed half of his beer in one swig. "The guy said he'd give me a ride and explain what the job was all about." Charlie stopped again. "Do you have anything to eat?"

"There's bread in the bread basket and a couple slices of baloney in the fridge."

Charlie rose and went to the fridge, followed by Moira.

"Make it snappy, Charlie. I need a few hours of sleep. I worked hard today and I have to get up at six tomorrow morning."

Charlie started to make himself a sandwich.

"What was the job all about?" his sister asked.

"It looked so simple...I just had to get ten one-hundred-dollar bills changed for twenties; that was all."

"They were *counterfeit?*" Moira asked, suddenly alerted.

"I don't know. I was robbed." He bit into his sandwich and finished it in a jiffy.

"Who is this guy, and why does he want his money back in such a hurry?"

"I don't know his full name; he goes by Sam."

Moira pondered the case. Charlie had an uncanny ability to get into trouble.

"Where do you sleep now?" she asked.

"At a shelter on York. They're kind to me."

Moira hesitated a few minutes. To perform well in her job she needed concentration and stability. She had to stay away from Charlie, or she would lose it.

"Tomorrow afternoon I'll go to the bank and ask for a loan," she said. "Come to Tim Hortons at 1:00 p.m. sharp; it's on the same street where the shelter is. I'll give you the money." As Charlie rose, she added, "Sunday morning I pick you up for church. And then we're going to have a long, long talk."

Moira strode away and into her bedroom. She was back moments later with a set of towels and a blanket. She tossed them on the sofa.

"Take a shower Charlie. Then wash and dry your clothes." She was going back to the bedroom when she called out, "Your cap too!"

✲ ✲ ✲

Fourteen

Detective Gordon Stevenson slammed the phone down, the air displacement sending some of the loose papers lying on his desk onto the floor. He emitted a long-suffering sigh.

Peggy O'Brian picked up the sheets of paper. "More problems?" She sorted them and deposited them back onto her boss' desk.

"It's mission impossible, that's what it is." He drummed his fingers on top of the phone. "If they want to find out who injured Charlotte Gassman they have to move quickly, and what does the OPP do? They sequester Charlotte's cat!" He tugged at the collar of his undershirt to breathe easier.

"The cat? What did the cat have to do with anything?"

"When one officer went to talk to Lucy Fairweather—the part-time maid of Mrs. Gassman—the cat jumped on him and scratched his trousers. As he tried to pick her up by the neck she scratched his hand."

"That's why they took the cat away?" O'Brian asked, astonished.

"No. It's more complicated than that."

"I thought so, since you stayed on the phone more than half an hour."

"The results from the blood found in Gassman's house show that another person was present when she fell or was pushed against the low table and injured her head, and that confirms what the owner of the corner store said, that around half past eight a red Corvette drove by toward the Gassman's house, which is the last one on that road."

"What does that have to do with the cat?"

"Long shot. They hope to find a link between the Corvette's owner and the unidentified blood in Gassman's house. Maybe the owner got some scratches too."

"Very long shot. What about Dalton?"

"He drives a Lexus, and apparently the cat targets only strangers. The brother would hardly qualify as a stranger. He and his sister are close."

O'Brian paced back and forth then stopped.

"How much is this sister of his worth?" she asked.

"Thirty million, maybe? In that range."

"She can't talk?"

"No. The doctors don't think she'll ever recover."

"So the brother inherits if she dies?"

"We don't know. He has power of attorney for both her health and her finances. He had signed all the papers at the hospital—that's the reason we know. He has also requested that his lawyer, Mr. Victor Maclaren, be present if anybody wants to talk again with Lucy Fairweather. The woman was very distressed about what happened, and understandably so, I'd say. Taking the cat away was an aggravation. She thought they were going to destroy it."

"Did they return the cat?"

"Not yet. They want to carefully examine her nails in case they have a suspect down the road. But they promised Lucy to bring her over soon."

"What do we do now?"

"Little to nothing. At the moment we've been asked to cooperate. The case is out of our jurisdiction."

"Is Fred Dalton a suspect?" O'Brian asked.

"Not at the moment. He could become one if his sister dies and he's the principal beneficiary."

Frederick Dalton sat near the bed where Charlotte was lying. His sister's life escaped from her body in spurts, each spurt longer than the previous one. The green line that monitored her heart flattened for a while, then picked up again. The hospital had called Fred at the On the Front Restaurant, as Charlotte had deteriorated significantly. Her body had begun to retain water. He had stayed in her room all night, knowing that the moment of supreme detachment was near.

From time-to-time a nurse tiptoed in, gave a look at the equipment, and patted Fred on the shoulder. The doctors knew that the medical science couldn't do anything for the patient and let nature take its course. Fred had experienced a similar situation when his mother had died after a long agonizing illness.

The flat line on the monitor became longer, the spikes less frequent. Fred kept his sister's hand clasped in his, as if he wanted to snatch her away from death. Her hand had been cold for a while, and when Fred glanced once again at the monitor, he saw that there were no more vital signs.

He let go of her hand and genuflected in prayer.

He couldn't say whether he'd been in that position for a few minutes or an hour, when somebody tapped on his shoulder. It was Mary Gervasio, his secretary.

He rose and Mary hugged him tightly, pronouncing the usual words of comfort. Holding him by the waist, she escorted him out of the room and into the corridor. She opened the briefcase she had left near the door and extracted some papers.

"We need your signature before noon," she said. She gave Fred a pen and lay the papers on top of the briefcase, keeping it up and flat in front of him.

"Thank you," Fred said, and signed. "I have to take care of the funeral arrangements. I'll drop by the office probably late in the afternoon."

Mary had already placed the papers back in the briefcase. "Sorry for your loss, Fred. Let me know if I can do anything for you. I'll wait for you at the office."

Then she left.

A member of the hospital personnel approached Fred.

"Mr. Dalton, please come with me," she said. "There are formalities that need to be taken care of."

The news of Charlotte Gassman's death reached O'Brian's desk at lunchtime.

Stevenson munched on a grilled chicken sandwich, fighting the leaves of lettuce that slipped out from all sides of a big bun. A tomato slice had already fallen on the wrapping paper spread on his desk.

"How come they called you?" he asked O'Brian, and deposited the remains of his sandwich on the paper, his attention focused on the constable.

She stood beside her boss' desk.

"I have a friend at the hospital," she replied. "Fred is on his way to London. Do we bring him in for questioning?"

"Uh, uh, wait a minute…we aren't in charge of the case." He finished off the last bit of his meal and wiped his fingers clean with a paper napkin. "At the moment there's only an inquest. However, I got a bit of interesting news this morning. The blood under the cat's nails doesn't match the drops found on Charlotte Gassman's carpet…those that don't belong to Mrs. Gassman."

"So there might have been a third person present that night. It's imperative that we find the owner of the red Corvette who was around Gassman's property."

"That person may have seen something. However, Gassman's house is in a cul-de-sac; the driver might have just driven there by mistake and turned around."

"But the owner of the corner store only saw it going up; she closes at 9:00 p.m. She didn't see it coming back."

"Maybe she didn't notice," Stevenson said. "But, yes, the Corvette's owner is a person of interest."

✳ ✳ ✳

Fifteen

Nicholas Samuel Falcone was very pleased with himself. Everybody still thought of him as a misfit, a loser, a guy who lived on other people's wits in order to get through the day, and he liked to keep up that image. It was the best guarantee that nobody would find out the truth. His farmhouse, a dilapidated dwelling in urgent need of repairs, the shabby shed on the side and the old windmill with three vanes missing, confirmed the presumption of his low social status. The truth was that he had come into money. Nobody, but *nobody* knew how it had happened, and he wanted to keep it that way.

One day he had wandered along the shores of Lake Huron, walking on the wet sand, pondering whether life was worth living. That day he felt low, betrayed by his parents, who had left him very little to live on. It was twilight and nobody was in sight. As he reached a shallow bay surrounded by sand dunes and shrubs, he spotted a medium-size, inboard-motor boat, its prow well set in the sand. He had approached it, called aloud for its owner, and then, when he had received no response, proceeded inside. A man sprawled on the floor, dead. At first he felt repulsion, but his ever-present sense of greed prevailed. Nobody the wiser, he had opened every one of the boat's drawers, cupboards, and storage spaces he could spot. Underneath the dashboard lay an old green bag that contained another bag, the latter made of heavy plastic and sealed. He had broken the seal, opened it, and found what he had never expected to see. He had left the green bag on the boat and reached his house with the other bag on his shoulder. It had been an hour-long walk— the most pleasant walk of his life.

He should keep going with his plan of putting his exceptional find to profitable use.

Stretched out on his old recliner, he was ready for a good, cold drink when the phone rang. He quickly rose to answer.

It was Tessa. She had been calling him at least once a day, worried about the condition of the Gassman woman. He would have to listen to whatever rubbish she spun. Tessa and her old-fashioned idea of making money by catching a wealthy husband. To keep up the pretence of being short of money, he had accepted Tessa's proposition to help her befriend Fred, and had gone to see Charlotte Gassman to convince her to give a surprise party for Fred's fortieth birthday. Regrettably, the encounter had not turned out as he expected.

He set the phone on his shoulder while he reached to open the fridge and get a can of ginger ale. He opened the can and sipped it, hearing, in the background, Tessa's non-stop rambling. He picked up the phone again.

"Yeah, yeah," he replied. "Don't worry. Everything is under control."

"But I read it, Nick. It was in the paper. The police are looking for the owners of red Corvettes."

"You told me that yesterday. Don't use the car for a few days."

"Have you been listening to me or not?"

"Yes."

"Charlotte *died*, Nick! It's a murder investigation now!"

"I see," Nick said coolly.

"What should I be doing?"

"Give me some time to think about it. I'll call you back."

Nick put the phone back in its cradle, and drank his ginger ale. He walked toward the kitchen window and looked outside. The situation was tricky. It would take no time for the authorities to make a list of all the Corvettes in Ontario and check on their colors. They had probably done that already. Soon they would bring in Tessa for questioning. She could become a liability.

Moira's head was spinning. Too many things were happening all at once. She had gone to The Werkstein early in the morning for a last look at the contract for the construction of the hangar. That done, as Mary typed in the last few prices, Moira had hurried to the Ausable Credit Union, where she usually banked, to bargain for a low-interest loan of a thousand dollars. Last year the old manager had granted her a loan for buying a new car and she hoped to talk him into lending the money she needed now. Unfortunately, the old manager had retired and the new one, a woman in her forties, had kept shaking her head. Moira had no substantial collateral.

"A woman working in a construction company?" the manager had asked with a tone that betrayed incredulity close to disdain. "How long do you think you'll last?"

She had declared her a high-risk customer, so Moira had to take what she was offered: a one-year loan at twelve percent interest. She was unhappy with the deal, but the urgency of settling Charlie's problem had overshadowed all other considerations.

She had driven to Tim Hortons, where she had found Charlie happily seated at a table, enjoying a croissant sandwich with a latte. With relief she had noticed that his appearance was much improved from the night before. He had shaved his wild beard and collected his huge mass of blond-reddish hair in a ponytail. Standing in front of him, she had given him a short sermon on being careful and ordered him to avoid dealing again with the crook who had asked him to exchange large bills for twenties. Charlie had nodded convincingly and finished his latte. Moira had no time or energy to spend with him, so she had secured the envelope with the money inside his coat pocket and reminded him to be ready for their Sunday meeting.

She needed to spend the afternoon filing all the documents that had accumulated on her desk, but as soon as she entered the main office, she found out about Charlotte's demise.

"When did it happen?" she asked Mary.

"Just after you left. We tried to reach you, but your cell was shut off."

It was true. She had received crank calls, and she had so much on her plate that she didn't have time for nonsense.

"Do we know where the funeral will be held?" Moira asked.

"In London. Fred asked me to arrange the visiting times at the funeral home. He went to see the pastor of St. Peter's to decide on the readings; they believe that St. Mary would be too small for the ceremony."

Moira slumped on the chair in front of Mary's desk.

"How was he?" Moira asked.

"Sad. Tired. He looked exhausted, actually. He was up all night."

"I can imagine. He looked beaten last night and he was hoping for a good night's sleep. Well, the doctors didn't expect Charlotte to recover. Neither did he."

"Right. It must be hard, though. First he loses his wife, then his sister only five weeks later."

"Hard, yes. My brother, Charlie, gives me a lot of problems, but I would miss him if he died."

Mary looked closely at her. "Have you had any lunch?"

"Not yet."

"What do you mean, 'not yet'? It's three thirty!" Mary rose. "I'm going to get you a chicken wrap and a salad. A coffee, too." She strode purposely out of the office.

Moira closed her eyes. She chased away the image of Charlie, dead. She wanted to have a normal life; being with Charlie on equal terms had not worked out at all, but she would miss him if he suddenly disappeared from the earth. She understood how Fred must have felt when Deborah died. When Charlotte had been injured and slipped into a coma it must have been even worse.

Somebody was shaking her shoulders.

"Are you okay?" It was Fred, bent over her.

She looked up. "Oh, hi, Fred. I'm fine. Just tired." She patted his hand. "Sorry for your loss. I learned about Charlotte only moments ago."

Fred murmured, "Thank you" and dragged Mary's seat from behind the desk to sit closer to her. "I know you bore a lot of the load with the hangar project. I wasn't here to help, and the other two are slacking off more every day." He gave her a concerned look. "You should take a few days off."

Moira straightened her back against the chair. "I just need a good night's sleep."

Fred still wore yesterday's suit; it was crumpled, and his tie had spots of coffee. He needed a good night's rest too.

"When is the funeral?" she asked.

"The day after tomorrow. The police asked for an autopsy."

✫ ✫ ✫

Sixteen

Detective Gordon Stevenson entered the Investigative Response Unit area with firm strides and tossed *The London Free Press* onto his desk with a satisfied expression.

"I deserve a cappuccino," he said, and moved toward the hall where the new Shaerer coffee machine had been installed.

"I'll get it for you," Peggy O'Brian said. "I was thinking of having one too."

"Ah, ah...You want to know why I was late, eh?" As Peggy nodded, he said, "Pay for the coffee and I'll tell you."

When Peggy returned, Detective Stevenson stood beside his desk, his arms crossed behind him. He turned as he sniffed the coffee's wonderful aroma.

"Fred Dalton is Gassman's heir, together with two charity organizations, which get a million dollars each. The part-time help, Lucy Fairweather, also gets some money; even if Mr. Dalton couldn't say how much."

Peggy stood in front of him, two coffees in her hands.

"Aren't you giving me mine?" Stevenson asked, stretching out his arm.

Peggy complied, an astonished look on her face. "How did you get this information?"

Stevenson laughed, and whispered, "My personal charm."

"Come on, no attorney would give out that information before the reading of the will, and there's no formal request from the authorities to have a copy of it."

"I know. I know all that. There's no case yet, so no court can authorize the viewing of it." Stevenson sipped his coffee and invited Peggy to do the same. "Drink, or it'll get cold."

"So, how *did* you get the information?"

One last swig and Stevenson finished his cappuccino. "Exquisite," he said. "And when it's free it tastes twice as good. So guess; use your imagination."

Peggy looked at him blankly.

He sat behind his desk. "Simple. I saw Mr. Dalton and asked him."

"And he told you?"

"Well, he was surprised with my request. I told him there was an ongoing inquest and the names of the beneficiaries could help us proceed in the right direction. He had no problem with spelling them out." Stevenson grimaced.

"He'll be mad at you once he discovers that it was a shortcut to get him on the list of the suspects."

"He might." Stevenson drummed his fingers on his desk. "I like the guy. Either he's a very canny criminal who plans and recites every gesture and every word with the craft of a consummate actor or he has nothing to do with any murders."

Peggy remained silent for a moment before saying, "The police will have a hard job pinpointing a guilty party. Do you think we'll be involved in the inquiry?"

Stevenson squeezed his paper cup and tossed it in the center of the garbage basket fifteen feet away.

"Marginally, I believe. In any case we'll both go to the funeral. You can practice what you've just learned in the course about profiling."

The phone rang and Stevenson picked it up, cutting off the second ring. He looked at Peggy and pointed at his phone. "Ten-four." *Ten-four* or *roger* were the answers the London police used to acknowledge a received message. "We'll start right away, sir. No, we didn't receive any fax." He looked at the fax machine at the end of the long room. "It might be coming in right now." He deposited the phone in its cradle.

Peggy had already fetched the document. She handed it to Stevenson, who glanced at the paper and rose.

"I'll take this with me," he told Peggy. "It's the list of people who own red Corvettes."

"Too bad I can't come with you."

Stevenson gave her an inquisitive look as he grabbed his coat.

"It's my turn to shadow Mr. Fred Dalton." Peggy said, a mischievous look on her face.

"Oh, I understand." He glanced at the big calendar sprawled on his desk. "Today it's the last time."

"Mmm-hmm."

"Anything substantial?"

"No. This past week his routine was frantic, but monotonous. From his lawyer to his accountant and to his office, every day; sometimes back to his lawyer late at night. In the evenings he went twice to a grocery store and three times to a fast food outlet."

"I didn't think we'd discover anything, but you don't seem to mind the job."

Peggy laughed. "It surely wasn't heavy work, and the man isn't hard to look at. He has nice blue eyes."

Stevenson gave her a reproachful look, and called for Santos Lopes.

The red brick walls and black roof; the prominent mansard; and the round extension protruding at the front, paneled with long stained windows, gave Tessa Wilson's house a unique look. Stevenson and Lopes parked their cruiser around the corner, determined to handle the upcoming meeting as a friendly visit.

While Lopes rang the bell, Stevenson stood on tiptoes and looked into the garage through the row of glass wedges on top of the door. He looked at Santos and shook his head. "No car."

He joined Lopes at the main entrance. The door was a striking combination of craftsmanship, art design, and modern technology; the metal frame encompassed a central piece of beveled and frosted glass interlaced with inlays of gold and silver; two side panels sported floral decorations.

"How much would a door like this cost?" Santos asked.

Stevenson shrugged. "Probably thirty thousand," he whispered. "Bear in mind that it has to suit the owner of a Corvette."

"Who is it?" a voice asked from the inside.

"London Police Service," Stevenson said, with his baritone voice. "We're looking for Ms. Tessa Wilson. We think she may help us."

The door opened. Tessa Wilson made a grand appearance in a red robe that opened at the front, her long, wavy hair grazing her neck. Her hazel eyes looked directly at one officer, then at the other. "I am she."

"May we come in?" Stevenson asked, and quickly introduced himself and his partner.

Tessa hesitated, then nodded. "Yes, but make it brief. I was getting dressed for a party."

"We will. It's our information that you own a 2008 Corvette. Is it still in your possession?"

Tessa shrugged. "Yes. Is there a problem?"

"Where is it?"

"I took it to the shop. A few scratches, you know...it needed a paint job."

"Scratches? Did you have an accident?"

"Oh, no. It's just that...I just like to keep it in top shape, that's all."

"What garage?" Stevenson asked.

"Savino's Body Shop."

Stevenson was inside, but Lopes was still on the threshold. Stevenson moved forward and gestured for Lopes to do likewise, then closed the door behind him.

Tessa moved back a couple of steps.

"Anything else?" she asked.

"Yes. A red Corvette was seen approaching the premises of Mrs. Charlotte Gassman on the evening of August the fifth. Were you around that place between eight and nine?"

Tessa's cheeks reddened. "I...I don't remember."

"Did you know Mrs. Charlotte Gassman?"

"Yes." She nervously tugged at her belt, and pulled one side of her satin robe over the top of the other.

"Have you ever visited Mrs. Gassman?"

"Yes, of course...on occasion."

"Recently?"

Tessa looked blankly at him.

"By any chance, August the fifth?"

"I don't know whether or not it was that evening, as I said." With firm steps she walked between the two men and opened the door. "Now if you'll excuse me, I have things to do."

"I understand. Thank you for your time."

Stevenson moved outside, followed by Lopes. They walked briskly to their car.

Santos sat in the driver's seat. "She's the one. She knew the victim and she has the right car." He started the engine and put the cruiser in gear. "What do we do next?"

"We'll go to Savino's Body Shop; I know the place. Go back to Wonderland Road. It's just a ten-minute drive."

When they arrived at the garage an acute odor hit their nostrils.

"What's that terrible smell?" Lopes asked.

"Trichloroethylene."

"Tri-what?"

"The basic chemical used in paint thinners." Stevenson winked at his constable. "I finally can show off some of the stuff I learned in my two years of chemistry."

Soon a woman in a green coverall and yellow helmet met them at the front.

"May I help you?" she asked, in a friendly tone. The name tag on her outfit read *Guendy.*

Stevenson and Lopes introduced themselves as they appraised the surroundings.

"We're looking for a red Corvette," Stevenson said, and read the license plate from the sheet he held in his hands.

Guendy waved them inside the working area. "It's there, but it won't be red for long. Ms. Wilson wanted it repainted."

"Oh, is that right?" Stevenson neared the car. "What color?"

"Silver; it'll be a big job. Red is one of the most difficult colors to cover up." She laughed. "I told her she might end up with a silvery-pink looking car."

"Did she mind?"

"No. She was tired of red, she said, and wanted a change."

"Do you mind if we look inside?" Stevenson asked.

"No, but it's been cleaned to the bones, just this morning, inside and out."

When Stevenson and Lopes walked back to their cruiser it was six o'clock.

"Our Ms. Wilson beat us by less than twelve hours," Stevenson grumbled, as they headed back to Headquarters. "Of course, there might not have been any trace of blood. We can go home, since Ms. Wilson will be out by now. We'll go back another time and give it another try. She was very uneasy when we were there. If we push a little harder we might get something significant out of her."

"Without a warrant?"

Stevenson laughed. "We don't have one and we can't get one. We're in the loop but we aren't in charge of the case. We were asked to check on the red Corvettes' owners, Santos, so that's what we'll do; we'll be tactful but unrelenting."

Seventeen

Not everybody who had lined up for Charlotte Gassman's religious service could enter St. Peter's Cathedral Basilica. Some stood on the front steps, ready to follow the service in that position. Fred glanced at the crowd as he joined the other five pallbearers to carry the coffin into the building. As the song *On Eagle's Wings* resounded through the air, he marched through the nave in cadence with the others and stopped to place the coffin in front of the altar.

He took a seat in the first pew. The priest covered the coffin with a white cloth, symbolizing the cycle of the Christian faith from baptism to death. So the Mass began, with selected readings and songs of the faithful. Fred's mind wasn't with the process, however; he wandered through the untimely death of his parents when he was only eight; the tough times he and Charlotte, his senior of sixteen years, had gone through to overcome the difficulties of living on a limited income based on their parents' life insurance. Fortunately, Charlotte had been old enough to assume parenting duties, thus saving him from going to a foster home.

Charlotte, though a beauty, did not have the carefree youth most people had. She had dated late. At thirty-four she had met Werner Gassman, a German entrepreneur who had come to Canada to expand his business. A fifty-year-old widower with no children, Werner had fallen in love with sweet Charlotte, and had soon decided to liquidate his investments in

Germany and start a new construction company in Canada. That was how The Werkstein was born. The business had boomed and the marriage had been happy, if not long. Werner had died when Charlotte was only forty-eight, leaving her a very rich widow.

Fred knew she had missed her partner deeply and, unfortunately, had spent countless hours longing for a presence that was no more. Volunteer work in charity foundations had filled part of her time, but after arthritis had advanced and severely limited her mobility, she had retired to her villa on the shores of Lake Huron and hoped for her friends to come visit her. Recently, her shopping sprees took her only as far as London or Sarnia.

Fred listened as the pastor dispensed the eulogy with warmth and conviction. For some time Charlotte had not attended the services of her parish, but she had continued to support the church's many activities. As the priest took a seat at the far end of the altar, Fred felt overwhelmed with emotion. He had buried Deborah, and now he was bidding farewell to Charlotte. He had no more family, he realized, with sudden and deep sadness.

The pastor's words, the unfolding of the funeral ritual, and the presence of the mourners around him seemed unreal, as if it were all happening in a faraway world. He felt enclosed in a foggy bubble that protected him from the lacerations caused by Charlotte's final departure.

The Mass ended and, once more, Fred lined up with the other front pallbearer. As quietly as they had entered, they carried his sister's mortal remains out of the church and loaded them into the funeral home's limo.

Fred took his place in the next car, ready to surrender to Mother Earth the remains of the person who had been sister and mother all in one to him.

The reception at the Delta London Armouries on Dundas Street took three long hours; there was speech after speech, most commending Charlotte Gassman's participation in charitable work. After the last cup of coffee was served, the mourning crowd started to disperse, while Fred stood up to shake hands and receive renewed condolences.

At the end of the line stood Moira, who inched up to him and set a hand on his arm. The jacket of her black suit was open at the front, showing the ruffles of a white blouse; a necklace bearing a small silver cross adorned her neck.

"I came with your Lexus," she said. "I could take you home, or you can take your car and I'll get a ride."

Fred was about to answer when Tessa approached him from the other side, her statuesque figure taking up most of the space available in front of him. Nick Falcone was behind her, and both ostensibly ignored Moira's presence.

"I'm here for you, Fred. I'd like to take you to my place and make you feel comfortable." Tessa's voice was suave, almost seductive.

Fred was about to reply when a huffing and puffing Lucy Fairweather shook Fred's free arm.

"Mr. Dalton, you have to help me! Those two officers want to take me with them." She pointed to Detective Gordon Stevenson and Constable Peggy O'Brian.

"Oh...I see. One moment, Lucy. I have to talk to my friends first." He looked at Tessa. "Thank you, but as you can see, I have more chores to do." He took Moira by the arm and stepped a few feet away from everybody. "I'll take the car. I saw it when I came in; it's parked at front, right?"

Moira nodded, took a pair of keys out of her black purse and gave them to him.

"Thank you for everything, Moira."

Moira murmured, "Welcome," and scampered away, her little purse hanging low near her hips.

Immediately Lucy hung on his arm, soliciting his attention. Her long skirt touched the ground; her sweater was two-sizes too large and her gray hair was gathered at the back by a pink ribbon. With her weather-battered skin and puffy eyes she looked older than fifty-five. She had been working at Charlotte's for the last ten years, but he wondered how much help Charlotte had really gotten out of her recently. He knew that, from time to time, Charlotte relied on a specialized company to do some of the cleaning or other work around the house.

"So what's the problem?" Fred asked.

"They want to take me downtown."

"Did they say why?"

Lucy shook her head. "They also said that Mrs. Gassman's cat Sultana is dangerous."

"Oh? Why?"

"They kept her for four days—only God knows where—and when they came to return her to my place she...she bit me." Lucy lifted her right sleeve and showed a gauze patch fifteen centimeters long.

Fred was tired; he looked around, hoping to see Victor Maclaren, his lawyer, but all the guests were gone and the only people he could spot were the two police officers, standing on the threshold of the main entrance. He had seen them leaving immediately after the religious service. Now they were back, and he wondered why. He didn't feel like talking with them.

"The cat—"

"Lucy, for the time being let's set aside the cat's problem. About the police request...I don't think it's a big deal to go with Detective Stevenson, but if you don't feel comfortable with it, tell him you want to talk with my lawyer first. I'll give him a call tonight; I'm sure he'll contact you tomorrow." He patted Lucy on her shoulder. "I'm exhausted, Lucy. I need to go home."

Fred waved at Detective Stevenson and strode off through the side exit on his left.

Tessa stood near the passenger side of the 2008 Dodge Dakota, waiting for Nick to open the door. Her light-weight black dress outlined her slim waist and full breasts.

"Hop in." Nick helped Tessa climb inside his pickup truck.

"Couldn't you get a better ride?" Tessa gathered her flimsy skirt into her lap.

"What do you mean by better? It's the only V8 in its class. It has a lot of power and it's not bad on fuel."

"It isn't suitable for the occasion. The Armouries is one of the best hotels in town."

"Well, first, nobody notices what I drive, and second, I can't splurge on cars."

"You should get a job."

"Why don't *you* get a job?"

"I have one. Two days a week."

"Really?"

"What do you mean *really*? Don't be sarcastic! I have a job and it's a technical one!"

"Technical?" Nick couldn't hide his sarcasm.

"Yes. I transfer pictures from VHS tapes to DVDs. There, I said it. I operate a machine for that."

Nick turned to look at her. "I'm impressed."

They were silent for a while, then Tessa said, "Did you see how Fred treated me? Like I was nobody!"

"He was tired; he had dark circles under his eyes. Don't make a big deal out of it." He paused and concentrated on disentangling his vehicle from the many cars leaving the parking lot. "He ignored me; that's not like him. He must have been exhausted."

"He had time for that redhead, Moira."

"Yes, just to get a pair of keys."

"At least he talked to her." Tessa pouted.

Nick kept quiet until they arrived at Tessa's house.

"Like to come in?" Tessa asked.

"Sure, I never refuse an invitation from a beautiful woman."

As soon as they stepped inside the living room Tessa approached the angled bar located in the farthest corner and poured herself a rum and Coke. She sat in one of the arabesque-upholstered chairs and stretched her legs onto the low table in front of her. Nick took a stroll to admire the photographs of the several landscapes that hung on one of the walls.

"Your ex-husband's work?" he asked Tessa.

"Yes. Walter was an amateur photographer. Didn't sell much, unfortunately."

"I see." Nick reached for the bar and poured a snifter of brandy. He sat in the black leather couch opposite Tessa and sipped his drink.

Tessa sighed audibly. "I can't think of any way to get close to Fred," she said with a touch of frustration in her voice.

"Be reasonable. He's in mourning. Give him time, for heaven's sake! We'll find an occasion or two to meet him socially."

"I'm bugged by that shrimp of a woman, Moira; she can see him every day."

"Don't make a big issue out of nothing. She works there; that's all. I don't think a man like Fred would seriously consider dating her."

Tessa downed her drink and went for a refill. She took two bags of potato chips out of the drawer underneath the bar counter and tossed one onto the low table. She sat in the same chair where she had been sitting before and opened the other bag. She alternated munching a few chips with sipping her drink.

"At the end of the reception I saw two policemen waiting at the door."

"I saw them too. Charlotte's maid said they wanted to talk to her."

Tessa guzzled her second drink. "One of them came to see me," she whispered.

Nick sat up. "Who came to see you?"

"The policeman you saw at the hall. He was with a younger fellow; he asked me if I owned a red Corvette."

Nick leaned across the table that separated him from Tessa.

"They came *here*, to your *house?*" he asked.

Tessa nodded. "They asked me if I was at Charlotte's the evening she was injured."

"And?"

"I told them I didn't remember."

"Good." Nick relaxed his back against the couch and finished his brandy.

"I took the car to a body shop to have it painted a silver shade."

"Why?"

Tessa shrugged. "One, I was sick of red; two, I thought I could avoid any inquiry about a red Corvette."

Nick rose, clearly upset.

"But that wasn't smart! Having it repainted will make them suspect that you really were there that night!"

Tessa stood up and faced Nick.

"*We* were there, Nick, and *you* were the only one who entered her house!"

For a moment Nick stared at her; then he threw his glass against the wall and left.

✵ ✵ ✵

Eighteen

Moira had a hard time recognizing her own brother. At the Men's Mission they had given him clean clothes—second-hand jeans, a shirttail-out pleated shirt and a pair of sneakers that seemed brand new. Charlie looked like a normal handsome young man. She had felt proud to walk to church with him. After Mass she had taken him to her apartment and left him there watching TV while she went shopping.

Now she had returned and it was time to find out what the thousand dollars was all about.

"Charlie, you have to tell me everything, and I mean *everything*!" She raised her voice. "I'll ask questions and you have to answer."

"Sure," Charles replied, and sat on the ottoman close to the sofa, a big smile on his face.

"What's the name of the man who entrusted you with the one thousand dollars?"

"Entrusted? What do you mean?"

"The man who gave you the money, Charlie."

"Sam."

"Okay, so this Sam gave you that amount of money without knowing you?"

"Yes. I had to go to the Royal Bank on Richmond and exchange a bunch of big bills for twenties."

"Oh, I see, and where was this mysterious Sam while you entered the bank?"

"A few feet beside me."

Moira stood in front of him. "And you were robbed while Sam was watching?"

"It's more complicated than that."

Moira crossed her arms and waited.

"There was a long line and a woman came in with two children and a baby carriage. They made a lot of noise and commotion and lined up behind me."

"And?" Moira pressed him.

Charlie stretched his arms wide in sign of surrender. "When I was in front of the teller and looked for the money I couldn't find it. My pocket was empty."

"What did you do?"

"I said I was robbed, but the cashier didn't believe me. I looked for Sam; he came from behind and dragged me outside."

"I see."

Moira sat on the chair in front of him, pondering what Charlie had told her. The mother of the three children may have staged a con act, but Sam himself may have retrieved the money and then accused Charlie of losing it. The second option seemed more likely than the first one, since Charlie's demeanor would not induce any robber to stage a complicated act. Sam—whoever he was—probably was an experienced con man.

"Now, this is what you're going to do. You don't do anything else ever with this Sam no matter how much he begs you to go places with him or promises you money or asks you to do things. Clear?"

Charlie nodded.

"And second, you go to work at the fairground starting tomorrow morning. I got a job for you. You stay at the shelter until I think of a better solution. Clear?"

Charlie nodded again. "Yes. Thank you, Moira. I love you." He looked at the clock on the bookcase. "The baseball game is already on. Can I watch it?"

"Sure. I should be going anyway. 'Bye, Charlie."

For the third day in a row Nick had gone to the Men's Mission and Rehabilitation Centre on York Street to see Charlie Johnson, and for the third time he had come out empty-handed. The manager had been quite kind but he had neither denied nor confirmed whether Charlie was there. When Nick had peeked inside the large room that served as a refectory he had not seen him.

The situation was getting critical. The money he had found in the mysterious boat was of dubious provenance, probably hot, and he should assume that most financial institutions and several shops would be supplied, sooner or later, with a list of serial numbers. It was imperative that he avoid using that money himself. Charlie was the ideal person; if questioned, he couldn't explain the source of the money and he didn't know Nick's full name. He needed to find Charlie or somebody like him who would exchange the hundred notes. Now that he was rich, he should play it safe.

He wondered what had happened to the boat, named *The Catalina,* and its dead skipper. There had been no announcement in the media of a ship abandoned on shore, so either it was still there or some of the dead man's friends had come to take it away. If the latter, he could figure out how enraged they must have been once they realized that the money had disappeared. He mentally retraced what he had done when he was aboard the boat and how much evidence of his visit he had left behind. Well, crooks don't have up-to-date databases as the authorities do, so his fingerprints wouldn't mean anything but his shoe prints might give him away; he should get rid of those shoes as soon as possible.

The serious problem was that he needed cash, and Charlie was the ideal person to exchange big notes into smaller ones without raising immediate suspicion. He wouldn't play the trick again of stealing from him and blackmailing him afterward if he didn't pay him back—that was good only once—but now that he had spent the one thousand Charlie had given him to help buy his second-hand pickup he needed fresh cash. *Where is he? Is he even still living at the shelter? Maybe he's at the bowling alley on Oxford West.* He quickly drove there to look around and inquire whether anybody had seen Charlie Johnson recently. No luck. Annoyed, he hopped back into his truck.

His cell rang and Nick answered. It was Tessa.

"My Corvette isn't ready yet, and I need a ride," she whined.

"Serves you right. Having it repainted was a stupid idea."

"You're always so hard on me. Would you come around and take me out for supper?"

"I can come, but you have to buy."

"Why don't you get a job?"

"Why don't *you* get a job? You sit at home all day thinking of ways to con some man into marrying you."

"I told you, I have a job, two days a week."

"Get one for a full week; it pays more."

Tessa was silent for a moment. "Come over, I'll cook supper."

Wonderland Road was close to where Nick was, so he could easily drive to Tessa's place; he would have an opportunity to find out whether the police had made more inquiries about the driver of the Corvette seen at the Gassman house the evening Charlotte had been injured.

"Okay, but I had a problem paying with a hundred dollar bill at Dollarama. Would you have any change for it?"

"I normally use plastic. I don't know if I have that much money in my wallet."

"Can you check?"

"Okay," Tessa said wearily. She was back a few minutes later. "Yes, I have a few twenties and a few fives. Come over."

Nick glanced in the rear-view mirror. It had been a hot and humid day and he had spent enough time outdoors to become all sweaty and untidy. Not good enough for going to Tessa's. He stopped at a gas station, took a clean shirt out of his backpack and slipped into the washroom. He took his shirt off, washed his face, torso, and hair, and dried himself with paper towels. The clean shirt could stand a bit of ironing, but it had to do. Feeling presentable, he went back to his pickup and drove to Tessa's place. He would get a free meal and a hundred dollars he could spend without fear of being questioned.

Tessa was waiting for him. Her white slacks adhered perfectly to her well-shaped legs and the bright green blouse clung to her like a second skin. Her hair, gathered in a ponytail, made her look younger than her forty-four years. Nick kissed her on the cheek and together they walked into the dining room.

"Supper is ready." She gestured Nick to sit down.

"First I'd like to exchange the money, so I don't forget. You can't believe the troubles I had just trying to pay with a hundred dollar bill."

Tessa was nonplussed, but left the room and came back with her wallet from which she extracted a handful of bills.

"Here." She carefully placed the hundred in her wallet.

"Business is done," Nick said, and sat at the table.

Tessa wasn't the best cook in the world; the pasta was overcooked and the carbonara sauce was a poor imitation of the real thing, as she had used bacon instead of pancetta, but the White Zinfandel was nice and cold, suitable for a hot day.

"So, when will your car be ready?" Nick asked.

"Tomorrow for sure. When I pick it up I'm going to see an old aunt of mine. She lives in Montreal."

"Hoping to inherit?" Nick asked with a grin, as he refilled his glass.

"Not for a while. She's only sixty-five and in good health, but the visit will be a change for me. Fred is too busy to be pulled into any parties or other social events. I'll give the idea of conquering his heart a rest, and ease up a little."

"Good idea. More visits from the police?"

"Strangely enough, no." She gave him a look of complicity. "You're safe, for the time being."

"I'm always safe. I don't own a Corvette. Nobody can pinpoint me there at that time."

Tessa rose and set a can of toasted almonds on the table. "Well, I can."

"Are you threatening me, or what?"

Tessa shrugged. "Just reminding you that we're partners. I'll keep quiet if you help me get close to Fred." She tossed a few almonds into her mouth. "What really happened that evening? Did you hurt Charlotte?"

Nick rose and stood in front of her. "You're an idiot! And you don't know who you're dealing with!"

He strode off and got into his pickup. Tessa was dangerous. He kept her around in order to have a cover, in order to make people believe that he was in bad financial shape, but she was on the way to becoming a serious problem.

I might have to do something unpleasant, he thought.

✵ ✵ ✵

Nineteen

As he entered his office on Trafalgar Street, Fred thought, *It's incredible that I'm still sound of mind after all that happened last week.*

He had spent hours at the lawyer's office after the reading of his sister's will. He'd had a long meeting with Charlotte's accountant for tax purposes, and had arranged for the transfer of the money that was in the joint account into one of his. He had hired a company to clean all the blood stains in Charlotte's house and had put one of her neighbors in charge of looking after the premises. He had sold his old home to a young couple on the condition that he would have the remodeling finished within a month.

What had taken so much out of him, however, was Lucy Fairweather's disappearance. Detective Stevenson had called him five times asking about Lucy and her possible whereabouts, and with one excuse or another he had managed to keep Fred on the phone for more than half an hour each time. On top of all that, he missed his sister. She had been there all his life, and was the one person who had judged the people around him by the same standards he held. He set his feelings aside and hoped the current week would turn out better than the previous one.

"First things first," he said to himself.

As he was away from his office too much to take care of the business properly, he should put somebody capable in charge. Unfortunately he had little choice; Verge Bristol was the best man, going by seniority and knowledge. The idea didn't appeal to him, but it would be only for a short time, a month to start with; he would extend that period if the need arose. He called Verge on the phone and asked him to come to his office.

Verge Bristol entered, took off his yellow helmet, and hung it by its interior straps on the corner of the chair in front of him. As usual in the summer, he was dressed in a pair of jeans and a short-sleeved shirt.

"Have a seat," Fred said, taking place in his swivel chair.

"Hi, Fred. I was going to ask you if you need extra help." He sat on the other side of Fred's desk.

Fred glanced at him with mixed feelings. Maybe this was the time to talk frankly.

"In the past months I found out that there have been some changes in terms of subcontractors, materials and their costs." He paused for effect. "Of course, changes are often necessary when one sub goes broke or the material agreed upon is not available or not deliverable in time." Fred looked directly into Verge's eyes. "However, in most cases I didn't find a valid justification. This is an irregularity that isn't the best of practice."

Verge's face reddened, but he kept quiet.

"As you can guess, at the moment I'm very busy, so I'd like you to take over my job—say for a month to start with."

"Sure, I'm glad to help."

"Find out why these things happened and talk to the people responsible. There will be a five thousand dollar bonus for the extra work."

"Fred, I don't know what to say. I didn't know there were unauthorized changes."

"After a contract has been signed, nothing should be changed except for the reasons I just spelled out, and all changes should be documented."

"Of course, of course. I've been busy at the construction sites, so sometimes I didn't really check those changes, but you're right, they should occur only when there's is a reason." As Fred gave him a severe look, he added, "A damned good reason, I mean."

"Great. I'll send an email to everybody in the company to inform them of the change and I'll have a second desk put in this office. You start tomorrow. We'll meet from time to time; I'll call to let you know when." Fred rose, giving Verge a clear sign that the meeting was over.

"Sure. Thank you, Fred. I appreciate the bonus, even though it isn't really necessary."

"You're welcome. Take care."

Verge Bristol had just walked out of his office when a worried Mary Gervasio and Detective Stevenson appeared in the doorway, side-by-side. "Sorry, Fred. Mr. Stevenson didn't want to be announced. He just walked past me."

"That's fine, Mary. Discretion isn't a police virtue." He patted Mary's shoulder and closed the door after her. "So, Detective Stevenson, can you make it brief? You called me several times already, and I believe I answered all your questions. I can't imagine anything else you can learn from me." Fred stood, waiting.

"Can we sit down?" Stevenson asked.

Fred went behind his desk and sat in his swivel chair.

"As you know, Lucy Fairweather has disappeared. We need to find her."

Fred let out a soft laugh. "That's one of the reasons we have a police corps, to find missing persons."

Stevenson waved off his remark. "The neighbors have been of little help. They described her as a fairly peculiar person, with strong mood swings. Lucy's previous employer, a fast food outlet, let her go because of her inability to cope with the customers. It's my conclusion that your sister was the only person she worked for in the last few years."

"It could be. So...?"

Stevenson leaned toward Fred across the desk. "What I'm going to tell you isn't something we normally disclose—"

Fred cut in right away. "Please, please! Don't take me into your confidence," he said, sarcastically.

Stevenson didn't bother to acknowledge Fred's remark and continue. "I have to, in order to convince you to help me. The blood found in your sister's dining area and bathroom belongs to Lucy. We checked with the hospital where Lucy had surgery last year. There was a match, so we got a court order to search her house. We're running a DNA test. We'll know the results in a couple of weeks."

"Are you saying that my sister was injured during the course of a fight with Lucy?"

"It looks that way, but things are more complicated. The blood we found under the cat's nails belongs to yet another person. We think that more than one person met with your sister that night. Maybe there was a meeting of some sort? This conjecture is supported by the fact that a lot of the lights were turned on inside the house; even the three layers of the big chandelier were lit." He paused as if expecting some reaction from Fred, but Fred remained impassive. "Something had been going on that night." He paused again. "Aren't you anxious to find out what that *something* was, so we can catch your sister's killer?"

Fred rolled his eyes. "Until now I believed my sister was injured in a fatal fall, so I've had no reason to be eager to catch her so-called killer. At night my sister lit the chandelier when a guest came to the house. She did it for me, too."

Stevenson nodded. "I understand, but you must know something more about your sister's maid...or maybe you can give me the names of some of Mrs. Gassman's close friends? They may add a bit to the scenario we're trying to reconstruct."

"The people who went to see her regularly were the managers of the two charity organizations she worked with and supported: one is Elisabeth Ross, the chair of Welcome Among Us, an organization for recent immigrants, and the other is Bernard Morteson, the father of Charlotte's doctor and chair of The Safe Harbour, an organization for people who can't live alone. Then there's Brad Rowe, the man who took care of her yard and ploughed the snow in the winter. I can ask my secretary to dig out their addresses and phone numbers for you."

"Thanks. Do you know of anyone else who's been to see your sister, somebody a bit out of the ordinary?"

Fred nodded. "There was an old friend of my late wife, Tessa Wilson, who visited her a few times recently. She wanted to organize a party with the gang Charlotte and I chummed around with when we were young."

"Anybody else?"

"Not that I can think of."

"Those names and phone numbers could be of help. Any idea where Lucy could be staying? The more time passes, the more difficult it may be to find her."

"No. I really never knew much about Lucy." Fred rose and took Stevenson to his secretary's desk. "Mary, dig out the addresses of the two organizations Charlotte gave money to, and those of Theresa Wilson and Brad Rowe."

He waved the detective goodbye and briskly stepped back into his office.

He sat in his chair and stretched his legs over the desk. Keeping his cool during Stevenson's visit had been hard; first, the man had burst into his office, and then had insinuated that he didn't care about catching Charlotte's killer, as if Fred had no feelings for his sister. Stevenson needed information to carry out his job, and yet he adopted an antagonizing attitude toward him.

What did he imply? That he, Fred, knew more about Charlotte's death than he had let out? What an absurdity! Surely, he wanted the perpetrator, if there was one, caught and brought to justice—but first the police had to come up with more evidence than they had collected so far.

Forget about Stevenson, Fred told himself. He should go to the job site on Admiral Road and see how the construction proceeded.

Verge Bristol lifted up a corner of his shirt and used it to dry the drops of perspiration glistening on his forehead. *Oh boy! Fred knows about our hush-hush deals!* He was not completely surprised; Fred had the ability to catch anything out of the ordinary—from a shingle out of place on the roof to a price out of line on the spreadsheet—just by glancing at it. *I was a fool to listen to Alain...*

His heart pounding, Verge entered the office he shared with Alain Alstein and Moira Johnson and gestured for Alain to follow him. He took him to the conference room and shut the door.

Alain sat in one of the metal chairs situated around the long table and anxiously looked up at his colleague.

"What's so urgent?" he asked.

Verge sat close to him. "Fred called me into his office. He knows what we've been doing."

"But we—"

Verge put up his hand. "Don't ask me how he found out. The fact is that he knows. He probably checked the orders. The man is smart."

"But when did he have time? He's been so busy!"

"That doesn't matter; we have to stop cheating. That's final."

Alain wiggled in his chair. "I can't. I need money."

"You just have to stop taking those trips to Vegas."

"We don't go there anymore. We've been to Sarnia and to the Falls."

"Same thing. Stop gambling."

"It's the only way I can keep my marriage together."

Verge rose. "Change wife then. No more fiddling with prices, subs, or materials, period."

"Why are you being so harsh?"

"Because what we've been doing is illegal and I want to keep my job. It's that simple." He rose and pushed his chair underneath the table.

Alain blinked in distress. "I thought Fred was too busy to go around checking everything like he did before Deborah's accident. And after she died, I thought the police would do a bit more investigating."

"And why did you think that?"

"First, because in most of the cases the spouse is involved and second... because—"

"Because what?"

"Because I made a couple of calls to the police."

"Calls? What kind of calls?" Verge stood close to him, his face red with anger.

"I just suggested that they shouldn't exclude the possibility that the husband did it," Alain's voice trailed off to a whisper.

"Oh my God!" Verge stared at his colleague. "What kind of person are you? Insinuating that Fred could have killed his wife! He catered to her every whim no matter how strange! I'm ashamed to ever have called you my friend!" Verge stormed out of the room.

Around five o'clock Stevenson arrived at the London Police Service headquarters. Peggy O'Brian was still there, eager as usual to find out what Detective Stevenson had discovered.

"What's new?" she asked, trying to hide the curiosity in her voice.

Stevenson waved his cell in the air. "Took some pictures and emailed them to myself." He fiddled around his computer and downloaded the photos he had taken at The Werkstein while Mary had gone to the storage room to retrieve the files of the charity organizations Charlotte had been supporting.

"Our Mr. Dalton is in the clear," Stevenson said, and pecked on the print key.

"How did you find out?"

"Go get the printouts, Peggy. They're the pages of the planner regarding Fred's engagements for the last month. The evening Charlotte was injured he was meeting with Mr. and Mrs. Gardener about the sale of his house. Eight o'clock in the evening. He'd told them it was the only time he was free. I already checked with the Gardeners. They confirmed the day, time, and location."

"He's already found a buyer?"

"I guess so."

"Oh." She stood, stunned.

"The printouts, Peggy? Go get them; I'd like to put them in the dossier."

Peggy soon hurried back with a sheaf of papers and handed them to her boss. "So if we go by the book and exclude Dalton and the two charity companies, the only beneficiary left is Lucy Fairweather. She gets a million dollars, and she's on the run."

Stevenson sighed. "Fred doesn't have a clue where she could be, and neither do the neighbors we interviewed."

"Bad for us."

Stevenson closed the folder where he had stored the copy of Fred's monthly planner. "Look at the bright side. Where can she go? How long can she stay away? If she killed Charlotte for money she'll have to surface to get it, and when she does, we'll be there."

Twenty

Fred climbed into his white Lexus and drove to the construction site on Admiral Road in the east part of London. The Werkstein was one of the few companies still very active in spite of the economic crisis. The work was proceeding well, Fred noticed with satisfaction. Thanks to the current recession there were no delays in the delivery of materials and the subcontractors all turned up on time.

He looked at the first house near the entrance of the twenty-unit complex The Werkstein had contracted to build. Two men installed brown shingles on the roof and another stuffed insulation into the walls. Fred entered the two-story, three-thousand-square-foot house-in-the-making. It would fit his needs well in terms of space and location. He should decide soon whether to buy it, so he could meet with the architect and have some input on the final layout of the interior. He stepped outside and into the barely outlined backyard; he admired the grove of locust trees that flanked the edges of the property, thus providing the house with plenty of privacy.

He felt the need to have a nice place he could call home. *I'll come back next week*, he thought. *Give the house a second look, and then decide on the acquisition.*

He retraced his steps, waved at the foreman, who was busy instructing a couple of construction workers, and drove away. He placed a call to Brad Rowe, the neighbor looking after Charlotte's property, and informed him that he would be at the house. He drove to Port Franks and, for the first time after his sister's death, entered Charlotte's house. The place seemed strangely empty, devoid of soul. Charlotte hadn't been in good health in recent years, but her spirit had always been vibrant, her attitude toward life, positive.

He moved to the patio and sat in one of the lounge chairs, his gaze drifting over the vast extent of water in front of him. The weather was warm; the leisure activities around the shores and on the lake were at their peak. He had always loved this place. It was home. In the past he had enjoyed taking a swim, spending time in meditation or simply having a chat with his sister. He missed her, and he missed having a family, people who cared about him, people he could spend time with and share happy hours with. What was in store for him?

The jiggle of hinges stopped his musing; somebody was reaching the backyard through the walking path that flanked the house. Brad Rowe, Charlotte's neighbor, came into view.

"I saw your car drive in, Mr. Dalton. Thought I'd come to have a chat with you."

He sat in a chair close to Fred. A retired policeman with a lean body and an erect carriage, Brad was in his sixties, and liked to keep busy by doing chores for his neighbors.

"Nice of you, Brad."

"We had a lot of commotion around here. The police are looking for Lucy, as you probably know."

"Do I? I got one call after another, asking questions I can't answer."

"I always wondered why your sister kept rehiring her. She didn't present herself well. I mean, forget about the old clothes, sometimes I believe she didn't have a bath for a week. Her own place and yard were a mess."

"She lived very close, and that was an advantage. By the way, did Lucy ever mention any relatives she liked to visit?"

"Not a soul. I wonder what happened to her."

"We'll let the police worry about it, I guess."

"She said she'd take care of Sultana, Charlotte's cat, but she let her loose, free to wander in the neighborhood."

"Where is she now?"

Brad looked at the ground, then back at Fred. "I took her to the animal clinic, Mr. Dalton. She was nasty and attacked people. I believe they put her to sleep."

Fred sighed. He should have thought about Sultana, but with all that had happened he had forgotten about the cat.

"Did the police talk to you?"

"No. They asked questions around; three times they talked to my friend who owns the variety store down the road; she'd seen a car driving up on the evening Mrs. Gassman was injured."

"Oh, I see." Now he understood why, since the beginning, Detective Stevenson had suspected that Charlotte's injuries might be the result of an act of violence and not of an accidental fall.

"Can I get you something to drink?" Brad asked.

"No need; I won't be staying long. I'll look around and see if there's anything urgent that needs to be done or repaired."

Brad hesitated and then said, "If you want to rent this house, just let me know. I know of a couple of people who would like to spend the summer in this beautiful place."

"At the moment I haven't decided what to do." He paused, then took out his business card and handed it to Brad. "Send your bills to this address, for the time being."

Brad nodded, said goodbye, and left the same way he had come.

Fred freed his iPhone 3G from his belt and opened it. He clicked on Voice Memos and dictated the date and place, then walked around inspecting the premises with the eyes of an expert. He recorded items that needed closer attention. The trellis had partially caved in and needed to be replaced; the picket fence should be painted and the stones covering the walking path should be leveled. He didn't bother inspecting the roof and the painting of the exterior walls, as The Werkstein had taken care of those items last year. He checked the main and side doors; they were solid wood and could stand a couple more winters with no problems. When he finished recording the information he closed his iPhone, locked up the house, and got in his car.

✳ ✳ ✳

Twenty-one

Lucy Fairweather decided she would go back home. She had spent four days and nights in a shed near what she believed to be an abandoned farmhouse, living on a sack full of food she had taken with her. She couldn't endure the hardship anymore. She was thirsty and hungry; her clothes, impregnated with dry sweat, sand, and dirt, stuck to her body uncomfortably. It was time to make a move.

She walked to the lake and followed the shoreline toward her old house. It was hard dragging her feet on the sand, and up and down many dunes. She would, though, approach her house unseen, crossing through the Gassman's property.

It was just 7:00 a.m. when she reached her backyard. To her surprise a double chain with a heavy lock barred the entrance. She brushed cautiously along a sidewall and glanced at the front door. There was a lock there, also. She retraced her steps and looked at the window below grade that opened onto the basement. She took a shoe off and broke the pane with it. With the same shoe she brushed aside all the glass shards that had fallen outside. She put her shoe back on and turned around, then slowly slid down through the window until she touched the floor.

She rushed upstairs and into the kitchen and turned on the sink tap. To her surprise, there was no water. She flipped the switch on the wall to discover that there was no electricity either. All that hard walk for nothing! She slumped, disheartened, into a chair.

For a moment she entertained the idea of going to the control panel outside and turning on the switches that regulated the water and power supply, but she thought that could be dangerous; somebody might be keeping an eye on the place. She abandoned the dream of a nice breakfast and a good bath and walked over to the pantry. She found a can of tomato juice and drank it in one big gulp, then ransacked all the goodies she could see on the shelves and put them in a garbage bag; she went to her bedroom and changed into clean clothes. She would wait until twilight to go back to her refuge.

Still unable to find Charlie Johnson to help him change large bills into small ones, Nick Falcone had toured the airports in Ontario and Quebec, stopping at the exchange booths to convert some of his money into a different currency. He had the equivalent of fifteen thousand dollars safe in his backpack when he had approached the booth at Terminal 1 of Pearson International. The employee on duty had taken the hundred-note bills, set them against the light, and then compared their serial numbers with a list in her possession. Nick had managed to get his five hundred dollars in US money, but immediately after he had decided to put a stop to his operation. It could be dangerous. He had returned home, satisfied with his partial achievement.

From far away Nick spotted a silver Corvette parked in front of his farmhouse. *Oh, oh,* he thought. *What in the world is Tessa doing here?* Of course, he liked to see her and have a good time with her, but maybe he had been too hasty to tell her where he hid the house key.

He parked his pickup outside. He opened the main door slowly to avoid the usual squeaking and entered the large family room. He deposited his carry-on onto the floor and looked around. Tessa sprawled on the old sofa, an empty glass in her hand and a bottle of whisky on the floor. Nick tiptoed to the basement and checked on his money, which he had hidden in an out-of-order old freezer. Everything seemed to be in order. He retraced his steps, took the carry-on to his bedroom, and walked to the family room to have a drink.

Tessa stirred and then yawned. "You're home, finally!" She rose and straightened her skirt. "Where have you been?"

"On a trip. Weren't you supposed to be in Montreal?"

"Yes. I was there but I only stayed three days. I got bored. My aunt has her crowd and her things to do: bridge, exercise classes, quilting. Nothing

I was interested in, so I came back. I called you yesterday and today. Since you didn't answer, I came over to see whether you were okay."

"I forgot my cell at home."

"So what was the trip all about?"

"Nothing in particular; just visiting old friends."

"Oh. Any good news?"

"No, but I thought of a way to get close to your precious Fred Dalton. You remember how the boys used to come over here to practice shooting? The trap house is still up. Come on—you can see it from the kitchen." He took Tessa's hand and led her in front of a little window above the sink. "See it?"

"It looks like a big box."

"Of course. Fred was good at it. I could give him a call and ask if he'd like to come over. I don't know whether he's kept up with the sport, though."

"It might be worth a try." Tessa rubbed her breasts on Nick's back and hugged him around the waist. "Come back to the family room," she murmured.

"Good idea, I was thinking of having a drink." He turned around and meekly followed her.

"I can pour it for you. Whisky?"

"Yes."

Tessa offered him a tumbler filled with a generous amount of bourbon. She took a sip from the glass and handed it to Nick, then caressed his cheek and neck.

"What do you have in mind?"

In response she rubbed her breasts against his chest. "I was thinking of a bit of relaxation, the two of us together." This time her hands were at work on his chest and below. "Aren't you interested?"

He had to give it to Tessa; she knew how to seduce a man. Nick sipped his drink. "Maybe."

Tessa took a step away from him and, looking intensely in his eyes, unbuttoned her blouse in slow motion, one button after the other.

As Nick moved forward, she put her hand up.

"Not yet. First we have to create the proper atmosphere."

Here we go, Nick thought. *She has a fixation with candles. No candles, no sex. But I haven't got any candles in the house!*

Tessa reached for her big purse and extracted a handful of candles, from short to tall, and a box of matches. She set a couple of candles on the low table near the couch, a couple of little ones on the side table near the floor lamp, and three big ones on the fireplace mantel, then lit them all and stood back to admire her handiwork.

"Now things are in place," she purred, satisfied.

Nick deposited his drink on the coffee table, pulled her close, and freed her of her loose blouse and skirt. In one swift move he tossed her on the couch and knelt over her.

"Now that the candles are lit the show can commence," he crowed.

With one hand he caressed her temple down to her jaw line, and with the other he drew her closer to him. He kissed her hungrily, one demanding kiss after the other. He felt her tongue dancing with his; her body arched to make contact with his hips. He stopped kissing her, unhooked her lace bra, and took one nipple between his teeth to softly nip on it. He then bent over her to lick her bare tummy.

Tessa moaned, then drew him up close to her chest. She tugged at his shirt and unbuttoned it, but fumbled as she tried to loosen his belt.

Nick helped, and soon his shirt and belt found their way to the floor. He pulled her panties off, then paused for a moment to look at her voluptuous body, made to please a man's sight and touch. Memories of past pleasures overwhelmed him, creating urgency in his body. He hurried to free himself of all garments, and dug a condom from his trouser pocket. In one smooth movement he rolled it on.

"Aren't you being too hasty?" Tessa asked. "Don't you like—"

"Not this time." He pulled her legs apart. "Maybe the second time around."

He entered her—as he expected, the way in was moist and slippery. She arched her back tightly against him, wanting him deeper, and Nick obliged. He thrust and thrust; she soon came, her moaning replaced by a loud wail. Gripping her hips, he continued to thrust, and Tessa, as if by silent agreement, moved rhythmically with him until she came again, and Nick with her.

"You're amazing," Nick said moments later, as they lay very close to each other on the couch.

"You aren't bad, either." Tessa reclined her head in the crook of his neck.

In no time they were asleep.

With a colorful afghan tightly wrapped around her body Lucy Fairweather looked at the two cars parked outside the farmhouse. When she had left this morning, nobody was in sight.

"Oh my God!" she whispered. "There're people living in the farmhouse!" She squatted behind a clump of tall grass and waited.

It was fairly dark when a tall woman exited the house and waved good-bye to a man. She climbed into the sports car and left.

Lucy waited a bit longer, in the hopes that the man would also leave. Fat chance; soon lights appeared inside the first floor and music blared from the house. Walking a fair distance from the house, Lucy entered the shed and set camp there.

Her mind wandered back to the terrible night when she had found Charlotte sprawled half on the floor and half on the low marble table, her eyes closed and the cat curled at her feet. She thought the woman was dead, and so she had gone to the roll-up desk to get the cash Charlotte kept in the bottom drawer. She had taken all the bills she found there and had started to count them when Charlotte's voice startled her.

"What are you doing? Robbing me? Call for help! I'm injured!" Charlotte had straightened her back up and had tried to rise.

"I thought you were—"

"Call 911!" Charlotte had ordered, and, placing her hands on the floor she had begun to lift herself up.

Lucy had panicked. She had served time and couldn't afford to be reported. With one rapid move she had grabbed the silver candelabra on the desk and rushed toward Charlotte. In the small lapse of time it took her to winch up the heavy object, Charlotte had clutched at her ankles, pushing her against the edge of the marble table. But even the cut on her leg hadn't stopped Lucy. The heavy candelabra had fallen on Charlotte's neck, sending her to the same reclining position in which Lucy had found her.

Lucy sighed at the memory. *Bad luck…in my life I've had only bad luck.* Exhausted, she lay on the makeshift bed of straw and old rugs and fell asleep.

✲ ✲ ✲

Twenty-two

When Nick Falcone woke up the following morning, he felt good about his life and himself. Things were definitely going in the right direction. He had money, even if it needed to be processed before being used; he had a woman who enjoyed sex with him, and he had a place to live. *Not bad at all*, he concluded. He should start organizing the days ahead. He would take ten thousand dollars of the *good* money to a bank. He could say it was the result of having liquidated all the assets he had accumulated while he was out west. He would keep the remaining five thousand in the house. That thought triggered the consideration of securing the premises. He should buy a couple of deadbolt locks for the doors, then get a few iron bars and install them on the basement windows.

Whistling the tune of *You Belong with Me,* by Taylor Swift, Nick showered, dressed, and then took a walk in the fields. The farmer who had bought the field from his parents had planted beans, and they were now coming to maturity. In the east corner was a stagnant pond surrounded by cannas and tall grass on one side and thickets on the others. On the west side, thick woods needing thinning out marked his property's boundary. Following the dry brook on the southern side, he turned back toward the house. The nearby shed was kept together by metal sheets of different colors that didn't line up with each other; he should dismantle it—it wouldn't take more than a day. He should buy a used trim saw so he could cut the weeds, bushes, and climbing shrubs that had clamped the house in a green vise.

Nearer the house he looked at the small part of land that was still his, where he and his friends, and his father before them, used to practice target shooting. Nick had become pretty good at it and a few times managed to even beat Fred Dalton, who had a keen eye and a perfect tempo for hitting a flying target. He wondered if Fred still practiced that sport. He should find out, because that would be a way to establish some contacts with the man Tessa had decided to conquer.

He hopped in his truck and headed for London. He should go to the shelter where Charlie was staying, again. He shouldn't wait too long before exchanging a few more hundred dollar bills. Actually he should make the exchange a regular weekly operation until all the money was recycled.

He drove to York Street and looked for the Men's Mission and Rehabilitation Centre, the place Charlie referred to as "the shelter." The three-story yellow-brick construction soon drifted into sight. He parked his Dakota at the rear of the building and looked around. The wall surrounding the outside staircase sported colorful murals; a little lady swept the steps, her broom about three inches taller than she was. As Nick greeted her, she stopped working and pushed her heavy glasses up the bridge of her nose.

"Yes, I know the young man." She reciprocated Nick's smile. "He has a job. He's out to work."

"Where?"

"I'm not sure, but I heard him talking about the horse races at the Fair. Last night he stayed there to watch them."

"The Western Fairs Raceway?"

The little lady shrugged. "That's my guess."

Nick thanked her and went back to his vehicle. *So Charlie has a job... that'll make it more difficult to convince him to do any work for me.* Last time, when Charlie had given him back his money, he was shaking from head to toe, and with good reason since Nick had threatened to kill him. *That wasn't a wise move,* Nick thought. *Still, I have to try to contact him.* He drove east until he met Rectory Street.

When he reached the large parking lot he stopped the engine. As he stepped out of the pickup he marveled at how much the compound had expanded since he had left Ontario. Several modern-style constructions now alternated concrete or brick walls with glass sidings. He passed through the revolving door of the main entrance and took the stairs to reach

the Carousel Room at the Top of the Fair. This was a three-level restaurant, devoid of patrons at this time of day, and supervised only by a young
woman seated behind a counter. He asked permission to look around and
descended the few steps that separated him from the large glass wall which
provided a view of the entire racetrack.

In a far corner of the parking lot adjacent to the track were three piles of
sand. Charlie Johnson worked on one of them, shoveling sand into a wheelbarrow. The entire compound was fenced off, with the longest segment of
the fence bordering the public road.

He saluted the woman behind the counter and walked to his car. An
hour later he returned, carrying a toolbox and wearing a helmet and an
orange vest with green stripes on the back. He walked close to the fence,
extracted a few tools from the box, and carefully looked around. He worked
on the junction of two adjacent fence pieces until he created a wedge
between them. When he thought nobody was watching, he sneaked into
the compound.

Charlie was pushing a wheelbarrow and didn't stop when Nick called
him, so he got closer. Nick was surprised by Charlie's new appearance; no
hair peeped out of the hard hat and he'd shaved his thick beard.

"Charlie, it's me, Sam," he said, and grabbed him by the arm.

Charlie lowered the wheelbarrow and looked at him. "I don't want to
talk to you."

"And why not? We had a good time at the bowling alley."

"You wanted to kill me."

"Oh, that! I wasn't serious, you know? I just wanted my money back;
that's all."

Charlie picked up the handles of the wheelbarrow and moved on.

Nick stopped him again.

"Listen, I know you like to watch the races. Why don't I come back
after you quit work and take you up there?" Nick pointed up toward the
Carousel Room. "We can have a couple of beers and follow the races. We
can even place a bet directly from our dinner table!"

Charlie put down the wheelbarrow again and looked to where Nick was
pointing. He took off his helmet and raked his hair, then shook his head.

"Why not?"

"My sister, Moira, would be mad, and she's real nice to me." He turned
around and, once more, he picked up his barrow. "She isn't like you."

"Wait, wait." Nick barred Charlie's way. "I have an idea. Tell me where your sister lives, and I'll go talk to her."

Charlie hesitated and Nick rode the wave. "Everything will be okay, I assure you. I'll explain that we had a misunderstanding." Charlie didn't react. "Do you know the name of the street where she lives?"

"King Street."

"And the number?

Charlie shrugged. "Don't know. It's a tall building near the corner with…" He paused, trying to remember. "Rectory."

"Good enough," Nick said, and tapped him on the shoulders. "And her name is Moira?"

"Yes. Moira Johnson."

A man wearing a white helmet was walking toward them. Nick waved at him, and said, "Just looking after the fence. All in order."

He quickly entered the building and followed the way the man had come out.

Nick never had any intention of meeting Charlie's sister; he just wanted to get more information on Charlie, his family and his whereabouts; maybe he could use both brother and sister for recycling the money.

Shortly after eight o'clock the following morning Nick parked outside Moira Johnson's apartment building. He had gotten her physical description and the make of her car from one of her neighbors, and had no problem recognizing the Hyundai as it emerged from the underground garage.

He followed her to the nearby Superstore and watched her, careful not to be seen. She checked the price of each item she planned to choose, put others back on the shelf and then stopped at the butcher's counter to order some fresh cuts. Clearly Charlie's sister wasn't poor. Nick wondered why her brother was living in a community center which was supported by the government and set up to help the less privileged. He bought a copy of *The Globe and Mail*, walked out of the store, and waited outside for Moira to finish her shopping. Finally she appeared, carrying two green boxes full of groceries. While leafing through the newspaper Nick gave her a quick glance. Those red curls peeping out of the beige scarf looked familiar, even if he couldn't remember whether he had ever met her.

He concluded Moira was off limits. He would have to work on Charlie alone. The young woman looked in control of her life, so it would be difficult to con her. In a couple of days he would return to the Western Fair and convince Charlie to spend some time with him. He looked at his wristwatch. *Too early to go back home. I'll go see if the old St. Thomas Gun Club is still in existence.*

He hopped in his pickup. Forty minutes later he stood in front of the club, located at the back of Cowan Park in Central Elgin. From a distance he saw ten trap houses and the marked spots where the shooters would stand, ready to aim and fire.

There was no action in the field so Nick entered the modest clubhouse. He started a conversation with an old geezer who told him that the club welcomed new members, that it was very active, as few clubs of this kind existed in the neighborhood.

"I'd like to join," Nick said, tentatively. "But I don't know if I'm good enough for this club. I haven't shot for more than ten years." He looked at the walls. "I see a lot of trophies and banners with championships. Which levels of members do you have?"

"All levels," the man replied. "People come here to enjoy themselves. Good company and good sportsmanship." He walked out and was right back with a flyer and a form. "Here." He handed both to Nick. "This flyer gives you some information, and there's an application in case you decide to join."

Nick thanked him and left. One stop at the Home Depot for a couple of locks and then he would head home.

As he negotiated the last bend before reaching the farmhouse Nick realized how his feelings had changed over the arc of the day. In the morning he had felt like a king in control of his reign. Now a vague sense of insecurity, an uneasiness that he could not completely explain, nagged at him. He parked his Dakota in the carport and entered the house.

The water was running somewhere; he quickened his steps to the bathroom on the upper floor. He opened the door and parted the shower curtains.

Sprawled on the floor was the naked body of Lucy Fairweather, a jet of water hammering her stomach. Water had overflowed onto the floor and trickled out of the bathroom as the drain couldn't keep up with the influx.

Nick stepped inside the shower and turned off the tap. Then he stood there, shocked.

✳ ✳ ✳

Twenty-three

With one hand Detective Stevenson held his cell phone to his ear, and with the other he fanned a sheet of paper. He listened attentively, from time to time asking a question. When Peggy O'Brian walked by, he gestured her to come close. Soon afterward he turned off his phone.

"Do you know when they're going to give us some air conditioning?" Stevenson asked.

Peggy shook her head. "Still trying to find out what's wrong. Not too soon, I'm afraid."

"I don't mind the heat, but when the humidity is high, I get a headache and a big one—like the one I have right now." He looked at his wristwatch. "One more hour to go."

Peggy stood hesitantly close to his desk, as if she wanted something, but was afraid of asking a question.

"Okay, okay, you want to know about my call. Lucy Fairweather is dead. They found her body on a dune, close to shore, about twenty kilometers from Port Franks."

"Drowned?"

"Don't know. The autopsy is set for the day after tomorrow. Time of death is estimated at about three days ago." He tugged at his moustache. "There goes our primary suspect."

"Suicide maybe?"

"Possibly, but I'd exclude it if she knew of her inheritance. More likely an accident. Somebody also broke into her house." He sighed audibly. "We're left with the owner of the Corvette, who *might* know or have seen something about the fall of Mrs. Gassman—a very long shot at this point."

"What do you think's going to happen?"

"I don't know. We just have to wait for the autopsy report." Stevenson drummed his fingers on the desk. The phone rang, and Stevenson picked it up. "Interesting." He listened for more than fifteen minutes, then added, "Very interesting."

When he turned the phone off, Peggy asked, "What was so interesting?"

"Go get me the frozen patch for my poor forehead. I'll tell you when you come back."

"What's so interesting?" Peggy asked as soon as she returned, handing him a towel and a bag of frozen peas.

Stevenson placed the bag inside the towel and wrapped it around his head before replying.

"This morning the coast guard helped a boat, *The Catalina*, stranded midway between the Canadian and American shores," Stevenson said. "They provided some fuel and fined a Mr. Oscar Clark for not having a craft operator card—a boating license. They were ready to let him go when the OPP informed them that a corpse had been swept ashore in the Pinery. They asked Mr. Clark to follow them. He is now at the OPP Detachment in Grand Bend, and the boat is being searched."

"So…?"

"The call I got was from a friend of mine at the detachment in Grand Bend. He was wondering if this corpse and that of Lucy Fairweather could be connected."

"Interesting."

The phone rang again and Stevenson snatched up the receiver. As before, he listened a lot and spoke little. When he was finished, he said, "The mystery thickens. Oscar Clark has a police record, so they're going to do some digging." Stevenson reorganized the loose papers on his desk. "I'm going home. Tomorrow we'll get a bit more information. My friend promised to keep me posted."

For the fourth day in a row Nick Falcone anxiously leafed through *The London Free Press*. The second page carried the discovery of Lucy

Fairweather's corpse. He was eager to read the details. Afraid that her presence in his house could trigger unpleasant inquiries, he had dressed her with the clothes and shoes he had found in the bathroom, loaded her into his pickup, and taken her to the dunes near the shore. It had been dark, and a sudden thunderstorm had made unloading the corpse a cumbersome operation. Once at home Nick had washed all the floors. It was morning when he finished; he then took the old floor mat in front of the entrance to the dump. The heavy downpour that followed had washed away any footprints Lucy might have left on the ground.

The newspaper reported briefly on the woman's role in Charlotte Gassman's life and the emergency call she had made when she had found Charlotte injured and sprawled on the floor. Lucy's corpse had been found half-buried in the sand only a few meters from where Nick had deposited it. There were no details, not a word that would explain why Lucy had taken refuge in his house. Disappointed, Nick folded the newspaper. Clearly, he should have thought of some good locks to keep intruders out, long before he had. *But why did the old woman wander so far away from her home? Is it possible that she was connected with the owner of the boat, The Catalina, where I found that pile of money? That would spell trouble, but there's nothing I can do about it for now.*

He picked up the application form he had received at the St. Thomas Gun Club. *Maybe it would do me some good to have a hobby.* He wondered again whether Fred still did any shooting. He rose from the sofa and went to the kitchen to make an instant coffee. When that was ready, he took it to the family room and sat again on the sofa. He opened his cell and dialed Fred's phone number at The Werkstein.

Mary Gervasio, Fred's secretary, answered promptly. Nick introduced himself and, when he heard that Fred wouldn't be in his office for a while, asked for Fred's private number.

"I'm not sure I should give it to you. You're Mr. Falcone, you said?"

"Right. I'm an old friend of his; I knew his late wife, Deborah, and his sister, Charlotte. Don't you remember me? I was at the reception that followed Mrs. Gassman's funeral." He waited, expectantly.

"There were so many people." Mary sounded uncertain. A few seconds passed. "Well, here's his cell's number." She read the number out to him.

"Thanks so much," Nick said, and hung up. He called Fred right away.

Fred seemed surprised, but Nick didn't give him much time to elaborate on his motive.

"I'd have called you before, but I thought you might be too busy to talk to an old friend. I want to tell you again how sorry I am about Charlotte. She was very dear to me. I've been to her place so many times that I considered her family, like an aunt."

"Thanks. She left a big empty space in my life."

"I can believe that. That's one of the reasons I called you, to take your mind off things, if I may. A few days ago I went to the gun club in St. Thomas and I remembered the good times we had together, you, me, and Mr. Gassman. Maybe we could go shooting together."

"Oh, I haven't done much shooting since Deborah's accident."

"And I didn't do any when I was out west. Maybe it's time we start over."

"I'm not a member of the Ontario Rifle Association anymore; I even sold my shotguns. I didn't want to have any weapons in the house with Deborah so sick."

"I understand. Well, I have two. Remember my parents' farmhouse? I live there now."

"Oh, yes. I remember." He paused. "I took time off from work so I could take care of all the private matters that followed Charlotte's death." Fred paused again. "Actually tomorrow I don't have anything planned after two o'clock. Would the afternoon be convenient for you?"

"Perfect. Three-thirty? I'll put up a target and get plenty of target sheets ready."

Twenty-four

Pleasantly surprised by Nick's call, Fred looked forward to trap shooting again. It had been the only sport he'd practiced with regularity; it was something he could do alone in the little time he managed to get away from work. He had started to trap shoot using a cheap pump-action gun of unknown denomination, and later he had bought a Stock Remington 870 with a 28" barrel. After Deborah's accident he had given away his shotguns, but he had packed all his shooting paraphernalia in boxes and stored them away. The urgent desire to own a place he could call home surfaced again. He could actually buy a parcel of land and get an architect to design a house the way he liked it, but that would take time. He really should just buy the unit he'd looked at the other day, in the complex The Werkstein was finishing up.

Happy with his decision, Fred tightened the knot of his tie and grabbed the coat draped over the back of the chair. He was ready to leave for the meeting with Welcome Among Us, one of the organizations Charlotte had been supporting, when his cell phone rang.

"Have you seen the article in *The London Free Press?*" a non-identifiable voice asked. "Lucy Fairweather is dead. How come so many people around you die?" A click terminated the communication.

Fred snapped his cell shut and then went to the entrance hall where a pile of unopened mail lay on the floor, most of which was still addressed to his sister. There were a number of copies of the local newspaper, so he hunted down the news about Lucy. There was nothing, but then he realized that today's newspaper had not been delivered yet to his door. He slipped on his coat and left the apartment. He entered the superintendent's booth and asked for today's newspaper.

"Oh, sorry, Mr. Dalton," the man said, sheepishly. "Please forgive a bad habit of mine. Your sister didn't come down often, so I used to read her newspaper before delivering it to her door." He folded the paper he had on the counter and handed it to Fred.

"Well, maybe now you should bring it over as soon as it arrives, since at the moment I live here." Fred gave him a chill look, and left.

Once in his car he opened the newspaper and looked for the news about Lucy. Yes, he thought with dismay, Lucy was dead and her body had been found in puzzling circumstances. He sighed. *I should take a vacation. Stevenson's calls will probably triple.*

For the last couple of hours the countryside surrounding Nick's farmland had resounded with the shots that Nick and Fred had fired, silence falling only when the two stopped to reload their guns. Now quiet had returned, as the two men retired inside the house.

"That was fun," Fred said as he finished cleaning the gun on the kitchen counter. "But I don't think it would be worthwhile to repair the trap house. All the metal parts are rusty, and the rotating mechanism is broken."

"You're right. Besides, going to a club is more fun. We could enter a competition once we're a bit better."

"A bit better? Look here!" Fred pointed at the poster-size sheets where several concentric circles were painted black on a white background. "Only ten percent dead on center and another twenty percent on target. All the others were astray. We even hit the tree ten feet away!"

"I admit there's room for improvement." Nick put locks on both of the guns and placed them in their cases. "The guns weren't too bad though." He cleaned the kitchen counter from the gunpowder's residuals.

"No, they're similar to my old Remington. If I stick with this sport, I should buy myself a gun."

"Good idea. Something to drink?" Nick asked, and opened the fridge.

"Oh, yes. I'm thirsty."

"I have an idea." He handed Fred a Labatt Blue. "Why don't we go see the club in St. Thomas? Then we can have supper in town."

"I don't think I'm presentable." Fred sat on one of the high chairs in front of the counter.

"I'd offer you one of my shirts but I think it'd be too big."

Fred laughed. "It definitely would be. I've lost weight in the past months."

"And I put on thirty pounds since I left for the west."

"I noticed. I almost didn't recognize you at the reception after the funeral. I thought it might be you but I wasn't sure."

Nick sat close to Fred and finished his beer. "Let's drive to the club and have a look around. If you don't feel comfortable going out for supper, we can go to a take-out."

"Some other time, maybe." He finished his beer. "Thanks for looking me up. It was a surprise and a pleasant break."

"My pleasure."

Fred rose and they both walked outside. "Not a bad place you have here."

"When I came back after my parents' death, the place was a mess—it still is, as you probably noticed. I didn't do much, since I'm not sure I'll be setting camp here."

Fred gave a knowledgeable look around. "The brick walls are in good shape but the roof needs to be replaced before the cold season—several shingles are missing, and others are loose." He paused. "So what did you do when you were in the wild west?"

"Worked in a shipyard in Vancouver, and in a can factory when I was in Calgary. Good money but long hours."

"Never got married?" Fred asked, as he opened the driver's door of his Lexus.

"No, I'm a free spirit. I don't want to be on a leash." He realized Fred didn't talk much about himself—actually he never did, now that he remembered. Maybe he would open up if he asked about his marriage. "It must have been hard coping with Deborah, after the accident."

"It was. I couldn't do anything for her. Nobody could, actually." Fred stared into the distance. "She was so full of life, and then one day there was little left in her, just enough consciousness to realize what a terrible state she'd been reduced to."

"They never found the owner of the truck who pushed her against the tree. Right?"

"No. It happened at night, and they found Deborah in the morning. The truck driver had all that time to disappear."

"It must have been terrible for you, too."

Fred shrugged. "For me? I couldn't feel sorry about myself. One look at Deborah and any self-pity would disappear."

"I understand." He paused. "Well, life goes on. I'll call you soon for another shooting session."

"You do that." Fred waved goodbye and drove away.

Nick watched until Fred's Lexus disappeared beyond the first curve. *Mission accomplished. We're as much friends as we've ever been. He doesn't have the faintest idea how much I've changed in the last few years.*

Things were falling into place; now he should find a way to exchange more of his hundred-dollar bills. Charlie still remained a possibility, even if his sister would be on guard. All at once he remembered where he had seen those red ringlets: at Charlotte's funeral. She was an employee of The Werkstein, he realized with disappointment. He needed to tread carefully.

✷ ✷ ✷

Twenty-five

Verge Bristol was exhausted. He had just returned from a two-hour meeting with the bonding company that The Werkstein normally used. Strongly determined to get the same deals Fred had gotten in the past, Bristol had bargained hard. He had realized that the company tried to take advantage of his inexperience. At the end of the two hours, however, Bristol had obtained bonds for the two upcoming jobs, each worth around three million dollars, with the same premiums The Werkstein had paid in the past. He had never realized how much work went through Fred's desk until he had taken over his job. The extra five thousand dollars Fred had promised him would surely be welcomed, but he wished he would be able to go home before dusk at least a couple of days a week.

He looked up as Alain entered the office.

"What's this barging in?" Verge asked. "Don't you know how to knock?"

Alain, his face red with anger, slumped in the swivel chair and spun it toward Verge. "That snake of a female midget! You won't believe what she's done!"

"Moira?"

"She found out about the sub I replaced and called Fred about it! I heard her leaving a message on his phone."

Verge rose and stood in front of his colleague. "We agreed there wouldn't be any more fiddling with the prices or the subs. So first, what did *you* do?"

Alain looked down, downcast. "I was in a bind. I needed five thousand in a hurry."

"Five thousand! And who did you replace?"

"The guy doing the drywall for the hangar. The guy I got is a good guy. He'll do a good job. Nothing to worry about."

"I'm not going to worry about the job, and surely not about you. Fred will probably fire you, and that's the end of the problem."

"You have to talk to him, explain the situation. I can't lose my job, Verge."

Verge shrugged. "The best I can do is to keep quiet for the time being, but if Fred talks to me, I'll have to explain that you and your wife have a problem. That's as far as I can go. If he asks me to fire you, I will."

Alain's face reddened even more. "If you do, I'll spill the beans; I'll tell him about all the other times we did it together."

"He already knows. Putting me in charge of the business was a way to test me; what he expected me to do was to stop doing it and stop anybody else who tried. The drywall for the hangar isn't up yet. I'll take care of it; I'll call the original sub and explain that there's been a clerical error. Get ready to refund the money to whoever paid you."

"I don't have the five thousand!"

"Borrow it then. It's your problem, Alain."

"I thought we were friends!" Perspiration gathered at his hairline; he dried it with the corner of his checkered shirt. "I can't understand how Moira caught on."

Verge rolled his eyes. "Not only are you a crook, but you're an idiot. She did all the pricing for that job. There was no call for tender. Everything was done directly from this office; she approached the subs mostly on Fred's advice. The legitimate sub probably called Moira and asked for an explanation. She checked and confirmed the original agreement, then contacted Fred. Clearly she doesn't trust me."

"Please, Verge, help me!"

Verge turned Alain's swivel chair to face the door. "Get out. I started cheating on your insistence when you joined The Werkstein. Then those calls you made, trying to implicate Fred in the death of his own wife! How can anybody do something that low?" He shook the chair to make Alain move. "Get out!"

Alain rose, shoved the chair away, and strode out, slamming the door behind him.

Concerned and saddened by the behavior of his former friend, Verge paced back and forth. He remembered the day Fred Dalton had first entered that office as the boss, a week after the death of Werner Gassman, Fred's brother-in-law. Fred had worked in the construction industry in several capacities when he was still a student and after he had joined the company. To his formal engineering training he had added hands-on-experience. He had acquired an appreciation for how much time each job required, and Gassman had involved him in office work just a year before his death.

By the time Fred took over, The Werkstein had acquired an excellent reputation in the field. Fred became a cautious innovator. One of the first things he did was to give Verge a raise and, soon after, as the business boomed, he had agreed to hire Alain Alstein, whose wife had found life in Barrie too boring and wanted to move to London. Alain was a good estimator, fast with figures and fun to be with. In no time he and Verge had become friends, as their wives enjoyed shopping together.

However, the occasional night the four of them spent playing poker had become two nights a week, and Verge had soon realized that playing cards had become an addiction for the Alsteins, not a pleasant pastime. Then, one day he had discovered that Alain had substituted a sub with a friend of his. He should have marched directly into Fred's office, but instead he had gone along with the cheating and cashed in on the profit. Alain's excuse was that everybody in the industry did it, but he, Verge Bristol, knew better.

"Well, the past is behind me now," Verge murmured. He stopped pacing and went back to work.

The hot, humid weather had carried into September. Fred flipped the steaks and smeared them with barbecue sauce. Nick Falcone had made a social call and Fred had invited him to see his acquisition on Admiral Road.

"You said rare, right?" he asked Nick, who had just finished inspecting Fred's new house.

"Yes, but be sure the potato is well cooked."

Fred nodded. "Get ready with your dish. Two minutes and yours is done."

"How come you bought a house in a subdivision? I thought a general contractor would build his own, something special to advertise his trade."

"I just wanted a nice place to live and I don't need more business...not at the moment, at least."

"Lucky you! But, of course, you're rich."

"That's why I could afford this new barbecue, a Weber Summit." Fred smiled. "Actually it was on sale, being the end of the season." He deposited the steak on Nick's paper dish and cooked his a bit longer.

"Beer?" Nick asked, and opened a cooler by the picnic table.

"Yes, thanks."

In no time they were sitting at the picnic table, savoring their steaks and the potatoes strewn with sour cream.

"A sprinkle of chives on top of the sour cream would have made this dish perfect."

"Good enough for me." Fred wiped his mouth with a paper towel. "You can't imagine how much I enjoy having a place of my own, and an old friend to share a meal."

After a moment of silence, Nick said, "You need a female companion." As Fred didn't respond, Nick continued. "What about Tessa? She's a beautiful woman, and she's looking for a stable relationship."

"She isn't my type, really." He paused. "And that isn't all. I always wanted to have a family, so I'd prefer somebody a bit younger."

Nick wiped his dish clean. "Then you have to start looking around— the St. Thomas trap shooting club sure isn't the right place for romantic encounters."

Fred laughed. "Surely not. I thought they would at least have a nice clubhouse, but instead it's just a big shed."

"What about the Hunt Club? That would suit your financial status."

"Me? The Bricklayer? I've done all the humble jobs in the industry." He laughed. "Including sweeping tons of dust for days and days."

"Oh, but the club would welcome you: The Bricklayer made it in life."

"Thanks for the kind words." Fred collected the paper dishes and threw them in the plastic garbage bin. "I like real things and real people. I don't think I'd appreciate the atmosphere of that club."

Nick rose and picked up the ball cap he had deposited on the bench of the picnic table.

"It was just a thought. I have to be going. Should we trap shoot every week? Say Tuesdays?"

"Definitely."

"My place, three o'clock?"

"Yes. By then I'll have my own gun."

"Perfect," Nick said, and strode off.

Fred cleaned the grill and turned off the barbecue, then took the cooler inside. Everybody involved, subs and employees of The Werkstein alike, had worked overtime to finish his house quickly. The carpeting on the upper floor remained to be done and the windows still had a big white S painted on the panes. He had moved all the boxes with his personal belongings into the large rooms on the main floor and installed his bed in the master bedroom, which opened onto the backyard. He would spend the evening opening boxes and placing what little furniture he had kept where it looked best. An interior decorator, scheduled to come next week, would make suggestions on the kinds of drapes to install for the windows and the two patio doors. Then he would see what furniture he should buy to make the place look like a real home.

In doing so he hoped to gain a sense of belonging and stability.

✽ ✽ ✽

Twenty-six

Fred realized with satisfaction that he had a day without appointments; it was time to go and buy a gun. He remembered the shop where he had bought his first Remington, so he moseyed on to Aylmer.

The town was an interesting mixture of cultures with a prevalence of Mennonite settlements. Most of these, Canadians who had returned to their homeland from Mexico in the seventies, had joined the much older Amish community established in the east of town.

Fred parked his car in front of the Gun 'N Gadgets building, and marveled at how little it had changed over the years. It sported the same lateral sidings, bricks on the lower portion of the facade and a disappointed hunter painted on the windowpanes. He had called ahead, so he was not surprised when the door opened as he approached the entrance.

"Come in, come in, Mr. Dalton. Nice to see an old customer coming back—for whatever reason."

"George is your name, if I remember correctly."

"Right on the dot."

"Years back I bought a nice Remington here, and I'd like a similar one for the same job—trap shooting."

"Plenty of choices." George turned around to choose a few models from a large selection that took up an entire wall.

Fred indulged himself. He took his time looking at the shotguns George had put on the counter, then focused on the Remington 870 and 887, both pump action types.

George disappeared into the back of the shop and came back with a rifle. "Give a look at this beauty. One day you may want to do a bit of hunting, and this rifle will serve you well. It's a Thompson G2 Contender with interchangeable barrels; one uses rim fire cartridges, the other center fire rifle cartridges for hunting."

Fred took it in his hands and looked at it with interest.

"It's a nice gun and yours is an interesting proposition; there're a lot of wild turkeys near my sister's place close to the lake. Maybe one day I'll get a hunting license." He looked at George and tapped on the rifle. "I bet it's expensive."

George laughed. "It is, but it's worthy. Each barrel comes to about eight hundred dollars."

The door opened and Fred looked toward the entrance. A tall woman wearing a huge pair of sunglasses walked in.

"Come in," George said, and moved to welcome the new visitor.

It was Peggy O'Brian.

Fred found himself very close to her as she approached the counter. The shop was small, and hunting paraphernalia took most of the available space.

"What a nice surprise!" Fred deposited the gun he was holding onto the counter. "I almost didn't recognize you without your uniform."

"It's my last day of vacation." She raised her sunglasses on top of her curly hair and picked up the gun Fred had just deposited. "Interested in guns?"

"Just a bit. I decided to go back to trap shooting. I shot for years when I was young."

"Oh? I practice skeet shooting." She looked at him with interest.

"Competitions?" Fred asked.

"When I can, yes."

"So what brings you here today?" Fred asked.

As Peggy studied the gun, Fred studied her figure. Her tight jeans clung to her slim legs and her pink T-shirt revealed the round curve of her breasts. The woman intrigued him, and he was going to find out a bit more about her.

"Ammo." She snapped the gun closed.

George must have known that already, as he had set a box of shot shells in front of her.

"Can I buy you a drink?" Fred asked.

"I don't drink."

"Something to eat, then?"

Peggy looked at him intently. "Why do you ask?"

"I have some free time, and I wouldn't mind some company."

Her hazel eyes hadn't left his face.

"If you don't intend to arrest me, of course," Fred said, to break the impasse.

Peggy threw her head back and laughed. "I'm not on duty, so you're safe, but I don't know if it'd be proper to accept—"

"And why not? Your boss bought me lunch when he wanted to pump me for information. He was very diplomatic about it, but that's what he did."

"Oh, I see." Peggy took a wallet out of her back pocket and deposited ten dollars on the counter.

"So consider my invitation a way to reciprocate the courtesy."

Peggy gave him a sidelong look. "Since you put it that way..." She looked at the white-metal watch that took up all of her wrist. "Oh, oh. Can't do it today. I have another engagement."

"Tomorrow? We can make it dinner, then."

Peggy emitted a quick laugh. "You're a fast operator, aren't you?" She collected the change George had put before her.

"So...?"

"Tomorrow will be fine." She paused. "But I warn you, I eat a lot."

"Since you don't drink, I might still come out on top."

Peggy laughed aloud and gave him an open, cheerful smile. "Okay. Come to Headquarters at six o'clock, then. Park on Williams Street; I'll come down."

"Wouldn't you prefer that I pick you up at home, maybe a bit later?"

"No need, but thank you for the offer." She turned to the shop's owner. "'Bye, George. See you next month."

"Nice girl," George said, as soon as Peggy was out of earshot. "Comes from a family of five. She worked hard to become a police officer. Her passion is target and skeet shooting, but she hasn't the time to compete. Probably not the money to travel either."

"I see." Fred tapped on the Remington 887 and took out his credit card and the firearms license. "I'm going to take this gun."

"Not interested in the wild turkeys?"

"Maybe later; and four bricks, please."

"Four bricks? You really plan to do some serious shooting! That's a thousand shot shells!"

"That's right. I'm back for good."

In no time George entered the data into the computer and gave Fred a paper and a receipt to sign. "You've bought a nice gun, Mr. Dalton. I'm sure you'll enjoy it…and, remember, I have the G2 Contender in stock."

Two days of rain had cleared most of the humidity in the air and restored the temperature to a comfortable twenty-four degrees. Stevenson was himself again, full of energy and zest. When Peggy walked by, he gestured her to come closer.

"Big things happened while you were away." He ticked off two. "Fingerprints on Oscar Clark's boat besides those of the owner. Most of them belong to the deceased found on the beach at the Pinery. The boat is registered to Oscar Clark, who has a police record in three different provinces. And that isn't all." He waved the remaining finger in the air. "Another set of fingerprints belong to an old resident of this province, Nick Falcone. He became a kind of celebrity when he danced in the nude on the beach." Stevenson expected Peggy to inquire about Nick's performance; instead she said, absently, "Interesting findings."

"What do you mean interesting? It's sensational! Very seldom do things come together this way! It usually takes months of investigation to link one finding to another."

"Right. And the result on Lucy Fairweather's autopsy?"

"Not yet. I expect it any time." Stevenson looked at the constable with curiosity. "Your hair looks different."

"I was tired of the flat color. I got a new cut and some highlights."

"Looks nice; it seems like you have twice the hair you had before." He paused. "Anything new on your side?"

"Not really. The usual invitation to a competition south of the border. I can't go, unfortunately; it's the same day as my little sister's wedding."

Stevenson knew that Peggy stayed on the force mainly because of the money and the physical training she would get as a member.

"Well, there's some clerical work to be done. Nobody touched it while you were away." He gave Peggy a pile of folders and loose sheets. "Enter the new data into the computer and update the old records." The phone rang and Stevenson snatched it up. He listened attentively. "Thanks." He hung up and turned to Peggy. "Lucy's death is attributed to a head injury followed by or concurrent with a massive stroke. Had she died at home, they'd be inclined to think of natural causes, but since she was found in the sand dunes, they're going to investigate the case." He paused for a moment. "Since she died before the conventional thirty-day period elapsed, her allocated inheritance reverts to the estate. Our Mr. Dalton gets another million."

"Good for him." She tapped on the folders and papers in the crook of her arm. "I'll have this job done today." She briskly moved to her desk and began typing.

At quitting time Peggy disappeared without saying goodbye. *Strange*, Stevenson thought. *She never forgets to say goodbye.* He gathered his coat and was on his way to the main exit when he saw her coming out of the Ladies' wearing a dress, its soft material fluttering around her body as she quickly walked back to her office. Now he understood her absent-minded state. The young woman had a date.

I hope it's a good one, he thought, and left for home.

Twenty-seven

Dundas and the nearby streets were still congested with traffic. Fred had to circle a couple of times before finding a parking spot near the London Police Service. A few minutes later he saw Peggy walking in brisk steps toward his car. A shining scarf dangled down her side. He slid out of the car and opened the passenger door for her.

"I almost didn't recognize you. You look great."

Peggy gave him a quick look. "Thanks." She entered the Lexus.

"Where to? You choose the place. I have no preference."

"The Keg?"

"Fine, just guide me." He eased into the traffic and followed Peggy's instructions. "So tell me about skeet shooting."

"Not much different from trap shooting, just more complicated."

"In what way?"

"There are eight stations—two houses, one ten feet high, the other three and half—located at the end points of the field. Seven of the stations are positioned along a semicircle, and the eighth is set in the middle point of the line joining the first and the seventh house." She paused and then added. "There's also a difference in the shells: we use number nine shot for skeet, and less for trap."

"You're right, it sounds complicated. What gun do you use?"

"A double-barrel Beretta 686 White Onyx, twenty gauge. I bought it used, of course." She met Fred's eyes when he turned to her as he stopped at a red light. "I couldn't afford it new; I'm not like you who could buy a new one every month."

Fred put the car in motion. "Yes, I could now, but not when I was your age. My first one was a non-denomination gun. It fired, and that was all it did. I didn't go to any clubs; I just went shooting in the field with friends."

They had arrived. Fred parked his car in front of the building. The Keg was in the old Canadian Pacific Railway Station, properly restored to house a restaurant. As they entered, a hostess welcomed them and showed them to a table; soon afterward a waiter arrived to take their orders for drinks and placed two menus on the table. Fred ordered a Black Russian; Peggy, who had asked for an iced tea, almost immediately hid her face behind the menu. Fred wondered whether inviting her out had been a mistake. Were they standing on opposite sides of some hidden social divide? She, the working girl, and he, the rich man? Was she viewing his wealth with acrimony? That would kill any relationship before it started.

He sipped his drink and looked around. The inside of the building had been restructured to give the restaurant a modern appearance. Two big pipes traversed the length of the hall to provide air conditioning. Painted brown, the pipes fit well with the color of the ceiling and the walls. Venetian blinds on the large windows protected the patrons from too much light. Pictures of celebrities hung on the walls.

When Peggy put down the menu he asked, "What are you getting?"

"The 'zesty salmon,' with rice."

"Make it two," Fred said to the waiter, who had appeared at their table. The young man collected the menus and walked away.

"I just moved into a new house and am not yet organized for doing any cooking. Most of the time I slam a piece of meat and a potato on the barbecue. Tonight is a nice change."

"Don't you have anybody to help you with house chores?"

"Not at the moment. For the last four years a housekeeper and at least one nurse permanently moved around my wife and me. There was no privacy, so I became eager for space, or at least eager to have only people around me I can connect to."

Peggy looked at him, no emotion on her face.

"So tell me, why did you accept my invitation?" Fred asked.

Peggy bent her head back and laughed. "I wanted to find out what it was like to go out with a rich man."

"So it was curiosity? And I thought it was my good looks!"

Peggy's cheeks reddened. "That, too."

"That's better."

The waiter brought their food and they both tackled their entrees with fervor.

Peggy routinely scooped a forkful of rice followed by a bite of salmon, hardly stopping to drink her tea. Then, almost suddenly, she held fork and knife in the air.

"Why did you ask me out?" she asked.

"Well, you intrigued me when I met you at Headquarters. You looked professional—I mean like a police officer—but there was a feminine side that peeped through the way you shook your hair and the way you gestured. When I saw you without uniform at the gun shop, it confirmed my first impression." He finished his drink and took a sip of water. "Don't you have a boyfriend?"

Peggy shook her shag and resumed eating.

"Then maybe you can give me some lessons on shooting. I'm pretty rusty. I haven't done much of it since—well, since my late wife had her accident."

"Where do you practice?"

"At my friend's farmhouse, at the moment. He's rusty, too, so we've postponed joining a club."

Peggy pushed her empty plate aside. "If I do, I'd have to tell Stevenson that I'm seeing you."

"Oh? Why?"

The waiter stopped by their table, and Peggy ordered two desserts: a mocha ice-cream and a lemon blueberry cake.

Fred didn't want any dessert and ordered a coffee.

"Why so?" he asked again, after the waiter had walked away.

"Well, it's just that your sister's accident is still an open case. At the moment we're only marginally involved...nevertheless, Stevenson should know."

"Hmm. I have no problem with that. Your boss likes me. I don't think he'll object." Fred examined the young woman one more time. She seemed a lovely person; he should get to know her a bit better. "I have an idea.

Come to see my new house so you can tell your boss that you've taken the opportunity do to more checking on me."

Peggy laughed. "Not only are you a fast operator, you're also an experienced one."

Fred joined her in laughter. "I'm not forty for nothing. Ready to go? It's a nice place, you may like it."

Peggy gave him a big smile. "Why not? But first let me eat my dessert."

Stevenson drummed his fingers on the desk, slightly worried. Peggy was not at her desk, and normally she came in early. He hoped she hadn't run into trouble with her date. She bonded easily with people and had been born more to raise a family than to enforce the law. She had no luck with the opposite sex, unfortunately. The last man she had dated had dropped by her place in the middle of the night because of a road accident. He had set camp in her little apartment for two weeks straight with the excuse that he needed to recover from his multiple bruises, none of which was visible. At the end, Stevenson had dispatched his squad to kick him out.

As he reviewed the messages that had come in while he was away, Peggy finally showed up with a cheerful look on her face."Here I am," she said, and stood in front of Stevenson.

"I see. Had a good time last night?"

Peggy cocked her head sideways. "How to you know I went out?"

"Detective's intuition, but you didn't answer my question."

"Yes, I had a good time."

Stevenson was ready to deal with his work when Peggy added, "However, there's a problem."

Oh no, not again, Stevenson thought.

"You remember what you told me last time? To stop looking for men who draw on my sympathy and look for somebody who can stand on his two feet?"

"Yes..."

"I did."

"Good. Then where's the problem?"

Peggy set her arms on the edge of Stevenson's desk and leaned forward. "I went out with Fred Dalton."

"What?"

"He said you liked him. You even bought him lunch when you wanted to get information out of him."

"Well, not on purpose. He was sitting at a table at Burger King drinking tea. I saw him, ordered two Whoppers, put one in front of him and said, 'You look like somebody who didn't eat yet.' So we started a conversation." Stevenson paused, still very surprised. "It was professional...I should say it was a means to get him to talk, which he did. Nothing personal, but going on a date...that might not be appropriate at this time."

"But we aren't in charge of the investigation into his sister's murder, and he's never really been a suspect in connection with his late wife's death, right?"

"Right," Stevenson said tentatively. "But you've told me you have no use for wealthy people."

Peggy wrinkled her nose. "I'm going to make an exception." She scampered away to her desk.

Stevenson rose and followed her. He needed to know the level of her involvement.

"Do you plan to see him again?"

Peggy nodded, and began pecking on her computer.

"To do what?"

"Relax, Boss. I put him down for classes on shooting, private lessons."

"Does he practice skeet shooting?"

"No, just trap shooting. I met him at the gun shop in Aylmer. He didn't play much while his wife was in a wheelchair, and he wanted to start over."

"That's all?"

Peggy smiled. "No. Tomorrow night I go to his new house and help him choose the curtains. An interior decorator will be there too."

"Hmm. Don't you think you're moving too fast?"

Peggy rolled her eyes. "He's pleasant company, Gordon, and he's very handsome." She closed her eyes. "Tall, slim, dark hair, blue eyes—"

"He's graying fast," Stevenson remarked, casting his last dart.

Peggy smiled. "Yes, and that little gray adds a touch of charm, don't you think?"

Stevenson sighed. "I see there's no point in talking to you."

✵ ✵ ✵

Twenty-eight

M oira flipped over the manila envelope, surprised that it didn't bear a return address on either side. *It could be bad news*, she thought with apprehension, as she looked for a letter opener. She didn't need any more aggravation, as the last few weeks had been very tiring. With Fred away she felt isolated, almost abandoned. She hadn't expected him to put Verge Bristol in charge of the company, then basically disappear.

She slid a letter opener along the envelope.

"Jesus!" she exclaimed aloud, as newspaper clippings fell onto the floor.

Others were still inside, together with a sheet of paper on which capital letters had been pasted. They read, *GET READY TO PAY. I HAVE THE TAPE.*

She slumped on the antique-pink sofa, disheartened. For the last ten years she had feared that the person who had made the tape would surface and ask for a ransom. *But why now?* Maybe the blackmailer had gone to jail and had no way to contact her before? Or maybe Charlie had recently talked about the tape with somebody who decided to take advantage of the situation? Maybe no tape existed and somebody was trying to cash in on information that was completely public. Eagerly, Moira examined all the clippings taken from *The Barrie Examiner* and other newspapers. Hmm. Nothing new except the information that the blackmailer claimed to have the tape.

Moira rose and fixed herself a double vodka. She sat again on the sofa and sipped her drink without tasting its flavor, patiently waiting for the alcohol to appease her nerves and put her to sleep.

The following morning she rose early and drove to the Men's Mission and Rehabilitation Centre on York Street. With the excuse of a family emergency, she got her brother out of bed and into her car. She drove to the nearest parking lot and killed the engine.

"The truth, now. Did you talk to anybody about——" She abruptly stopped and glared at Charlie. "About our secret?"

"Oh, sis, don't be mad. You know I can't cope with that. I'd do anything for you."

It was true, anything except keeping his mouth shut or following any other order. *Limitations of the human spirit*, thought Moira bitterly.

"The truth. Did you talk to anybody at the Men's Mission about what was supposed to remain our secret forever?"

"No. At the Centre they don't ask personal questions, just how they can help you."

"Did you talk with anybody at the Western Fair?"

Charlie shook his head, but Moira knew he was guilty from the way he behaved. He trembled, perspired heavily, and avoided looking at her.

"Charlie: I have to go to work, and I know you said something to somebody. Who was it?"

With his sleeve Charlie mopped away the droplets of perspiration that broke out on his forehead.

"Sam. He came to see me and took me out for a treat at the Dairy Queen. It was good...*really* good."

She should have known that crook would not leave such easy prey as her brother alone.

"Do you know his last name?" she asked.

"No."

"Where does he live?"

"Don't know." Charlie gave her a sidelong look. "He said he'd talk to you and everything would be fine."

"Talk to me? How? Did you give him my address?"

"Yes."

Moira banged both hands on the steering wheel. She should have refused to help Charlie when he had shown up at her door. He was a liability and now they were both in trouble. She had to think quickly.

"Is he coming back any time soon?"

"I don't know."

Moira took her personal cell out of her purse and set it in her lap.

"If he shows up again, call me right away, but don't let him see that you're calling me. Go to the washroom when you make the call."

Charlie nodded.

"Repeat what I said."

Charlie repeated it, his head down.

Moira grabbed his chin and twisted his face toward her.

"Do you understand that we're in trouble? Don't you ever again say a word to *anybody* about what happened at our old place! Not a word!" She let go of his chin, sat back from the steering wheel and pointed at her phone. "Press this key to call me at the office. Understand?"

Charlie nodded again.

She gave him the phone, turned the engine on and drove back to the Men's Mission to drop him off. On her way home she stopped at a Staples outlet to buy a new cell. Then she called The Werkstein and said she was not feeling well—after all, it was the truth. She would have time to think about how to deal with the blackmailer's threat.

Gordon Stevenson was glad to leave the house and go to work. His home wasn't a home anymore. His wife had endured one miscarriage after another. She had suffered both physically and mentally, and he knew she felt less of a woman because she couldn't bear children.

Sad heritage of an ancient culture that cast women in a fixed mould, Stevenson thought. After they had decided to stop trying, Stevenson had hoped she would find peace and divert her attention and energy toward other goals. Unfortunately, that had not happened; on the contrary, she had slipped into a depression that seemed to deepen with every passing day. He couldn't do much to help, the psychologist had said, except offer his support. He had done so, but the situation had taken a toll on his spirit. Last month his wife had gone to visit her parents in Nova Scotia, and he had no idea when she would be back. His home was just an empty space, and he was happy to get out of the house.

Stevenson found a fax on his desk and he read it carefully. The OPP Detachment in Grand Bend was overloaded, and would like him to join the on-going investigation. If he agreed they would follow the official channels and request his presence to his superiors. As Peggy walked by Stevenson gestured to her to come over. He let her read the fax.

"What do you think?" Stevenson sat behind his desk.

"I'd go. Lucy's and Charlotte's deaths have similarities; maybe it's the same perpetrator." She paused. "That mysterious boat, *The Catalina*, may be the key to the case. You have to be there if you want to help out; here we're all cut off."

Stevenson drummed his fingers on the desk. "I was thinking the same thing." He got on the phone and called his friend in Grand Bend. When the call was over, he looked at Peggy. "There's only one little problem. I won't be able to keep an eye on your romance with Fred Dalton."

Peggy threw her head back and laughed. "That's an advantage for me. You're too conservative in your advice."

"Conservative? Because I warned you about the dangers of this relationship?"

Peggy crossed her arms. "Spell it out: what are these terrible dangers?"

Stevenson cocked his head left and right. "Nothing on the surface. But when two people belong to different social environments a long-lasting relationship may prove to be difficult." He looked at Peggy, at her happy face. "But I wish you all the luck in the world, Peggy. You deserve it."

"Thanks. And I wish *you* luck with the new assignment."

She sauntered back to her desk.

✳ ✳ ✳

Twenty-nine

When Arthur Saldini, a close friend of the Gassmans', had asked Fred to build a hangar for storing his ultra-light planes, Fred had mentioned that several companies offered installations of pre-fabricated steel hangars at a convenient price. Arthur, however, wanted an old-fashioned building, with real foundations and brick walls to agree with the style of his old country house, located in the outskirts of Lucan.

After the call he had received from Moira concerning the attempt to switch a sub, Fred had wondered how the project was coming along and had gone to inspect the building, which was due near completion. When he arrived at the site, he noticed that the construction was finished, except for the fifty-foot door, which he couldn't see anywhere. At first he wanted to call The Werkstein, but then he thought it better to drop by the office and talk to Verge Bristol or Moira Johnson in person. He drove into London at a leisurely pace, admiring the many fields of corn and beans, and the green pastures that flanked Highway 4.

When Fred entered The Werkstein, Mary Gervasio immediately welcomed him. "Verge is out to inspect a new job site. And Moira called in sick for the day."

Fred walked into his office and sat at his desk. To his surprise, Verge had made a three-page report highlighting the most important results that the company had achieved in the past weeks. The project on Admiral Road was almost finished, the excavations for the new complexes were under way, and there was a call for tender for a mall, which would house a superstore and numerous small shops. Fred looked for the folder related to that project and spent a couple of hours familiarizing himself with it.

Things are moving at the right pace, Fred thought when he finished reading. Verge was in favor of bidding for the mall and so was he. If they got it, they would have one big job in an enclosed area and could keep working even when the weather turned to its worst. On a separate page he found a note on the hangar project, in which Verge explained that the wrong door had been delivered and had to be returned. The new one, of the correct dimensions, would be shipped next week. Fred nodded his head in satisfaction with the way the work was proceeding and also that Verge had not disappointed him. He hoped things would continue in the same fashion for the days ahead. He looked at his wristwatch. *Time to get a bite to eat then go home and change.* The interior decorator and Peggy were due at his house in an hour.

I never imagined that drapes could be so expensive, Fred thought as the interior decorator finally left with her load of albums, samples, and measuring kit. She had come an hour late, and now he and Peggy had little time to be together, as Peggy had an early morning shift. They sat in two easy chairs, opposite each other, Peggy sipping a cola, Fred a beer.

"So, where do you see yourself in five or ten years?" Fred asked.

"About where I am now, doing the same job, and target shooting in my spare time."

"No plans to have a family?"

"Kids, you mean?"

Fred nodded.

"I'd love a couple of them, but where would I find the time? Those little monsters need a lot of attention. When I visit my two older sisters, who have little ones, I'm swamped with requests- -playing, pushing them on the swing, singing and taking them places. I hardly have time to have a conversation with my sisters." She paused. "Now I have a question for you. Why do you keep inviting me out?"

"I want to offer you more than one opportunity to check up on me and report to your boss. Maybe it will advance your career."

Peggy rolled her eyes. "Then you have to give me something substantial. Tell me some secrets about yourself. I can't fill in a report about the cost of the curtains."

"Oh, yes, you could, and entitle the report 'How to legally rob a guy.' "

"That's true. The lady was very persistent, and some of those expensive curtains she wanted you to buy were so heavy and clogged with pattern that they wouldn't look nice in a modern house like this." Peggy finished her cola and deposited the empty can on the glass-topped table. "So tell me about your romantic life."

Fred laughed. "It's very brief. When I was young I worked all the time. In the summer I spent my free time on the lake, with my sister's family and a bunch of friends. I dated on and off. Then one late summer evening I took Deborah out for a ride. We were married soon afterward."

"Were the two of you happy before the accident?"

"Yes, I'd say so. She helped organize parties for an outfit in town. Sometimes she stayed at the parties as an animator, dancing with old folks or playing games if it was a birthday party for kids." Fred stared into his bottle for a short moment. "Saturdays were her busiest days, so we set aside Sundays and most of the Mondays for being together. It worked." Fred finished his beer. "So, when can you give me that private lesson we agreed upon?"

"The day after tomorrow...say five-thirty at my place? I'll take you to a field where we can practice as long as we want. We'll have light for a couple of hours." Peggy took a card and slid it over to the other side of the table. "Here's where I live."

Fred pocketed the card. "Supper together after the lesson?"

Peggy rose and brushed Fred's nose with the paper napkin she had in her hand. "Be careful, or I might think you're interested in me as a woman, and not as a coach."

Fred rose slowly. "I promise I'll clear out any doubt you have on the matter after the lesson." He walked her out and to her car.

When he re-entered the house Fred sat in the same chair where he had sat before, not ready to call it a night. Questions raced through his mind. *Am I moving too fast with Peggy? Do I like her enough to start dating her regularly? Am I just trying to fill my solitary evenings?* The time he took off work had seemed a blessing after having to run left and right for all the chores springing out of Deborah's and Charlotte's deaths. Now, with all the main legal issues settled, he had more free time than he needed. The invitations he received were mostly business-related, but he felt the need for closeness, the need to care for someone and have someone care for him.

He rose to get a second beer out of the fridge, then turned on the television. *Time to see what's going on in the world.*

When Moira reached the door of the office she shared with Alain Alstein, the man moved quickly toward her.

"We have to talk."

For a moment she just stood there, perplexed, but Alain took her arm and led her to the conference room.

"Want a coffee?" Alain asked her.

"Sure. Just cream, please."

She sat in one of the chairs and deposited her purse on the table as Alain placed the order for coffee over the phone.

"I'd like to talk to you about the project for the mall. Fred okayed it; we should start working on it soon." Moira kept silent and Alain continued. "I know that you consider different suppliers for each material specified by the architect and then you suggest the best buy." He stopped as Mary Gervasio entered with a tray and the two coffees.

"Nice to see you're back," Mary said to Moira.

"Thanks!"

Mary placed the coffees in front of Alain and Moira and left.

"So what's the problem?" Moira asked after the first swallow of coffee.

"I have a couple of suppliers I'd like you to consider."

"I will if they're any good."

Alain wiggled in his chair. "I guarantee you they're good."

After a moment of silence, Moira said, "You want me to rig the submission."

Alain didn't respond right away, but he looked her in her eyes. "There's a reward for that. Three thousand each."

"It's unethical," Moira murmured, and took another sip of her coffee.

Alain shrugged. "Everyone does it in one form or another."

"Why don't you make this suggestion to Fred?"

"Fred is out of the loop, temporarily he said, but probably forever. It's something we should arrange between the two of us. I'll take care of Verge.

He's too busy to do any checking; he can hardly cope with all the work involved in being the boss."

"I don't like it, Alain. I won't go for it."

"Come on, Moira. Everybody knows you have problems with your brother. He can't really have a normal job and you're stuck supporting him. You need the money as much as I do."

"The answer is still no." She stood and left the room.

Alain's menacing words drifted out behind her: "You'll regret turning down my offer!"

Thirty

Once at home, Moira stretched out on the sofa, trying to unwind. She had worked all day, setting aside, for the time being, Alain's suggestion, and his attempt to intimidate her. Now, however, isolated from the outside world, her feelings exploded, anger taking the lead. *So he's out to control me, but is he also the blackmailer? He needs money, so he has motive. What about this mysterious Sam? Is he the one who claims to have the tape?* She had to fight a battle on two fronts, not knowing which was more dangerous. She could, of course, resign and disappear, as she had done years ago when she left Barrie and took off for Windsor and then London. But that had not helped her as Charlie had followed her in spite of his promise to remain up north.

Moira banged her fists on the nearby coffee table, trying to defuse her anger. She rose and made herself a drink, then gulped half of it in one swallow, furious at herself for not foreseeing the damage Charlie could do. *And I saved his life!* Thinking back to the accident, she wondered who might have seen the events of that terrible afternoon. At that time the police had mentioned that they were aware of the existence of a tape, but they had never been able to get a hold of it. Had it been a trick to induce Charlie or her to spill the beans? For some time she thought that Ryan, Charlie's little friend who used to wander in the woods filming wildlife, could have captured some images of the accident, but Ryan had never come forward and the tape had never surfaced. That accident still hounded her, Moira realized with dismay. *And this fellow who pasted the blackmailing message in capital letters…how much does he want?*

The ringing of a bell shook her from her torpor. She went to the intercom box and punched the *Listen* button. It was Charlie.

"Hi, sis. I tried to call you, but you were already gone at the office."

How forgetful of her; she had a new cell and Charlie couldn't call her at home.

"Can I come in?"

"Are you alone?"

"Yes."

She let him in and went to open her apartment door.

Charlie, his face as happy as she'd ever seen, waved a ten in the air. "You're going to be proud of your brother." He hugged her.

"Let me be the judge of that."

She grabbed the purse she had left on the console table at the entrance and rooted through its contents until she found her new phone. She asked Charlie for the one she had given him earlier, and stored her new cell's number into Charlie's, then showed him which key to press if he wanted to call her.

Charlie assented and pocketed the phone, took off his ball cap, deposited it and the ten on the kitchen table and walked over to the fridge. With a Coke in his hands he slumped on the sofa.

Moira stood in front of him and crossed her arms.

"What's this all about?" she asked.

"Sam came. I went to the washroom and tried to call you. I couldn't, so I listened to what he had to say."

"So…?"

"First, he gave me the ten, just for myself, and then asked me to see him tomorrow morning. He'd like me to exchange two hundred dollar bills at the bank. He'll stay with me so nobody can rob me this time." He sipped his Coke with sheer pleasure. "I came here to tell you, so you know and see that there's nothing bad about Sam."

"He threatened to *kill* you, Charlie!" Moira shouted.

"He said he was joking about that."

"Sure, sure." She couldn't buy anything this Sam had told her brother, but maybe she would have an occasion to see who the man was. Tomorrow was Saturday, and she didn't need to be at the office. "Which bank?"

Charlie opened his arms wide. "Don't know."

"Do you know the time?"

"In the morning."

Of course. The banks close in the afternoon. She would have to be at the mission before nine o'clock. "You can go with Sam this time." She looked sternly into his eyes. "But this time only, understood?"

Charlie nodded and finished his drink. "Can I stay for supper?"

Moira looked at the clock on the wall. It was eight o'clock and she hadn't had much to eat since breakfast. "I'll cook spaghetti. But you'd have to leave soon afterward. I have work to do."

Bands of rain and unrelenting gusts had battered London and the vicinity for two days straight, making it impossible for Fred and Peggy to go shooting. Things had not panned out as Fred had hoped. The next two days he would be busy working with Verge, planning a strategy for the upcoming cold season. The following day was the regular time he spent with Nick at his farm. He actually enjoyed going there, shooting the breeze, and remembering old times. Their aim had improved considerably since the first time. He was thinking of an excuse to call Peggy and have a chat with her, when his cell rang.

"Mr. Dalton, I wonder if you can spare a few minutes of your time. I'm in front of your house, parked on the road," Stevenson said, his voice suave, yet assertive.

Fred laughed inwardly. *He's checking up on me, not as a suspect, but as Peggy's date. If I decide to date her regularly, I'll have to cope with Mr. Gordon Stevenson's presence. I'd better start now.*

"Yes, I have a few minutes, but don't stay on the road, come up to my garage door. There's still a lot of dust as trucks move in and out of the compound to finish off the road."

"Thank you; you're a gentleman."

Gordon wore plain clothes, a light coat over a white-and-blue striped shirt opened at the neck. He was six feet tall, with an athletic build; his presence was imposing, but not intimidating. *He knows how to control people without letting them know what he's doing*, Fred thought, as Gordon walked inside.

"Come to the rec room. I still don't have much furniture, but there're a couple of comfortable chairs." He walked ahead of his guest and sat in one, gesturing Stevenson to the other.

"I won't take much of your time. I wonder what you can tell me about Ms. Theresa Wilson."

"Tessa? I knew her when I was young. We were friends for seven, maybe eight years. There was a group of us—five or six guys plus the usual fringe who join any party in the neighborhood—who went swimming together, did a bit of fishing, practiced body surfing, went to rock concerts, danced together—"

"In the nude, on the beach?" Stevenson interjected, amused.

Fred laughed and nodded. "I wasn't there when it happened, but I heard about it. It happened only once. It was a night event dedicated to Indian dances; everybody had to wear a costume and paint their faces and part of their bodies. One of my friends, Nick, painted his whole body, but he forgot about the costume." He stopped to remember. "Nothing would have happened if he had stayed on my sister's premises but, excited by the applause he drew from the audience on the public beach, he ventured away. First he danced half-way in the water, so nobody remarked on his nudity, but then with the full moon...well, you can probably guess what happened."

Stevenson nodded. "The police came and took him in."

"Well, as I was saying, we played together. Tessa was one of the regulars until she got married."

"Still married?"

"No. She divorced not long ago. Her husband was Walter Wilson."

"What did he do?"

Fred laughed. "His main job was spending the family money. He was a photographer, but he found it difficult to get established professionally."

"You mentioned before that she was a friend of your sister Charlotte. Right?"

"Oh, yes...when Tessa got divorced she moved back to London. She came to see my wife about once a week and, at times, my sister. As I said, my friends and I chummed together at my sister's place in Port Franks."

Fred stopped to follow Stevenson's eyes which were taking in the environment. "My friends more than me, since I was busy working my butt off."

"I know you've worked hard all your life. Did she have any reason to visit your sister on the night of the accident?"

Fred weighed his answer. "Probably. She was determined to convince Charlotte to throw a big party for my fortieth birthday, something I found inappropriate because of my wife's recent death."

Stevenson nodded again. "Do you think she'd have any reason to harm your sister?"

"I can't think of one." Normally Fred would ask his guest if he wanted coffee, but he didn't want to invite Stevenson to stay longer than necessary, although the man didn't seem to have any intention of leaving.

"That about wraps it up." Stevenson didn't move, just looked around. "On another note, I heard that you're taking shooting lessons from one of my officers."

Fred laughed. "I knew you'd get around to that." He wondered if he should let Stevenson know that he was poking out of his territory, but decided against it. He looked at his guest. "I like Peggy. I'd like to know her better."

"She gets hurt easily," Stevenson said with an enigmatic undertone.

"I won't hurt her. I'm a poor shot, but not that poor. I'll make sure she stays behind me when I aim at a target."

"Fred, you know what I mean."

"Yes, I do." He paused for a moment, Deborah's image as a radiant bride gliding through his mind. "There's always a danger in a relationship, Gordon. You think you got the best there is in the world and then destiny plays a terrible trick on you. I know from experience."

Stevenson sighed and nodded. "Time for me to go. Thank you for seeing me." He rose and quickly walked out.

☆ ☆ ☆

Thirty-one

With her mass of red curls tied together underneath a baseball cap, Moira waited patiently to see who came to get Charlie at the mission. She had parked on the road, ready to follow the mysterious Sam. Around 10:30 a.m. a blue pickup truck entered the premises and stopped at the back of the building. A tall, husky man, wearing jeans and a gray coat walked through the lateral door. An uneventful half an hour went by. Fortunately she had taken with her a thermos full of coffee and a bagel with cream cheese. She drank some coffee and chewed off a morsel from the bagel. Finally Charlie appeared out of the door, followed by the man she guessed to be Sam, and both climbed into the blue pickup. Moira slipped on a raincoat, lifted the collar high, and turned on the engine.

As the pickup truck moved east on York Street, Moira swiftly turned around and followed it. Soon the pickup stopped at a Bank of Montreal branch. Once again Moira parked on the street, but this time she stepped out of the car and followed Charlie and his companion into the bank. She stopped at a side counter and began filling one of the application forms lying there, and watched the duo in her peripheral vision.

Charlie stood in front of a wicket, with Sam a few feet away watching Charlie's every move. Some discussion occurred as Charlie presented the teller with two bills. Moira guessed that the bank was reluctant to carry out a transaction for somebody who was not a client; she saw Charlie shooting a desperate look at Sam, who gestured for him to leave.

The two men climbed into the pickup and soon stopped at another financial institution. This time Moira waited outside, a good thirty feet away from the entrance. Twenty minutes later Charlie and Sam re-emerged, a satisfied look on their faces. They had managed to exchange the hundred dollar bills, Moira surmised. She followed the pickup to the Men's Mission, where Sam dropped off Charlie and then continued west. On Oxford Street he turned left on Wonderland Road and, shortly after, drew up in front of the garage door of an expensive house. He either had arrived home or he was visiting somebody he knew well. Moira wrote down the address on a piece of paper and turned away. She would do her usual Saturday shopping and come back later.

It was past four o'clock and the blue pickup still sat in the same spot where she had seen it last. Moira was growing impatient. Maybe Sam lived here, even if he hadn't parked inside the garage. Then again, the owner of such an expensive home wouldn't need to carry out the exchanging-bills charade. She had almost decided to go home when Sam stepped out of the fancy main door and slid into the pickup. Moira waited until he was about a hundred meters ahead of her before starting to follow him. Because of the intense traffic, Moira was not concerned about being spotted until Sam left the city on Highway 4, driving a good fifteen kilometers per hour over the speed limit. Moira would have to match his speed to stay with him and see where he lived. She decided it was too dangerous, so, as she passed Arva, she turned into a side road, circled around, and headed home.

The gravel road that led to Nick's house climbed straight up at first, then meandered among the cultivated fields. At the last bend Nick spotted an OPP car parked in front of his farmhouse. It was too late to turn around, so he slowed down and decided to assume an annoyed, distant attitude.

He parked his pickup in the carport; from the back of the vehicle he lifted up the trim saw he had bought the day before and plugged it into the power outlet nearby, as if to ensure that it worked properly.

An officer approached him.

"Mr. Nicholas Samuel Falcone?" the officer asked.

With thin, gray hair, not quite six feet tall and with curved shoulders, the man was probably close to retirement.

"Yes."

"Can we talk?" The officer raised his voice to top the decibels delivered by the saw in action.

"That's what we're doing, I think."

"Can you turn off that noisy tool?"

Nick complied, but not before cutting down the tufts of grass around the carport.

"Thanks. Can we go inside and sit down?"

"I prefer not; I just came back from the west and found that my late parents' house is in terrible condition." He pointed with the saw. "See all those weeds? It'll take a week to clean them all up."

The officer moved closer to Nick. "Do you know Oscar Clark?"

"Never heard of him."

"Ever been on his boat, *The Catalina*?"

Nick's ears pricked with attention. They had information related to the boat where he had found the money.

"I've been aboard dozens of boats," he replied. "In general I don't ask who the owner is."

"We found your fingerprints on and underneath the dashboard of his boat."

"And you're here because of my fingerprints? I've been to Port Franks a few times since I returned; maybe I was aboard the boat this fellow owns. Who knows? I don't recall his name."

The officer got a photo out of his pocket. "This is his picture. Do you recognize him?"

Nick took it in his hands, read the name *Oscar Clark* penciled at the bottom and studied it.

"No." He handed the photo back to the officer.

"A few days ago we fished a man out of the water not far away from here. We have evidence of his presence on *The Catalina*. We're investigating his death." The officer extracted another photo from his pocket and handed it to Nick. "Better luck with this one?"

"This is a dead man?"

"Yes."

Nick recognized him. He had reached over his body when he had searched the boat to see whether there was anything valuable to steal. He shook his head and gave the picture back to the officer.

"Okay, thank you, sir. I'd also like to look inside your house."

Oh good Lord! He'll find the bag.

"I don't see why. I mean, I have nothing to hide, but it's a question of principle."

"Okay," the officer said. "We might come back with a court order and then we'll be doing a thorough search."

"Whatever." Nick said nonchalantly. He entered the house and closed the door behind him. He didn't move any farther until he heard the car leaving. *Saved, but for how long? Tomorrow morning? Probably Monday morning, since they won't disturb a judge on Sunday for a pair of fingerprints. But where can I stash the money? Bury it? No, they would spot right away that soil had been dug and repacked. In the out-of-order trap house? Too close to the house.*

Nick collapsed on the old sofa. He felt depressed. He couldn't think of a secure place. *Maybe I can find somebody to keep it for the time being, but who? Tessa? No, she's too nosy. Charlie? Too easy to rob. Who else can I trust?* He couldn't think of anybody.

Nick couldn't sleep. It was still dark when he rose and descended to the basement, illuminated only by a light bulb hanging on a wire. It was full of old farming tools, pipes of different sizes, pails, and empty boxes. He selected two cartons in good shape and cleaned them of the dust accumulated over the years. He loaded them onto his pickup, then re-entered the house and took a shower. At nine o'clock, dressed in clean jeans and a sports shirt, he climbed into his pickup and set the bag with the money on the passenger side. He would patrol the region until he found an outfit with storage for rent open on Sunday. His plan was simple. He would store the empty boxes and his money in a rented storage space and mail the lease to his old address in Calgary, so that no compromising material could be found in the house. *A fool-proof plan*, he concluded with satisfaction. The police could search and search, but they would not find the slightest link to the money, or the boat, or whatever they searched for.

✳ ✳ ✳

Thirty-two

The work was proceeding well, Fred realized as he left the office. Verge had gathered the announcements of the tenders concerning two medium-size jobs and made comments on each. One was an elementary school and the other a bank branch, with deadlines for both in the next month. He should keep an eye on those in case the contract for the big mall didn't materialize. With the recession lingering and the cold season approaching, the competition was fierce, but his company had always managed to beat most of the bidders to a tender in good, as well as in bad times, so Fred was hopeful that The Werkstein would win the contract for the new mall in London east. Pleased with Verge Bristol's performance, he had asked him to carry on as acting manager for another month. He had seen Moira, exchanged a few words with her outside the usual business conversation, and got the impression that she was deeply troubled. He found her behavior unusual, but dismissed it thinking that the changes in the company had probably upset her—something he regretted but could not avoid.

The weather forecast was for more rain, so he wondered whether he should go to Nick's farm for the weekly shooting practice. He decided to go home, have lunch, and call Nick from there.

He sat at the kitchen counter with a grilled-cheese sandwich and a glass of tomato juice and opened the local newspaper, which now was delivered

to his new home. An article about the recent events at Lake Huron contained a call to the public for any information on the police findings. Two
bodies had been discovered on the shore near Port Franks: an unidentified
male ten days ago, and Lucy Fairweather. The police couldn't exclude foul
play from either case. A short description followed of the inboard-motor
vessel, *The Catalina,* and its owner, Oscar Clark. The police were looking
for any information that might provide a link among the three persons.

Fred read the article twice, flabbergasted. Lucy had been a suspect in
his sister's death and now her name was surfacing in the investigation of
another crime. Did Charlotte harbor a felon? Probably nobody would ever
know. Lucy was dead, so she could not speak for herself. He'd hardly known
her; still, because she had been part of his sister's life, she was closer to him
than a total stranger. She had been interred without any special ritual, so
Fred had asked his lawyer to plan a memorial service for her. After what
he had just read, he hoped that the service wouldn't attract undesirable
attention.

He was still immersed in his sad thoughts when Nick called.

"I read the newspaper. What a situation is developing in Port Franks!
Did you know Lucy well?"

"Hardly, but it still hits home," Fred replied. "I can't believe she could
be involved in something criminal."

"Something really strange happened over there." He paused. "I'm
afraid there won't be any shooting today since it's already raining here. I
was thinking of taking a couple of days off and wondered if you were game
for it; a bit of distraction would do you a lot of good."

"Where?"

"Niagara Falls. Plenty of things to see and do over there, good or bad
weather."

Fred didn't answer right away. "Sounds great, but first I have to call
my lawyer and finalize everything for Lucy's memorial, which is scheduled
for Tuesday next week. There wouldn't be many people and I'd like to be
present. I should also keep in touch with my office."

"I understand." Nick paused. "I have an idea. Why don't I come over
to your place? It'll give you time to make your calls and then we can take
off. Two, three days max. We'll be back in time for the weekend and for the
memorial. I'll come with you."

Fred took a moment to ponder whether that was feasible. He could make it work, he decided. "Okay, come on over. And thank you, Nick. You're a real friend."

Fred had plenty of time to talk to Verge Bristol and Mary Gervasio and gather what he needed for a two-day stay. He threw everything into his carry-on. Next, he placed a call to Peggy. He told her of his planned excursion.

"Will you have time to go to the shooting range when I get back, weather permitting?"

"Of course. Just call me when you get back...and supper together afterward?"

"I wouldn't miss it for the world." He paused, pleased that she didn't play games. "Why don't we set a time for supper and then go shooting if we can?"

"Good idea. Saturday okay? I'm free."

"Perfect. I look forward to seeing you again, Peggy."

"Me, too," Peggy whispered.

Moira had worked hard to price the project for the mall; the blueprints were overloaded with notations, making it difficult to grasp the most important features of the would-be building. On the other hand, the specifications were at times vague, forcing her to place one call after the other to the architect's office to get clarification. She had worked all day and into the night hours for five days in a row.

After the chase she had given to Sam's pickup on Saturday, she had not had any occasion to observe him. He hadn't contacted Charlie. The only link she had was the house where he had spent about three hours the past Saturday. Moira decided to take some action, feeling that Sam was probably the blackmailer. She wanted to know more about him. When she left work, she drove to the residential area on Wonderland Road, hoping to spot his pickup. She made a couple of rounds, hoping to see light inside the house she was casing. Dead end, she concluded with disappointment as she headed for home.

She retrieved the mail from her mailbox, entered her apartment, threw her purse on the console, kicked off her shoes, and went to sit on the sofa. As she leafed through her mail she found flyers, a coupon book, the phone bill, a subscription renewal to *Readers Digest*, and an envelope with no sender. She rose and mixed herself a vodka with orange juice. After sipping half of it, she slid open the envelope. This time the message was typed.

I have the tape. Two thousand dollars by Sunday evening. I'll let you know where to drop it off.

Moira threw the paper and the envelope on the floor. How was it possible that this fellow had gotten hold of the tape? She closed her eyes as painful memories flooded her mind. *The tape...*

In a bad mood, her mother could be the meanest person on earth, beating Charlie over the head when he couldn't understand what she wanted him to do. She would beat Moira too, but Moira had learned how to avoid the worst by staying in school after hours or working at the drugstore down the road until supper time. That day, as she walked home, she had seen her mother going after Charlie with a big stick. Charlie had run for the creek, which had been severely engorged by a recent storm. Before jumping over, Charlie had tripped over the root of a nearby tree and fallen on the creek's edge, landing with his face in the water. Her mother had started to pound mercilessly on the boy.

Moira hadn't done much. She had pulled her mother off Charlie, pushed her aside and, as her mother tried to come after her, she pushed her into the creek; she helped Charlie to spit water first, and then helped him to stand. She heard her mother screaming and fighting the current as she was taken downstream but she had felt no need to call for help. She and Charlie had walked back to the house without saying a word.

Moira opened her eyes. Had Ryan filmed the accident? Had he given or shown the tape to somebody else? The police, during their lengthy interrogation, hinted that they were aware of the tape and its content. Moira stood her ground. She had reached the scene in time to see Charlie in trouble; she hadn't realized her mother was being swept away by the fury of the water.

Had someone really recorded the deadly push she had given to her mother?

Ryan Costello, a friend of young Charlie's, a couple of years her brother's junior, used to come around with an old camcorder. After school he wandered for hours in the countryside, filming birds, squirrels, groundhogs and the occasional deer. He often stopped at her mother's house to get a glass of milk with cookies and to show what he had recorded during his wanderings. Moira had seen him taking off for the bushes the afternoon that her mother had the so-called accident. After that day he had never shown up at the house again, not even once.

Moira reopened her eyes; she felt no remorse for her crime—only anxiety for the possibility of punishment.

Nick Falcone congratulated himself for his good planning, good thinking, and excellent results. The trip to Niagara Falls had been a success. Fred had been a cheerful companion, ready to explore what was normally offered to a tourist, and he had even accompanied him to the Fallsview Casino. He hadn't placed any bets but he'd roamed around observing people. He had let Fred pay with his credit card and reimbursed him later with the big bills he was so anxious to unload. He would have liked to stay for the weekend, but Fred had an engagement for Saturday evening, and so they had returned to London in the morning. He had dropped Fred off at his house and now he found himself with nothing to do. He was in town, so he called Tessa and asked if he could drop by. She agreed.

Tessa, still in her nightgown, was cooking pancakes. She was in a talkative mood and told him how much she had enjoyed watching the races at the Western Fair and placing a couple of bets.

"I went there a few times. I liked the food and the crazy atmosphere. One night I ran into Jeanette Alstein. You know...Alan's wife? Alan's one of Fred's guys, over at The Werkstein. Anyway, I think I'm going to go out with her for lunch some time, and see if I can pump her for the skinny at Fred's job. Maybe that will give me an in with him!"

The coffee maker made its final gurgle and Tessa poured coffee for both of them. She brought the pancakes to the table along with the syrup. "Help yourself." She spread soft butter on her serving.

"You might get a lot of gossip. Not very useful, probably."

"Probably, but she's a pleasant person, and I don't mind company when I go to do the Fair, especially since you aren't interested in coming. What have you been doing lately?"

"Well, I contacted Fred, as we planned. The idea of target shooting took off, and we're ready to make a habit of practicing once a week." He paused and poured plenty of syrup on his pancakes. "Then I asked him to take a couple days vacation with me to cheer him up. The man is still down, almost lost. We went to the Falls."

"Why didn't you ask me to come along?"

Nick shook his head.

"Tell me why I wasn't invited!" she asked peremptorily. As Nick kept eating in silence, Tessa repeatedly banged the fork on her dish. "The real reason, Nick!"

"Well, the problem is…Fred isn't interested in a woman of your age; he wants a younger woman so he can have kids. He wants a family."

After a moment of icy silence, Tessa exploded. She threw her pancakes at him first, then the plate itself. As Nick ran for the door, she started throwing the candles she kept on almost every piece of furniture. Fortunately, her aim was poor.

Telling the truth had been a mistake, Nick concluded as he found safety outside. Tessa would cool down in a week or two; no need to worry. He climbed into his pickup.

As he drove home he mentally reviewed his financial situation. The bulk of the money he needed to launder was stored in a rented place and nobody knew about it. If the police stormed his premises, they would find a ton of dust and a lot of rusty tools ready to be taken to the dump.

On Highway 7 he noticed that a car was tailing him and so from time-to-time he glanced into the rear mirror to keep track of it. Finally, when he turned into the gravel road that led to his home, the suspicious car continued straight on. He looked in the rear mirror once again. The tail had disappeared, and he nodded in satisfaction.

As he straightened out the steering wheel after the last bend he spotted a police car and a van parked in front of his house. His first instinct was to take off, but he knew that there was no way out. Clearly they had obtained a warrant and had gone ahead with the search. The door of the shed stood wide open and a man in plainclothes carried stuff from the shed to the van. *What could they have they found? There was nothing in that dilapidated shed!*

He slowed down and parked his pickup in the carport, then got out and nonchalantly approached the closest officer.

"What's going on?" he asked.

His hand on his holster, a second officer joined the first one.

"Mr. Nick Falcone?" he asked.

Nick nodded.

"We need you to come to the station so we can ask you a few questions."

"Fine, but what're you doing inside the shed?"

"We found several items we believe belonged to Ms. Lucy Fairweather. You need to clarify a few issues: who brought them in, when, and why."

Nick closed his eyes and shook his head. *I should have looked in the shed when I found her in the shower. She must have been staying in the shed, but why?* He didn't have the slightest clue, but could he ever convince the police?

Moira had discreetly watched the house on Wonderland Road until Sam had entered the place. She had then taken off for Arva and waited there patiently. An hour later Sam's blue pickup had appeared and she had started the pursuit. Only when the pickup had turned into a gravel road had she desisted and continued straight. A few meters ahead she had stopped on the shoulder and waited. Moira knew she should turn around and come back tomorrow in plain daylight when it would be easy to look for neighboring farmers and ask them to whom the blue pickup belonged, but she was out of time. It was Saturday and the blackmailer wanted the money tomorrow.

She turned around, thinking of following Sam's tracks. Before she moved on, however, a cruiser, a van, and the blue pickup came down the road, negotiating the curve slowly enough for Moira to see that Sam was inside the police car.

She held her arms up in jubilation. She didn't have to worry! If Sam was the blackmailer, he would have enough on his plate to forget about threatening her, at least for the time being.

✼ ✼ ✼

Thirty-three

The place Peggy had chosen for target practice was an isolated field with two benches in one corner and three targets set at different distances. It had started drizzling as soon as she and Fred had arrived; after the first few shots the weather had changed for the worse, forcing them to take shelter inside Fred's car.

"It looks like we'll have to suspend our lesson," Fred said. "Should we wait and see if it stops?"

"By all means. The forecast calls for scattered showers, not steady rain." Her cell rang and Peggy opened it and listened carefully. "Ten-four," she said, and shut the phone. She gave Fred a disappointed look. "A bad road accident, and one of my colleagues is sick. I have to go. Please take me home, so I can change quickly and rush to the site."

Fred put the car in gear. "Do I have a good reason for speeding?"

Peggy laughed. "You do, but if you meet with a cop, he'll have a good reason for fining you."

"Just a bit, then." He turned around and took off right away. "We'll have to think of an alternative to shooting. We keep having poor weather conditions or other problems." He looked at Peggy, whose eyes were full of excitement. "The afternoon and evening are shot, so I'll go to my office now and see if there's anything urgent that needs to be done; this way I'll be free all day tomorrow. How does it sound for you?"

"Good, except if this emergency drags into tomorrow. But I like to go to church in the morning. It's Sunday."

"Me, too. What about coming over to my place in the afternoon? I don't have much to do, maybe shuffling around some furniture to make room for my new bar. Otherwise I'll just be thinking about the backyard and what to plant so that it'll look nice in the spring. No must-dos."

"Wonderful. We'll do whatever we feel like doing, no plans; I like the idea. Can you look after my gun? Cleaning, etc.?"

"No problem." He pulled up in front of her house. "Be careful. I count on seeing you in one piece tomorrow."

The time at the office had been very productive. Only two of the ongoing jobs were delayed because of poor weather; the others remained on schedule. The pricing for the mall was almost completed, and Fred noticed that Moira hadn't made a special copy with her annotations. He wondered what could be wrong, or whether her behavior merely resulted from having to report to Verge Bristol. *It would be a pity if she left*, he thought. She had done excellent work and had extended herself beyond the call of duty to help keep the company on the right track. She deserved a raise. He would talk it over with Verge to determine how much would be appropriate.

At midnight he quit working and headed home. The huge box with the new bar was in the garage. Anxious to see how it would fit in the big rec room, which was at the heart of the house, he carried the box inside, removed all the packaging, and assembled the bar. The round front, lacquered a shining white, opened in the middle, showing a set of drawers on the left, shelves for more than two-dozen bottles in the middle and a special shelf with holes for hanging glasses upside down on the right. The top was a black-and-white marble imitation made of a special plastic material. Fred was satisfied. Tomorrow he would move it into a corner and clean up the box and wrapping.

Sunday morning went by quickly; he had breakfast; caught the ten o'clock Mass; cleaned Peggy's Beretta and his new Remington and lingered around the house, once more satisfied with its recent acquisition. He then took his last cup of coffee to the veranda and sat there, taking a leisurely look around. Gray clouds amassed low in the sky, promising another ration of rain.

A rap on the door reminded him he should install a bell. He saw Peggy's slim silhouette through the glass part of the main door.

"Hello, stranger," Fred said as he opened the door. "Happy to see you made it and that you're still in one piece. You look wonderful."

"Hi, Fred." She shrugged off her nylon jacket and threw it on top of her gun, which was standing flush against the wall. In spite of the cool weather she wore a pair of white shorts, a sleeveless yellow top, and a pair of high-heeled sandals. Taking in the sight, Fred didn't move.

"Are you going to let me stand here?" she asked.

"Sorry." He moved aside and they both walked into the rec room. "Anything to drink? I have plenty of juices and soft drinks."

"Nothing at the moment." Peggy looked at the bar. "Fancy." She opened it and turned toward Fred. "It's empty!"

"You don't drink, so I wasn't in a hurry to stock any liquor. I still have a bottle of whisky in the cupboard."

Peggy moved toward the patio door and examined the curtains. She closed them and re-opened them.

"They did a good job, and that green valance perfectly matches the color of the leaves on the beige fabric." She looked at the floor. "And it coordinates nicely with the carpet."

"I had a good adviser."

"I was glad to be of help." Peggy opened the patio door and walked outside. "I like a veranda; it cuts a bit of the sunlight, but it lets you sit outside without being concerned about the weather." She took a few steps in the open. "Big backyard."

"Yes. Plenty of trees already. They were here before we started building, so I'm not thinking of planting any others. A couple of flower beds and then grass—what do you think?" Fred neared Peggy from behind and brushed her neck with his lips.

Peggy turned around and looked at him intently. "Planning to seduce me?" she asked in a soft tone.

"Not really. I'm too rusty. I hoped you'd do it."

Peggy laughed. "I don't believe you."

"But it's the truth."

She put her arms around his neck and kissed him. Her lips were soft and warm, the scent of her body inviting. Fred pulled her close and returned her kiss.

"Should we go back inside?" he asked.

Peggy didn't respond; she closed her eyes, her hands caressing his neck and face. She kissed him again, one kiss after another, without giving Fred time to repeat his question.

Fred hugged her around the waist and gently dragged her inside.

"How am I doing?" Peggy asked when she opened her eyes.

"Not bad." Fred's voice was a husky whisper. "But you still have too many clothes on."

Peggy took a step back and removed her top. "Better?"

"Too many, still."

Peggy unzipped her shorts and let them slip to the floor. "You have to help with the rest."

Fred glanced at her body, half-naked before him. Clothing didn't do justice to her. He drew her into his arms, his hands running across her back. He unfastened the clasps of her bra and bent over to trace small circles around her breasts with his tongue and brush their tips with his lips. He held them in his hands, then took a nipple into his mouth and swirled his tongue around it.

"Not bad for a rusty lover," Peggy whispered.

Fred didn't respond as his hands streaked up her hips and freed Peggy of her panties. He stopped for a moment and contemplated her body.

"What's wrong?" Peggy asked.

"You're a centerfold, Peggy. You're the most beautiful woman I've ever seen."

Peggy kicked her sandals off and folded her body around Fred. "I'm happy you like me," she murmured.

"I want you, Peggy. I want all of you."

Peggy held his face in her hands and kissed him. "Take me, Fred. All of me."

✠ ✠ ✠

Thirty-four

When she woke up early Sunday morning, Moira felt well-rested; she was confident that, with Sam stuck at some police station, her troubles about the tape were on hold. She dressed in a pair of Capri pants and a beige hoodie and drove to the Men's Mission to fetch Charlie and go to church. To her surprise, he was outside, pacing back and forth. When he saw her, he waved the cell she had given him earlier. Moira gestured to get into the car and drove out of the compound and toward St. Mary's Church.

"What happened?" Moira asked.

"The cell kept ringing, and a voice kept asking for you. All morning."

Moira froze. *The blackmailer!* Charlie had her old phone. That was why she had not received any calls.

"Last night too?" she asked.

"Yes, twice last night."

"What time?"

"Don't know."

"Was it dark?"

"Yep."

Then he couldn't be Sam.

"Same voice?"

"Yep." He looked at his sister. "Are we in trouble?"

Moira took time to weigh her answer. She couldn't speak freely with Charlie; he might misunderstand and react in an unpredictable way.

"I hope not. Did the man, I mean the voice you heard, say anything?"

"Once he said not to play games. That's all."

They arrived at St. Mary's, and Moira sneaked her Hyundai between a pickup truck and a Lincoln Mercury. She exited the car but Charlie didn't move.

"Charlie!" Moira called. "Let's go; we're late."

Charlie slowly complied, frowning. "I did wrong, eh?"

"No. Don't worry." She forced a smile. "Let's go hear some good words." She took his arm and led him into the church.

They were halfway through the Mass when Charlie's phone rang. Moira abruptly unclipped it from his belt and hurried outside. She opened it and waited.

"I want to talk to Moira," a guttural voice growled.

It could belong to a man as well as to a woman, Moira noticed. "Speaking."

"Have you got my money ready?"

"Money? What for? For a phantom tape?"

"The tape is real, I can assure you."

"Then make a copy and mail it to me."

She shut the phone, set it on vibrate, and re-entered the church. She joined Charlie, who was already kneeling on the kneeling-pad. If the black-mailer was bluffing she had shut him off; if he had the tape she had bought herself some time, which she would spend to find out his identity and how to prevent him from harming her brother and her any further.

Lucy Fairweather hadn't led an active social life, so there had been only a short ceremony at the funeral home. Very few people had attended and Fred wondered why Nick had not shown up, as he had promised. In this very same room he had seen Charlotte for the last time, immobile in her final rest inside the coffin. Remembering a farewell given to a dear person was always a sad occasion; however, today the remembrance of his sister seemed to appease him instead of saddening him—the vision of Charlotte sliding away with levity.

The time he had spent with Peggy had given a new dimension to his life and disclosed a brighter horizon. A sense of freedom and anticipation took hold of him. Peggy had broken through the numbness that had pervaded his body and mind since the day he'd realized Deborah would never recover from her accident. His numbness had been a form of defense, a natural reaction to minimize the tragic situation and the resulting hardship he had to face. With her vitality and openness, Peggy had driven a wedge into the shell of his lethargic state.

He smiled as he remembered the time they had spent together on Sunday. They had rolled in the sheets, eager to discover each other's body, and sex had been only a part of the play. They had talked nonsense; when he had confessed that he was ticklish at the waist, she had gone after him until he had fallen out of bed. It was a homecoming, and that feeling was still vivid two days after they had been together.

Immersed in his thoughts, he didn't notice that the music had stopped and the lights had been dimmed. He rose and followed the funeral home director on his way out; he thanked him and quickly headed home.

As he approached his house, he spotted the silhouette of a police car. When he clicked on the remote to open the garage door, Peggy, in uniform, got out of the car and waved at him.

Fred joined her. "I'm innocent, officer."

"That'll be up to me to decide," she said, with mocked authority, and gestured toward the house. "I'm on my break, so why don't you invite me in?" She waited for Fred to open the main door. "I tried to call you, but you didn't answer."

"I was at the memorial service for Lucy. I left my cell in the car."

"Sorry about Lucy, even if we're pretty sure she was involved in your sister's death." Peggy put her arms around Fred's neck and pecked on his lips. "I have only a little time left before going back to work. Just enough time for a drink."

Fred pulled her toward him. "What about tonight?"

"On duty until late. But tomorrow I have some free time." She gave him a mischievous look. "The forecast is for good weather; ideal for practicing target shooting."

"That's what you really want to do?"

Peggy laughed, disengaged herself from Fred's arms, and moved toward the kitchen. She got a can of ginger ale out of the fridge and opened it.

"I'm thirsty."

"Only for a drink?"

"It's all I have time for right now. Tomorrow afternoon, then?"

"By all means. Call me and let me know the time."

Peggy nodded, drank the last few drops of her ale, and deposited the empty can on the table. She was almost out the door when she turned around and reached for Fred who quickly opened his arms.

"I was waiting for a proper goodbye," Fred murmured, and sealed her mouth with a light kiss. *It's wonderful to be wanted*, he thought, as Peggy leaned against him, her eyes closed. He brushed her eyelids with his lips and then relinquished his hold. "I'll be thinking of you."

"Me too," Peggy said and left.

✧ ✧ ✧

Thirty-five

By the time dawn arrived, Moira had a plan. She called the main office at The Werkstein and left a message saying that she had an urgent family matter to take care of and she would be away a couple of days. She gave the phone number of her new cell and asked to be contacted only if something urgent came up. She wrote a note for Charlie with a similar message and put it in an envelope together with a ten. She would drop it off at the Men's Mission on her way to Barrie.

She packed clothes for a couple of days, her toiletries, and a sandwich for her imminent trip. In no time she was on the road, on her way to find out a bit more about Charlie's old friend, Ryan Costello.

After her mother's death, Moira had wanted only one thing: to leave town and put everything behind her. At that time, Charlie's seizures were not as severe as they became later; he was able to work as a janitor at the local elementary school. As soon as the police had released on their grip, Moira had listed the prefab house for sale and started selling the furniture and household furnishings piece by piece. Three months later the real estate agent had found a buyer who had gladly taken over the low-interest mortgage on the house, and Moira, finally free, had contracted board and lodging for Charlie and then attended college with what remained of the proceeds from the house sale. She had hoped never to see that old house again, nor her old neighbors, nor anything connected with her hometown, Barrie.

Located on Kempenfelt Bay, Barrie boasted a population just short of two hundred thousand. A rapidly expanding city among the many in the Greater Golden Horseshoe, Barrie offered great business opportunities and an enormous choice of entertainment, from swimming and surf sailing on Lake Simcoe in the summer to hockey and ski-dooing in the winter.

Young Moira had never thought of leaving Barrie. Her ambition was to attend Georgian College, get a degree in Engineering Technology and, once established, enjoy the many leisure activities the city offered: entertainment at the MacLaren Art Centre and Gryphon Theatre and concerts and performances at the Barrie Molson Centre. Unfortunately, life had a way of changing the best laid plans.

When Moira arrived in Barrie, she was exhausted, but more determined than ever to do what she had in mind. She took a room at the Days Inn. The night didn't bring much rest, as images of her mother struggling in the rough waters kept disrupting her sleep. It was a disturbing vision that troubled her often, and sudden immersion in the same environment where the fatal accident happened made that vision more poignant. She had suspected this would happen; that was one of the reasons she had never wanted to return to Barrie.

When morning finally arrived, she stopped at the elementary school where Charlie had worked. The principal had no time for her, but his secretary, Rose Holton, was available. She looked very much the same as Moira remembered, except that her hair was streaked gray and a few wrinkles marked her forehead. She received Moira with a friendly handshake and invited her to sit across from her at her desk. She immediately apologized on behalf of the school board for laying Charlie off; he had become unreliable, showing up only half the time for work. Moira was well aware of this fact as she had been in contact with the school at the time Charlie's alertness started to deteriorate. Moira wanted to know about Ryan Costello, whether he had graduated and gone on further in education. So after more chatting on Charlie's condition she veered the subject toward Charlie's friends, and asked who was still in town.

The secretary, however, responded vaguely to Moira's inquiries, and immediately asked questions about Moira's job. Was her work interesting? They heard she had graduated from the University of Windsor and was doing important work. How was it to hold a job in a construction company? Moira answered politely, and tried once more to steer the subject onto Charlie's friends. Rose Holton asked again about Charlie's health and whether he had been able to hold a job recently. So Moira gave a lengthy explanation about the ups and downs of her brother's condition; he had been able to deliver mail for a while, until the old curse had hit again, making him forget where to go for a few days in a row. He had lost that job, but now he worked at the Western Fair in London. There was another digression on which kind of job Charlie was doing at the Western Fair, and then the secretary seemed satisfied. She rose and made coffee for both.

Rose sat back in her chair. "You want to know about Charlie's friends, you said? I don't remember any, except Ryan Costello. He was Charlie's buddy."

"Yes. Charlie asked about him."

"He has his own shop in town, on Richmond. He sells and repairs cameras—any kind." She looked at Moira. "You remember that he used to walk around with that old camcorder?" She smiled at the memory. "He'd take pictures of everybody and everything. The school had a problem making him understand that it was not appropriate to film people in their homes without their consent."

"I know. We were quite friendly with the Costellos; I'll tell my brother he's still in town and still busy with photography." Moira took a couple sips of her coffee and started to rise.

"Oh, do you have to go so soon?"

"Well, there're a few people I want to see before going back to London."

"Are you going to be around tomorrow?" Rose looked at her planner. "We could have lunch together."

Moira hesitated. "I'll call you tonight and let you know if I'll be in town for another day." With that, she left.

Moira drove to Richmond Street and circled a few blocks before spotting Ryan's shop. Wedged in between a pizza take-out and a discount store and four feet away from the curb, the sign Photos and Cameras was hardly perceivable. She parked her car on the street and strode to the entrance. The front door stuck, but a hard push activated the musical chimes and signaled her presence. The shelves on two walls advertised digital and traditional cameras by showcasing their empty boxes. Framed photos of weddings, graduations, and parties hung on the other walls, clearly promoting Ryan's work as a photographer.

Ryan appeared from a door at the back of the store. He was in his twenties, short with a baby face and vivid brown eyes behind his metal-framed eyeglasses.

"Moira Johnson!" He walked toward her with his hand extended.

"You recognized me?" Moira shook his hand.

Ryan hesitated a bit. "Difficult to forget your curly, red hair. How have you been?"

"Not bad. As you probably know, I went to school soon after I left Barrie; now I'm working in London."

"Good job?"

"It pays well, but it's a lot of work and responsibility." Moira looked around, thinking how to bring up the subject of the famous tape. "Charlie often asks about you. The two of you used to wander in the woods together."

"Yes, I remember. Charlie was very good at spotting birds for me to film with my camcorder."

"You must have had a ton of pictures and films by the time you finished school."

"Yes, indeed. I went to work with Black's Photography in downtown Toronto to learn a bit of the trade from the commercial point of view, then I came back here and set up my shop."

"That's wonderful." Moira's gray cells were at work to find a way to ask about the tape.

"My dream is to be a freelance photographer, but it's difficult to make a living with that job alone. I'm swamped with demands in the spring and early summer, especially for weddings, but there's less in the fall and zilch in the winter."

"I can understand." Moira approached the walls and looked at the framed pictures. "You do very nice work, but you were very good even at a younger age. You took a lot of pictures of this town and the countryside."

Ryan laughed. "Yes, I did, until the school told me I could film all the wildlife and all the trees and pastures I wanted—but not people in their homes. That was illegal without people's permission." Ryan paused. "At first I didn't believe them, but then one day the police came to our house and asked to see my tapes."

"Oh?"

"Yes. They asked my mother. She didn't believe in my talent as a photographer and dismissed the idea flatly, denying that my tapes could contain anything interesting. But the police came back the following day when I was home and asked me directly. By that time I had hidden the box with the tapes together with my zoom lens in the doghouse. They wanted to see my camcorder, which, of course, had only a brand new tape inside."

"Naughty boy. I know the town is planning a big celebration for next summer, inviting citizens to supply old records and pictures. I bet your old stuff would be useful."

"Oh, yes, it could be. You see, I sent out all the pictures and the short films I took to a company in London. They'll evaluate the material and build me a portfolio. I hope to boost my reputation and work for an advertising agency, temporarily putting on hold my dream of full-time freelancing. I'm getting married next year." Ryan pulled a chair from underneath the counter and invited Moira to sit. "You look tired."

Moira collapsed on the chair. The incriminating film, if it existed, was now in the hands of strangers. She would never find out who those people were.

Ryan looked at her with concern. "But you didn't come to my shop only to talk, right?"

"No. I wanted to ask you if you ever took pictures of our old place. The prefab house near the creek? I'm making a family album."

"I did. But right now I have no way to trace them. I'd have to wait until the portfolio is completed; it will take three to four weeks."

Moira summoned all her strength and rose. "Thank you, Ryan. I'll have to wait, then. I'll give you a call in a month or so." She thanked him, shook hands and left.

Back at the hotel, Moira slumped on the bed, disheartened. It was foolish to think she could get information about one particular tape after so many years; a tape that was now out of reach but still constituted a threat. She tried to examine the situation with lucidity. Ryan had not reacted like a person who had seen a murderess in front of him. He had been friendly, and the fact that he had never stopped at the house after her mother's death could be because she and her brother knew that he was taping not only wildlife but people as well. Having the police inquiring about his hobby might have put a temporary stop to his chumming around with Charlie. However, even if Ryan had not seen her push her mother, he could have filmed the action with his zoom lens; he may not have played the tape afterward in order not to raise suspicion at home; after all, his mother might have kept an eye on his photographic activities. *But what about these people who are supposed to evaluate Ryan's pictures and build him a portfolio?* By now they might be aware of what happened, and they could be part of the current blackmailing.

Tomorrow, before returning to London, she would call Ryan and see whether she could get the name of the company evaluating his work.

Thirty-six

The London company with Ryan's tapes was called Off Broadway, a pompous name for a tiny office located on the second floor of an old building on Queens Street. Moira cautiously approached the shop door, hoping to get the name of the company's owner. There wasn't any. Through the tinted glass door she saw two silhouettes bent over a desk, shuffling around what she guessed were pictures. When Moira heard steps coming down from the floors above, she quickly descended the stairway and walked outside. She didn't want to be spotted. With her short stature and red hair, anybody who gave her a quick glance would be able to identify her.

She returned to her car, where she noticed that a van had parked on the road while she'd been gone; it carried the inscription Off Broadway and a phone number painted in large characters on the rear window.

She entered her Hyundai and called the company, requesting an appointment, possibly after office hours. She told the person who answered the phone that she wanted to find out whether they could help promote her career as a graphic designer. She was put in contact with Mr. Michael Sullivan, who gave her an appointment for the following day at eight o'clock.

Things are working out, Moira thought. She would have plenty of time to think about what to say to Mr. Sullivan and find an excuse to be alone in his office and snoop around. Moira drove to The Werkstein, dodged Mary

Gervasio, who expressed concerns about her family problems of two days before, and put in a solid day of work. The pricing for the mall on the east side of London was due the following week. Late in the evening she went to see her brother to tell him what to do the next day, when they would both drive to Off Broadway. Her last stop was at a shop specializing in party supplies, where she bought a dark wig.

At five o'clock the following day, Moira was checking all the prices she had gathered so far when Alain Alstein approached her. With Verge Bristol in Fred's office almost permanently, he clearly didn't feel the need to ask her to follow him to the conference room.

"You should think about my offer," he said in a low voice. "I know you have problems with your brother; some extra money would come in handy. I do have the names of a couple of subs who wouldn't raise any suspicion and would give us about five grand each." He blinked his eyes nervously.

Moira had worked hard all day and still had to perfect the act she had in mind for her meeting with Mr. Sullivan. She didn't want to entertain a lengthy conversation.

"I have a good reputation in this business," she said, evenly. "I wouldn't compromise it for a lousy five grand." She leaned over the monitor of her computer, checked a few lines on the spreadsheet in front of her, and then clicked on the *Print* key.

Alain still stood there when she filed away the printout. She ignored him, grabbed her purse, and left the office.

Moira had prepared a sheet with questions for her upcoming interview even if she wasn't obviously interested in any of the answers. Shortly before eight o'clock she parked her car on Queens Street and, for the last time, reminded Charlie of the role he was supposed to play. She lowered the visor of Charlie's baseball cap; pulled out her cell and pointed to the number he had to click.

"In twenty minutes." Moira showed him where his watch's hands would be. "Understood?" Most of the time Charlie knew the time, but on this particular occasion she wanted to be sure he would place the call twenty minutes from now.

"Yes." Charlie gave her a big smile. "And when you come back we'll go to the Dairy Queen?"

"Sure thing," Moira replied and stepped out of the car.

Contrary to her expectations, the man who welcomed her at the door was an older man with a long white beard and thick glasses.

"Michael couldn't make it tonight," he apologized. "But I'm sure I can be of help. This business was mine before I handed it over to my son." He gestured Moira to a chair and sat on the other side of the metal desk. "I'm Jacob Sullivan, and I know you're interested in our services." He extracted a folder from the main drawer and opened it. "This is the best package we have. Ad in the local newspaper for five weeks, ad on a locally accessible Internet provider of your choice for a week, Web page design and its maintenance for a full year." He turned around the sheet so Moira could read it.

"Interesting. And the price?"

"Four thousand."

"Hmm. That's a bit steep for me at this time of my career. I do have a nice job but I'd like to set up my own business. Do you have anything else?" She looked at the huge clock that carved its space between a forest of posters of all sizes and styles. Only fifteen minutes had gone by, so she needed to look at another package.

Jacob placed another few sheets in front of her, describing a new package that was similar to the previous one, but for a shorter period of time.

Moira looked at it. "I was hoping for something more personal and more technical."

"Like an evaluation of your expertise?" Jacob asked.

"Yes, yes. You just took the words out of my mouth."

The phone rang and Jacob grabbed it at the second ring.

"What? What are you saying?" He paused and brought the phone closer to his ear. "Yes, this is Off Broadway. My van is being towed away?" He paused and listened a bit longer. "That's impossible! At this time of night I can park there as long as I want. It's well after six o'clock!" His face was red, and the hand holding the phone was shaking. "Thanks. I'll come right down." He deposited the receiver in its cradle and rose. "I can't believe this. They're towing away my van! Stay, stay. It'll only take a minute. I'll go down and be right back."

Without another word he left the office and headed for the stairs.

Excited, Moira looked around; it was hunt time. The file cabinet in the office would contain the most recent material, she surmised, so she excluded it from her search. She swiftly moved into the adjoining room. There was a table with several boxes, one set on top of the other and each identified by a proper name. The three biggest ones carried the script *Ryan Costello*. Moira opened the first one to find only a huge number of CDs and DVDs. She put aside that box and opened the second; it contained some CDs at the top, floppies and tapes at the bottom. She lifted a few tapes, noticing that dates were written on their sides. They were more recent than the ones she was interested in, so she closed that box also, set it on top of the first one and opened the last one. Inside there were only tapes. She was ready to lift up a few, when she heard the old man scuffing his feet on the staircase, swearing against whomever had played such a prank on an old man.

Moira reshuffled the boxes into their original position and returned to the main office.

"You wouldn't believe it! There was nothing wrong with my van. No tow truck in sight! It was a joke, and in bad taste if you ask me!" He took a white hankie out of his trouser pocket and dried the perspiration on his cheeks. "So where were we?"

"You just gave me two folders, one with a nice package but a bit pricey for me; the other, the one for twenty-five hundred, seems very appealing." Moira focused her attention on the front sheet and tapped on it. "Yes, this looks good. What would be the time frame?"

"Three to four weeks."

"That long?"

Jacob wiggled in his seat. "I should really ask my son; I'm not in the loop anymore and your expertise is a bit unusual."

"I see; no problem. I need to think about it for a few days."

"Yes, do that; then give us a call. I'll make sure my son is here; he can give you more details about the promo."

Moira took the folders with her. "Thank you for your time. I'll be in touch."

The following day Moira entered The Werkstein building with her spirits up. She hadn't received a tape in the mail, and her trip to Barrie had not been a total failure. She had found useful information, and another trip to Off Broadway might produce an even better result.

She was early, and hoped that she wouldn't meet anybody on the way to her office. Fat chance. Mary Gervasio was already there, an exciting look on her face.

"Come here, Moira! Come!" Mary pulled on her coat sleeve.

"I have work to do," Moira said, feebly.

"Just a few minutes! Come to my office!"

Reluctantly, Moira complied. "So what's so exciting?"

"I convinced Fred to throw a house-warming party! Next Saturday, open house from five to nine o'clock." She took a card out of the tray that lay on her desk. "Sign here, and be sure to come! We all plan to be there."

Moira felt as if she had been plunged abruptly into another world. It seemed that the problem of the tape had obliterated everything around her.

"Are you okay?" Mary asked.

Moira nodded. "Remember the bug I had a few months ago? I got it back. It isn't a big deal; it just makes me very tired."

"I understand. And that emergency you had? Was it a family matter?"

"Yes, it was about my brother. I told you about his condition, right?"

Mary nodded. "Seizures, and a bit slow, if I remember correctly."

"It's difficult for Charlie to hold on to a job; sometimes I don't know how to help him."

Mary gave her a sympathetic look. "I believe you, poor child." She patted her on the back. "The big job closes in three days; after that you'll have a bit of time to relax." As Moira turned to walked away, Mary hastened to add, "No gifts of any sort, Moira. That was the condition Fred set before agreeing to give the party."

Moira nodded and walked to her office.

✵ ✵ ✵

Thirty-seven

Mary Gervasio had been with The Werkstein since the founding of the company; she still remembered the small office where Werner Gassman had interviewed her for the position of secretary. After twelve years of marriage she had found herself alone with two boys to raise; she was not certain her secretarial skills were up-to-date enough to guarantee her a job. Werner, however, had immediately offered her a probationary employment; during this time Mary had worked extra hours to become familiar with the office computer software and communications equipment. Within a year she was hired full-time. She had seen the company grow from a few employees to twenty full-time members with another twenty seasonal workers. She considered the company her home, as now her two sons had moved to Toronto and had families of their own.

When Fred had bought his new house, she thought it would be the right time to let him know how much the company's employees liked him and that they wanted to join in the celebration of his new beginning. Fred had been reluctant at first, but at the end he had agreed.

Today Mary had arrived at Fred's house to give one last touch to the party arrangements. A catering company had provided food and soft drinks; she artfully lined up the trays with snacks and hors d'oeuvres on two picnic tables, covered by white tablecloths for the occasion. A small table on the side held a variety of alcoholic beverages. From her bag she extracted several stacks of disposable glasses and set them in front of the bottles and cans. She tossed a couple of colorful garlands onto the ceiling light fixture, and set the big banner with *WE LOVE YOU FRED* stenciled on it across the bar. She opened the half-dozen folding chairs she had unloaded from her car and set them flush against the walls. Finally she walked into the kitchen and filled two big coffee makers—they were ready to be plugged in—then took the temporary license for alcoholic beverages from inside her purse and pasted it on the fridge door.

She took another critical look at the large room and, satisfied, she went home to get dressed for the occasion.

Fred, who initially had mixed feelings about having a house-warming party less than three months after Deborah's death, was happy he had agreed to it. Yesterday he had learned that the contract for the shopping mall had been awarded to The Werkstein. The fifteen-million dollar job guaranteed that even his part-time employees would work through the winter. It was clearly a cause for celebration, as it had been in the past. Combining the two occasions made it more palatable for him to throw a party.

Tonight was the night. He looked around, happy that his employees were enjoying a spirit of camaraderie, then delved into the snacks with pleasure. Moira had arrived late and was the only one who seemed almost reserved. He approached her.

"I heard that your brother is in town and you're worried about him. Mary mentioned that he's in poor health."

Moira sighed. "He's a bit slow and suffers with seizures." She paused and looked at Fred with a sweet smile. "I'm trying to see how I can get him a good accommodation, one he feels comfortable with. He'd like to live with me, but I can't work when he's around me; I can't concentrate at all." As Fred nodded sympathetically, she added, "Mary must have told you I took some time off. I made up for the time lost by working evenings."

"Yes, yes, I know. Verge told me you had everything ready by the tender's deadline. Just let me know if I can help with your personal situation."

"Thanks. Recently I couldn't do much snooping, though; I was too busy pricing."

"No problem. I looked at the current contracts and submissions, and I didn't spot any irregularities. None so far. Perhaps Verge Bristol got the message and will keep things straight from now on."

"That would be great."

"I see your glass is empty. Want a refill?"

"Yes. Orange juice and vodka, please."

Fred was adding juice to the spirit when Peggy appeared on the threshold. He quickly handed the drink to Moira and hastened to greet Peggy. To his surprise, she was accompanied by Detective Gordon Stevenson; neither was in uniform.

Before Fred could say a word, Peggy took him aside.

"I couldn't leave him alone. His wife let him know she won't come back to London. She's staying with her parents, indefinitely it appears. The man was devastated by the news. Gordon has been very good to me."

Fred nodded and moved to give Stevenson a warm handshake.

"Glad you're here. Peggy's friends are my friends." He stood in the middle of the room. "Folks, I'd like to introduce you two friends of mine, Peggy O'Brian and Gordon Stevenson. Some of you have already met them. They do police work, but they assured me that tonight they'll not arrest or interrogate anybody. Please welcome them."

There was a warm applause, and Fred took both by the arm and led them to the refreshment table. He poured straight scotch for Gordon and lemonade for Peggy.

"You look great in your blue outfit," Fred whispered to Peggy. It was a simple dress of soft fabric, with a huge silvery belt that delineated her slim waist.

"Thanks," Peggy answered. "Are all these people employees of your company?"

"Yes, all the full-time and their spouses, of course."

"Nobody else?"

"Unfortunately not. The friend I practice trap shooting with seems to be unavailable. I tried to call him a couple of times, but I got no answer." He paused. "I may have to drive up to his farmhouse and see what happened."

"Where does he live?"

"On a parcel of land about twenty-five kilometers from Port Franks."

"Close to your sister's house?"

"No. Charlotte's was right on the lake; my friend lives inland, where the farming land starts. He doesn't have much property around the house, but enough bushes and shrubs that we can set up our targets and shoot as much as we want."

Mary Gervasio approached Fred from behind and tapped on his arm.

"May I have a word with you?" she asked.

Fred excused himself with Peggy and followed Mary to a corner of the room.

"Something's wrong with Alain's wife, Jeanette," she whispered. "She drank too much, I think, and she's getting louder and louder."

Jeanette, in an ankle-length, red dress was resisting Alain, who was trying to take her glass away from her. In spite, she threw her drink in his face and hurled the plastic glass across the room.

"Leave me alone!" she screamed. "I told you she's the one! I recognized her!"

People had stopped their cheerful chattering, making the room more receptive to Jeanette's shouting.

"Please, Jeanette, come with me," Alain said softly.

Fred neared the couple and stood in front of Jeanette.

"Let me take you to the kitchen and give you a cup of coffee." He put a hand on her arm, while Alain took her other arm.

Jeanette freed herself of both holds. "You want me out of here, right? You don't have to grab me! I can leave by myself." She purposely marched toward the exit, followed by Alain. Before reaching the archway that separated the hallway from the rec room she did an about-face and screamed, "I tell you, she's the one!"

Fred followed Alain outside. "Can I do anything to help?"

"No. She gets rowdy at times. When she has one too many she feels people are after her, in one fashion or another. She'll calm down as soon as we're home."

He quickened his steps to the car Jeanette had already entered, then got in and drove away.

Detective Stevenson had joined Fred.

"Everything okay?" he asked.

Fred nodded. "Just some bad family business. They'll work it out. Let's go back inside." He quickly moved to the CD player and put on some music. He gestured to Mary. "Time to bring in the cake and the champagne."

While Mary sliced the three-layer cake, Peggy whispered, "Do you have any idea about who was she talking?"

Fred shook his head. "Not in the least."

Once at home, Moira walked straight into her bedroom and threw her little purse on the bed. What should have been an occasion to relax and take pride in what had been for the most part her achievement ended up being an exhausting outing. Alain Alstein had avoided her, and Verge and most of the other employees, accompanied by their wives, had exchanged only a few words with her. She had experienced the same situation at previous gatherings. Being the only professional female in a group of males wasn't an easy situation. In addition, she had been troubled by the idea that the blackmailer could be among the partying crowd and therefore had exhausted herself in the effort of scrutinizing the behavior of the guests, at times capturing bits of their conversations.

Days of hard work, the threat posed by the tape and dealing with Charlie had drained her emotionally. Without getting undressed Moira slumped on the bed and fell asleep.

The following Monday she stopped by Mary's desk, carrying two coffees and a box of doughnut holes, of which Mary was particularly fond. She sat opposite her and, after commenting about the success of the party, said, "Too bad about the scene Jeanette Alstein made. Do you think Fred got very upset about it?"

"No. My first boss, Mr. Gassman, often said that Fred wasn't really a tough guy, but that he was very resilient. He can cope with the worst situations without letting them bother him." She paused, sipped her coffee and savored a couple of Timbits. "That's how he managed to deal with his wife's sickness."

"I heard that Jeanette is not only a drinker, but also a gambler." Moira sipped her coffee slowly, attentively watching Mary's reaction.

Mary retreated into the role of the perfect secretary. "I wouldn't know. I always found her pleasant when she comes here to see Alain. I never exchanged many words with her, however."

Moira finished her coffee and looked at her wristwatch.

"Time to go to work. Both Fred and Verge decided on a restructuring job; it's about a bunch of storerooms out of town, on a piece of land Fred bought some time ago."

"I heard that. This place is always busy."

The phone rang and Mary waved Moira goodbye as she picked up the receiver.

✳ ✳ ✳

Thirty-eight

From the OPP Detachment in Grand Bend, Nick placed another call to Tessa; she hadn't answered the first two. Finally she did at the fifth ring.

"I don't want to talk to you," she said, as soon as he identified himself.

"Tessa, please, I'm in trouble."

"Really? Or is this some kind of scam?"

"No! I need your help. It's about Lucy."

"She's dead, so what could be the problem?"

"The police found some of her clothes and her purse in the shed near my house. I had no idea she'd camped there, but they don't believe me. They keep questioning me."

"And what does any of this have to do with me?"

"I need you to come down here with a lawyer; I don't know anybody."

After a silence on the line, Tessa said, "First, you have to tell me what happened when you went to see Charlotte, that evening she got injured."

"Tessa, I didn't do anything. It was an accident."

"What kind of accident? I want to know!"

"Okay, okay. I asked her about throwing a party for Fred's fortieth birthday, as you and I agreed. She objected and I insisted. Then out of the blue her big cat came out of nowhere and attacked me. It scratched my hand and my arm. I got upset, grabbed the cat and tossed it away. Charlotte screamed at me and tried to catch it. She lost her balance and fell backward." Nick paused. "I got scared. I left and asked you to take me home. That's all."

"But you should have called for help, instead of leaving!"

"I know, but what's done is done."

"That's easy for you to say! Charlotte was my only entry into Fred's new life, idiot!"

"I understand. We'll find another way to get you close to him. Now, do you want to help me or not?"

"I'm not sure."

"Come on, Tessa! I'll make it up to you. I'm here, detained at a police station, without having done anything wrong. I have no idea why Lucy chose to hide in my shed!"

"Okay, I'll see what I can do."

"Come down too, please."

"And why is that necessary?"

"You have to tell police that you saw me greeting people coming in with their boats in Port Franks and that I was invited to join two groups of boaters for a ride. Remember? Two invitations in one single day! I told them about those occasions and you can confirm them."

"And why is that important?"

"I'll explain when you get here."

"Okay, but you owe me big time!"

Nick Falcone waited patiently for the last formalities to be completed. They were going to release him, but he would have to be available for more questioning. Tessa was growing impatient, sipping her second can of cola.

"Why do we have to wait? They said you're free to go, right?"

Nick shrugged. "They have to fill in the release form. Sit down, Tessa, it can't take much longer."

"I hope not. I'm really tired. Last night I was up late playing the slot machines. I won a bit." She yawned and finished her cola.

"You went alone?"

"Yes. You meet people if you stay long enough."

"Anybody interesting?"

Tessa shrugged. "Not really. Last time I saw only lonely older people."

An officer appeared on the threshold and gave Nick a piece of paper, which Nick folded and silently put in his pocket. He linked arms with Tessa and strode off.

"Your truck?" Tessa asked.

"I'll get it back tomorrow."

Tessa gestured him into her shiny silver Corvette.

"Fred would never talk to you again if he ever hears about Lucy being in your shed for days!"

Nick sighed. "I know, and I'd actually started enjoying spending time with him."

"What's going to happen next?"

"I don't know. The lawyer said he needed a couple of hours to examine the evidence they have against me; he'll call me later." Nick sighed. "At least he managed to get me released."

"Meanwhile...?" Tessa asked.

"Meanwhile, I keep a low profile and work around the house."

The Corvette's tires squealed when Tessa took the last half of the bend that led to Nick's farmhouse. She rocketed the car over the parched terrain for the last hundred meters and then abruptly stopped in front of the old house, spreading dust all over.

A Lexus was parked on one side of the house.

"What the heck? Fred is here!"

"Looks like." Nick exited the car.

"Wait. What are you going to tell him?"

Nick neared Tessa on the other side of the car.

"That I had some urgent business to take care of and had to go away. Maybe I'll say that the police have questioned me, but I won't mention Lucy." He looked at Tessa who was checking her makeup in the car mirror. "Agreed?"

Tessa put new lipstick on her lips and nodded.

Fred emerged from the side opposite where he had parked his car.

"Hey, strangers! Where are you coming from?" Fred hugged Tessa and then shook hands with Nick. "What happened to you?"

"Urgent business," Nick replied.

"You didn't leave a message for me and I couldn't get you on the phone. Happy to see that you're okay. And driving a fancy car!"

"I had a problem with my pickup, so Tessa gave me a ride."

"I don't want to intrude. I just came by to see whether you were at home. Now that I know that you're okay, I can leave."

"No, no! We were thinking of going out for a bite to eat, right Nick?"

Nick grinned. "Actually, I have a better suggestion. While don't you two go? I need to get a shower and relax a bit."

"That's a great idea! I haven't seen you much recently, Fred. Now I'll have a chance to remember the good times we had together, when we were both young and foolish." She gave Fred a captivating look and took his arm, then turned back to Nick. "I'll leave the Corvette here. Just bring it over tomorrow sometime."

A bit surprised, Fred looked at Nick. "Give me a call when we can go back to practicing."

"Oh, tomorrow afternoon will be fine, Fred. Just come on over."

Nick watched as Tessa tapped Fred on the shoulder, said something, and then threw her head back in a laugh. As Fred opened the door for her she shook her colorful mantel off and tossed it on the back seat. She took her time entering the car, moving her curves around Fred. *The female tiger is on the hunt*, Nick thought as he watched the Lexus disappear down the road.

Nick was glad to have some time for himself. He really hadn't wanted to hire a lawyer, but his position was deteriorating by the day. At the first interview the police had asked one question after another, but had let him go the following morning. Then they had come to the house and done a second search, leaving nothing unturned. When he thought their inquiry was finally over, they asked him to follow them to Port Franks and look at *The Catalina*—the boat where he had found the loot—and asked him what he had been doing there.

"Having a drink," Nick had answered.

He shrugged off all other questions. Then he had been dragged to the London Police Service and interviewed by two other officers. Just when he had thought his ordeal was over, they had come to his house one more time and taken him to the OPP Detachment in Grand Bend. He had overheard two officers discussing the charges against him; it was then that he had called Tessa and asked her to come down with some legal heavyweight. To his surprise, she knew of the famous Bruno Heisman.

A man in his sixties, Heisman was five-foot-five, bold, with a gray goatee, metal-rimmed eyeglasses, and piercing hazel eyes. He had walked into the police station with secure strides, carrying a metal briefcase that he had almost slammed on the counter. He had talked only half an hour with the chief of police before gaining Nick's immediate release.

The lawyer turned out to be good, both in the legal field and good at looking after himself: his fee was six hundred an hour. He was costly, but worthwhile. It had paid off to ask Tessa, Nick concluded, even if now it would come out that he wasn't as poor as he claimed. He had chosen the better of two evils.

Nick showered at length, dressed in jeans and a sweatshirt, and then poured himself a drink. He was about to turn on the television when the phone rang.

It was Bruno Heisman. In his guttural voice he explained the situation. The authorities didn't have a case against him, but they were trying to build one. A detective from the London Police Service had been attached for the occasion, and his investigative reputation was excellent.

"Keep in mind that that they have two corpses—Lucy Fairweather's and that of an unidentified man. They suspect a link between them, and they believe that link is you. Lucy had camped in your shed, and her body was found close to that of the dead man. Also, evidence of the dead man's presence was found on the boat—*The Catalina*, if I understood correctly—where they also found your fingerprints. They won't give up easily. The police will try to get more information out of you." The lawyer paused as if he was fatigued. "The good news is that they don't have any of your fingerprints on Lucy's purse or on any of her objects found in the shed, and there's no trace of her in your house or truck. So they'll insist on investigating your casual boat rides with people you didn't know well. They'll ask what the reasons for the rides were; what business you had with these people." The lawyer paused again. "That's all for the moment. For now we just wait for their next move. You'll receive my initial bill soon. Have a nice evening, Mr. Falcone."

☼ ☼ ☼

Thirty-nine

Gordon Stevenson drummed his fingers on the desk that the OPP in Grand Bend had temporarily assigned to him. The inquest into Lucy Fairweather's death was at a standstill. Evidence of natural death was overwhelming and her disappearance from her house gave credibility to her involvement in Charlotte Gassman's fatal injuries. Avoiding the authorities was, in Stevenson's judgment, an implicit admission of guilt. Finding her body on the sandy shores of Lake Huron raised questions, but those questions were probably going to go unanswered. Detective Stevenson twisted his dark moustache with both hands. *Time to let go.* He looked around when the door opened and Peggy O'Brian entered his office.

"What a nice surprise!" Gordon gestured toward a chair in front of him. "How come you're here?"

"Got a free day," Peggy replied. "I thought I'd pay you a visit and see how the shared investigation is going."

Gordon laughed and lowered his head.

"It's going nowhere," he whispered. "We thought we had a good subject we could squeeze, and were almost successful when the famous Bruno Heisman showed up at our door. He countermanded our efforts, at least for the time being."

"I can understand that; Heisman is hard to handle; but did you have strong evidence?"

"Unfortunately not, only circumstantial, but I'm convinced the guy knows more than he told us. Also, he plays poor—you should see how dilapidated his place is—but he could hire Heisman. That doesn't figure."

"Absolutely not." Peggy took a pencil from Gordon's desk and began flipping it between her fingers.

"So what's new with you?"

Peggy kept quiet.

"Come on, Peggy, there's something you want to get off your chest. Is it about our friend, Mr. Dalton?"

Peggy cocked her head left and right. "I saw him at the Oscar Steak House in the company of Tessa Wilson."

Gordon bolded up tight. "Compromising attitude?"

"No. He was signing the credit card bill, but that woman was twisted around him, tapping on his shoulder and touching his arm. She was smiling, laughing, and shooting languid looks at him."

Gordon laughed. "Have a heart. It was her occasion to court thirty-plus million dollars. She has to maintain an expensive house and a luxury car."

"You're no help."

"Sorry, I couldn't resist. I hope you didn't give into the temptation to follow them."

"No."

"Good. Jealousy isn't a good ingredient in a relationship."

"I was on duty until nine o'clock." She looked sheepishly at Gordon. "But after my shift I went to his house."

"And?"

"He was home. You know where he lives, right? In the first house near the entrance of the new compound. He hadn't closed the drapes so through the sheers I could see his silhouette moving around. He was alone."

Gordon kept quiet for a moment.

"Tessa Wilson is one of the few people who dared to visit his late wife. They've known each other for quite some time. I wouldn't give too much importance to an occasional get-together. Had he been interested in that woman he wouldn't have courted you. Tessa was available long before you came around."

"Hmm." She pouted. "She wore a short, tailored dress that advertised her body; she didn't have a coat, but a shiny mantle with all the colors of the rainbow. She wrapped it around her body, showing off her long legs."

"I've seen the woman, Peggy. I went to her place with Lopes when we were looking for the red Corvettes' owners; she was still in her robe. She's a striking woman, no doubt about it." He stretched his arm to stroke Peggy's hand. "But, I repeat, Fred would have already made a move if he was interested. Obviously he isn't, so don't worry. By the way, how come the two of you aren't shooting today?"

"This is the day he goes practicing with a friend of his. Somebody he used to trap shoot with when he was young."

The phone rang and Gordon snatched it up. Peggy waved him goodbye and left the station.

When she entered her apartment, Moira was very tired. After she had finished the pricing for the mall she had hoped for a couple of weeks of light work; instead Fred Dalton and Verge Bristol had agreed to take on a restructuring job out of town to fill time until the foundations for the mall could be laid out. *Work, work, work...*She tossed her little purse on the kitchen table, took a cracker from the nearby basket, and sat on her sofa. Her gaze landed on the unopened mail she had left on the side table the day before. It was normal mail; no little packages or cushioned mailers that could contain a tape. Relaxed, she opened the first one: it was a coupon book, so she selected the ones she might use and set them aside. The second piece of mail was a funding request for the handicapped; she had contributed enough to help the handicapped, namely her brother. She slid open the next envelope. Moira's heart skipped a beat: it contained a numbered sequence of black-and-white prints from her past. In the first one she was pushing her mother into the creek's raging water; in the second her mother was suspended in mid-air; in the third her mother was struggling to come ashore; in the fourth Moira was standing, impassively, as her mother disappeared under the strong current. Moira closed her eyes. If the police got hold of these pictures she would probably be arrested immediately.

The prints were taken out of context, however. Moira had run toward the creek alerted by her brother's high-pitch howling; on her way to the scene she had watched her mother beating Charlie with a big stick; when she had finally arrived Charlie's head was already under water so she had yanked her mother off Charlie and, when her mother came after her, she had shoved her into the creek. She had first helped Charlie to spit water, and then helped him to stand up. After that Moira had taken a long breath and watched her mother being swept downstream, without feeling the need to call for help.

The memory of that scene had hounded her almost every day of her life.

A strip of paper in the same envelope contained the request for money: *Two thousand dollars by next Sunday. A call will follow.*

Moira rose and helped herself to a four-ounce vodka. She sighed and took a long swallow of her drink. So somebody had come across that infamous tape. But who was he or she? Back on the sofa, she pondered the situation. *Clearly, the blackmailer couldn't make a copy of the tape, so his access to it was only temporary and partial. Evidently, this was recent.*

Everything pointed to Off Broadway. It was essential that she get the names of all the people who worked there.

Moira had just entered The Werkstein when Mary Gervasio ran to her.

"Fred wants to talk to you. Just go in." Without another word she shook Moira's white jacket off her, and gently pushed her toward Fred's office. Dumbfounded, Moira knocked at the door, which was ajar.

"You wanted to see me?"

"Come in; come in." Fred came to the door to greet her. "Take a seat, Moira."

She sat slowly.

Fred moved to the other side of his desk, took an envelope from the incoming basket, and waved it in front of her.

"This is a bonus for the extraordinary work you've done. Your efforts were instrumental in winning the big job."

Moira took the envelope.

"Also, I talked it over with Verge Bristol, and we concurred that you deserve a raise. It'll be five hundred a month, starting next month."

Moira felt a lump in her throat and fought back the tears in her eyes. Now that everything was going well, she probably would end up in jail.

"Thank you so much," she managed to mumble.

"Another thing. Mary told me more about the problems you're having with your brother. I think I can help."

Moira couldn't refrain from crying; she just nodded as a sign of acknowledgment and thanks.

Fred took a card from the main drawer of his desk. "You should contact this organization—The Safe Harbour—they can help find a group home for your brother. I know the manager, Bernard Morteson." He paused and Moira dried her tears with her sleeve. "Anything else I can do for you?"

"Oh, yes...I'd like to take a week off." For the first time she looked directly at Fred. "If it's not too much to ask."

"No problem, Moira. I intend to come back to work pretty soon." He rose and neared Moira. "Just go home and let me know how it turns out with your brother."

☆ ☆ ☆

Forty

The Star of the Night on Exeter Road was open all night. Most of the regular costumers would leave after the last show, but truck drivers would come in all night long. The food was rich with plenty of flavor, and the coffee was brewed fresh every half hour.

The bartender cleaned the countertop one more time, looking at the lady who sat alone in the farthest corner. She had come in at eleven o'clock and ordered one drink after the other, paying for each drink with plastic as it was served. At one point the owner had chosen to put a hamburger with French fries and coleslaw in front of her, hoping she would stop drinking, eat something, and clear out. She had nibbled at the food, then asked for another drink, which he hadn't provided. Her cell had rung four times, and she hadn't answered any of the calls. Now her head was on the table, her auburn hair half on the platter.

The bartender neared the woman and tapped on her shoulder.

"Lady, it's almost morning. You can't stay here any longer. Give me the number of a friend I can call."

She gave him her phone and pointed to a number.

"The name?" the owner asked.

"Tessa."

The man clicked on the number.

"Yes?" a sleepy voice answered.

"Your friend is at The Star of the Night and needs a ride."

"Who would this friend be?"

The bartender looked at the woman. "What's your name, sleepyhead?"

"Jeanette Alstein."

"It's four o'clock in the morning!" Tessa Wilson cried aloud.

"I know. Please come get her. She can't move on her own." He closed the cell and walked to the counter. He was soon back with a black coffee. "Drink it," he said to Jeanette, with authority.

Half an hour later Tessa Wilson walked into the shop, neared Jeanette, and bent over her.

"What happened?"

"I lost a thousand dollars."

"It doesn't help to get plastered. You don't get your money back; you only get into more trouble."

She took Jeanette's coat from the back of the chair and helped Jeanette slip it on. She almost dragged her out of the bar and into her Corvette.

"I don't want to go home," Jeanette whined.

Tessa turned on the engine. "And why not?"

"We're broke."

"You told me your husband makes good money, so how can you—"

"It's complicated, and it's all the fault of that woman."

"Your husband had an affair?"

"No. He and his friend Bristol used to rig the submissions and everything was going well. Then this midget of a woman who calls herself an engineer walked in; everything still went well for a while, but then the boss discovered what they'd been doing. It has to stop, he said. So Alain and I can't go to Vegas for the weekend, anymore."

Tessa put the car in motion, and Jeanette continued.

"I know that woman...Moira Johnson. She's a killer. She killed her mother."

"What are you blathering about?"

"It was in the newspaper when it happened, about ten years ago. The police knew it; they couldn't prove it, but I know she did it."

"Come on, Jeanette, you're talking nonsense."

"Am I? She's a monster, I tell you, and she plays the sweet girl with Fred. I'll bet she has something going on with him."

Tessa stopped the car. "What did you say?"

"There was a party some time ago. She was the only woman without a partner and as soon as she walked in Fred hurried to pour a drink for her. I tell you, there's something going on between them."

"What kind of party was it?"

"The company has a party every time they get a job over ten million... and this one was a *big* one." Jeanette reclined her head on the headrest.

Slowly, Tessa resumed driving. "Jeanette, I want to know everything about this woman." As Jeanette didn't answer, Tessa shook her arm. "Do you hear me?"

"Yes..."

"Jeanette?"

But Jeanette was sound asleep.

Nick looked out of the kitchen window, a mug of coffee in his hand. Outside a squirrel gathered the walnuts, still green, that had fallen from the black walnut trees. Its cheeks swollen with its harvest, it furtively dug a hole in the ground and buried its winter supply. Old leaves ripped off trees by recent rain covered the lawn almost completely; the beans, planted in the fields that once constituted the family farm, had been harvested and winter wheat had been planted. Fall had arrived and the cold Canadian winter was about to start.

Nick took a sip of coffee. *Will that lawyer be able to get me out of trouble permanently, or should I pick up my money and flee the country?* He had started to like his new status and the old house. For the first time in his life he felt the need to set roots. The phone rang, and he looked at the caller ID: it was Tessa. He had no special inclination to talk to her, but from now on he would have to address her concerns, no matter how ridiculous. He picked up the phone.

"How come you're up so early?"

"I had to rescue a friend of mine, Jeanette Alstein. I told you we go gambling together from time to time. Right?"

"Yes. Her husband works at The Werkstein."

"Right. She's also the one who talked her boss into hiring me. Anyway, she told me Fred's having an affair with that shrimp of a redhead who works for him as an engineer."

Nick was taken by surprise.

"Oh...well, I wouldn't know."

"But do you know if he has a girl?" Tessa's voice had a high pitch.

"No, I don't, and he doesn't talk much about his personal life, Tessa. He never did, even when he was young."

"Can't you follow where he goes?" When Nick didn't answer, she added. "Nick, you have to get busy. You owe me. I want to know if he's seeing Moira."

"I'll try." He paused. "By the way, how come you know that big shot, Bruno Heisman?"

Tessa hesitated. "I had a little problem with one of my aunts; the one who lived in Stratford. I often went to the Shakespeare Festival and spent the night at her place; the last time I was there she died in her sleep. The police made a big fuss. It was a ridiculous situation and the police kept asking a ton of questions." Tessa paused. "They made a big case just because her will was in my favor. So I hired Heisman and he extinguished the inquest after two meetings."

"I see." Nick wondered what the case was all about. "It's good for me that you knew him and he didn't mind coming down quickly."

Tessa laughed. "He's another guy who owes me one."

Thanksgiving had come and gone, leaving Fred with a sense of emptiness. It was the first time in his life he had spent that day by himself. With Deborah in a wheelchair the celebration had never been as cheerful as in his youth, when Charlotte dedicated hours to decorating the house and cooking a meal with all the foods reminiscent of a successful harvest. But even after Deborah's accident, Thanksgiving had been an occasion for cherishing and honoring family ties.

Ignoring the occasion had been useless. The decorations had sprung up like magic at the beginning of the week, reminding passersby of the approaching festivity, and Fred had seen them all on his way to work and back home: a couple of huge pumpkins in front of a door; a scarecrow in the middle of the lawn; corncobs, wheatears and butternut squash artfully set in a small wheelbarrow; pumpkins of any size intermixed with corn stems spread on the doormat of a house's entrance.

This year nobody had invited him for dinner, and Peggy had been unavailable, pleading an extra shift for the day and a late family reunion out of town. Fred had spent the day at home; he had hung the Norman Rockwell pictures he particularly fancied in the rec room and a mirror in the entry hall; and he had started to cut the sheets of spruce wood he would use for paneling the basement walls.

And so Thanksgiving had passed.

By the time Peggy agreed to go target shooting, Fred had repeatedly sighted his Remington, had become familiar with its snappy recoil and refined his aim at the St. Thomas Gun Club. No wonder that he had managed to hit the three targets, each set at a different distance, eighty per cent of the time. Peggy had fired away, hardly talking to him or giving him any suggestions.

"Supper together?" Fred asked, as Peggy kept practicing in spite of darkness.

"Maybe."

"What do you mean maybe? I'm hungry." He folded his rifle in its case, and closed it. "I'm going to sit on the bench."

Finally Peggy walked to the targets and lifted off the target sheets. She folded them under her arm and joined Fred.

"I'm hungry, too," she said, and deposited her Beretta in its case.

The trip to The Keg on Wellington South was a silent one. Once they arrived Fred ordered a beer and Peggy a glass of grapefruit juice. After the waiter left with their orders of prime ribs, Fred looked at Peggy.

"What's wrong?" he asked.

"Nothing," Peggy murmured, and stared at the table.

"Come on, you can do better than that. Tell me what's bothering you." He lightly tapped on her hand.

"Would you tell me the truth?"

Fred laughed. "It depends on whether it's the police officer or the woman who's asking."

"You mean you'd lie to the police?"

"Of course not. I just wouldn't talk. Keep quiet, that's all. So is the officer inquiring?"

"No."

"Then fire away."

"I saw you having dinner with a woman. She was all over you."

Fred withdrew his arm. "Oh, that! I went to see Nick, my old friend, at his farm, and Tessa, a girl I chummed around with when I was young, was there. First, the three of us were going out for supper, then my friend

Nick said he preferred to stay home." He shrugged. "So I was trapped; I took her out."

"She's very sexy."

"Yes, she is."

"Would you go out with her again?"

"Not if I can avoid it without being impolite. She was my late wife's closest friend." He reached to stroke Peggy's hand. "No need to be jealous; I don't have any interest in her."

"And you have an interest in me?" Peggy opened her eyes like a child in search of reassurance.

"Not anymore. My instructor doesn't talk to me."

"I mean...you know what I mean."

"No. Tell me."

"Why do you invite me out?"

Fred withdrew his hand and tapped his lips with his index finger. "Let me think. I like to have company when I eat."

"Is that all?"

"Oh, no. I also like to have a friend at Headquarters, in case I get a speeding ticket."

A small smile cracked on Peggy's face. "Anything else?"

"I can't think of any other reasons at the moment. I'm too hungry to think. But by the time I take you to my place something else will probably pop into my mind."

Peggy gave him an open, big smile. "You like to tease me."

"That isn't the only thing I like to do."

✵ ✵ ✵

Forty-one

Two days of playing sleuth had finally paid off. Moira had found out that the secretary at Off Broadway was Jeanette Alstein. As such, she had access to the infamous tape. But how had Jeanette recognized her? After all, the shop was in charge of evaluating Ryan Costello's work; that should not involve the secretary.

She must have had some prior information. She knew something that made her dip into a pile of tapes, search for a special one, insert it into the computerized converter and make prints out of it.

Would Jeanette expose me if I don't pay? Definitely, yes. After all, she's a gambler and everybody knows she makes big bets. She probably needs money.

Moira decide to start following her and discover how she spent her free time.

The phone rang and Moira answered it. It was her brother.

"You promised you'd take me to McDonald's for a Big Mac," Charlie grumbled.

Moira had forgotten about it. "I'll be there in twenty minutes." She closed her cell.

Charlie—all her troubles started with her brother. She remembered how much she had wanted a sibling to play with and how happy she was when baby Charlie was born. She'd had to wait three years until he was finally walking and trying to catch a ball. Soon, it became apparent that the kid was slow, but that didn't bother her, as he always smiled and was eager to please her. Then her father had left, and her mother no longer had an adult to pick a fight with, so she had turned against her kids. She couldn't accept the doctor's verdict: that the learning curve for Charlie's brain was only slightly pointing upward.

Moira sighed at the memories, then gathered her purse and descended to the underground garage to get her car. She should concentrate on the driving and forget all the pain that she and her brother had suffered in their childhood.

After lunch at McDonald's, Moira took Charlie to the group home to meet with the director. It was a brief meeting that left the three of them satisfied. There would be a vacancy in three weeks, and Charlie seemed enthusiastic to go live with other young folks. When he had seen people playing basketball in the courtyard Moira had a hard time convincing him that he had to return to the Men's Mission and stay there a little longer. She finally managed to get him in the car with the promise to take him out for supper before the week was over.

With the most imminent chores dispatched, Moira returned home to ponder her predicament. She knew who the blackmailer was, but did that information help her any? Would it be a one-time payment or would she demand money on a regular basis? Where could she get help? Her cell rang and Moira looked at the little screen, hoping to recognize the number. It was unknown. With shaky hands she answered. A guttural voice asked her to listen carefully to the instructions for the drop-off. The sum requested was now three thousand dollars.

Monitoring Jeanette Alstein's movements at night might provide useful informa-tion, Moira thought as she stationed herself a hundred meters away from the Alstein home. It was past 9:00 p.m., and Moira was ready to call it quits when the garage door opened and a car took off at a sustained speed. Moira followed it and moved close behind it as the car passed the intersection at a green light. The driver was a woman, and she assumed it had to be Jeanette. Only one gambling house existed in London, and Jeanette was not driving toward the Western Fairs Raceway; instead she turned on Oxford Street and soon stopped in front of a bar. Moira parked her car in a neighboring street and approached the site on foot. The dark windows and the discreet illumination didn't allow her to look inside. She regretted not wearing her dark wig; she thought it might not be wise to enter the bar, so she returned to her car.

The following night Jeanette followed the same route, and entered the same bar.

Moira followed her again, this time wearing shoes with spiky heels, a long gown, her black wig, and plenty of necklaces that hung around her neck and over a black shawl. She didn't hesitate to enter, and sat on a stool at the counter. A big mirror carrying the insignia of the Molson Canadian Brewery allowed her to look at the table where Jeanette and another woman sat. She ordered a beer and sipped it slowly, avoiding conversing with the men who had come to sit near her. *So Jeanette has a friend*, she thought. *It will be interesting to see what happens next.* She paid for her drink, walked outside, slipped into her Hyundai, and then patiently waited until Jeanette came out of the bar, shook hands with the other woman, and walked toward her car.

It was after midnight when Jeanette arrived home. The snooping hadn't done much to improve Moira's knowledge about her presumed blackmailer; so far she hadn't learned anything that could help her avoid depositing the payoff money Sunday night in Victoria Park. Tomorrow she would follow Jeanette one more time, and then decide what to do.

Flattened against the Kiwanis Memorial Monument, Moira kept up her surveillance. At nine o'clock, as instructed, she had placed the black garbage bag near the biggest cannon, a relic from one of the many battles the British Empire had successfully fought. It was bitterly cold; even her coat, which covered her down to her ankles, didn't manage to keep her warm. She repeatedly bent her fingers, as they were getting numb. Those were the only movements she allowed herself to make.

The sound of two lovers laughing and talking reached her from nearby Richmond Street; a car's horn sounded as the car crossed the intersection with Central; the bell of the nearby church tolled nine thirty. By now Moira was sure that the blackmailer was Jeanette, as she had witnessed the little accident Jeanette had last night. After all, she had been part of it, even if involuntarily. She would wait another few minutes—just to be sure her husband wouldn't collect the bag, which, of course, was empty. All of a sudden the wind picked up, and she smelled a strong odor; within a few seconds she knew the distasteful truth: a skunk lurked in the vicinity and was approaching. Suspiciously, she looked around, and in the dim light spread by the far-away light fixture she saw a big white stripe swaying sideways at her feet.

Moira couldn't take it any longer. She leaped away, and in doing so she provoked the animal's prompt defense. Its long spraying range centered the back of her coat.

Moira was still laboring in the night hours, trying to get the smell not only out of her clothes, but out of the apartment. She had heard of the awful smell of a skunk's spray, but always thought the stories were exaggerated. She'd been wrong.

Washing and washing again didn't help, so she waited until the drugstore where she usually shopped opened. Ignoring the looks of the people she met, she strode to the pharmacy's counter and explained her predicament. The pharmacist didn't know much about the problem either, but he would go on the Internet and find the proper remedy. He disappeared through the backdoor, and returned half an hour later.

"Got a recipe for the treatment," he said with satisfaction. "Mix three cups of three-percent hydrogen peroxide, one quarter cup of baking soda and one teaspoon of liquid soap."

"Great." Moira was relieved. She was already moving away from the counter when the pharmacist shouted, "You may have to repeat the treatment."

"How many times?" Moira asked, disheartened.

"Until the smell disappears."

Oh, that was good news! Moira bought the hydrogen peroxide and hurried back to her apartment. She cleaned and cleaned until the awful smell disappeared. It was late morning when she finally slipped into bed.

Nick Falcone had two urgent matters to deal with: one, he had to call Fred and get him to open up on his private life; two, he had to contact Charlie and see if he could exchange a few more hundreds. Fred answered right away; the season for target shooting was over, unfortunately, but he was thinking they could work together at some projects, one day a week. Fred had the paneling of his basement in mind, and knew that Nick could use his help remodeling his old kitchen. Tuesday was agreed upon, the same day they had previously reserved for shooting. If a nice day came along, they could still practice for a couple of hours, Fred had added.

Nick accepted with enthusiasm, since spending a full day together would give him plenty of time to find out a bit about Fred's private life. Happy about his little accomplishment, Nick walked outside and began clearing the yard of old branches and leaves. Around four o'clock he drove into London to the Fair, hoping to see Charlie come out at the end of his shift. He waited until dark, but he didn't see the young man. The place was getting busy, and Nick thought he'd be safe buying a couple of souvenirs and having a bite to eat, each at a different place. In doing so he could exchange three of his hot bills. He was ready to return home when his cell vibrated. It was Tessa. She was stressed out, and need some company. Nick complied and drove to her house.

The door was unlocked; Nick let himself in. Tessa sat in a corner of the black leather sofa, still in her coat, her hair in disarray. She held a mug with both hands.

Nick knelt close to her. "What happened?"

"I just got back from the hospital. I told you about Jeanette, right?"

"Yes. Is she hurt?"

Tessa nodded and deposited the mug on the coffee table. "An accident...a dislocated shoulder and bruises on her face."

"Sorry." Nick looked inside the mug; it was empty. "Would you like a refill?"

"Yes. I'm very cold."

Nick walked to the kitchen and came back with two coffees. He handed one to Tessa and sipped on his own as he sat close to her. "Do you know what happened?"

"Not really. She fell, or she was pushed, or hit. I couldn't get a straight answer." Tessa took a long swallow of her coffee. "We fought last night. When I arrived at the bar where she wanted to meet, she was plastered, so I told her off. In her condition she couldn't give me any useful information, and she was endangering herself."

"What kind of useful information did you expect?"

"Jeanette grew up in Barrie, and she claimed she'd heard of Moira Johnson. At one point she was suspected of killing her mother by pushing her into a river."

"Was she ever charged?"

"No. For some time the police questioned a boy who apparently had filmed the murder, but the tape never surfaced. Jeanette claimed she had found it."

"That sounds strange."

"Yes. I don't think she's very stable. I told her I wasn't interested in anything else she had to say. She became upset, and I left."

Nick stroked her shoulder. "Have you had supper?" Tessa shook her head. "Let me cook something for you."

"Just a bowl of soup."

"Fine. I'll call you when it's ready."

Forty-two

Fred Dalton was back in his office, looking at the last two months' earnings. The company was doing great; a glance at the statistics that he received monthly from the Ontario General Contractors Association showed that The Werkstein did particularly well compared to others of the same size. The leave he had taken from his work had given him time to settle his sister's affairs and set his life on a new course. All taken into consideration, he realized how much the company had become an intrinsic part of his life. It had given him an extremely good living at any level of employment, had given him a great sense of achievement when he had become the major player, and constituted a challenge that made him feel alive. Moreover, the well-being of twenty full-time employees and of many part-time or seasonal workers depended on the existence of The Werkstein. He was ready to return to work—though maybe for fewer hours than before, as he wanted to spend time with his friends, and hopefully with a companion. He would call a meeting and determine how to redistribute the responsibilities of running the company.

Two hours later Mary Gervasio, Verge Bristol, Alain Alstein, and Moira Johnson gathered in the medium-size conference room. Single tables were set next to each other to form a long table; framed photographs of the major construction projects The Werkstein had completed, each tagged with the project's name and year, covered the largest wall. Opposite was a large window; on another wall hung the portrait of Werner Gassman, the founder of the company.

Verge had unfolded the screen at the end of the room, in case Fred had a formal Power-Point presentation in store, and Mary had put bottles of mineral water on the table. Soon after Fred appeared, everybody took a seat.

Mary sat close to Fred, a pen and a pad in her hands, ready to transcribe the minutes.

"This is an informal meeting," Fred said, and put a hand on Mary's arm to abstain her from taking the minutes. "First of all I'd like to hear what all of you have to say, how you view the company at this stage of growth, and what changes could be beneficial."

Alain Alstein was the first to speak. "I'd like to go part-time. My wife had an accident last week and she's still in the hospital." He lowered his gaze to the table. "She's addicted to gambling, and when that doesn't turn out to be successful, she drinks." He sighed. "I put a lot of effort into earning more and more money to pay for her problem, but maybe what she needs is more company...more attention from me. More care, I believe."

"Sorry to hear about your wife, Alain." Fred paused. "What kind of accident did she have?"

"She wasn't too steady on her legs when she came out of the bar; she tripped over the curb and fell on the road. It isn't clear whether a car was also involved. She has several contusions, but nothing's broken."

"Will she have to stay long in the hospital?" Fred asked.

"One more day, but she'll have to take it easy once she's home."

"I can see that you want some free time. Granted."

"I appreciate it."

"Your request comes at a critical moment, since we're involved in a big project, but we can take care of the situation. I was already going to propose we hire another engineer and an extra foreman, so now that becomes a must." Fred turned and looked at Verge. "Would you like to remain in charge of the office when I'm away?"

"Yes. It was hard at the beginning, but now that I've got the hang of it, it takes me less time to get things done."

Fred looked again at the others. "Moira? Moira?" he repeated as Moira didn't seem to be listening. "Anything you want to say?"

Moira raised her eyes toward Fred. "If we get another big job like the mall, it'd be nice to be able to count on an additional member. Somebody junior but capable of taking in the bid and adding the last prices on the fly." She paused. "We can't use our cells because of fear of a breach in security. We have to be close to the place where the bid has to be handed in and, at the same time, find a land-line phone to check on the latest price updates. That part takes a lot of time."

"I can see. We should look into getting a secure cell or a satellite phone for that specific task. I'll do that." He clicked on his iPhone and texted a note. He looked at each member in turn. "So we agree about hiring two extra members?" They all nodded, and Fred went on. "Verge, can you start advertising the positions?"

"Sure. Times are tough; we'll have no problem getting a kid out of a good school and hiring an experienced person to supervise the jobs." Verge stopped and then asked, "Are you going to go public? The company has reached a fair size."

Fred answered quickly. "The answer to that is no. I'm not ready to open The Werkstein's stock up to trade in the stock market. There's only one reason to sell shares, and that's to raise capital. But I don't need to go public to raise capital: I can use my own money. So there's no reason to give up any control of the company by selling shares." Nobody commented, so Fred asked, "Anything else any of you want to say?" When he got no answer, he continued. "I'd like to handle the company's profits in a different way; to distribute a part of these to the employees on a yearly basis. I haven't figured out, yet, how to do it, but this practice has been used successfully elsewhere. I have to do a bit of research." He turned to Mary Gervasio. "Is the amount of work still reasonable for you, Mary?"

She shrugged. "It's fine, since I like to be busy. I do secretarial work for six people—will be seven after the hiring—the others are in the field. For these, all I have to do is to order some special equipment or check up on the delivery dates. As a rule, our accountant takes care of all purchases."

Fred looked around to see if anybody else wanted to speak.

"Well, I'm always available if any of you has a problem. Just give me a call if I'm not at the office." Fred rose. "Alain, maybe we can talk about your reduced hours. Come to my office."

Outside the building Fred found Moira was waiting for him, a big plastic bag hanging on her shoulder.

"What are you doing out here in the cold?" he asked her.

"I was on my way, when I remembered that I forgot to thank you for talking to the group home about my brother." Together they walked toward the entrance of the parking lot. "Charlie got all excited when he saw younger people playing in the yard and in the game room. The director told me they'd have a place in a few weeks, but yesterday she called and said Charlie could come in right away. I got new clothes for him. I'm going to pick him up right now."

"I'm glad I could be useful." He looked around. "Don't you have your car today?"

Moira shook her head. "Had to take it into the shop. It'll be ready the day after tomorrow. I'll catch a bus."

Fred lifted Moira's bag off her shoulder, took her arm, and led her toward his car.

"Let me give you a ride. Where's your brother staying at the moment?"

"The Men's Mission on York Street."

Fifteen minutes later Moira stepped out of Fred's Lexus.

"I'll grab a cab to go to the group home, Fred. It'll take awhile to gather Charlie's stuff and be sure he gets a good shower."

Fred was out of the car carrying Moira's garbage bag.

"Are you sure?"

"Yes, but thank you so much."

Fred accompanied Moira to the door, patted her shoulder, and handed her the bag.

"Good luck," he said. He waited to walk to his car until she disappeared beyond the side door. It was then that he bumped into Nick Falcone.

"What are you doing here?" Fred asked without concealing his surprise.

"I was going to ask you the same question." Nick laughed. "Are you going broke?"

"Not for a while. I just took Moira to see her brother. She had to take her car to the garage. Do you have time for a drink? I know of a bar not far from here, where they make a fantastic pumpkin Martini, suitable for a fall day like this."

"Why not? The person I was looking for is busy, so I'm free. I'll follow you."

"I can't see a thing," Nick complained as he bumped into a table at The Lampara, the bar in the east of London famous for its exotic cocktails. Intermittent lights flashed here and there, making it difficult for the eyes to adjust. A soft beat resounded from the back.

"It's part of the ambiance." Fred sat on a stool at the counter.

Nick took a place close to him as Fred talked to the bartender.

"Do you come here often?" Nick asked.

"Not anymore. I used to when Deborah was alive; it's very close to where I lived then."

"They advertise a show." Nick squinted to read the poster that hung on one of the walls.

"Yes, but it's late at night."

"Nice show?"

"I wouldn't know. I stopped here on my way home, so too early for it."

"You must have lived like a monk."

"More or less."

Their drinks arrived, and they both sipped.

"Nice flavor," Nick said. "What's in it?"

"I don't know exactly...some vanilla vodka and pumpkin schnapps for sure."

Nick sucked on the cinnamon stick that came with the cocktail. "Are we staying for the show?"

"Oh no, not me. I have work to do at the house."

"You don't have to live like a monk, anymore."

"But I don't."

"Have a girl?"

Fred laughed. "Nick, you're too curious. First you tried to fix me up with Tessa, and now this question. Are you in the business of playing matchmaker?"

"Just trying to be useful," Nick said, and quietly finished his Martini.

On his way home Nick tried to extract the truth out of Fred's elusive answers. If he was having an affair with Moira, he was careful in advertising his relationship; the scene he had witnessed at the mission, in fact, didn't reveal any feelings. When they worked together in their spare time Fred talked mostly about sports: target shooting and hockey. He emphasized how anxious he was for the return of the warm season, when he would be able to practice boogie boarding and body surfing. He didn't seem interested in much else, and he hardly mentioned any outings to a theatre or other social event. He had returned to work four days a week, and Nick wondered what he planned to do in the remaining three. So far he had little to report to Tessa, and that would not please her.

He parked his pickup in the carport. On his way into the house he noticed that his mailbox was overflowing with papers. He grabbed all the mail, entered the house, and tossed his load onto the low table and his coat onto the sofa. He made himself an instant coffee and turned on the television. He slouched on the sofa and began sifting through the pile of mail. Most was advertising; he threw that to the floor. Then he found a letter from his lawyer. The first page was an invoice for three thousand four hundred dollars; the next page described his services; the last page contained a brief legal advice: *Be available to answer any questions the police may throw at you, insisting on the answers you had previously given. Clearly the police have doubts about the veracity of your story, but doubts don't constitute proof.*

Nick sighed and looked again at the invoice. It was a lot of money, but it was a cheap exit from his two major predicaments: the finding of Lucy's belongings in his shack and his fingerprints on *The Catalina*.

✽ ✽ ✽

Forty-three

Sipping on a gin and orange juice, Moira relaxed, knowing she didn't have to worry about Charlie anymore. Her brother had become strangely daring, at times even resentful, because she hadn't let him stay with her. She felt relieved that Charlie now had a place he could call home. The last time she had spoken with the director of Charlie's group home, she mentioned that a certain Sam might come around and try to take Charlie for a ride and, potentially, cause trouble for Charlie. The director, Ms. Sandra Tremonti, assured her that she would keep an eye on Charlie's visitors. Moira was comforted by the thought that Sam didn't know Charlie's new location, and that it would take him some time to find it.

One problem solved, she thought, with some relief. Jeanette's accident had temporarily stalled the blackmailing. A week ago she had hidden in Victoria Park and waited to see who would pick up the black garbage bag that she had deposited near the commemorative artillery. She had expected that nobody would show up, and no one did in the half hour she had been there. Because the blackmailer hadn't voiced any complains about the lack of money in the bag, and hadn't contacted her anymore, Moira was sure that Jeanette Alstein was the blackmailer.

Things were falling into place. She only needed to eliminate that terrible tape. Once she got her Hyundai back she would put her plan into action.

The following day she left the office early, and took a cab to the garage. She paid the bill for the new side mirror, filled the tank with gas, and left. At home she changed, and hid her hair under a gray wig. With a baseball cap, boots twice the size of her feet, and a checkered coat, she could be mistaken for a squat, rough man.

She drove to the Off Broadway shop and introduced herself as having been sent by Ryan Costello from Barrie. Chewing tobacco, Moira tried to keep her voice as low as she could, and her tone firm and resolute. She was to take back one of the boxes with Ryan's photography records.

Michael Sullivan was in the office busy with a client and asked his father, Jacob, to take care of the problem. Jacob hesitated at first, asked again for an explanation, and Moira gave it to him.

"There's a commemoration of the town's history. Ryan needs the old tapes to mount a small show. He only needs them for a week, but he needs them now."

Jacob seemed confused and went back to talk to his son. When he returned he grumbled about how busy the office was, with one employee away on sick leave. Still grumbling, he got a sheet for Moira to sign, and pointed to the box with Ryan Costello's old tapes.

Pounding on the floor with her man's boots, Moira left Off Broadway with the box that, she hoped, contained the tape that incriminated her. She shoved it in the back seat of her car and drove away.

When she arrived home Moira was drowning in perspiration. Carrying the heavy box, compounded with the anxiety she had experienced during the stunt had made her nauseated. She kicked off her boots, the ball cap, and the wig and knelt beside the box. The label, pasted on one side of each tape, carried a date, so she nervously tossed the ones she was not interested in onto the floor. Her movements became more and more frantic as she dug deeper into the container.

In no time she was confronted with the bottom of an empty box.

She took off her coat, sat on the kitchen floor, and went through the tapes carefully, examining them one by one. The incriminating tape was nowhere to be seen.

She felt sick to her stomach. Overwhelmed with rage she repeatedly kicked the empty box. Soon despair replaced anger. She was trapped. Somebody had the tape, and she couldn't see any reason that somebody would hold onto it except with the intent to harm her.

Nick was puzzled by Tessa's behavior. For the last few days she had become obsessed with questions about Fred's life and behavior. He was seeing Fred either at Fred's or his own house to do carpentry work, but he had no idea how Fred spent the rest of his free time. Tonight, to break the impasse, Nick had invited Tessa for supper and then to a play at the Talbot Theatre. A parody of *The Taming of the Shrew* in a modern setting had been quoted in the local newspaper as a delight to the audience.

The show over, they walked to Nick's pickup truck in silence. The first snowfall had arrived, making the sidewalk and parking lot slippery. Tessa, wearing boots with high heels, leaned on Nick's arm for stability.

"Are you going to invite me for a nightcap?" Nick asked, as he put his vehicle in gear.

"I don't think you deserve any," she replied, and yawned.

"Come on, Tessa, don't be so hard on me."

"Nick, let's face it; you have nothing to offer me. You're broke, you can't get me close to Fred, and you can't even tell me if he's seeing that redhead after hours." She paused. "I need to get married; otherwise I'll be broke in two years."

Nick drove in silence until they arrived at Tessa's house. He helped her out of the truck and accompanied her to the door.

"You said you had a part-time job. What happened to it?"

"It's temporary. They had a huge amount of tapes to be stored on DVDs. The work will be over in a month or so." She entered her house and kept the door open. "Well, come in...just for one drink."

Tessa shook her mantel off, turned on the gas fireplace, and sat on the chair close to the fire.

"Make me a rum and Coke," she said, pouting.

The flames cast uneven light in the sitting room; the chiaroscuro created special effects on Tessa's striped dress. The black vertical stripes made a sharp contrast with the red ones, which shone vividly; it looked as if her body had been cut into bloody slices.

Nick made the drink, handed the glass to Tessa, and made one for himself.

"I'm sorry to disappoint you; it just that the only time I saw Fred with Moira was when he gave her a ride to the place where her brother lived. That was all. Then the two of us went to have a drink." He sat close to Tessa and stretched his hand to caress her leg.

Tessa didn't move; she just sipped her drink, staring into the distance. "The money I got from Walter—my fucking ex—is almost gone, and the inheritance I got from my aunt will only carry me another couple of years." She moved her leg away from Nick. "I'm not getting any younger, Nick; I have to get a new husband while I still look great." She turned to face him. "Can't you follow Fred or something?"

Nick took his time to reply. "Tessa, even if we get to know all Fred's moves, I can't create an occasion for you to be with him. He and I do carpentry work at each of our houses in turn. We go target shooting when the time allows it. You don't do either."

"But there must be a way I can see him, have an occasion to talk to him...When I think about that shrimp of a woman seeing him every day I get mad, so mad you can't believe! I wouldn't need too many occasions to...to get him to like me. I went out with him when we were young. He was fond of me."

The conversation was going nowhere, so Nick changed the subject.

"I got Bruno Heisman's bill. Thirty-four hundred dollars; the man is expensive." He finished his drink and set his glass on the low marble table. "How did you get to know him?"

"An interlude in Saint Lucia. He'd just divorced his second wife."

Nick emitted a soft laugh. "How come you let him go? He makes a pile of money."

"I didn't know who he was; I just saw a little man in need of company. I was starved for a bit of attention. He pledged his undivided love if I had sex with him. So I did, more out of boredom than anything else. He never said a word about his job." Tessa sighed, audibly.

"When did you find out?"

"Three months after I came back from my trip. By that time he had remarried."

"I see. Was he the one who swiftly settled the trouble you had with your aunt's will?"

"Yes. He's the one."

Nick rose.

"Thank you for the drink. If I get a brainstorm about Fred, and his whereabouts I'll let you know."

Finally, Tessa could visit Jeanette Alstein, still in the hospital. Pneumonia had set in, and nobody had been allowed to see her until the fever had completely disappeared. Today she was in a semi-sitting position in her bed, two pillows behind her head, her arms on top of the blue sheets and blanket, a cast on her right shoulder. In the penumbra of the hospital, petite Jeanette looked like a ghost of herself, her eyes deprived of sparkle, the white bandage on her forehead accenting her pallor.

Tessa dragged a chair close to the bed and sat on it.

"How is the sickie doing?" she asked in the most cheerful tone she could muster.

"Not too good."

Tessa took her hand and shook it. "Come on, come on...you're going to be out of here in a couple of days."

Tears raked Jeanette's face, and she didn't make any effort to dry them.

"I'll have to have counseling, they told me." At last she turned to face Tessa. "No more going to the Fair, and no more going to bars in the evenings."

Tessa petted her hand. "You still have your work; they like you there. They tried to get me to fill in for you, but I couldn't do much. So cheer up." Jeanette didn't react to her words, so Tessa continued. "Are you going to get some compensation because of the accident?"

"No. The car didn't stop, and there was a witness, the owner of the bar, who said that I caused it."

"*You* caused a car to hit you on the road?"

"I don't remember much, except that I was walking home and I lost my balance. The bar owner said that I stepped off the curb and swung my bag outward. The oncoming car put the headlights on and avoided me but the car's left mirror hit my purse." She paused as if she was extremely fatigued. "My purse had shoulder straps, so I was twisted around and I fell. My shoulder took most of the impact." She cried again. "It's my right arm, so I won't be able to type for a while. I can do other jobs, but at the shop I'm the only one who does secretarial work. And I can't drive."

"The driving is no problem. I can pick you up, since Off Broadway asked me to come in everyday for the time being; they're overloaded. By the time they don't need me anymore, you'll be in great shape." Tessa clutched Jeanette's hand. "Spirits up!"

"Easy to say...Alain took time off work because of my accident and now he's only going part-time. We still have a big mortgage on the house. I'm worried."

Tessa let go of Jeanette's hand. "All you have to think about is getting better. Alain knows what he's doing. What he chose to do may be the best for both of you."

Jeanette stretched to get some water. "It's all the fault of that terrible red-haired bitch. Things started to go bad since she joined the company."

Tessa's ears pricked with interest. "What do you mean?"

"Don't make me talk about Moira Johnson. If I could, I'd strangle her. She plays the professional, perfect employee, but I think she played up to Fred. Alain is sure that she spied on him and other fellows, and I think she's been having an affair with Fred." Jeanette coughed and drank more water. "Even before Fred's wife died."

"Oh, tell me! Tell me!"

Jeanette lowered the headrest. "Another time, Tessa. I'm too tired now." Jeanette closed her eyes and fell asleep.

Forty-four

It was after hours when Gordon Stevenson paid an unexpected visit to the London Police Service. Peggy O'Brian saw him walking in the corridor and approached him.

"How's the investigation going?" she asked, keeping her voice down. Her coat parted in the middle, showing a pair of tailored black pants and a shiny top; clearly she was ready for an evening out.

Gordon laughed quietly. "Not too good. We spent an enormous amount of time investigating and interrogating the suspects—pardon me—the persons of interest. It's quite evident that everybody lies, but the lies, all together, are close to a scenario that might have happened. But there's no way we can contest their fabrications without solid evidence." Stevenson sighed. "And we don't have *any* evidence, as a matter of fact."

"That bad, eh?"

Stevenson nodded. "The key man, a one Mr. Falcone, has a super defense layer. Falcone hides behind him, so there's no point bringing him in and asking him questions. Falcone didn't deny that he may have been aboard *The Catalina,* among many other pleasure boats in that circuit along the coast of Lake Huron. This fits his life style: he's a playboy." Stevenson saluted a fellow officer who was walking by and then resumed talking. "Lucy Fairweather's death, in view of no other emerging factors, has been declared due to natural causes. Falcone may have removed the body; however, Falcone's statement that he didn't know she was hiding in the shack, corroborated by the absolute lack of his fingerprints on any of her personal effects, seems to clear him." He stopped. "What I told you is what we put in the official report."

"What about the owner of the boat?"

"Oscar Clark? He was fined for minor violations to the marine code. Nobody claimed the corpse abandoned on the shore, so it was buried at the municipality's expense. There was strong evidence of a massive stroke, so no need to go any further. Another death from natural causes."

"Well, at least your time in Grand Bend was pleasant, I hope."

"Yes, it was. Nice colleagues to work with and a beautiful town." He paused. "It was also a break from my thinking about my wife being away indefinitely." He looked at Peggy. "Now, what about you?" He glanced at her long dark pants and shiny top. "What about your romance with our rich friend?"

"We went out a couple of times." As Stevenson clearly expected more, she added, "Once to a hockey game in Toronto, and once to a shooting event."

"That's all?"

"More or less. Oh, we went shopping together for a drawing-room suite."

"Who chose it?"

"The manager knew Fred and came to talk to him, so I wandered in the showroom by myself and listed a few sets that would go well in his big room."

"And he agreed to get one of those?"

"Yes."

"Pretty engaging, if you ask me. Do you have reservations about your relationship with him?"

"He's a man difficult to...to assess? He hardly ever answers directly; he likes to joke. I don't know what he really thinks."

"I noticed that, too, when I interviewed him those couple of times."

"The only thing I found out, indirectly, is that he'd like to have a family." Peggy glanced at her big wristwatch. "I have to go, or I'll be late."

Stevenson's phone rang. "I wish you the best, Peggy," he called out, before opening his cell.

Led Zeppelin's *Stairway to Heaven* was playing when the passenger door opened and Peggy slipped into the seat.

"Sorry I'm a bit late. How do I look?"

Fred looked her over and grinned. "Not bad. Your eyes are too blue and your hair is too blond; otherwise you're fine." He pecked her on her cheek and began driving.

"I mean...you know what I mean. I've never been to a board meeting."

"Relax. The chairperson of Welcome Among Us, Elisabeth Ross, is a kind old lady; she wants new blood in the organization, and I couldn't refuse to be part of it, considering that she and Charlotte were close friends. Maybe you'd like to have a role in it, too, if you like the idea and have time. You could contribute much more than I ever could. I know about bricks and concrete, but I know nothing about immigrants."

"I'd like that. It's just that—" She took a deep breath. "Since I started going out with you, I don't have a life of my own anymore."

"But we hardly see each other twice a week, and sometimes not even once in a week!"

"That's the problem. Even when I don't see you, I'm thinking of you," she whispered.

Fred threw his head back and laughed. "That's good, eh?"

"Laugh, laugh! You enjoy the power you have over me. Right?"

"Immensely." He stopped the car. "We're here."

The meeting at Welcome Among Us was brief and to the point. The non-profit organization, established by the late Werner Gassman, an immigrant himself, had seen its work double in the last few years, and Elisabeth Ross had to resort to the Food Bank to provide families without income with a weekly supply of groceries.

Fred listened attentively and made only a few remarks. Near the end, the chairperson asked Peggy whether she would be interested in becoming an active member, and Peggy, to Fred's surprise, had accepted with enthusiasm.

Back in the car, Fred asked, "Are you sure you want to do it?"

"Yes. They need more help in the winter, and this is the time I don't do much target shooting." She held her head high. "Besides, it'll help me not think so much about you."

"I can't win all the time. Elisabeth was delighted to have you aboard." He drove for a stretch and then asked, "Where to now?"

"I'd like to try those new fancy chairs of yours. See if they're comfortable."

"That's a great idea. We can also check the new security system. I didn't want one, but it was the fastest way to get rid of the salesman. He was trying to convince me to sell that feature in all our new houses, and to convince me he installed it in my house free for a full year."

"Lucky you."

"I hope I never need it."

Tim Hortons was very busy, but Tessa and Jeanette had been able to find a table for two away from the main passage. Gray roots were visible in Jeanette's hair, in strong contrast with her longer auburn hair. She wore no lipstick and no polish on her nails. As a splint held her right arm in a fixed position, she made some awkward movements to get some newspaper clippings out of her purse. She pushed her empty coffee cup out of the way and put the sheets in front of Tessa.

"See what I mean? There was a lengthy investigation of the death of Moira's mother; allegations she often fought with her mother and that, in the end, she killed her by pushing her into the river. Alain and I were living in Barrie at the time. I followed the story."

Tessa examined the newspaper clips carefully. When she was finished with the last one, she said, "Nothing came up at the inquest?"

"No, they never got hold of the tape that'd prove her guilt."

Tessa returned the clips to Jeanette. "Maybe there wasn't one."

Jeanette shook her head. "I spoke with a poacher, back then. He'd been out in the woods getting some rabbit or a wild turkey out of season. He saw both Moira and her mother near the creek, and he saw a kid who took pictures in the neighborhood. The kid was far away, but he had a zoom lens on his camcorder. Now the big coup!" She paused as to give emphasis to what was coming next. "I got hold of that tape long enough to make these prints."

Jeanette extracted four sheets from her purse. In the first one a young, short woman was pushing an older woman into a river; in the second the older woman was suspended in mid-air, her long gray hair caught in the wind; in the third the older woman was in the river, making convulsive movements; and in the fourth the younger woman was standing still, her back to the camera.

Tessa drummed her fingers on the table. "Where is the tape? These prints prove little, if anything."

"I left it on the windowsill of the main office at Off Broadway. I had just used it, when Mr. Sullivan called me and sent me out on an urgent errand." She stopped and sighed. "That night I had the accident and never went back to the office."

"We have to get that tape," Tessa said with authority. "And you're sure that Fred and Moira are having an affair?"

"Well...indirectly, yes." She looked straight into Tessa's eyes. "Swear you won't repeat what I'm going to tell you to *anybody*."

Tessa raised her right hand. "I do."

"Alain and Verge, together, had this little thing going that made us a pile of money, to use the subs we knew instead of those in the contract. When we found out Moira was reporting to Fred, Alain offered her a piece of the action. She refused."

"Hmm...I start to see your point."

"Exactly. She's determined to please Fred. What other reason would she have to neglect a five-grand handout? Because she's aiming higher. There's something going on between them, I tell you. Sex and money are traded there."

People walked by and stood close to them, so the two friends suspended their conversation.

Tessa rose resolutely and murmured, "We have to find that tape."

☆ ☆ ☆

Forty-five

Nick had just gone past the last bend when he spotted a car parked on his front lawn. He glanced at his wristwatch; he didn't think he was late. He was expecting a crew to come work on the roof, but he didn't figure they would come with a car. As he drove nearer, two men, dressed in dark suits, stepped out of the car. Immediately, Nick smelled trouble. Too late to turn around, he kept driving and parked his vehicle in the carport. Slowly, he took his coat from the backseat and got out. He walked to the back of his pickup and unloaded the trimmer he had just bought.

The two men approached him.

"I'm Oscar Clark," said the shorter man. "We'd like to have a talk with you."

Nick deposited the trimmer on the nearby bench.

"About what?"

"Let's go inside," said the second man. "It's too cold out here."

Nick tried to assess the situation. Oscar Clark was the owner of *The Catalina*. He was probably connected with the large package he had taken from that boat. He walked to the door, opened it, and let the two men in.

"What seems to be the trouble?" he asked, nonchalantly.

In the small hallway, the two men opened their coats to let Nick see their guns.

"We want the money. The full million dollars," Mr. Clark said.

"What money?" Nick asked.

"The money you took from my boat."

Nick sat on the little stool close to the side window.

"I didn't take any money from any boat. I've been aboard many boats, as I told the police. Possibly I was on yours too, but never alone."

Oscar Clark gestured to his friend. "Search."

"Be my guest. The police came and searched my house high and low and found zilch. Besides, do I look like a man who has any money?"

A truck carrying red shingles, and a pickup with *The Werkstein* painted on the side, pulled up out front, along with another truck dragging a scaffold. Voices drifted into the house as a crew of seven men, with orange jackets crossed by green stripes, populated the front and sides of the house. From the rapid succession of sharp commands it was clear that they were trying to unload both the scaffold and the shingles as close to the house as possible. Finally Nick heard a shout.

"Get that fucking car out of the way!"

A knock sounded on the door and a man with a yellow helmet walked in. For a moment he looked surprised, then stared at Nick.

"Mr. Falcone?"

"That's me." Nick rose.

"We're here to replace the roof; we'd like to start right away, but we need someone to move that car." He pointed to the beige Cadillac. Just before he turned around he stopped and looked at the guns peeping out of the men's belts. "Those guns—you can't have them, you know. You can't walk around with a pistol if you aren't a policeman."

Both men closed their coats; Nick Falcone took advantage of the diversion and followed the foreman out.

One worker was eyeing the Cadillac. The truck with the hefty load of shingles was ready to move in, thus barring the way to the Cadillac.

"No, No!" Oscar Clark shouted and ran to his car. "We're leaving."

The goon rapidly slipped into the driver's seat and put the car in gear; maneuvering around the truck in front of them they sped off.

Still very nervous, Nick stayed outside watching the men at work. At five o'clock the crew left, saying they would come back tomorrow to continue the job. Nick thanked them and walked inside.

It was a clear, crisp night that made him appreciate having a place to retreat in comfort. He got a Bud Light out of the fridge and clutched the key of the storage locker where the unspent part of the million dollars was stashed.

Today he had been saved by the arrival of the construction crew, but he couldn't rule out another visit in the near future. Unfortunately, his name, among others, had been mentioned by the media in connection with the two dead bodies found ashore. Those men would be back, and soon. He needed a safe place to hide, at least for a while, but first he had to convert some of his hundred dollar bills. With Charlie out of reach, he had to resort to another stratagem.

The following morning he made a stop at the storage locker and extracted thirty thousand dollars from the moneybag. He drove to the first casino on his way to the States. He got poker chips for five thousand dollars, played a hand of Caribbean poker in which he lost thirty dollars and then went to the bar to have a drink. There were visible cameras in many places, and he knew that there were also very small ones that couldn't be spotted by the naked eye. He lingered among the tables, played at one slot machine for a dollar a piece and then at another for fifty cents. After three hours he approached the cashier and cashed in his chips. Nobody asked any questions. He arrived at the second gambling house at six o'clock that night, bought another five thousand in chips, played a little, had dinner, sat at a table for a stud poker game and, when the crowd saturated the place he went to cash his chips.

"Excellent night," the cashier said.

"You don't know the full story." Nick pretended to be desolate.

For a moment the cashier looked at him mystified as if he was afraid of having to listen to a lengthy tale. Soon after he put his head down and began counting the amount due in twenty-dollar bills. Nick repeated his small operation once more. At the end of the second day the small package of thirty-thousand dollars that he had comfortably held in his pockets took all the space inside his backpack. Most of the cashiers had been too nervous to ask questions, but Nick had several answers in store to justify the little time spent betting, such as "I thought about my wife and came to my senses," and "I wanted to see if I am really cured of gambling," and variations on the same theme.

He was on his way home when he got a ring from Fred.

"Tried to call you before," he said.

"I had my cell turned off. I was on a short trip. What's new?"

"It's about your roof. When we took all the old shingles off, we realized that they'd been set on top of an old roof, now completely rotten. They used to do that, in the old days; now it's against the building code. So I ordered my guys to dismantle the old roof. I won't charge you for that."

"Thank you."

"Now, the bad news. There's only a little section of the new roof on, nothing else. If you go home it will be like sleeping under the stars, and it's a bit cold for that. Why don't you come here? The guest room will do for a couple of nights. There're no drapes, but at least it's nice and warm."

"That's great. Thank you, Fred."

"Don't worry if you're late; tonight is hockey night. I'll be watching two games, one in the east and then the one from Calgary. I'll be up."

Nick was already on the gravel road that led to his parents' house, so he kept going; when he was in front of the house he gave a look to see how the new roof was shaping up. It was too dark to appreciate the full impact of the change, but by eliminating the structure underneath the roof would acquire a flatter shape and give his house a slicker look. Satisfied with what he saw, he made a swift U-turn and drove to Fred's. He parked outside the garage and rang the bell.

"It's open!" Fred shouted from the garage. "I have a little work to do in the backyard. Make yourself at home."

Nick entered the kitchen and made himself a cup of instant coffee. He took it to the large rec room and sat in one of the new chairs, ready to watch the first period of the hockey game between Calgary and Vancouver. Then, all of a sudden, he heard a voice.

"The million dollars, smart ass, and now!"

Nick turned and faced the same two guys who had come to his house two days before.

"I don't have it, I told you. I've never seen a penny of your money."

Oscar Clark took the remote and set the volume as high as he could get it, then approached Nick.

"We need to do a bit of convincing."

He motioned with one hand and the goon began pounding on Nick, first on his chest and stomach, then on his face. Nick fell to the floor. He tasted blood in his mouth and wondered how long he could take such a treatment.

"Give me some water," he murmured.

The goon moved to the kitchen and came back with a cup; only at the last second did Nick realize it was the hot water he had warmed up for his coffee. He turned his face sideways and up just in time to protect his eyes.

"More water?" the goon said and laughed, immediately joined by his boss' raucous laughter.

A first set of shots made the goon lose his concentration and drop the cup he was holding; a second series, aimed at Oscar Clark's shoes, made him lose his balance and roll on the floor. As the goon tried to get at his gun, Nick called up all his strength, rose, and tipped the coffee table on top of him.

Clutching his trusty Remington 887, Fred walked into the rec room and swiftly got hold of the goon's gun, while Nick got Clark's gun.

"You fellows have no business breaking into my house." Fred's voice was edged with steel. "I'd kick you out, except that the police are on their way and I don't want to disappoint them." He gestured toward the goon with his shotgun. "Sit." He turned toward Oscar Clark. "And you, stay where you are." He pointed his gun at the intruder to give strength to his commands.

"Oh Fred, thank you so much!"

Fred was looking around to see if there were other people in the room.

"There were only two of them."

"Sure?"

"Yes."

"Good. I'll still keep my gun at the ready—you never know—but you can do some work for me. With your free hand, open their wallets and get enough to cover the damages to the wall and floor." He paused to make some mental calculations. "Make it a good thousand, maybe twelve hundred."

The sirens of the police cars were getting louder. As the first police car pulled into the driveway, Fred said, "Do the house's honors, Nick, while I put my shotgun away." Fred disappeared through the door leading to the garage.

A few days later Peggy and Fred were spending the evening together. Peggy set her herbal tea on the low table and opened a bag of corn chips. A bowl of salsa was already on the table, together with Fred's whisky.

"Can I stretch down close to you?" she asked.

"Only if you don't tickle me," Fred answered, and moved closer to the back of the sofa.

They were all set to watch the third period of a hockey game, but several commercials were still flashing on the screen, so Peggy turned off the volume.

"I think you used your shotgun to intimidate the two mob guys." Peggy tapped on Fred's nose, "But you didn't tell that to the police."

"They didn't ask. They were very discreet."

"Didn't they ask about the damages?"

"Sure; it was clear that there was a fight, and Nick's condition proved it without doubt; they had to sew him up with four stitches, and one of his ribs was broken. The crooks! Coming into my house! My house is my castle—anybody with good intentions is welcome; anybody with bad intentions should stay out, or I'll kick him out."

"I never thought you were so belligerent."

"Only when they touch what's mine."

"The police were very happy to apprehend Oscar Clark and his goon. They'd been going around visiting cottages and houses in the Port Franks area, intimidating people and accusing them of having stolen what was theirs. Finally they've been caught. The police were very grateful to you, even if they won't let you know that they were." Peggy paused and sipped her tea. "How did you know there was trouble?"

"A car I didn't know was parked nearby and an awful noise was coming from my house. I was outside, winterizing the barbecue. I peeped in through the kitchen's window, so I got my—" Fred laughed. "I mean, so I took some action."

Peggy giggled. "You used your Remington."

"Shush. By the way, I should go to Gun 'N Gadgets and get the G2 Contender George has in stock."

"Oh, oh. Are you serious about hunting?"

"Something like that."

"I think I'll stick to target shooting. I wouldn't have time to go hunting." She paused. "Oscar Clark claimed that he'd been robbed while he was in this house."

Fred laughed and tapped on Peggy's nose. "But you can't believe what people like Clark say, right?"

Peggy deposited her cup on the table. "Right," she agreed, and cuddled up to Fred, ready to watch the third period of the Montreal Canadiens versus the Toronto Maple Leafs.

✻ ✻ ✻

Forty-six

Alain Alstein was impatiently waiting outside the office Verge Bristol and Fred now shared. Finally Verge arrived and opened the door.

"What's up?" Verged asked. "You're early."

Alain slumped in the chair in front of the desk. His face was red, and he clenched his hands together nervously. "You won't believe this!"

"What happened?" Verge took his coat off and sat opposite him.

"Moira is gone for the rest of the week. She's helping Fred with one of his pet projects."

"Yes, I know. So what's the problem?"

"The problem is that I'm stuck training the new fellow, that snot-nose fresh out of school, that's the problem! She should do that, since she's the last one to join the company."

Verge shrugged. "Fred wants her to work on a special project, and he's the boss. I was busy, too, going around the job sites and showing the new foreman how we operate."

"You justify everything. Since you moved into this office you've become like him."

Verge laughed. "Maybe it was Fred's trump card. Giving me his job, so that I'd feel and act like him. I wouldn't be surprised; the man is pretty clever, you know."

"So I have to train the new guy?"

"Yes sir."

"Why can't he work here and let Moira take care of the training?"

Verge sighed. "Fred always liked to take on a small job and do it all. It's fun, he used to say. He would do it at home. He stopped after Deborah's accident; clearly he couldn't concentrate at home. When Moira came, he associated her with every design-and-build he got. The last one was the hangar for Mr. Saldini. He's set up a nice office in the basement of his new house—I've seen it—so he went back to his old practice, and he needs Moira for the pricing."

"How long will it take?"

Verge shrugged. "I don't know. One, two weeks? These are never big developments."

"Two weeks! I'll have done all the training by then!" Alain, redder in the face than when he had come in, rose and strode off.

The day was bright and sunny, and Tessa and Jeanette had managed to find a table close to the windows, thus enjoying the illusion of a summer day. They each tasted an almond croissant, together with one of Tim Hortons' famous lattes.

"I like your hair streaked blond; those bangs across your forehead make you look younger."

"I'm going back to work tomorrow. I have to be in shape or they'll look for somebody else." She was wearing a pair of suede slacks and a soft orange jacket. "So this is our last afternoon outing," Jeanette said with a touch of regret.

"I hope you'll have better luck looking for the famous tape than I had." Tessa shrugged off her leather coat, revealing a high-collared gray sweater. Her long earrings ended in two huge pearls that attracted attention to her beautiful face. "I looked around, but my job confines me to a corner of the office. I can't maneuver freely."

"I know, but don't worry. I'll go through that office with a fine-toothed comb, I assure you." She sighed. "I want to nail that bitch. Not only is she a murderer, she's also ruined Alain and me financially. On top of that, she's hooked up Fred for good."

Tessa deposited her cup on the table abruptly, spilling some latte. "Do you have more evidence?"

"Evidence? Full proof, I tell you!" She took a big swig of her drink and dabbed her lips with the paper napkin.

"I'm listening! Don't keep me in suspense!"

Jeanette leaned toward Tessa. "Last week she went to work at his place for some mysterious project—Alain couldn't tell me what—and she'll keep doing that for another week!"

"She works at his *home?*"

"Yes! Don't tell me that there's nothing going on there. And at night too, or that's what Alain heard from Mary. Mary is the secretary at The Werkstein."

Tessa finished her latte in a hurry. "I'm going to find out what's going on. Tonight!" She grabbed her leather coat. "I'm going home to put on a pair of running shoes and then I'm in business. I won't let that shrimp of a woman grab a good catch like Fred."

"But Tessa, what's important is the tape; once we expose her, all her playing up to Fred will stop. She'll be in jail for the rest of her life." Jeanette buttoned her coat in a hurry, as Tessa was already marching out of the donut shop.

Tessa dropped off Jeanette at her place and drove home. She swapped her high-heeled boots with a pair of old sneakers, and drove to the vicinity of Fred's house, where she parked her Corvette.

It was getting dark, and she regretted not having brought a flashlight with her. On foot she approached Fred's house. A car was parked in front of his garage and there was no light in the basement where he was supposed to be working; instead, there was music and lights on the first floor. She rounded the house, hoping to get a look into the kitchen, but as she walked into the backyard she fell on the slippery ground. She cursed, knowing that the expensive leather outfit she was wearing was probably ruined beyond repair. By the time she got up and retraced her steps to the front of the house, the car that was parked there before had taken off. *If I ever get my hands on that bitch she will pay for my expensive outfit!*

Peggy was off duty, but she went to Headquarters just the same, as she wanted to practice at the indoor firing range. An hour later she walked over to see Gordon Stevenson, who had returned to his normal duties at the Investigative Response Unit.

"How does it feel to be back?" she asked.

Stevenson, wearing the traditional dark blue outfit with tiny red stripes along the trousers, looked more relaxed, almost younger.

"Good," he replied. "The time spent at the OPP Detachment helped me take a break from the situation at home. In a way, I got more accustomed to being alone. Of course, the investigation I was associated with didn't shed much light on the deaths of Charlotte Gassman or Lucy Fairweather…a sad story, but not an uncommon reality." He looked at the work that had accumulated on his desk. "It seems that I have a lot to catch up on, but first update me on your romance."

"Things as usual. The only news is that I'm involved in one of Fred's projects. He wants to see if it's possible to build an indoor target shooting range close enough to London to attract a lot of people, yet have it reasonably priced."

Gordon laughed. "Is he planning to make money on it?"

"I think so. He's fired up at the idea, and he managed to make me feel the same way. Most of the time I can be there only at night, so the woman who does the pricing comes in at night too. She seems not to mind at all; actually, I think she enjoys it." Peggy looked at her big wristwatch. "I have chores to do, so I'll be going. See you later, Gordon, and welcome back!"

The idea of an indoor shooting range was really awesome, and she was happy that Fred had come up with it. She was following the project as it took shape, step-by-step. She couldn't believe the time and effort that it took to evaluate its feasibility, and the enormous number of contacts Fred had to make. He consulted the bylaws related to sport facilities; he discussed with Verge whether a freestanding structure would be suitable to the case; thinking of a steel structure, he contacted suppliers to get an idea of the cost; and finally he had drawn a sketch of the pavilion with the approximate dimensions. At that point he had asked Moira to work on two things: a three-dimensional computer model of the pavilion and an evaluation of costs with a few different materials. Moira had worked on each step in conjunction with Fred, and they had produced the blueprints of the building Fred wanted to realize.

Peggy had been fascinated by the unfolding project, growing from an idea in Fred's brain to a model that looked real and complete. The only thing she couldn't see from looking at the various projections on the screen was whether the shooting range would be for trap shooting alone, or whether he had thought about her favorite sport, skeet shooting. She was anxious to find out. Moira had been excited too, as at first she had no notion what the purpose of that strange structure would be.

Yesterday Fred had met with the sound engineer; today he was scheduled to speak with the environmental inspector. Peggy had not seen him for two nights in a row, and she was looking forward to spending an evening alone with him. Moira, in fact, had to go see the director of the group home, as Charlie had been suffering from unusual tremors and convulsions and had been taken to the hospital.

When she arrived at Fred's house, Peggy noticed that the lights were on. As she entered, a wonderful smell of tomatoes and basil leaves greeted her.

Wearing a dark green apron, Fred was busy in the kitchen.

"Hi, love." He kept stirring the sauce on the stove with a wooden spoon. "I came home early and thought I'd make supper. I hope you like pasta."

"I do. Already done?"

"Of course not; pasta can't be cooked until the dining party is present! The water is boiling, though. Go to the lazy Susan and choose which kind of pasta you like."

Peggy complied. "I found some penne; it cooks fast, and I'm hungry." She deposited a box on the counter, near Fred. "So how were the two meetings you had yesterday and today?"

"To make the structure sound-proof all the way through the building might be very expensive; the sound engineer had some information on a similar one built in the States, where shooters stand inside booths; but that takes away the feeling of a sports club." Fed measured two small bowls of penne and dumped them into the salted boiling water. "Eight minutes and the food will be ready."

"What about the environmental man?"

"He told me how far the range should be from the populated area. No problem since I'm thinking of some land I own: thirty acres, most labeled as *hazard zone*."

"So everything's okay?"

Fred laughed. "Not in the least. The total cost is around one million and two hundred. We'd never make a profit."

"But people will use it all year around. You can set the membership high enough to cover the cost."

"If you charge more than twenty dollars an hour you'll get only a few people, and even they will go to open ranges as soon as the weather permits."

The pasta was ready; Fred strained it and then tossed it into the saucepan. He stirred it, set the saucepan on a metal holder and then on the table. "A couple of dishes, grated parmesan and we're in business. Will you grab the drink you like from the fridge? I have my beer."

They sat at the kitchen table and scooped a good portion of penne onto their dishes.

"Are you giving up on building the range?" Peggy asked.

"Probably."

"But you and Moira have done so much work!" She made some mental calculations. "Together, you've logged more than two hundred hours!"

"That's the construction business. You price a job at your own expense— spend hundreds of manpower hours on it, and then you don't get it. On average we get three jobs out of the ten we price; four when we're very lucky or have been very sharp at pricing."

"How do you do that?"

"Searching and searching for more economical but reliable subs— subcontractors, I mean—and looking for vendors who sell the materials specified by the architect at the lowest price."

"I see." Peggy was pensive. "And Moira is good at that, right?"

"Fantastic. The best I've ever seen."

"Better than you?"

Fred laughed. "I was probably better in my prime, but now she'd beat me for sure."

Peggy closed her eyes and inhaled deeply. "It smells wonderful," she said, and dug into her pasta. After a while, she asked, "Any news from Moira about Charlie?"

"Yes. They released him from the hospital. They found his condition stable and the same as before. Moira told me that they didn't want to give him more meds without a very good reason."

"Do you think she worries a bit much about Charlie?"

"Difficult to say. Moira has been always been convinced that there is more than the old attention deficit disorder."

✫ ✫ ✫

Forty-seven

Fred and Peggy watched the wire-frame model of the shooting range flash on the screen from different angles. The building resembled a gigantic seashell; the shooters stood on the low part, the targets on the high section. They played it over and over again; after a while they exchanged a knowledgeable look.

"It isn't like Moira not to show up," Fred said. "She was excited about the new quotes for the aluminum bars from a vendor in Toronto and anxious to enter the data into the computer. She thought they'd bring down the price so much that the total cost could be acceptable. She added that the project could be sold on the open market." Fred was clearly immersed in deep thoughts. "She doesn't answer her phone and she didn't let Mary know she had any problems. I'm worried."

Peggy nodded. "I checked with Headquarters. There were no accidents on the road, so the wisest thing to do is drive to her apartment and see what happened." As Fred didn't say anything, she added, "Let's go to my place so I can pick up my badge; it's useful for opening doors." She winked at Fred. "Sometimes, at least. I'd also like to get a coat, in case we're out for the night."

Peggy wore only jeans and a long-sleeve top that hung loosely on her body. She picked up her purse as Fred was already walking out of the basement and up to the main floor.

When they arrived at Moira's apartment on King Street it was past ten o'clock and they had a difficult time getting the superintendent's attention; he stared at Peggy's badge with skepticism.

"I can open the door and let you look inside. But you can't be out of my sight or touch anything."

He took Fred and Peggy along a dark corridor and stopped in front of number eleven. He fingered the many keys that hung on his chain, and finally found the one that opened Moira's door.

They took a couple of steps inside and then abruptly stopped, stunned. All the drapes were drawn; only a floor lamp was lit in the sitting room. Old VHS tapes were spread all over the floor of the kitchen and adjoining sitting room, and a big carton had been smashed against a wall.

Moira lay sprawled on the antique pink sofa, her eyes almost out of the orbits, her tongue sticking out, her hair in disarray, her white blouse rumpled, and a red mark around her neck.

"Oh my God!" the superintendent screamed. "You folks get out! Get out right away! I have to call 911!"

Fred shook his shoulders. "My friend is with the police. Don't worry!"

His eyes blinking and his hands shaking, the superintendent rushed out of the apartment.

Peggy bent over Moira and, to substantiate what was evident, she checked on Moira's carotid artery. Fred knelt close to her and was about to take Moira's hand in his, when Peggy stopped him.

"We can't touch anything," she said, and opened her cell. She strode away from the scene and talked on the phone for a few minutes. When she returned she tapped Fred on the shoulder. "Let's wait outside. I alerted Headquarters and then called Stevenson on his private number. He'll come down right away."

On her way out Peggy looked at the door's lock. "No forced entry. Either she trusted her killer enough to open the door or she was forced to open it."

They stood in the corridor until the forensics team arrived, and then they went to sit in Fred's Lexus. An hour later Stevenson came out of the building to talk to them.

"You should go home. Somebody was looking for something important in that apartment and either Moira Johnson was in his way or she surprised him. She's been strangled. I'll go interview the superintendent right now."

That night Fred couldn't keep his eyes closed for more than a few minutes. The image of little Moira, so frail, so pale, and so still, played and replayed in his mind. He had grown attached to her; even if they didn't see each other socially he considered her a friend he could depend on and had depended on for keeping his company in good standing. He regretted not having been involved a bit more in her family problems, as she probably needed support coping with her brother, far more than finding a suitable home for him.

Fred sighed as a feeling of inadequacy took hold of him.

People were dying around him; he wondered if he could somehow be the indirect cause of it. He should also get ready for a round of questioning regarding his personal relationship with Moira and the role Moira played at The Werkstein. There would be a repetition of what had been going on after Deborah's accident—he would probably have to face harsher questions because this was a homicide. As before, it didn't matter that he had an airtight alibi—the police never excluded the possibility of a hired killer.

Finally he rolled out of bed, showered, dressed, and walked briskly to the kitchen to turn on the coffee maker. He waited for the machine to gurgle and then poured himself a cup. He drank it eagerly and glanced at the wall clock. It was six-thirty, too early to go to work. He refilled his cup and descended to the basement and looked once more at the video of the shooting range.

Moira had put her heart into it, and her work wasn't finished yet.

He looked at the data that had been recently sent to that workstation and saw with surprise new quotes for the aluminum bars. He inserted the data into the master program for the pricing and waited until all the computations were done. Moira had been right; the final price was now around nine hundred thousand, roughly three hundred thousand dollars lower than the previous cost.

He ran the visualization program again and waited for the monitor to display the wire-frame image of the shooting range. As he expected, the model had not changed significantly, since the size of the bars was about the same.

As usual, Moira completed her task, he thought with a pang in his heart.

Upstairs once again, he drank an orange juice, grabbed his sport coat and his car keys. He wouldn't bother with exercise today, but would drive directly to The Werkstein.

When he arrived he could see Mary standing in the doorway, and could hear voices in the background. She took his arm and together they entered his office.

"What happened to Verge Bristol?" Fred asked. "Where is he?"

Mary slumped in the chair before the white plastic-top desk. "They've arrested Jeanette Alstein, and two policemen came here to take Alain to Headquarters. He was shaking like a leaf. Verge went with him."

For a moment Fred was without words. "Jeanette? How could Jeanette be mixed-up in this?"

"We were talking about that; we think it's what she said at the party, you remember?"

"I know she was drunk and Alain took her home, with some difficulties, I'd say."

"She screamed, 'I told you she's the one! I recognized her!' and she said that while looking at Moira."

"Oh, I remember the words, but I hadn't noticed she was in any way fingering Moira. But that wouldn't be enough to arrest her!"

"And then they came for Alain."

"Oh, I understand why people are so upset."

Mary rose. "Something important, Fred. The owner of the superstore called and asked when the construction is going to start."

"I see. Send in Verge as soon as he returns. The building permit for the superstore came in yesterday, and so did the report from environmental studies. We have to get moving in the field." Fred got rid of his coat and sat in his swivel chair.

"Fred, you don't look so good. Have you had breakfast yet?"

"No, and I couldn't sleep last night."

"I'll send for some food." Mary rose. "Very sorry about Moira. She slaved for this outfit from the first day she came."

Fred silently nodded.

Work had always been an emotional and mental refuge in his moments of trial, so he would concentrate on what needed to be done. He opened the main drawer and extracted the thick file with the specifications for the new job.

It was past four when Peggy called and asked him how he was holding up.

"I try not to think about what happened. I can't believe anybody would want to hurt Moira. I'm waiting to get information from you guys before I talk to my employees."

"A release is being prepared. It'll go on the air in an hour or so."

"Anything of substance? Does it say why Jeanette Alstein had been arrested?"

"No, but I can tell you what the superintendent of the apartment building overheard and leaked to the press, since it'll be broadcasted on the six o'clock news. The boxes in Moira Johnson's apartment came from a shop in town called Off Broadway, where Jeanette Alstein worked, and there's an indication that Moira was being blackmailed."

"Blackmailed? For what? And by who?"

"I don't know. By the way, I won't be part of the investigation."

"Oh, too bad. Can you at least explain the reason for such a drastic action as an arrest in the middle of the night?"

Peggy took the time to fill in the blanks, explaining the reasoning behind police actions. After the party at Fred's house, Stevenson had done some poking into Moira's background and her possible connection to Jeanette's life. He had discovered that they both came from Barrie, where Moira had been suspected of being involved in her mother's death, and that Jeanette worked at Off Broadway. Yesterday, when Stevenson had seen the box that belonged to that company and read the blackmail letter, he went into action. In most murder cases one has to follow the tracks right away and that was why he wanted to surprise Jeanette with an arrest, thus giving her the impression that the police knew more than what they actually did.

"I see. But why take in Alain also?"

"That's just the beginning. All members of The Werkstein will be interviewed and it'll be more of an interrogation for those who don't have an alibi for the time of the murder." Peggy paused. "I worked with Moira too, at your place, so I already had to give my statement."

"Makes sense, even if I'm not looking forward to spending more time at Headquarters. I spent enough hours over there for Deborah's case." He paused. "I shouldn't complain, though. Headquarters is where I saw for the first time a wonderful young woman disguised as a police officer."

"You remember, eh? I love you. Let's keep in touch."

Gordon Stevenson prided himself on being able to spot a liar from a distance. Jeanette Alstein may not have killed Moira Johnson, but she was the one who blackmailed her, he was sure of that. Moira had been killed between 5.30 p.m. and 6.30 p.m. and Jeanette had asked to leave Off Broadway at 4.30 p.m. with the excuse of an urgent errand. When he had asked her for an explanation, the woman had gone into a frenzy, and he had to suspend the interrogation.

He could detain her for twenty-four hours, after which he had either to charge her or release her. Stevenson twisted his dark moustache with both hands, as he usually did when puzzled. He then looked at the tape they had made soon after her arrest. She had admitted to nothing except the errand she'd used as her excuse to leave her office, picking up a couple of fish fillets at the Burger King takeout. There was no tape to validate her story. A window of opportunity existed during which she had no alibi, as her husband had left the office at six o'clock.

Stevenson was tired. He had spent the night piecing together the facts and trying to recreate a possible scenario. He looked into the interrogation room. They had given Jeanette a bottle of water and a sandwich; she had drunk the water, but hadn't touched the sandwich. She had asked for a lawyer, and he was supposed to come in shortly.

Stevenson made up his mind. He had to drill into Jeanette that the proof of blackmail was irrefutable; lying about it, if she had not killed Moira, would make her a strong candidate for murder. She might not grasp the implication, but her lawyer would catch on quickly.

He walked into the corridor and grabbed another cup of coffee. It was the third of the afternoon and he hoped he wouldn't start shaking.

From behind, Peggy tapped him on the shoulder.

"I got you a chicken sandwich with coleslaw. I bet you didn't eat much all day."

"No, I didn't. Thank you." With his free hand he grabbed the brown paper bag Peggy offered. "Where are you going?"

"Richmond…a truck accident. Take care, Gordon."

And Peggy was gone.

Santos Lopes came running and stopped in front of Stevenson.

"The lawyer for Mrs. Alstein has arrived and he wants an hour with his client in a private room."

Stevenson sighed. "Fine. Tell him not a minute more. Then send in Mr. Alstein. I want to have a second talk with him."

He ate his sandwich, but neglected the coleslaw. He waited until Lopes was back and ready to tape the meeting with Alain Alstein before he opened the door of the interrogation room and sat in front of Mr. Alstein. He started right away.

"So, Alain, this morning we talked about your whereabouts at the time of the murder. Now I'd like to know about your professional relationship with Ms. Moira Johnson."

"What about it?"

"Was she liked at the company? Did she make any friends?"

"Oh, that. People didn't like her a bit. She made a big deal because she could use some graphics software and clicked on a program that showed the buildings in 3D—something that any real estate agency can do."

"I see. So she didn't make any friends?"

"Hmm, no. Except—" He paused. "Expect the boss. She played up to him and he fell for it."

"You mean Mr. Dalton?"

"Yes, of course. Since the beginning he gave her the design-and-build projects to do, small projects that don't require a call for tender."

"Why did he do that?"

"Because he could choose vendors and sub-contractors as he pleased, without consulting us." He paused again. "If you ask me, it was a reason to make her work at his house, if you know what I mean."

"Which house? The one he lived in when he was married?"

"No, of course not. The new one."

"But you said Mr. Dalton gave her all those special projects since the beginning. That means from one and one half years ago to the present. He only moved to the new house a couple of months ago. So what special project are you talking about now?"

"That crazy thing about a shooting range."

Stevenson paused. The man had a lot of resentment against Moira Johnson. He didn't have to dig any further.

"Mr. Dalton has no official girlfriend?"

"Not that anybody knows about."

Stevenson drummed his fingers on the table. He had gone to the party offered by The Werkstein in the company of Peggy, and people had assumed that she was with him.

"So you believe there was something more than a working relationship between Mr. Dalton and Moira Johnson?"

"I'm sure."

"And that was why the employees at The Werkstein didn't like her?"

"That, and others. She would never talk much during coffee breaks; nobody knew anything about her, except that she had a demented brother."

Stevenson kept quiet for a moment, thinking how tough it must have been for Moira to work with such a colleague as Alstein. "That'll be enough for the day, Mr. Alstein. Oh, just a moment…what did you have for supper last night?"

"Jambalaya. Jeanette had cooked it the day before, and we ate the leftovers."

Stevenson couldn't hide his satisfaction. Jeanette's alibi failed to match up to that. "You're free to go home."

"With my wife?"

"Not quite. I need to talk to her a bit more."

Stevenson stepped out and entered the room where the interrogations were routinely recorded on video.

"Santos?" he called. "This is over. Get Mrs. Alstein and her lawyer."

Stevenson went to get a bottle of water, and after Santos had taken his position before the video camera, he entered the interrogation room for a new showdown. He introduced himself to the lawyer, Mr. Donald Norton. The man was in his fifties, medium height, with slightly curved shoulders, straight gray hair combed back, and metal-rimmed glasses.

"I hope you had a good talk with your client and advised her wisely."

"I did."

"So where do we stand? On all the lies that Mrs. Alstein had scooped out so far, or do we get the truth?" Stevenson guzzled half of the water from his bottle.

"Mrs. Alstein is no killer," the lawyer said.

"When I'm finished with this water, I'm going to file charges against Mrs. Alstein." Stevenson gave her a harsh look.

Jeanette was pale, her black outfit accenting her pallor. She couldn't meet his glance, and turned her gaze toward the lawyer.

Mr. Norton cleared his throat. "Mrs. Jeanette Alstein admits to having sent that letter and the four prints, but she stands firm in denying having anything to do with Ms. Moira Johnson's death."

Stevenson shook the bottle he held in his hands. "We're getting somewhere. So the charges will be blackmail and lying to the police." Stevenson looked at the lawyer and then at Jeanette. "Agreed, Mrs. Alstein?"

Jeanette faintly nodded.

"Agreed, Mrs. Alstein? I want to hear your voice."

Her eyes blinked back tears. "Yes."

"Fine, we'll prepare the statement and she can sign it."

"Just a moment, please," the lawyer cut in. "Could you drop the charges for lying? She was taken out of her bed in the middle of the night. She has just recovered from a car accident. Can you?"

Stevenson looked at the lawyer and then at the woman. "Just one question—what was the urgent errand you had to do, Mrs. Alstein, when you left work early?"

Jeanette looked at her lawyer, who assented. "I'd found the tape from which I'd taken those pictures. I wanted to see the entire sequence."

"I want that tape," Stevenson said, keeping the excitement out of his voice. "An officer will come with you to get it." He finished his water. "Then we'll drop the lying."

He left, and waited outside until Lopes turned off the tape. When Lopes joined him he said, "Get the statement ready and show it to me so I can read it over. Then ask Mrs. Alstein to sign it."

"Me?" The younger officer's Adam's apple started to jiggle.

"Yes, you. There's nobody else around here." His phone rang. He listened to the speaker on the other end. "That's what I figured." When he turned off the phone, Lopes was still there, clearly hoping for a reassignment. "Go!" Stevenson shouted.

Stevenson went to sit at his desk and opened the container of coleslaw. The call from forensics had confirmed what he had suspected. Moira had been strangled with probably only one hand; there was no evidence that she had fought with her killer.

☆ ☆ ☆

Forty-eight

Stevenson had a good night's sleep. He had needed one, because he was going to have a friendly chat with the head of The Werkstein, Frederick Elliot Dalton.

He had left Fred waiting twenty minutes so far, even though he knew that wouldn't rattle him. He figured Dalton was probably using that time calculating how to make more money. Stevenson sighed. He hadn't moved any closer to solving the case since yesterday. The only remaining suspect was Jeanette Alstein, and the time frame and her physical characteristics did not match the evidence.

Finally Stevenson entered the interrogation room with firm strides.

"Good morning, Mr. Dalton." He took the seat in front of him, then opened the folder he had in his hands and looked up at Fred.

Gray suit with a white shirt and a blue tie—Stevenson guessed he had come to Headquarters dressed as he would for a formal meeting.

"Good morning," Fred replied.

Stevenson glanced at the first sheet in front of him. "Let me check some information about your company. Annual gross income of about twenty million?"

"Yes."

"Still worth about six and a half million in solid and liquid assets?"

"A bit more, actually."

"How much more?"

"About a million." He smiled. "We had a very good year."

Stevenson took note of the change. Even if the interview was taped, he liked to write down the salient points as he listened, a quick reference for later.

"How is it split?"

"Land and equipment: about three and half million, as before; working capital has been recently raised to three and half million; and the remaining half is still in the bank. I have to think about how to invest it."

Stevenson was busy writing and didn't look up for his next question.

"There're six people working at the office, and fourteen regulars in the field?"

"Fifteen in the field as of last week."

"Only the employees at the office interacted with Moira Johnson?"

"Yes."

"Tell me what they do."

"Mary Gervasio—"

Stevenson interjected. "Just tell me what they do; I'll get the names when I interview them."

"We have a secretary, three engineers who provide estimates for the tenders and check on the job sites, an accountant, and a computer specialist who comes in the afternoon and stays until late—he updates the software on all our computers."

"So you have one more than you had when we interviewed you last. You've already replaced Ms. Johnson?"

"No, we hired two extra persons about a month ago."

"I see. So, tell me something about Moira Johnson."

"Moira joined the company about nineteen months ago; to an engineering degree she added a specialization in the CAD/CAM systems and had worked in that field for about two years. She was the best candidate we interviewed at that time and we hired her."

"When you say 'we' do you mean 'you'?"

"I consulted the two people she'd have to work with, and they agreed."

"Do you do performance evaluations in your company?"

"Not really. Six people worked in the office, the others in the field. I know who's doing what and how well."

"So how did Moira perform, vis-à-vis the two other employees..." Stevenson glanced at the sheets in front of him. "Verge Bristol and Alain Alstein?"

"Very well."

"Why did you ask her to do those special projects...?" Stevenson glanced again down to his sheets. "The so-called design-and-build projects?"

Fred wiggled in his chair. "From time to time we get some projects that make us good money." Fred laughed. "I mean *really* good money. Sometimes business people need a new building in a hurry, something, in general, that will cost less than or about a million. To go through tender would take time, and they don't have it. So they give me a call and ask if I would do it all. I hire an architect, have the design ready in two to three weeks, and build it in a few months."

"So why Moira?"

"Both Verge Bristol and Alain Alstein were marking time, and in our business we can't do that if we want to stay afloat. They didn't learn any of the new software that helps both the pricing and the visualization of a building. Moira did that in a jiffy, and she searched the market. She offered alternatives for the material, some sturdy and expensive, others just adequate. Our clients feel in control when we do that. They can choose."

"Is it right to assume that Bristol and Alstein resented Moira's presence?"

"Yes."

"Enough to kill or plan to eliminate her?"

"I don't think so."

"Do you know anybody who would want to harm her?"

"No."

"Where were you on November fifteenth, between five and six-thirty in the afternoon?"

"Gone to see a parcel of land I own, near Lucas."

"What was your interest?"

"It's about thirty acres, twenty of which are hazardous land; you can't build anything on those. On the other ten there's a row of storage sheds, most of them dilapidated. The owner didn't pay any rent for six months, and I was going to see how many were still in use."

"Anybody saw you coming or going?"

Fred shrugged. "I don't think so."

Now Stevenson would ask the critical question.

"Did you have an intimate relationship with Moira?"

Fred's eyes blinked with surprise. "No! I have—" He stopped. "My interests are elsewhere."

Stevenson leaned on the desk to look Fred in the eyes. "Because if you had, I'd find out. And if you had, I can think of a nice scenario. Moira was your lover when your wife was alive; she served you well at that time, but now you wanted to break it up. As you said, your interests are currently elsewhere." He paused for effect. "She blackmailed you, threatened to expose you, and you had her killed." For a moment Stevenson thought he had caught the man off guard, but it was only a brief moment...

Fred roared with laughter. "I think you're in the wrong business, Gordon; you should write fiction stories for a TV series."

It was late when Stevenson stretched his legs across a stool and clicked *Play* on the remote. The tape was old; the black-and-white frames often appeared a uniform gray color, and the pictures changed quickly and wavered as if the photographer was walking while he filmed. *So this was the tape Jeanette Alstein used to blackmail Moira Johnson.* On the screen all sorts of images appeared: trees dressed in their baby leaves, a blue jay jumping from one branch to another, a cottontail rabbit rushing under a grove of trees, a young fox ambling out of its den on trembling legs, two boys hitting a baseball ball. Stevenson grew impatient to see the frames related to Moira's crime. As the image of an engorged creek appeared, he leaned toward the monitor to get a better view. The pictures were taken from very far away. Near the edge of the creek a woman was brandishing a big stick, seemingly beating on somebody. A girl, entering the scene from the left, rushed toward the woman and shoved her aside and, as the woman tried to come after her, she pushed her into the creek. The girl quickly bent over the other person, whose face was submerged. Some blank frames followed; then the camera focused on the boy on the ground; the girl held up his head and he was spitting water. After a few more blank frames, the woman reappeared, struggling and yelling, her head bobbing in and out of the water, while the girl stood impassive on the shore. The noise of rushing water intermixed with human cries could be heard in the background. Then the camera moved up and focused on a hawk circling in the air in search of a prey, and that was the last frame of the tape.

Stevenson watched the last section of the tape over and over. Yes, the tape incriminated Moira, but the worst she could be accused of would be manslaughter or failure to provide help in a life-and-death situation.

But how is all of this tied to Moira's murder? Usually it's the blackmailer who gets killed, not the victim. Tomorrow he would pay a visit to the Off Broadway shop and see if they could tell him who had taken the box with the tapes that had been found in Moira's apartment. Did Moira pay somebody to do it? If so, he should find out who he or she was.

Stevenson rewound the tape and called it a night.

Forty-nine

Ten inches of snow had come and gone, and Nick Falcone wondered what it would be like to reside in a house without heat. When he had called a company to repair the several stretches of broken pipes, they had told him that the old furnace didn't comply with the new safety regulations and needed replacing. The installation of a new central heating system would require knocking down walls and tearing up floors, and the total cost would be around twenty thousand dollars.

Nick had just paid for the new roof and didn't expect to have more repairs to do. He needed two things: to get a job, and find Charlie or somebody else willing to play his part. He would try once more to find Charlie, as it would take time to find another suitable person and then train him. He spread an afghan over his body and unfolded the newspaper he had just bought at the grocery store. The investigation on Moira Johnson's death took half of the third page and gave a lot of details about the murder and the search for persons of interest. He kept reading, hoping to find something about Moira's brother. There was nothing. Now that the vigilant sister was out of the way, it shouldn't be difficult for Nick to make Charlie do what he wanted him to do. Charlie didn't work at the Western Fair anymore; at the Men's Mission and Rehabilitation Centre they had been tight-lipped. He felt that they knew something, but didn't want to talk.

A couple of minutes later a brainstorm hit him. He called the Men's Mission, introduced himself as the director of the funeral home in charge of Ms. Moira Johnson's burial, and asked if they could trace her brother's whereabouts. He was put on hold and waited until the supervisor came on the phone and asked which funeral home it was. Nick, well prepared, gave the name of an existing funeral chapel in London, keeping his voice charged with profound sadness, proper for the occasion. After much hemming and hawing, he finally got the name and address of the place where Charlie Johnson lived. He thanked the supervisor profusely.

Nick looked at his watch. It was early afternoon; he would drive to the group home and ask to take Charlie out for an ice cream. He would take him to the Dairy Queen and make him pay with a hundred dollars. After three ice creams he would have exchanged three big bills, even if at some monetary loss.

He counted on his GPS to take him to the address, but the gadget was busy acquiring the satellite signal. He had reached the outskirts of London, and the device still kept trying to download the current earth coordinates. He turned it off and on again, hoping for a miracle. It didn't happen. Annoyed, he stopped and extracted the London city map from the glove compartment. Finally he found Pond View Road and resumed driving. After he made a turn, three old houses of similar architecture drifted into sight. Each was three stories with redbrick walls and a mansard, and surrounded by a cedar hedge at the front interrupted in the middle by an arch with the script The Safe Harbour.

Nick looked at his watch. It was more suppertime than snack time, but he still wanted to see Charlie.

He parked his car on the road, passed under the arch, and neared the central house, which had a recessed front door. He climbed a few steps and entered a narrow hallway. On the right he saw a glass door with *Office* written on it and on the left, an alcove with mailboxes. Nick knocked on the door.

"Come in," someone inside said.

He took off his baseball cap, introduced himself as Sam Falcone, and asked whether he could see Charlie.

The nameplate on the desk read *Sandra Tremonti, Director*. The woman behind the desk, in her late fifties, looked at him in a rather cold way. "Charlie has been sick. He isn't well yet."

"Could I see him?"

"Not today. He's been sedated. He's asleep."

Nick managed to hide his frustration. He thanked her and strode out of the office. As he moved toward the exit, he noticed two cameras, one on each side of the hallway. His visit had been recorded, he noted with concern.

For the second time Fred walked out of his house hoping to see Peggy's Ford truck coming down the road. Nothing. They had not seen each other for two full days, and he already missed her tremendously. He re-entered the house and poured himself a Jameson whisky. He had loved the commercial of the old Irishman going after his barrel of booze in the middle of the ocean so much that he wanted to taste that particular brand. *Not bad*, he concluded after the first few sips. Then the rumble of Peggy's truck signaled her arrival.

He opened the door and went to greet her with a hug and a kiss.

"Finally, you're here!"

Peggy fished out a briefcase from the backseat. "I might have to do some work tonight."

"Let's go inside. It's cold out here. Besides, I want you to see the new fireplace. I got it installed today."

They walked into the rec room, and Peggy immediately approached the fire and warmed her hands close to the flames.

"It's nice," she said, looking at the hearth's natural stone and the mantel, a slab of red-and-gray marble. She turned around. "Your house looks more and more like a home."

"Happy you like it. Anything to drink?"

"Yes, a tea. Hot—I forgot my coat today."

They moved into the kitchen, and Fred asked, "What work do you have to do tonight?"

Peggy sat on one of the barrel chairs.

"It's mayhem at Headquarters. Everybody's upset about all the articles in the press, and the TV reports accusing the police of inefficiency. The detective sergeant came down hard on poor Gordon, who has to work with only a handful of people with expertise."

"I thought you were out of the investigation."

"Officially, yes; but everything's at a standstill and I want to see if I can discover something in Moira's life. In my briefcase there're photocopies of the articles about her mother's death; I hope to find information about her relatives, if she had any."

The water was boiling and Fred poured some into a mug on top of a sachet of Lipton tea. He set it in front of Peggy.

"Jeanette isn't a suspect anymore?" he asked.

"Yes, but they think a man finished her off. Jeanette might have been there, though."

"Not all perpetrators are caught," Fred said after a pause. "It's a matter of statistics."

"Yes, but this homicide follows a number of deaths that were labeled accidental, even if not everybody was convinced that they were."

"You mean—"

"Your wife's, Charlotte's and Lucy's."

"Oh no! I hope they don't start again with poor Deborah! Besides, the other two were handled by the OPP."

"Yes, but Gordon was there, cooperating. They count against him."

"I see. Maybe I can help you."

They both moved back to the rec room and sat on the new upholstered chairs.

"That would be great; what I have with me is all a matter of public record. We can split the papers; search for names, people the Johnsons knew. Here, get a marker in case you find any."

For a long hour they went through pages and pages.

"Can't you get into trouble doing this, working on an investigation when there's a conflict of interest?" Fred asked.

She shrugged. "Probably. If that happens, I'll ask for leave or just resign. I was already looking for another job."

"Oh. I didn't know that. That's interesting."

"Why?"

"I was thinking of offering you one, but I thought you liked what you were doing, and I didn't want to create a conflict."

"*You* offering me a job?"

"Not immediately, a bit later on."

"Hmm. I can't type as fast as a secretary, and I can't lay bricks." Peggy finished going through her set of papers and dumped them on the floor.

"Nothing. Zilch. Moira's mother didn't work anywhere, and the only names I found were the schools where the kids went."

Fred was still reading and Peggy squatted at his feet.

"Find anything?" she asked when he was finished.

"Nothing. I was thinking...the person who knows the most about Moira and the people around her is still Jeanette Alstein. They both grew up in Barrie."

"I know, but she fell sick and quit her job. Gordon can't pressure her, or he'll be accused of police brutality. But I feel the same. Somebody should follow her and see what she does and who she talks to. She's still a key player."

Fred caressed Peggy's hair. "Anything I can do for you? A snack?"

"Yes; something sinful, like ice cream."

"You must be warm by now, if you want an ice cream. I have several flavors in the freezer. Come with me."

They were licking on their vanilla drumsticks, when Peggy asked, "What was the job you were thinking of offering me?"

"Manager of the shooting range."

At first Peggy looked at Fred with incredulity, then she exploded in elation.

"Oh, Fred! You're going to build it!"

Fred finished licking his cone.

"You have time to consider my offer."

Peggy jumped off the chair and went to kiss his neck and ruffle his hair.

"Fred, that would be wonderful! You must really like me!"

He turned around, picked her up, and took her to the sofa. He gave her a long, passionate kiss.

"I wanted to do this the moment you came in. You brought me back to life, Peggy. Not only do I like you *very* much, I love you."

✫ ✫ ✫

Fifty

Detective Gordon Stevenson finished revising the last report of the day. He was tired and frustrated as he had never been before. His job entailed too much paperwork and too little recognition. He had interviewed all the employees of The Werkstein, and talked with Michael Sullivan, the owner of Off Broadway, and his father, Jacob.

Mary Gervasio had confirmed the animosity the two older engineers of The Werkstein had toward Moira; the recently-hired staff member had little time to interact with her to make any useful comments, and the accountant expressed neutral feelings toward her. Moira Johnson was not loved at the company, Stevenson had concluded, but each of them had an alibi for the time of the murder.

He hoped the interview at Off Broadway would bear better results, but things didn't click that way. The day a man had come to take the box with the old tapes they were understaffed as Jeanette Alstein was in the hospital. Jacob had handed the box to a short, rough-looking man who chewed tobacco. He couldn't add any other useful details. So Stevenson had obtained the address of the tape's owner, Ryan Costello, who lived in Barrie. Somebody would have to take his deposition and check on his alibi. Today he had tried to contact Moira's brother, but the young man was under sedation.

Stevenson was meditating on an early retirement when somebody tapped him on the shoulder. He turned and saw Peggy standing close by. "Go away. I can't bear your cheerful face."

Peggy sat close to him. "I asked for a leave and I got it."

"But we're understaffed!"

She shrugged. "I told them to give me leave or I'd quit. They really had no choice." She grinned. "So now I'm free to do some poking around for you."

"Leave? And how do you live without a salary?"

"Fred offered me a job."

"A job? What kind of job?"

"I'll tell you about it later. Now, I think I'll follow Jeanette and see what's cooking. You don't have to share much with me, only what you can."

"At the moment I can share plenty of frustrations." He sighed. "I don't have enough people to work simultaneously on the clues we should follow: finding the man who took the tapes from Off Broadway, interviewing Moira's brother, organizing an interview with the OPP for Ryan Costello, and yes, shadowing Jeanette. She knows more than she admits."

"I'll take care of shadowing Jeanette. Now, do you need anything to eat? You look exhausted."

"No. I'm okay; I got supper and was about to leave. And oh, Peggy, call me only on my private number."

"Sure. Keep up your spirits. 'Bye for now."

"Where are you going in such a rush?"

She giggled. "To buy myself a couple of eavesdropping gadgets...the kind the police can't use."

Stevenson glanced at her and then got his coat, wondering what kind of job Fred Dalton could have possibly offered her. He would soon find out. Peggy seldom kept a secret for long.

Charlie Johnson had an alibi for the time of the murder; he had been in his room, sick.

Stevenson doubted that the young man could provide any clue on his sister's murder, but just in case, he had taken Santos Lopes with him and driven to the group home on Pond View Road to interview him. When they arrived, they found Charlie in the game room, playing pool with three other people. Stevenson stopped on the threshold, observing his behavior;

Charlie didn't lack concentration, as he had expected. His shots were accurate and he seemed to understand the strategy of hitting the white ball just enough to sink the others and leave it in a good position for the next stroke. Charlie didn't win the game, but he was only a few points behind the winner.

When the game finished, he approached Charlie, showed his badge, and asked him to come with him.

Charlie nodded without saying a word.

They walked into the director's office and Stevenson asked Lopes to fetch three soft drinks. He sat on one of the chairs and gestured Charlie to do likewise. He waited until the drinks were handed out and Lopes took a seat in a corner, ready to take notes.

"Sorry for your loss, Charlie. I'm sure you loved your sister very much, so I came here to see if you could help me find her killer."

Charlie nodded again, but he didn't utter a word.

"How have you been?" Stevenson asked. He opened a can of Dr. Pepper for Charlie and one for himself.

"Sick. I've been sick."

"I know, and that's why I didn't come sooner." He paused. "Did you see your sister often?"

Charlie shook his head.

"When is the last time she took you out for a treat? I mean for an ice cream or a sundae or even a hamburger with French fries?"

Charlie opened his arms and shrugged. "I don't remember." He slowly sipped on his drink.

"Did you know where she lived?"

Charlie nodded.

"Where?"

"In a big building on King Street."

"Have you even been there by yourself?"

"Yes."

"What does the place look like?"

Charlie's face lighted up. "Nice. A kitchen, a place to watch TV, and a bedroom."

"Have you ever been there at night?"

"No. Yes. One or two times."

"Where did you sleep?"

"On the sofa, with pillows."

"Do you remember when?"

Charlie shook his head.

"Last week, a month ago?"

"When I came from Barrie."

"Did you remember when that was?"

"No."

"Did you like to stay with your sister?"

Charlie's face lighted up again. "Yes, but she didn't want me there."

"Where were you before you came to The Safe Harbour?"

Charlie frowned. "What's The Safe Harbour?"

"It's this nice place."

Charlie nodded. "Ah."

"Don't you like it here?"

Charlie shook his head.

"No? Why not?"

"I liked to work at the Fair. It was nice there." Charlie closed his eyes as if he was fatigued.

"Charlie?" Stevenson asked.

Charlie took his head in his hands. "Headache," he said. He set the can on the floor and leaned back in the chair.

Stevenson rose and patted Charlie on the shoulder. "That'll be all for today, my friend. Have a rest."

On the way back Stevenson asked Lopes, "Did you get down our conversation?"

"Yes, sir. I think every detail."

"Good. Make a note that we have to find out what he was doing at the Fair. I assume he meant the Western Fair." He paused as Lopes put the cruiser in gear. "Find out who Charlie's family doctor is and ask him to give me a call. So far we have only hearsay about his mental condition. I want a diagnosis."

"I'll take care of it," Lopes said. "Where to now?"

"Headquarters. It's past five, so you can get your car and go home. I'm going to have another look at Moira's apartment."

All the tapes, except for the one used to blackmail Moira, had been returned to Off Broadway. Moira's apartment had a neater aspect, although the aura of death still seemed to permeate the air. Stevenson wanted to have an idea of what kind of life Moira lived outside her work. The police had sequestered her address book, her laptop and her bank, credit card and telephone statements, and yet they had not found anything that could advance the investigation.

Her laptop revealed that she played Sudoku, and that most of the emails she received were job-related. Her address book contained the phone numbers of Pizza Hut, Pizza Delight, Super clipper—a hair salon and the two full addresses where Charlie lived: The Men's Mission and The Safe Harbour. The bank and credit card statements had been the most interesting in terms of pointing to her character, showing that she had never made any big purchases, except her car and a television set. Moira lived frugally.

Stevenson started with the bedroom. The bed had been made, and the linen closet had towels and bed sheets nicely lined up over the shelves. The bedroom closet contained a few pantsuits and a couple of skirts, blouses, and dresses. The bathroom was clean and without frills; on the counter stood jars of creams and one container with make-up; the medicine cabinet had pills for headache and stomach problems and one box of Tampax; there were no prescription medications and no perfumes.

Next, he went into the sitting room and searched for magazines and newspapers. She had a subscription to *Engineering & Technology*; several issues were stored underneath the coffee table. In a cheap wooden bookcase technical books stood; most had titles echoing her profession.

The girl didn't have much fun, Stevenson thought, as he moved to open the entrance closet. A heavy coat, a windbreaker and two vests hung on rudimentary steel hangers. On the floor were a green coverall, two pairs of women's shoes, and a pair of working boots with steel toes. Stevenson lifted up the coverall and measured it against his body. It was short, very short, and he could smell a vague odor of tobacco emanating from it. He then analyzed the heavy shoes: inside were two pairs of insoles.

Could this be the outfit she used to steal the box with the incriminating tape? Stevenson asked himself. Excluding Charlie from the suspect list because of his size, either Moira had sent somebody to steal the tapes, or Moira herself had done it. Stevenson twisted and released his moustache. If such a man existed he had to find him. Something may have gone wrong between him and Moira, so badly that it ended in violence.

He was still pondering the situation when his cell rang. It was a preliminary report from the OPP. The day of Moira's murder Ryan Costello had a photography gig at an anniversary party, from the time the cocktails were served until late at night.

He had never considered Ryan a valid suspect, because he had included the tape with all the others he had given to Off Broadway for creating his professional profile. If he'd ever intended to blackmail Moira, he would have done so a long time ago. The boy filmed so much when he wandered in the woods that he probably had never played that tape.

I'm stuck with no clues, Stevenson thought with frustration. *I hope Peggy's surveillance yields something of substance.*

Peggy O'Brian felt free as a bird and charged with positive energy. Today she would find out how Jeanette Alstein spent her free time. Jeanette had seen her at The Werkstein party; however, Peggy counted on her height and the vehicle she drove to pass as a young repairman in case Jeanette spotted her. Dressed in jeans, a big tartan coat and a white hard hat, Peggy parked on the same street where the Alsteins lived, lowered the tailgate of her Ford pickup, set two road markers on the tarmac, and started to measure the shoulder of the road. It was past ten o'clock when Jeanette's garage door rose and her car took the road.

Quickly, Peggy put the orange cones back into the truck and followed Jeanette to the nearby Coffee for Thoughts. She watched as Jeanette went into the café, got a large coffee, and sat in the far corner, her back against the wall. About fifteen minutes later a silver Corvette arrived. Peggy thought that Coffee for Thoughts was much too common to get the patronage of Corvette's owners, and watched carefully who climbed out of the car. A tall woman appeared; her long, wavy hair swayed slightly in the breeze. She wore a mid-sized white coat with black fur cuffs and black boots with heels. She swung her big purse as she slammed the car door. She entered the coffee shop and sat at the table with Jeanette.

Peggy put the pickup in gear and parked a bit closer to have a better view of the duo. She recognized the newcomer as Tessa Wilson, the woman she had seen having dinner with Fred. She got her camera out, set up the zoom lens, and began filming. The two women talked agitatedly. Peggy stopped filming and set up the eavesdropping gadget she had just bought. She could grasp only a few words; the window clearly reflected most of the sound inward. So she put the gadget in her pocket, got out of her pickup, and entered the shop. She stood in line to get a coffee, and studied which of the free tables would best allow her to eavesdrop.

She lowered her hard hat a bit more, sat at the table she had selected and opened her newspaper; in between two pages she hid her listening device and the attached digital recorder. Now she could hear Tessa's mutter quite well.

"Something doesn't make sense. Alain thinks Fred had an affair with Moira?"

"Fred did give her a special project to work on, with him, at his house. Why else would he do that?" Jeanette asked.

Tessa seemed to weigh her response. "Maybe it was something he didn't want other people at the office to know about."

"Could be, but I doubt it. Anyway, she's gone for good, so you're free to step in."

"It isn't that easy. Who from the office has access to Fred's house?"

"Verge. Verge Bristol goes there when there's something he wants to discuss with Fred, and occasionally Mary Gervasio takes some documents that need to be signed to his house. But that happens seldom, since Fred is back at the office four days a week."

"Hmm. Could you ask Verge to keep an eye on the situation? I want to know if Fred starts seeing another woman."

"I can't ask him that. The Bristols were good friends of ours once upon a time, but lately they've been keeping their distance."

"See if Alain can ask Verge some questions…or maybe he can ask the secretary."

"Mary Gervasio doesn't talk about employees' private affairs. She's a lost cause."

Tessa looked at her watch. "We'll discuss this problem some other time. I have an appointment down at the salon. I'm going to get a perm." She rose. "Keep your eyes and ears open. I want to know what Fred does, and with whom." Tessa left the shop and hurried toward her Corvette.

That's enough for the first day, Peggy thought. She hadn't gotten anything of substance, but she would be back tomorrow, and the next day, and the next. Now she had to pick up Fred and look at the piece of land he had in mind for building the indoor shooting range.

Peggy and Fred walked hand in hand along the ravine that surrounded the thirty acres of Fred's property.

"What do you think?" Fred asked.

"It's perfect. You can put the building on the ten acres; the hazardous land around it will buffer the sound of the shots well."

"That's what I thought. I'll have to wait for the spring to start building, but I can put the bulldozer on those dilapidated storage units right away. I can also widen the access road and get it all nice and ready for action."

As they walked past the units, Peggy tugged at the three doors that had a padlock. "Somebody still has belongings inside."

"The previous owner should have cleared them out. I suspect he kept renting the storage bins even after he sold me the land. Mary has asked him to give us a copy of the contracts so we can contact them."

They turned around and walked back to Peggy's Ford. Fred grinned.

"I see that you're disguised as a construction worker. How was your first snooping mission?"

Peggy laughed. "It took me all morning to discover that Jeanette and your old acquaintance, Tessa are friends."

"Oh, really? I wonder how they came across each other. And what were they talking about?"

"I couldn't capture anything at the beginning, but in the last fifteen minutes Tessa kept talking about how to get close to you."

"You must be kidding!"

"She was very serious. And she wants to know if you have a girlfriend."

"Maybe I should call her and tell her. I could save her some time."

"And spoil my fun? No way! I'm curious to find out how far she's willing to go."

They climbed into the Ford.

"How was your day?" Peggy asked.

"So-so. I talked to the employees at the office; then I drove to the building yard we have out of town and did the same. I mainly answered questions, mostly about Moira and the investigation. They were all quite shocked about what happened and upset that the police can't find who did it." Fred paused. "They want to raise money to make something in her name. Of course, they don't know about the tape, the blackmailing and her mother's...what should I call it? Accident? I wouldn't either, if it wasn't for you."

"It's nice that they want to express their feelings for Moira."

As they were driving home, Fred asked, "What do you want to do? Eat out?"

"I'd prefer to spend a quiet evening at your place. I can cook for a change."

"I'd like that very much."

Fifty-one

For three days in a row Nick Falcone called The Safe Harbour and talked with the female director. He still wasn't allowed to see Charlie, as he was sick. Nick was frustrated. Soon he might have to go and tour some casinos, as he had done before.

The new furnace had arrived, and the pipes had been downloaded in his carport. The dismantling of the old ducts proceeded vigorously, but with deafening noise. Nick couldn't stand it and decided to give another call to The Safe Harbour. The director was away for the day and so he spoke with her assistant. Nick introduced himself, said he was a friend of the family and was eager to help. He wanted to come over and cheer up poor Charlie. The assistant agreed that Charlie needed people around him, people he could relate to, so he granted permission to come visit him and take him out for an ice cream.

Glad to leave his noisy house, Nick jumped into his pickup and drove to Pond View Road.

Charlie was in the hallway, waiting for him.

"Hi, Charlie." Nick gave him a high-five. "How's my old friend doing?"

Charlie smiled and opened the door, ready to scout outside.

"Come back before five o'clock," a voice shouted from behind them.

Nick turned around, saluted the young man who stood in the doorway of the office, and followed Charlie outside.

Charlie turned up the volume of the radio as soon as Nick put the pickup in motion, and began moving his head to accompany the rhythm. Once inside the Dairy Queen, Charlie chose a strawberry sundae, went to the cashier, and paid with the bill Nick had given him. Nick stood close.

The cashier looked with surprise at both the bill and Charlie.

"It's his pay," Nick said.

The cashier gave Charlie the change without comment.

They sat at a table and Nick asked, "How do you like it at the new place?"

"No good," Charlie said between one scoop and the next. "Nothing to do."

"Don't you play games with the other guys?"

"Basketball if the weather is good. Days like today, just pool down in the basement."

It was only drizzling, but Nick could see why they wouldn't let the guys play outside—the cleaning of the clothes, socks, and shoes would require additional work.

"So what do you do all day if you don't play ball or pool?"

"Listen to music or take a walk."

"Do they let you go out by yourself?"

"No, only with one of the special guys."

Nick understood that Charlie missed the freedom he had at the Men's Mission.

"Where do you go then?"

"At the end of the street there's a park." Charlie finished his treat. "Can we go see the horses?"

Charlie missed working at the Western Fair.

"It's too late to go that far today. Know what? We'll stop at McDonald's; I feel like having some of those good chicken nuggets." He needed to exchange at least one more hundred. "I'll come back tomorrow or early the day after tomorrow, and I'll take you to the Fair to see the horses."

Charlie rose, ready to leave.

When Nick arrived home, the workers had left; the place was still cold, but at least he had quiet. Charlie seemed a little strange, Nick thought. It was the first time he had seen him after Moira's death. Before, he'd been happy, cheerful, and communicative; now he was withdrawn. He wondered whether the cause of the change was the confinement he experienced in the new home or whether he just missed his sister in the extreme.

He made himself an instant coffee and looked at the calendar on the kitchen wall. Tomorrow the plumber was coming, so he would delay seeing Charlie until the following day. He counted the change in his pocket: one hundred seventy-five dollars, a twenty-five dollar reduction on the starting capital of two hundred; only the government inflicted such a high penalty in the name of taxation! Next time he would take Charlie to a bank to change a couple of hundreds into something smaller, and then he would find an excuse to avoid taking him to the Fair. This kind of strategy was getting too expensive.

Stevenson stood in front of the bathroom mirror and trimmed his moustache, on the left first, then on the right, and then again on the left. He should stop trimming or he would end up with no moustache at all. He wondered whether he should get rid of it; in the past he thought it conferred him with authority, but as it had started graying, he wondered whether that still applied. His wife liked it, though. She remained with her parents in Nova Scotia, and had given no sign she would come to visit him any time soon.

The house seemed empty without her, and Stevenson thought how unfair the situation was; she didn't want a legal separation, yet she imposed it on him de facto. As soon as he had some free time he should go see her and discuss the matter. To add to his frustration, he missed Peggy, her impish laugh and cheerful attitude toward life.

He finished dressing and drove to Headquarters, thinking about the investigation. Peggy had managed to record only one conversation in the three days that she had been following Jeanette Alstein as the women had moved the time of their encounters to later in the day, when Coffee for Thoughts got very busy. He wondered whether Peggy would ever manage to hear something of substantial interest. Were the two women plotting something together or it was only a way to pass some time? He would believe they were just passing time, except that Peggy reported that their conversation was always animated and both women looked restless. He wondered what had brought them together. Jeanette had committed a crime and Tessa Wilson owned the Corvette that had been seen near Charlotte Gassman's home the night Charlotte was injured. Criminals tended to stick together, but at the moment he couldn't think of any excuse to interview either woman.

When he entered the Investigative Unit, Lopes came up to him.

"Charlie's doctor called and left his number. He'd like to talk to you before he starts his rounds at the hospital...that is, before ten o'clock."

Stevenson nodded, shrugged his coat off, and took out his cell. After the usual formal introductions, the doctor filled him in.

"Not much I can say about Charlie. As I told his sister many times, there's nothing I can do for him; he's slow, he has attention deficit disorder, and he suffers seizures. If he takes his medication, he's okay and he can work. I don't know why she kept saying that a specialist should see him, but to get her out of my hair I got him an appointment with a neurologist. He'll see Charlie in January."

Finally the doctor stopped and Stevenson asked, "What were Ms. Johnson's concerns?"

"Oh, nothing serious, really."

"Such as?"

"Charlie had mood swings and he was not cooperative as in the past." The doctor laughed. "The woman was pretty domineering, if you ask me. She probably couldn't boss him around, so she called on the doctor to fix it."

"Don't mood swings reveal that he was or was becoming bipolar?"

"Yes, but I didn't see any evidence of that."

Thinking that he couldn't extract any other useful information from the doctor, Stevenson thanked him and terminated the conversation. He drummed his fingers on the desk and then called for an appointment with the director of The Safe Harbour.

Ms. Sandra Tremonti was short, with soft, rosy skin. Her white hair was gathered in a chignon at the back. She rose to welcome Detective Gordon Stevenson, and asked him to sit on the settee close to a low table. She sat opposite him.

"Thank you for coming alone."

"No problem. As I mentioned to you on the phone, I just wanted to have a chat off the record."

"It's about Charlie Johnson, you said, right?"

"Yes. Anything you can tell me about his behavior?"

"Charlie is a nice guy, but he's accustomed to moving freely, coming and going, eating and sleeping when he pleases. You can't do that in a home. It's been difficult to make him understand that there are rules, and he has to comply."

"What's his reaction when you point out to him that he's misbehaving?"

"He goes to his room."

"Nothing violent?"

"No. Just a long face for a while."

"Any other reaction you noted?"

"Well, he wanted to work, so I sent him to the kitchen, but the kitchen staff didn't want him there. Too clumsy. He created more work instead of helping. He was hurt and stayed in his room for a day."

"How did he react when you told him that his sister had died?"

"He didn't talk for a day or so. He didn't eat either, so I called our doctor and he gave him a sedative. The day after he was back to normal, but then there was a relapse after you came down to talk to him."

Stevenson took his notebook out of his pocket. "Ms. Moira Johnson was murdered on November fifteen. Where was Charlie between five and six-thirty in the afternoon?"

"Your office already asked me that question. Charlie was in his room; he'd refused to come for supper."

"Do you think Charlie's medical condition is deteriorating?"

Ms. Tremonti took some time before answering. "I haven't had enough time to judge that; after all, he's been here only a few weeks. I think the change from The Men's Mission to this environment disoriented him. That's all I've noticed."

"Thank you very much for your time," Stevenson said and rose.

"My pleasure," the director said, and accompanied the detective to the door.

✧ ✧ ✧

Fifty-two

Finally, everything's under control, Nick thought. The furnace diffused wonderful, uniform warmth throughout the entire house; the water from the kitchen and bathroom sinks flew down the drain with unexpected speed and not a drop came down from the roof when it rained. Things were definitely going well.

After having washed and polished his Dodge Dakota for the upcoming trip, Nick filled his carry-on with clothes for a few days, already relishing the pleasant drive that would take him to tour a few casinos south of the border. He would stop at his storage unit to get a bunch of hundred dollar bills and then he would be on his way. He was ready to lock up when his phone rang. The caller ID showed that it was Tessa. Sighing, he opened his cell.

"I couldn't reach you all day yesterday," Tessa snapped. "I need to see you."

"Oh? What's so urgent? I was about to leave for a business trip."

"I need to see you. Come down tomorrow and take me out for supper. Be here at six. It's an important matter."

He heard Tessa's cell close.

Nick sighed. Now that everything was falling into place, why did Tessa suddenly have an important matter to discuss? Couldn't it wait next week? *Probably something about her fixation with Fred.* Nick sighed again. He couldn't ignore her; he owed her.

He walked into the kitchen and made himself an omelet. He had to reorganize his day. He didn't have enough clean cash to take Tessa out. She had expensive tastes. He looked at the clock on the wall. It was early enough that he could take Charlie out and exchange a few bills. He placed a call to The Safe Harbour and, after he received the okay to see Charlie, he drove into London.

As before, Charlie had waited for him in the hallway and scooted out before Nick had time to say hello to anybody.

"Wait, wait! Aren't you cold without a coat?" The clouds were low and dark and the forecast was freezing rain. Charlie wore jeans, a T-shirt underneath a long, orange-and-brown plaid shirt, and working boots.

Charlie shook his head and moved to open the passenger's side of Nick's pickup. "Let's go!" He slumped into the seat.

Nick followed him and began driving. When they came across a bank branch he stopped the car.

"Let's go to exchange a couple of bills," he said with a natural tone and motioned to open the door on his side.

Charlie yanked furiously on his sleeve. "I want to go see the horses!" he screamed.

"I can't take you today, Charlie, and the races are only at night."

"Not true. They also run in the afternoon."

Probably there were training sessions in the day, not that it mattered. "Charlie, I can't go there right now. We aren't going, and that's final."

He looked at Nick with fierce eyes. "You said you'd take me!"

"But I can't."

Charlie got out of the pickup, slammed the door, and began kicking the vehicle. Nick rushed to see what he was doing.

"Stop! You're ruining it!"

Charlie looked at him for a second and then punched him in the face. Nick fell against the side of the pickup. He had never seen Charlie in such a state of rage.

Charlie took off down the street, walking in big strides.

Nick touched his sore jaw. He had already thought of giving up on Charlie. Now it was definite. He re-entered his pickup and called Fred to find out what he was doing for the evening. He was at home planning to work on the paneling of the basement.

"I was just looking for some free labor. Come on over."

It was hard work to put a coat of varnish on the cedar paneling, but the result was rewarding: the look of wood gave the walls warmth, and the varnish made them shine.

Nick sat on the floor.

"My knee hurts, in spite of the padded knee caps." He glanced around. "I didn't realize how big your basement was. You painted three times what I did, in the same time!"

"It takes practice." Fred extended an arm to Nick and helped him rise. "Time for something to eat, and then we'll watch the game."

"I'm no hero in the kitchen, but I can put together something acceptable depending on what you have in the fridge and freezer."

"Great. Go ahead; I'll go clean up."

Thirty minutes later Nick deposited on the kitchen table a platter with fried shrimp, a tureen with rice Pilaf, a dish with steamed broccoli, and a small bowl of cheese sauce.

"You need to go shopping for food, my friend. All you have left are five frozen pizzas."

"I know. It's on my to-do list for tomorrow."

They scooped the shrimp with the rice onto their dishes, sprinkled the broccoli with the cheese sauce, and took their dishes along with a beer into the rec room. They sat on the sofa and turned on the television. Toronto played Tampa Bay. While the referee was dishing out a penalty, the local television station announced the forecast: freezing rain all night. The police advised people to stay off the road if at all possible.

"Oh my God," Nick murmured. "I forgot about the bad weather."

"You can stay here, if you prefer."

"I wasn't thinking of me. Let me make a call." Nick rose and went to the kitchen. He placed a call to The Safe Harbour.

"Yes?" a female's voice said.

"I took Charlie out this afternoon and while we were walking he took off on me. I wonder—"

"Charlie? I can see him from where I stand. He's sitting at the dining table, wolfing down a piece of chicken."

"Oh, that's great. I was worried."

"Don't have to worry about Charlie. He always comes back. He knows the city better than a taxi driver."

Relived, Nick returned to watch the game. When the first period was over, Fred looked over at Nick.

"What happened that you were so worried about the weather?" Fred asked. "Did you leave one of your girlfriends waiting in the park?"

"No. I never told you before, but I know Moira's brother, Charlie. A couple of times I took him out for a treat or supper."

"I didn't know that. How nice of you!"

Nick waved off the compliment. "This afternoon I went to the group home where he lives to take him for a spin. He wanted to go to see the horses at The Western Fair, and I didn't want to go; it's too expensive. When I refused, he became violent, kicked my pickup, and then walked away." Nick stopped for a moment, his eyes down. "I suddenly remembered that he had no coat; that was why I made that call."

"And?"

"He returned safely to the group home on his own."

"Oh, good."

After the second intermission they went to the kitchen for another beer.

"You said Charlie returned to the group home on his own?" Fred asked.

"Yes. The person who answered the phone said, 'Don't have to worry about Charlie. He always comes back. He knows the city better than a taxi driver.' " Nick paused. "Oh, wow! Are you thinking what I'm thinking?"

"Yes. Charlie might have found a way to sneak out of the home the night Moira was murdered. He probably knew how to get to his sister's place and get back to the home." Fred paused to think. "I have to alert Detective Stevenson immediately. He had some doubts about the alibi the group home provided. He was sick in his room, they said, which meant nobody had really seen him. Charlie may have found a way out, especially while the personnel were busy serving the evening meal between five and six o'clock."

✳ ✳ ✳

Fifty-three

As he drove to Tessa's house, Nick thought of how much pleasure he got from Fred's company. There was no tension, no criticisms of one another, and no conflict. If he wanted to keep him as a friend, he should change his lifestyle: get a job and stop lying and cheating.

It would be hard, though, Nick admitted with a sigh. It was almost changing his whole personality, and he wasn't sure he could do it. *Well, I'll think about it some other time. Today I have to go see Tessa.*

When he arrived he found her wearing a red-and-black striped jump suit and black slippers, with her hair hanging loose on her shoulders.

"Hello, gorgeous." Nick pecked her on the chin. "I thought we were going out tonight."

"I changed my mind." Tessa sat on the leather chesterfield and crossed her legs.

"Why? Because you know I'm broke?"

"You're always broke. You should get a job. The situation is serious, and we have to take action."

"Hmm. We can sit and talk about it—whatever 'it' is—but first I'd like to have a drink. Somebody punched me." He turned his neck so that Tessa could see a blue spot.

"So I see. It's not too bad."

Of course not, Nick thought. *Other people's troubles are never bad for Tessa.* He walked over to the bar and poured himself a double whisky.

"That's better," he said, and sat close to Tessa. "So what's the big problem?"

"You didn't tell me Fred has a girlfriend."

Nick had suspected it for some time, but he had hoped Tessa wouldn't find out. He jiggled the ice cubes in his glass, trying to gain time.

"I didn't know."

"What do you mean you didn't know? You see Fred every week!"

"Yes, but we work on our respective houses. I helped him panel his basement; he helps me with setting the tiles in my kitchen. He likes to work with his hands and I'd like to learn the trade."

"Jeanette—I mean Jeanette Alstein—set up a watch on Fred's house for three nights in a row—something *you* should have done—and she saw a woman going in late in the afternoon and staying until around nine o'clock at night. So Fred has a girlfriend."

"So? He's a free man."

Tessa took hold of his arm and shook it hard. "I want that man! Don't you get the message?"

Nick rolled his eyes. "If I want something I go out and get it."

"I know you're a man of action, and that's why I called you here."

"Oh, and what am I supposed to do?"

"Get that girl out of the way."

"And how am I supposed to do that? Set out a tape with a kind of male-bird call? Chip, chip, little female bird, come to me?"

Tessa didn't answer and rose to make herself a drink. Then she stood in front of him, a harsh look in her eyes.

"Kill her."

For a moment Nick was without words. Then he rose and set his drink on the coffee table.

"Tessa, I'm a con man," he said. "I'm no killer." He turned to leave.

Tessa threw her glass against his back and when Nick turned to face her, she took the drink that was on the table and threw it at him. The glass shards hit his face and marked it with blood. Nick grabbed Tessa and twisted her arms behind her back.

"Be thankful that today I'm in a good mood; otherwise I'd break every bone in your body."

He threw her to the floor and left.

Almost a week had passed, and Peggy hadn't learned one iota more than the first time she'd overheard Jeanette and Tessa plotting. She decided to change strategy. Instead of waiting parked on Jeanette's street she went directly to Coffee for Thoughts. Banking on the fact that the duo sat always on one side of the shop and, when possible, close to the windows, Peggy arrived early in the day. She attached her listening device under one of the tables, left, and returned before the big crowd invaded the place. She bought a big lunch, sat at the wired table, and nibbled at her food.

Finally Jeanette arrived, followed by Tessa. They talked to each other, looking at the crowd. There was a long line at the cashier, and none of the tables were free. After more talking, Tessa pulled on Jeanette's sleeve and dragged her outside.

Peggy freed her eavesdrop device from under the table, put the little food that was still wrapped in paper into her pocket, and left.

The Corvette already had reached the other side of the intersection and Peggy was afraid she would lose them. She guessed that they would look for another place to have their usual snack or early lunch, and drove straight on. She caught up with them on Dundas Street and, to her dismay, she saw that they had parked at the Armouries. No way could she enter that fancy place dressed as a construction worker in action.

Frustrated, she turned around and headed home. She wondered whether she had any talent for snooping, and was surprised at how much time it took to get close to subjects of interest. *What should I do next?* Last night Gordon had called her and asked her if she had any news. So, without seeming to approve of what she was doing, he was in fact depending on it. And she had nothing! She spent the afternoon keeping in touch with friends by phone and cleaning her little apartment.

The following morning she felt like a soldier in a trench, ready to jump out and fight the enemy. She wore a pair of flimsy trousers together with a soft blouse underneath the coverall, and brought a fancy jacket, a long scarf, and a pair of high-heeled shoes. She kept her eye on the road where the Alsteins lived and followed Jeanette to The Blackfriars Bistro. Here she parked; she shed the coverall and the hard hat; she looked in the rear-view mirror as she put a scarf over her hair and wound it around her neck. Dressed in her fancy attire she entered the restaurant.

The two friends were ordering a cocktail. The restaurant was fairly empty, and Peggy asked for a secluded place, explaining that she had asthma and would like to sit away from people who often wore scents or other cosmetic products. She mentally prayed that her high-sensitivity listening detector with attached recording would be worth the six hundred dollars she had paid for it. Once settled at a table in the far corner of the restaurant, she ordered a coffee and opened the menu in front of her. She made it stand so she could set up her equipment. It worked beautifully: the two women were exchanging views about the recent play they had seen at The Grand Theatre. When the waiter came to get her order, the device was in front of her, the earphones in her ears, and she was swaying her head to the music she was supposedly listening to. She pointed at a chicken wrap and a potato skin with bacon. The waiter nodded, took the menu with him, and walked away.

The two women were now in deep conversation and Peggy lifted her coffee cup to her lips without actually drinking. She wanted to avoid any background noise; she was listening with her earphones and recording at the same time.

"So you need the ten thousand by when?" Tessa asked.

"Next week."

There was silence for a few seconds, as the women scooped their soup.

"I can give you the ten, but you have to do a job for me."

"I already did what you asked me; I watched Fred's house, and that wasn't easy, since Alain is keeping an eye on me. He doesn't want me to start gambling again. Then I followed Fred's new friend at home. I've done a lot."

After another moment of silence Tessa asked, "Where did the ten-thousand-dollar debt come from?"

"It was an old debt I never told Alain about. It was only a bit over six thousand but I didn't pay, so it went up and up."

"I see," Tessa said. "Keeping an eye on Fred's house was a minor job." She paused. "What does the girl look like?"

"Nothing special. Tall and skinny, in her late twenties, maybe early thirties."

"Where is she from?"

"Aylmer. She lives in a tiny attic of an old house."

They ate more of their soup; Peggy was tense with expectation.

The waiter came. "Can you move that music box a bit?" he requested. He carried two big dishes, one in each hand.

"Sorry," Peggy said and smiled. She quickly made room for the two platters. "When I listen to music I don't see or hear anything else."

"I'm the same; my mother says I don't know the world exists when I listen to the beats. Watch out for the potato skin. It's just out of the oven," he said. Then he bowed and departed.

Peggy resumed listening, but there were no voices, only the clattering of dishes. She glanced down the hall to where the two women sat. A waiter moved the soup dishes aside, and set a sandwich in front of Jeanette and a salad in front of Tessa.

"What kind of a job?" Jeanette asked, as soon as the waiter was out of earshot.

Tessa lowered her voice. "That friend of Fred's has to have a little accident."

"Accident? What kind of accident?" Jeanette asked, her voice a high pitch.

"Keep your voice down, you idiot! Something that leaves her in a wheelchair or six feet under."

"But...but Tessa! That's murder!"

"Yes, it is."

"You're crazy! You don't know what it means to kill somebody! Your conscience will never let you sleep!"

"I know very well what it means. I killed my poor little old aunt. She was ninety-two and she didn't know whether she was coming or going. I just smothered her with a pillow." Tessa laughed. "And you know what? When I called the family doctor and told him that she'd passed away, he signed the death certificate without even looking at her."

"I can't believe this!"

"Believe it. It's true." Tessa paused and laughed. "And that isn't all. You know Deborah, Fred's crazy wife? I showed her how to punch in the security code that unlocked the big slide door that opened onto the pool area. One day the nurse didn't show up and she called me, so I told her to get outside and be ready, and I'd take her for a ride. When she came out, I sneaked in behind her and pushed her into the whirlpool. She liked that pool so much; it was good that she died in it."

Jeanette jumped up, shoved her chair to the side, and rushed out of the restaurant.

Peggy held her breath. She couldn't believe what she had just heard. She shot a look at Tessa. The woman appeared calm and poised; she asked for the bill, signed the credit card receipt and left. Peggy wasn't hungry anymore. She drank her coffee, now cold, and signaled the waiter to approach

"I'm sorry; I just remembered I have an appointment. Could I get two doggy bags? And the bill, please."

The waiter nodded.

Still shocked by what she had heard, Peggy drove to Headquarters. At the entrance she almost collided with Santos Lopes.

"Where's Gordon?" she asked.

"Getting grilled by the detective sergeant."

"Oh. Were you going out on an important call?"

"Not really. Anything you need?"

"There's something extremely important that Gordon should know. Could you ask him to join me in my truck? I'm parked outside. I'd prefer not to go to his office."

"Sure. I'll wait until he's finished with the brass, and then I'll tell him. Anything new about Moira's case?"

Peggy shook her head. "No, but I have something bigger."

"I'll get Gordon."

Over the last few months Santos Lopes had become more sure of himself, learned the ropes, and handled the simplest cases with ease.

Peggy thanked him and retreated to her pickup. Once inside she opened one of the boxes the restaurant had given her and tackled the chicken wrap. Within half an hour Gordon appeared, carrying two large paper cups in his hands.

"Hi, Peggy," he said. "Your snooping paid off?" He handed her one of the coffees.

"Uh-huh. Make yourself comfortable and listen to my recording. It's amazing."

Peggy took a big swig of her coffee and then opened the box with the potato skin and bacon. It was cold, but it tasted delicious.

When the tape played the part where Tessa asked Jeanette to eliminate Fred's girlfriend, there was no noise in the car. Both had stopped even sipping their coffees.

"Incredible! I felt Tessa was not on the level, but murder! I can't believe it!"

"The worst part is that we can't use it," Peggy said.

"Right. I'll take the whole thing with me; I might think of a way to nail this cold-blooded killer." He was ready to leave, when he said. "You should go stay with Fred. I'll send an officer to escort you home. Pack what you need for a couple of days and don't go back until this charade is sorted out."

"But I'd feel like I'm imposing and—"

"You know better. Give Fred a call." He opened the door. "Peggy, no more following or snooping of any kind. It's too dangerous. Since Jeanette refused, Tessa might hire somebody else."

After the last severe seizure Charlie had been hospitalized. For a week the doctors had categorically forbidden any visit by police. Stevenson had been waiting impatiently for his release and yesterday, finally, Charlie had returned to the Safe Harbor, apparently in normal condition.

Stevenson re-examined the evidence that pointed to Moira's killer: the faint contour of footprints on the entrance mat hinted at men's boots, and the pictures of Moira's corpse revealed that the pressure on Moira's neck had been caused by only one hand. Even considering that Moira was a small woman, he should assume that the killer was tall and fairly strong. Charlie fitted the little evidence Stevenson had. He called two of his strongest officers and sent them to take Charlie to Headquarters. No interview in the director's cozy office of the group home, this time. He wanted to put pressure on the young man and see if he could find out the truth and, maybe, extract a confession.

At ten o'clock Charlie sat in the interrogation room, and Lopes was ready to film the interview.

"Charlie Johnson?" Stevenson asked.

Charlie nodded and kept his eyes down.

"Last time you went to visit your sister, what did you two talk about?"

Charlie shrugged. "I don't know." He began shaking, and looked away from the detective.

"Are you okay?" Stevenson asked.

"Thirsty. I'm thirsty."

Stevenson called for two bottles of water to be delivered. Charlie opened his bottle and drank half of it.

Stevenson waited a moment and then asked again, "Are you okay?" As Charlie nodded, he repeated the question. "Last time you went to visit your sister, what did you two talk about?"

"Don't remember."

"Come on, Charlie, you went to see her for a reason. Did you ask her for money?"

Charlie nodded. "I needed money for the bus."

"Did she give it to you?"

"No! She didn't want me to take the bus."

"I see. Were you happy that she put you in the group home?"

"No."

"Did you ask her to let you go back to the Men's Mission?"

"Yes."

"And what did she say?"

"That I had to stay there."

"Were you upset about it?"

"Yes." He looked up. "Why did she lock me up? I couldn't do nothing there. They didn't let me out when I wanted, and they scolded me if I was late." Charlie was red in the face and his eyes blinked continually.

"Did you hate her for that?"

Charlie nodded. "She shouldn't do that."

"So that night, what did you do?"

"I grabbed her by her hair. She turned around and slapped me in the face, and then..."

"What happened then, Charlie? Did you grab her?"

Charlie nodded. "I grabbed her by her neck and squeezed. I yelled at her to let me go back. She didn't answer."

"What did you do next?"

"I threw her on the sofa. She didn't move. I took the money she had in her purse so I could take the bus." Charlie put his head between his hands. "Headache."

Stevenson sighed. The young man had all the problems his sister suspected he had.

"I'll call a doctor. He may give you some medication," he said.

He walked out of the room, and Lopes followed him soon after.

"Get him to sign the statement. Then get me the form for requesting a psychiatric evaluation. He isn't sound of mind, but he's still dangerous. We'll charge him for the murder of Moira Johnson." He took a few steps toward his office, then stopped. "Lopes?"

"Yes, Sir?"

"Do you know the procedure we have to follow for calling in a public defender? Charlie Johnson needs one."

"Yes, sir."

"Good. Follow it."

Fifty-four

Stevenson didn't sleep well that night, and woke up early. He drove to Headquarters, listened again to what Peggy had recorded, and formulated a strategy for the day. Around ten o'clock he asked to talk with the detective sergeant. He needed his approval before asking for an appointment with Amanda Parker, the crown prosecutor assigned to Janette Alstein's case. The woman was known for applying the law to the letter, with very little compassion for those who broke it.

Stevenson got a cappuccino to raise his spirits, entered his boss' office, and presented his case. At first, the detective sergeant didn't want to hear his strategy. Then Stevenson unfolded all the newspaper clippings that described the London office as inefficient and gutless. The clippings covered the arc of time starting with Deborah's death and ending with Moira's case. Of course, the police had just solved the latter, but the other cases had left many people wondering. If Stevenson's plan got the approval of the detective sergeant and the crown prosecutor, the police could pride themselves on their acumen, insight, and alacrity.

Stevenson didn't know whether he had presented his case convincingly or whether his boss just wanted to get rid of him after a full hour of animated discussion. By noon Stevenson had permission to ask the crown prosecutor for an appointment, and by early afternoon he had the appointment set for the same day at four o'clock.

Stevenson reviewed the statement signed by Charlie Johnson, signed the request for a psychiatric evaluation and went for a late lunch. He then took a long walk along Dundas, turned on Ridout and then onto Queens to reach the Ontario Court of Justice. This was housed in a 1974-building; the lower part, sustained by square columns, sported a long row of windows; the recessed upper section sprang up as a tower, giving the building a very distinctive appearance.

The officer on duty recognized the detective right away, and flagged him through the security doorway. Stevenson took the staircase to the second floor and entered the huge waiting hall. He had arrived a little early and was about to sit down, when an officer approached him and ushered him into Courtroom 3.

Amanda Parker was a woman in her sixties, dressed in a black suit, with a white blouse and a pearl necklace. Seated erect behind her desk, she exuded a sense of security and fairness.

Stevenson sat where he was told, introduced his credentials and made a clear premise. He wouldn't be here, had he an alternative to take a dangerous criminal out of circulation.

"Present your case, detective. I'll listen."

Stevenson took the tape Peggy had recorded and set it on the crown prosecutor's desk. "The problem is that this tape was not obtained lawfully." Stevenson lowered his eyes. "The police came across it by a lucky coincidence. We had, until then, no suspicion that this woman, Teresa Wilson, could have played a role in the death of Deborah Dalton."

He clicked *Play* and they both listened attentively.

The crown prosecutor looked at him, eyes sober. "So. You know you can't use it, and I know you can't use it. Why are you here?"

Stevenson edged forward in his chair. "Because there's a way to make it work, if you agree to one condition."

"Explain what you think can be done and why this office needs to be involved."

Stevenson looked straight into her eyes. "Let me get Jeanette Alstein to listen to this tape and tell her that if she testifies in court about what Tessa proposed to her we'll forfeit her recent charge of blackmail. Only this office can approve such an action."

The woman rose and paced back and forth, her rhythmic steps the only sound in the chamber. Finally she stopped in front of Stevenson. "I hate bargaining. Justice should never bend so low." She returned to her chair. "However, this woman confessed, and not only confessed, but took pride in having killed two people. We have in our hands the chance to bring her to justice." She looked at Stevenson. "Go for it, detective. I approve of the bargain, no matter how revolting it is to my sense of justice."

"Thank you, Mrs. Parker." Stevenson bowed slightly, put the precious tape in his pocket, and left.

Fred tiptoed into the guest room where Peggy slept. They had stayed up late last night, after a cruiser had brought her to his house. Gordon had previously called him and briefly mentioned that Peggy's change of accommodation was only a precaution; Peggy had refused to elaborate on the subject and Fred hadn't pressed her for more information.

He wrote a note explaining how to operate the security system, put the note on the night table and drove to The Werkstein.

Verge Bristol was already in the office, two volumes of specifications in front of him. "Hi, Fred. I'm happy you're here."

Fred took off his coat and draped it on the back of his chair. "Mild weather today, good for installing the roof on our mall," he said. "What's new?"

"Alain Alstein called; he'd like a two-week leave. He wants to talk to you but he isn't in right now."

"Why? He's on part-time already. What's so pressing?"

"He didn't want to tell me."

"All right. Let's give him the two weeks; then we'll review his performance."

Verge rose and neared Fred, waving the volumes he was reading. "We can't bid on these two jobs. It's too much work, and we don't have enough people to do it." He deposited the documents on Fred's desk.

"Verge, the jobs on the go are almost completed. The mall with the big superstore will be finished in the spring. We don't have anything else lined up after that."

"True, but I have to be on that job site often, and Alain keeps taking off. What can we do?"

Fred picked up the two tomes and gave them back to Verge. "Ask the new guy to prepare a bid for the first one and give it to me. I'll check it out. While I make the changes he can prepare the second one; they're two weeks apart."

"The new fellow isn't Moira, Fred."

"No, I realize that. She was exceptional. So maybe we don't make the usual ten-percent profit, but at least the guys in the field will have a job."

"So you'll take care of these completely?"

"Yes. No big deal. What else, Verge?"

"Ah…oh, yes. The architect for the mall called, saying that the owner would like to put arches in front of the main entrance, to form a kind of portico, and an archway inside the building to separate the superstore from the fancy shops."

"Oh, great."

"Great, you said? I studied the proposal, and we'll have to change a lot. The trusses are up, and we're taking advantage of the mild weather to start on the roof. The changes are going to throw off our setup, not to mention our schedule."

Fred thought for a long moment. "Did they forward a sketch of some sort?"

"No. I just got a call."

"Then we can make suggestions how to implement the changes they want."

"Are you going to go along with this? According to the contract we can refuse."

Fred tried to hide his impatience. "Of course we could, but the contract also has an important clause. If we agree to the changes, there'll be a markup of twenty percent." Fred smiled. "We can make money on those changes; *good* money, Verge. I'll talk to the architect." Fred closed his eyes. "I can see the portico as an annex to the already designed building. It extends forward with as many arches as the owner wants, with the pillars in natural stone or colorful bricks." He opened his eyes. "It'll be an improvement on the existing design. For the interior we can go along with anything, but I'll make some suggestions even there; clearly the owner wants the place to look nice, so he won't mind considering something expensive." He looked at Verge, who was just standing there with a grim face. "Cheer up, partner. You supervise the on-going job. I'll take care of the rest."

"Okay, I'll give these specs to our new employee and then I'll drive to the site."

Fred was about to call the architect when his phone rang.

It was Gordon Stevenson. "You're at work, Peggy told me." His voice was subdued.

"Yes, I'm back on the job. Four days a week, more if necessary."

"I need you to do something for me."

"Oh? Headquarters needs an extension on its building? I'm available. I like to work for the government. They pay late, very late but they never go broke. If you don't die first, you get to see the check."

"Fred, I'm in no mood to joke. I need you to stay with Peggy."

For a moment Fred was speechless. "I wasn't aware the situation was that dangerous."

"It wasn't, yesterday, but we've lost sight of our suspect."

"Could you tell me a bit more? I'm involved in something I don't know anything about. Please!"

"I can't say much right now. Please just stay with her."

"But I'm no bodyguard. Can't you assign an officer to protect her?"

"Not at the moment. We don't have anybody available right now. Maybe tomorrow."

"Gordon? Does Peggy have her Glock with her?"

"No, she had to hand it over when she went on leave." He paused. "Be sure all the doors are locked, that the security system is on, and that you don't open the door to *anybody* you don't know. I can come over tonight if you need to go out."

"No. I don't need to go out, and I'll go home right away. What I have to do, I can do on the phone for the time being." Fred paused. "Are you sure you can't tell me a bit more?"

"No. I'll call you later if I have any news."

The communication over, Fred grabbed his coat and drove home.

Stevenson drummed his fingers on the desk, anxious to receive notification that they could search Teresa Wilson's house and access her bank accounts. In spite of the watch set on Tessa's house yesterday, the woman had escaped surveillance. It probably happened when the one officer had finished his turn and the next was taking over. If that was not enough, there had been a delay when they had to look for a Justice of the Peace to authorize the search.

The notification arrived and Stevenson faxed it to Tessa's only bank, The Bank of Montreal, with a hand-written comment of his own. He waited a good half an hour before the bank's director transmitted the information he wanted. Ms. Teresa Wilson had performed only one transaction in the last week; she had cashed ten thousand dollars, precisely at five minutes after eleven this morning. Stevenson banged his fist on the desk. *The woman has hired a killer, and we have no clue who he or she could be.*

"They're waiting." It was Santos Lopes, standing behind him.

"Eh, what?"

"Jeanette Alstein and her lawyer are here."

"Right, right." He walked to the interrogation room while Lopes entered the adjoining room to tape the meeting.

The lawyer was pacing. Jeanette was seated, her face pale, her hair in disarray.

"I thought we settled the charges against Mrs. Alstein once and for all," Donald Norton said, his voice harsh.

Stevenson would have liked to punch him, but unfortunately he needed the cooperation of both Jeanette and her arrogant lawyer. "We did, but as I said to Mrs. Alstein on the phone, we'd like to discuss a better deal." He shot a captivating smile at both of them, hoping it wouldn't look as false as it was.

The lawyer sat and Stevenson took the recording machine out of his pocket and clicked *Play*. It lasted only a few minutes, but the lawyer lost his belligerence. He looked at Stevenson expectantly.

"We know that Mrs. Alstein is no killer, and we know she was flabbergasted by the proposal, but we also learned that Mrs. Wilson is guilty of a double murder. We had our suspicions, but we never came across evidence as good as this."

The lawyer cleared his throat. "So what do you propose?"

"That Mrs. Alstein testifies in court."

"In exchange for…?"

"Dropping the blackmail charge."

The lawyer looked at Jeanette, waiting for a response from her. As it didn't come, he nodded to her.

"Mrs. Alstein?" Stevenson said. "Yes or no, I don't have all day."

She lowered her eyes. "Yes, I'll do it."

Stevenson was already standing. "Let's make it crystal clear, Mrs. Alstein: if you don't testify that on the 18th day of December, while having lunch at The Blackfriars Bistro, Teresa Wilson offered you ten thousand dollars to kill Mr. Fred Dalton's girlfriend, the deal is off. Do you understand?"

Jeanette Alstein nodded.

"I didn't hear you."

"Yes, I understand."

Stevenson walked out, only partially satisfied. He had the means to send Teresa Wilson to jail, except for a minor detail. He had to catch her first.

✧ ✧ ✧

Fifty-five

When Fred woke up he realized that it was ten in the morning. He didn't remember ever having slept that late, even as a child. He had tossed in bed for most of the night and only in the morning had he finally fallen asleep. He blamed it on being asked to protect Peggy without having any idea of what kind of danger she was in.

Yesterday Peggy had spent most of the afternoon reading or watching TV, seemingly happy to do things she seldom had time for. Fred, seated on the sofa in front of her, had taken his sketching pad and outlined how the portico for the outside of the mall should look. After the first five drawings, he kept sketching about the same thing, but with a few variations in the details. After Peggy had called it a night, Fred had phoned Stevenson and left a message for him to please call back.

He had toured the house, checking windows and doors and retrieved his newly-acquired hunting rifle, the G2 Contender, from the garage. He had congratulated himself for buying a gun that used real bullets; he had freed it of all the locks that the law prescribed, loaded it with the ammo, and set it in a corner of the kitchen, partially hidden by a tea towel and an apron hanging close by. After all, there was a police officer in the house. Then he had gone to bed, but even the whisky he had eagerly consumed had not helped him fall asleep.

Finally Fred got up and, still in his pajamas, walked into the kitchen, guided by the smell of fresh coffee. He expected to see Peggy there but she was nowhere in sight. He called her and received no answer. He looked through the entrance door window and saw her holding the newspaper and chatting with a neighbor.

Suddenly an engine roared, followed by the sharp sound of a shot, and then another. Fred rushed to the kitchen to get his gun. He opened the main door. Peggy's legs protruded from one side of a bush, the remainder of her body was hidden. Another shot came from a car already in motion. Fred aimed and fired repeatedly. The car swayed sidewise but managed to continue its course.

He ran toward Peggy and bent over her. Blood poured from one of her legs.

"Peggy? Peggy?"

"Help me up. I don't think it's serious."

Fred threw the gun on the ground, lifted her in his arms, took her inside the house, and laid her on the sofa. He reached for the phone and requested an ambulance. He ran into the kitchen, grabbed a few tea towels, and pressed them on the wound to contain the blood gush.

"I'm making your sofa dirty," Peggy murmured.

"It doesn't matter. Did you see who was in the car?"

"No. I'd gotten the newspaper and opened it to see if there was any news about Charlie Johnson. I had just turned my back to the road. Fortunately whoever wanted to kill me had poor aim. Did you get him?"

"I hit the car; the rear window, I believe." He adjusted a pillow under her head. "I hear the siren. The ambulance is coming."

Fred sat in the waiting room on the second floor of the University Hospital, anxious to know when he could see Peggy. She was still sedated after the surgeon had extracted the bullet from her leg.

Stevenson entered the waiting room, his raincoat open, almost flying behind him.

"How is she?" he asked.

"The operation went well. They don't think her muscles will lose their flexibility, but one has to wait and see." Fred rose and stood in front of him. "I feel like punching you right in the kisser. What kind of organization do you run, that doesn't protect its own? You sent Peggy to stay with me; she needed a safer place to hide!"

Stevenson rubbed his forehead with his hand. "Peggy was on leave, and whoever was after her knew where she lived. I couldn't provide official protection and I was short of staff. I've worked sixteen hours a day for the last week and so have several of my colleagues. I couldn't ask any of them to volunteer for an extra watch." He looked into Fred's eyes. "It was poor judgment, I admit."

"Who knew Peggy was staying with me?"

"On my side, me and the officer who drove her to your house." Stevenson slumped in a chair. "Let's consider your side. Who knew she was staying with you?"

"Not a soul. Why is Peggy a target?" Fred shook Stevenson's shoulders and raised his voice. "I want to know everything that is going on, together with the names! Why is Peggy a target? What's the reason?"

An orderly walked into the room and approached the two men.

"What seems to be the problem?" he asked.

Stevenson flashed his badge. The orderly looked at it and nodded.

"Please keep your voices down. This is a hospital."

Fred sat close to Stevenson. "Talk. I want to get a picture of the entire problem."

Stevenson took a package of tissues out of his pocket, extracted one, and dried the drops of perspiration that slicked his forehead.

"It appears that an acquaintance of yours, Tessa Wilson, has an interest in eliminating Peggy."

"Oh? And the reason is?"

"Because she's in the way."

"In the way of what?"

"Of getting to you, Fred. She's fixated on the idea of marrying you."

Fred relaxed his back against the chair. "Oh my God! I knew Tessa wasn't well-balanced, but murder? She's crazy!" Images of the weird arrangements for Deborah's funeral popped into his mind.

"Oh no, she isn't crazy. She knows what she's doing, and she knows how to plot. Believe me, she's a first class criminal."

"How do you know all this?"

A tiny smile appeared on Stevenson's lips. "From some clever surveillance Peggy carried out."

"Oh, I see." He gave Gordon a penetrating look. "Did you tell me *everything*?" Gordon remained silent and Fred repeated. "Is that all that is connected with the attempt to Peggy's life?" Fred shook Gordon's sleeve. "Talk!"

Gordon exhaled audibly. "There's something else, but I was waiting…"

"Don't give me that crap of police business." Fred's voice had an unusually high pitch.

"No, I mean yes, it's something we don't want to divulge at the moment, but that isn't the reason. I was waiting for the right moment to tell you—" Gordon put a hand on Fred's shoulder. "Tessa killed your wife." As Fred looked blankly at him, Gordon added, "She was there when the nurse didn't show up and took advantage of the situation."

Fred blanched. "On my God…that's why she came to visit so often after she returned to London." He opened the top buttons of his sports shirt and rose. He neared the closest wall and banged his fists against it.

Gordon tapped him on the shoulder. "Fred? Fred?" he called out.

Fred turned halfway toward him. "People died around me, Gordon. I wasn't vigilant enough. I couldn't save Deborah, and I didn't keep an eye on Charlotte either. She needed help too. Both dead." He pummeled the wall again.

Gordon took him by the waist and away from the wall. "Calm down, Fred. You have to be in good shape for Peggy. Now it *is* *Peggy* who needs you."

Fred nodded. "How do you know that Tessa murdered my wife?"

"Oh, she was very casual about it; she told a friend of hers and Peggy taped the conversation."

"How did it happen?"

"The camera installed in the large room showed your wife going into the pool area. Tessa had told Deborah what combination to punch in to open the sliding door." Gordon rose. "She had it all planned, Fred; she just waited for the right occasion. A first-class criminal, no doubt about it."

A nurse walked in and suddenly stopped in front of Fred. She gave him a penetrating look. "Anything wrong?" she asked him.

Fred shook his head. "I'll be okay."

"You can come with me to see Ms. O'Brian, if you want."

Fred and Stevenson strode into the room where Peggy lay in bed with her head propped up on two pillows.

"Hi Fred. Hi Gordon."

Fred knelt close to her and took her hand. "How do you feel?"

"Not bad…like I slept too much. A bit of a headache too." She turned toward Gordon. "Did you catch whoever shot at me?"

Stevenson shook his head.

"And Tessa…did you get her?"

"Not yet. She isn't home at the moment. We've searched her house; there's food in the fridge and the door that opens onto the backyard wasn't locked. She'll be back. Soon or later we'll spot her Corvette." Gordon looked at his watch. "I have to go. Where do you want to stay? I can find a secure place for you."

Peggy shook her head. "I'd like to stay with Fred."

"Fine. There's a policeman outside this room and there will be a cruiser outside Fred's house." He saluted Peggy and left.

"I'm happy you'll stay with me. I'll take good care of you. Promise."

Peggy freed her hand and tapped on her cheek. "Give me a big kiss here."

Fred rose and leaned on top of her; he kissed her cheeks and her forehead. "More to come," he whispered, "as soon as you feel better."

Peggy smiled and emitted a long, audible sigh. "I don't think I'll be going back to work at Headquarters. I'd like something less…less stressful."

"Great idea. Did they tell you when you can go home?"

"Tomorrow." Peggy closed her eyes.

"I'll let you rest," Fred said.

Peggy nodded without opening her eyes.

It was the first evening in two weeks that Stevenson arrived home before ten o'clock. He looked around the house and discovered that his wife's nice indoor plants had been plagued by drought. One was reclining, its branches drooping over the edge of the pot; another was brown, yellow, and black; a third had no more leaves; and the spathiphyllum, the pride of the house, had been reduced to one single quivering stem.

He went to the kitchen and fetched a garbage bag and a pitcher full of water. He gave the plant with reclining branches a suspended sentence and watered it; all the others got the capital punishment and dignified sepulcher in a brand new garbage bag. Then the phone rang.

They had spotted Tessa Wilson's Corvette exiting the 401 and proceeding down Veterans Drive.

"Don't scare her off," Stevenson shouted into the phone. "Alert another cruiser to pick up the chase after the next three crossings when you'll turn away. I want to catch her as she enters her house. We have a search warrant, which will allow us to get to see whatever she's carrying with her into the premises. It's important!"

At the next question, "Do we arrest her?" Stevenson answered, "Of course you do. Take her to Headquarters and let her stew for a couple of hours. She'll call a lawyer. Let me know when the lawyer arrives, and I'll come in."

Stevenson relaxed in his La-Z-Boy. Things were falling into place, but the hard part would be to get Tessa Wilson's confession.

Stevenson arrived at Headquarters at two o'clock. Tessa Wilson hadn't said a word, except for her name and address. Her lawyer, Bruno Heisman, had been with her for over an hour, and the two of them were carrying on an agitated conversation.

Stevenson entered the interrogation room.

"We meet again." He took the seat opposite the lawyer and Tessa Wilson.

Heisman ignored him. "What are the charges against my client?"

Stevenson removed Jeanette Alstein's signed statement from his file and read it slowly, from time to time shooting a glance at the famous lawyer. Heisman's facial expression had gone from supercilious to attentive, and from attentive to impassive. *He knows his client doesn't stand a chance,* Stevenson thought.

"This is a statement Mrs. Alstein gave of her own will," Stevenson said. "It establishes that Ms. Tessa Wilson murdered Deborah Dalton and tried to hire somebody to eliminate Fred Dalton's girlfriend." He paused for effect. "Your client can count on clemency if she supplies this office with the name of the person she hired to shoot Ms. Peggy O'Brian and tells us how she used the ten thousand dollars she cashed yesterday morning."

The lawyer looked at Tessa, who shook her head.

"Fine," Stevenson said, and walked out. He waited until the lawyer had finished counseling his client. When Mr. Heisman came out, Stevenson walked a few steps with him.

"Mr. Heisman, we both know that your client is facing from twenty to life. The only chance she has to get parole is if she cooperates. Did you make that clear to her?"

Heisman stopped cold. "I know my job, detective," he said, brusquely, and left.

Tessa Wilson is a hard nut to crack, Stevenson thought as he headed home. He didn't care if it took a week to break her down. He was in a hurry only because her hired killer might be out to finish the job. Tomorrow the newspapers would carry the news of Tessa Wilson's arrest. For Peggy's safety he hoped that either the killer had not been paid in full, or that Fred had scared him off.

Fifty-six

That last casino ruined me...that fucking casino in Sarnia. Not even a big one, not even a fancy one. Nick banged on the steering wheel. He had left home with thirty thousand dollars and he had lost it all. He had started to play poker and had won. He had used some of the win to bet on a second round and won again. He had repeated the bet, and again had won. It was so easy! Then he lost a little and didn't think it would matter. But it did. By the end of the night the whole thirty thousand was gone.

The trip that was supposed to produce good, clean money had been a catastrophe.

He banged again on the steering wheel. He would go get fresh money from his secret deposit. He drove to Lucas and took the small road that coasted a ravine and climbed to a glade. A couple of miles along the road he met with a big truck, from which soil was being unloaded toward the ravine's edges. The truck took most of the narrow road. Nick stopped.

"We're making the road larger," one of the workers said. "It'll take another twenty minutes."

The truck descended in discrete steps, at each stop scooping down a fixed amount of soil.

Nick had to back up about half a mile. When the discharge was finished, he had to wait longer because the truck didn't turn around but climbed the small hill in reverse, clearly on the way to obtain another load.

When Nick finally arrived at the clearing where the row of storage units was supposed to be, he saw a bulldozer going back and forth, leveling the dirt.

Nick got out of his vehicle and gestured wildly for the bulldozer driver to stop.

"What are you doing?" he asked.

"Getting the ground ready for a new building."

"But that isn't possible! Where are the fucking storage units? I paid the rent for one!"

"Not my problem. I work for The Werkstein; talk to them."

"What did you do with the units?"

"We took them to the dump for metals, about thirty kilometers from here. They have big machinery to squash them flat." The driver put his bulldozer in motion. "Your storage is now smaller than a pancake."

Nick couldn't believe what he had just heard. All his money was gone! What would he do now? He swore and screamed and banged his fists on the steering wheel, all the noise superseded by the bulldozer's roaring engine.

He had to find a job, but what kind of job?

All of a sudden Tessa's shocking proposition loomed. He would accept it—if the price was right.

Inside Fred's large rec room, Peggy hopped from one bouquet of flowers to the next. There were white lilies, white roses, and white camellias.

"They're beautiful." She bent to smell the roses, then gave Fred a mischievous look. "Are you trying to seduce me?"

"Not at the moment. Just trying to keep up your spirits. I'm sorry about what happened, because, indirectly, I was the cause of Tessa plotting to kill you."

Peggy laughed. "From what she told Jeanette, it seems she has a habit of solving her problems in a fairly drastic way. First her aunt, then your wife, and then me."

Fred pointed at the new recliner he had just bought. "Sit down, Peggy, and see how comfortable this chair is." He sat on the floor, close to Peggy. "There was always something ambiguous in Tessa's behavior. When we were young, a group of us often met to be together, just to have fun. At times it seemed as though she took pleasure in hurting people's feelings."

"Do you think she was in love with you?"

"Heck, no! She was after me only after I made money and stood a good chance to inherit from poor Charlotte." Fred paused. "It'll be a big blow for my friend, Nick. I think they were close."

"Nick is the one who convinced you to go back to trap shooting?"

"That's right. We also see each other about once a week to work on our respective houses. He inherited a big farmhouse in need of repairs, and I like to work with my hands." He paused and tapped Peggy on the good leg. "How long do you have to stay in therapy?"

"Four weeks."

"Would you like to take a trip with me after your leg is okay?"

Peggy leaned toward him. "A big trip?"

"Let's say something about two weeks long."

"That would be wonderful! Where?"

"Up to you to decide. I never traveled much, so any place would do." He rose and put the remote for the television in her lap. "I should go do some work. We're short of staff and we have work only until spring. We need more projects for the summer; I'm going to review the quotes our new engineer prepared for a pumping station. I'll be in my office downstairs. Holler if you need anything."

Peggy gave him a big smile. "I have everything I need. I feel like taking a nap right now."

Fred kissed her on the lips and descended to the basement. He had become familiar with the structure of the project yesterday. The government had put a ceiling on the total cost. The tricky part would be to stay below that ceiling and still make money. He worked for a couple of hours, called the new engineer a few times and struck off the items that he didn't deem necessary. He would give it another look tomorrow and then it would be ready for submission.

It was getting dark when he went up the stairway and joined Peggy in the rec room.

She was on the phone. She put a hand on the speaker and mouthed, "Gordon."

Fred went to the kitchen and made two teas. When he went back Peggy was closing her cell.

"Something for the sickie." Fred gave her one of the mugs. "Any news?" He sat close to her.

"The great Mr. Heisman withdrew from Tessa's defense. This morning she was looking for another lawyer. Somebody came to see her, and one of the rookies let him have a talk with her; only later they discovered he wasn't an attorney at law. Gordon was fuming."

"Well, the charges will stand, if Jeanette doesn't want to go to jail."

"Tessa could say that she was joking. Gordon is right; we have to find whoever received the money from her. It'd be wonderful if the fellow was also the owner of a blue Chevy Impala. That was the kind of car from which the shots were fired, right?"

"Yes. Well, let's let the police worry about all this. By the way, at the office they asked me what The Werkstein is going to do in memory of Moira." Fred stopped, immersed in Moira's image.

Peggy drank her tea. "You could call the shooting pavilion the Moira Johnson Range."

"Great idea. My employees may like it."

Fred received a call from the cruiser stationed outside, asking if he wanted to see Mr. Nick Falcone.

"Let him in." Fred went to open the door.

Nick kicked off his new boots and got rid of the white parka he wore.

"I thought I'd dropped by to see if you need any free labor."

"Where did you get all the new clothes? From the north pole?"

"I went south of the border and did a bit of shopping. They had a big sale." He looked around. "Did I come at a bad time?"

"No. Come in. I'd like to introduce you to Peggy." He took his arm and led him into the rec room.

Peggy, reclined in the new chair, opened her eyes. "Somebody called me?"

"Oh, sorry, I didn't know you were asleep. Peggy, this is Nick Falcone." Fred gathered the crutches that were on the floor and set them beside Peggy, one on each side. "Nick and I chummed around together when we were young. We ran into some trouble together."

Nick laughed and shook hands with Peggy. "Almost drowned in the lake more than once."

Fred looked at Peggy, who seemed tired. "Maybe we should let Peggy rest. Come into the kitchen and have a beer."

"I'm okay now," Peggy protested and operated the lever to get in a sitting position, but Fred and Nick had already moved away.

"What happened to her?"

"Long story. Have you watched the news or seen the newspapers?"

"Heck, no. I just came back."

Fred opened the fridge. "Oh, oh...I have to get more beer. These are the last two." He gave one bottle to Nick and slid one on the table. As he walked to the door that opened onto the garage he shouted, "They've arrested Tessa. Murder and attempted murder."

"Oh my God!" Nick sat on a barrel chair. "I can't believe it!"

"Believe it; believe it; they have solid proofs."

Back from the garage with two cases in his arms Fred moved behind Nick to shorten his walk to the fridge. He looked at Nick's back once and then again. He paled. For a moment he couldn't utter a sound. He quietly stocked the bottles in the fridge door shelves. When he finally recovered from the shock he said, "I'd better take a beer to my girl too or she'll complain." He tried to keep his voice natural. He took a bottle and walked to the rec room.

"Go to my bedroom and lock yourself in," he murmured. "Call Gordon."

He returned to the kitchen. "So tell me what you've been doing in the States." He sat close to Nick and not far away from his new gun.

"Just visiting old friends." Nick guzzled most of his beer.

Fred looked at his wristwatch. "It's almost time for supper. This time it's my turn to cook."

"I don't know if I'll be staying that long, and you have a guest."

"Nonsense. Let me find the recipe for the chicken fricassee Peggy just gave me. It's somewhere in one of these drawers." With one hop he was in the corner where his rifle stood, loaded. He grabbed it and with it he rubbed Nick's back. "The handgun on your belt...put it on the table... slowly."

Nick complied. Then he suddenly turned, ready to throw his weight against Fred. The bullet was faster, though, and did its job. It pierced Nick's shoulder from side to side.

Nick screamed and fell onto the floor, bleeding.

✳ ✳ ✳

Fifty-seven

"Do you need transportation?" a voice behind Fred and Peggy asked. They turned around and saw Gordon smiling.

"Gordon?" Fred asked. "What are you doing here?"

They had just returned from a cruise in the Caribbean Islands.

"Waiting for you guys." He shook hands with Fred and hugged Peggy. "You look wonderful."

She wore a long dress and a black shawl with big white daisies embroidered on the upper part. A colorful necklace made of little shells adorned her neck.

"Come with me." He took Peggy's carry-on from her and walked in front of them. They were at Pearson International and Gordon had his car parked outside. "We were incommunicado for almost two weeks, and I was anxious to tell you the big news." Gordon unlocked the trunk and helped deposit all the luggage inside.

"I have news too, Gordon, and I'll bet it's much bigger than all of yours."

Gordon looked at Peggy quizzically. "What is it?"

Peggy held out her hand, palm down, to display her diamond ring. "Fred and I are engaged."

"Congratulations to both of you!" Gordon laughed. "I was always afraid that Peggy would get stuck with a guy who couldn't help himself, on the grounds that she felt sorry for him. Now look what she's done! Got herself the best catch in town." Gordon turned to face Fred. "She's a nice girl, Fred. She doesn't play games."

"I know, and I love her for that. I mean, *also* for that." He winked at Gordon. "And for many other reasons."

They all entered the car; Peggy sat beside Gordon, who took off for the 401 west.

"Now, tell us all the news," Fred said. "Starting with Nick. What's going to happen to him?"

"He didn't point the weapon at you, so possession of an illegal firearm is all we could charge him with at first."

"Did he say whether he was acting on behalf of Tessa Wilson?"

"No, just wait until I tell you the entire story. The man is street smart, but smart just the same. He denied any involvement in what Tessa had planned. Didn't know a thing. When he came to your house it was just for a visit. Yes, he had an old revolver that his parents had left in the house, but he never intended to harm you or anybody else. He said it was all a misunderstanding, so he wouldn't press charges against you for being injured." Gordon paused as he left the service road and merged into the express lanes. "Did I say that happened *at first*?"

"Yes, you did," Fred and Peggy responded, in unison.

Gordon emitted a contented sound. "That was at first. Then we checked his bank account. He had cashed a check for two hundred thousand dollars the day before he came to see you, drawn from Tessa's account. He'd managed to see Tessa by passing himself off as her new lawyer. It was a fault on our part, but it turned out to be our trump card." Gordon laughed, his laughter shaking his chest so much that he almost choked. "I love it when a criminal falls into a trap he himself has set up. It saves a lot of police work. They're both going to jail for a long time, no matter how good a lawyer each gets."

Gordon drove in silence until the traffic decreased in intensity. Then he looked at Fred through the rear mirror.

"It was a real bullet, the one that shot Nick Falcone." As Fred didn't say anything, Gordon continued. "You and I will have to discuss that point, but later."

"Did you find out about the blue Chevy?" Peggy asked.

"Yes. Alain Alstein was stopped for speeding on the 402, just before crossing the border in Sarnia. The car had been rented in Detroit. When we put two and two together, the car had already been returned; Alain had offered to pay cash for the smashed rear window. It took some time to find out where the car came from, but we managed. We contacted the rental agency and asked them to call the police. There were two casings inside. We had to file a few forms to get the car back to this side, but we'll get it. We called in Alain and drilled him for the whole twenty-four hours we're allowed to keep a suspect in custody before charging him, and he finally broke down. He admitted to having received ten thousand dollars cash from Tessa Wilson to pay for one of his wife's gambling debts. He didn't admit to having shot Peggy and we didn't find a weapon in his possession or in his house. The case isn't as strong as we'd like, but we're working on it."

Gordon stopped talking for a moment; the traffic slowed to a crawl and two police cars rushed ahead on the left shoulder.

"Tessa Wilson?" Fred asked.

"She got a public defender. Apparently none of the ones she called would take the job. She isn't saying anything."

"Do you think she'll serve time?" Peggy asked. "I have a personal interest in seeing her locked up for good."

"I think so. The detail that Deborah had found a way to sneak outside in spite of all the measures in place to prevent her from wandering around on her own is crucial. Nobody could explain how. She offered the only solution to the mystery."

They had resumed driving at normal speed.

"There's another mystery that I, as a detective, would like to solve. We recovered one casing from the shot you missed, Fred, when you aimed at the blue Chevy. They're pretty sure that it comes from a rifle bullet, like those used for hunting—in other words like those used when one wants to kill. Same thing for Nick Falcone's case." He looked in the rear mirror as if he expected an explanation. When this didn't come, he continued. "Fred, you go trap shooting, so you're licensed to use shot shells *only*."

"R...right."

"I'm really puzzled. I wonder where those bullets came from. Any idea?"

Fred weighed his answer.

"The case seems to involve some complex physics." He cleared his throat. "You should ask those big brains at the university. I'm just a bricklayer."

✡ ✡ ✡

The End

Also by Rene Natan

Mountains of Dawn

Cross of Sapphires

The Collage

Operation Woman in Black

The Jungfrau Watch

The Red Manor

The Blackpox Threat

Fire Underneath the Ice (co-authored by Sharon E. Crawford)

Made in the USA
Charleston, SC
11 April 2012